THE SANTORINI ODYSSEY

A NOVEL BY

PEG MADDOCKS

This book is a work of fiction. Places, events, and situations in this story are purely fictional. Any resemblance to actual persons, living or dead, is coincidental.

© 1999, 2003, 2004 by Peg Maddocks. All rights reserved.

No part of this book may be reproduced, stored in a retrieval system, or transmitted by any means, electronic, mechanical, photocopying, recording, or otherwise, without written permission from the author.

First published by AuthorHouse 04/21/04

ISBN: 1-4107-6606-3 (e-book)
ISBN: 1-4184-4065-5 (Paperback)

Library of Congress Control Number: 2003094770

This book is printed on acid free paper.

Printed in the United States of America
Bloomington, IN

ACKNOWLEDGEMENTS

I am immensely grateful to my husband Gene, my mentor and best friend who twice traveled with me to Greece. I fell in love with this beautiful country, especially the island of Santorini. My second trip to Greece was spent mostly on Santorini. its mysterious charm prompted me to write this modern-day odyssey.

I am grateful to the Santorini archaeologist, Katerina Reelas who guided me through the ruins of the Ancient City of Thera, (1400 B.C.) and the ancient Minoan city (B.C.1600) presently being excavated from its pumice grave.

I want to thank my friend, Nick Dadoldy, A Greek linguist who helped me with the Greek words used in the novel.

Special thanks to Eric Thiss, Serpent's Tail Company, for his guidance on reptiles.

To my good friend, Dr. Joseph Buckley, many thanks for your supervision of the medical areas in the novel.

To these very special women, my deep gratitude, my editors, Dinah McNickols, Sandy Pasqua, Jean Degler and Kenis Dunne.

The cover design by Maddocks & Co, Los Angeles.

To my readers, thanks so much for your support and suggestions: Rita Jansen, Evelyn King, Emma Kocenko, Camille Lane, Virginia Linnehan, Peg Maddocks, Jr., Madelyn Mason, Gail Myers, Rose Shepperd, Claire Spaulding, Nannette Strull and Agnes Sweet.

And to my family for their love and support: Frank Jr. and Pat, Frank 4 and Jen, Peg Jr. and Aaron, Nancy, Erin, Meg, Max and Ernie, Jaime and Bill, Sarah and Jesse.

DEDICATION

I would like to dedicate this novel to the friendly, high-spirited citizens of the Island of Santorini. For thousands of years their fortitude has sustained them through so many catastrophic disasters that would have had most deserting their homeland for a safer haven. I hope my readers will have the opportunity to visit Santorini and share in the pleasures of this special Aegean Island, I warn you, it will cast a spell over you.

PROLOGUE

The Greek Island of Kalliste—B.C. 1600

Growing more impatient, Orestes called upstairs again, "Hurry, Zoe! Aren't you and Philo dressed yet? There won't be any seats left, and I want to be able to hear what the speaker has to say."

"We're coming right down. I see the Egyptian and the High Priest walking toward the theater now." When Zoe and her son reached the bottom of the stairs, she looked at her husband with pity. "Oh, Orestes, I know how worried you are, everyone is. I pray the Egyptian will be able to tell us what is happening to our island."

"Let's go," Orestes' voice was terse as they hurried out toward the theater.

For centuries the gods had been generous to the thousands of Kallisteans and Minoan Cretans who inhabited this small island in the Aegean Sea. They had lived in harmony, peace and prosperity but something now menaced their island.

The theater seats were filled to capacity when Orestes and his family arrived, and they had to sit on a grassy knoll nearby.

The High Priest addressed the crowd. "My dear people, I would like to introduce my old friend Sokar, whom I met in Egypt many years ago. At my request, this famous traveler and scholar has come a great distance to help us understand why our island shakes and why foul-smelling vapors rise continuously from the demon crater at the other end of our island."

Sokar stepped forward and scanned the amphitheater, where the multitude anxiously awaited his words. "My dear Kallisteans and Minoans, sadly, I bear you bad news. After investigating the problems occurring here, I must conclude there is nothing you can do to save your island. I have knowledge of other places that have experienced the same warning signs. It's sad such a place of ample water, abundant food and thriving communities is in imminent danger of destruction."

Gasps of shock rose up from the audience.

"There is no hope that the rumblings in the earth might end, but in fact, they are the final warnings that a devastating disaster is about to happen. You must believe me."

Cries of fear mixed with angry protests.

"How do you know this?" a man challenged.

"Could our island stop shaking if we pray harder to our gods?" a woman cried out.

"Oh, Orestes, how terrible," Zoe moaned, "What will happen to us?" She buried her head against Orestes' chest and cried, holding Philo tightly.

Orestes' face filled with anger and bitterness. He yelled to the speaker, "We can't leave the island! Our lives are here. I'm a landowner and builder!" He broke away from his family and ran down to the stage, shaking his fist at Sokar. "You're frightening the citizens with your hopeless predictions. Give us proof of what you say!"

The crowd rose to its feet and roared, "Proof! Proof! Proof!"

The elderly High Priest held up his hands for silence.

"My good people, please! This learned man has seen what happens when this kind of evil strikes. We must trust him! Over the years, our lives have been so fulfilled, we have grown oblivious to the subtle warnings that should have alerted us to this impending disaster."

The Egyptian spoke again. "When your priest told me how long your mountains have been shaking, and of mariners who report unusual, churning waves in the waters, which, they say, are much warmer than usual, I knew what evil was lurking, waiting to explode below this island. Believe me, these signs are a prelude to catastrophe. Many of your older citizens have fallen ill, and some have died from the foul-smelling fumes that now permeate the island. I beg you to leave before it's too late!"

The Egyptian's last words caused chaos, the screams of terror and anger were deafening.

The High Priest tried again to calm the crowd and begged for silence. When he was allowed to speak, he announced, "We have no choice. We must leave before it's too late. We will offer sacrifices to Zeus and beseech the gods' intervention to help us escape from our island."

For the next few days the mood of the populace changed dramatically. The peace that had once been a keystone of Kalliste disappeared. People grew rebellious. Merchants charged customers higher prices. Shoppers tried to return recent purchases. Householders tried to sell their possessions. Orestes' tenants refused to pay rent. Haggling for passage aboard ships in the harbor turned violent. Many were injured, and some killed.

A few weeks later, the island shook violently in a thunderous roar. A huge column of steam seethed from the crater at the far end of the island. Buildings cracked and cisterns collapsed. Panic-stricken residents fled their homes and slept in the streets. That night the smoldering crater turned red as molten lava surged to the surface, sending boiling flumes cascading down the mountain. The next morning steady streams of pumice and ash spewed hundreds of feet upward, showering the island with a gray, powdery residue. The terrified inhabitants, taking only what they could carry, rushed to the shore, fighting for space on the few sailing ships and fishing boats left in the harbor. When the vessels, packed to capacity, were ready to sail, anguished cries of terror rose from the hundreds of islanders abandoned on shore. Boat captains promised to return for them, if possible. Donkeys, goats, sheep and swine left stranded on the shoreline sensed danger and plunged into the sea, trying to swim alongside the flotilla.

The High Priest chose to stay behind, and he blessed the departing vessels. Because his temple had been destroyed, Orestes, who was reluctant to leave all his properties, invited the priest to his home, which was still habitable. Each day the remaining islanders gathered on shore to pray for the ships return. They wore blankets on their heads as ash continued to fall. On the third day, an enormous volcanic boulder jettisoned from the fiery crater. The High Priest saw it coming and pushed young Philo, who was standing next to him, out of harm's way as the boulder crashed beside them. Its impact was so powerful that it lifted the frail priest into the air, and he fell headfirst back to earth, breaking his neck.

His followers were devastated.

Orestes and Zoe were so thankful that the High Priest had saved their son's life, they begged the others to help them bury him. "We must carry our priest up to the mountain where his burial chamber and sarcophagus have been prepared in the event of his death."

The frightened citizens were reluctant to make the hazardous journey.

Orestes challenged them. "You all know that was his wish to be buried there. The gods will punish us if we don't."

"That's true!" Zoe added. "But if we bury him there, I know the gods will reward us for giving him the proper burial he asked of us."

The crowds complained.

"But it's such a long way up the mountain. It will take too long to get there."

"We could be trapped up there."

"If we're not here when the ships return, they'll leave without us."

Trying to encourage them, Oreste said, "The volcano is erupting on the other end of the island, not here. We can make it. The elderly and a large group of you warriors could stay here and wait for the ships. "There are more of you than them. If necessary, use weapons, force them to stay." then in desperation he declared, "If the rest of you won't give our High Priest the honor due him, then my wife, my son and I will carry him up the mountain alone." Orestes didn't wait for an answer. He rolled the priest's body onto a blanket and motioned Zoe and Philo to help carry the corpse up toward the mountain.

Suddenly, there was a second roar as another gigantic volcanic boulder burst from the crater, soared skyward out to sea and landed in the water a half mile away from the multitude.

"It's an omen!" an old woman screamed.

"The gods are warning us to bury our High Priest properly!" another yelled. "We must do it!"

The crowd pushed forward to catch up with Orestes and his family for the trip up the mountain.

When they reached the cave, they made their way into the deep cavern temple. There, in the sacred altar room, they entombed the High Priest into his sarcophagus along with his favorite treasures and religious objects that he had stored there. They prayed and performed the necessary rituals that would ensure his safe passage into the next world.

As was the custom, a few artists in the group hastily painted wall murals depicting the priest's death and the destruction of the island. As they left, they sealed the tomb with large pre-cut limestone slabs. They quickly made their way out of the cave and raced down the mountainside to the shore under a heavy rain of ash.

Two days later, the gods answered their prayers and a fleet of ships emerged through the thick blizzard of volcanic dust. The remaining residents hastily boarded the vessels and sailed away from their doomed island.

Their rescue came none too soon, for that night the final catastrophic upheaval began. The island shook violently, and fiery rivers of molten lava exploded over the rim of the crater, flowing over the island, coursing to the sea. Thousands of volcanic boulders hurled skyward, then crashed back to earth. Thick clouds created by boiling black ash turned day into night. Lightning flashed through the darkness. The island rocked wildly. A final explosion of incredible magnitude disintegrated the center of the island, and it sank into the sea, creating tremendous waves that surged outward for hundreds of miles. The once beautiful city of Kalliste, buried under tons of ash, disappeared. forever.

The Grotto of Hermes and Heracles

CHAPTER ONE

Santorini, December 1994
(The Greek island of Santorini was named in honor of Saint Irena who was martyred. In ancient times the island was called Strongyle, Thera and Kalliste, the beautiful island)

Kristos raced into his house yelling, "*Mana, Mana*, quick, you have to come with me up to the ruins! I've discovered a cave!" Kristos raced into his mother's weaving room and pulled at the sleeve of her sweater.

Without turning to look at her son, Dora Kaldara scolded, "Kristos, how many times have I told you not to disturb me when I'm weaving? Why do I have to keep reminding you how easy it is for me to make a mistake if my work is interrupted, even for a minute?"

Flailing his arms and running around the room in a frenzy, Kristos cried out in frustration, "But *Mana*, yesterday's earthquake made a big hole in the back wall of the grotto of Hermes and Heracles, and I can see steps going down!"

Dora Kaldara smiled to herself and stopped peddling the treadles. She straightened up, placed both hands on her lower back and massaged it to ease the stiffness. She always found it difficult to chastise Kristos; most of the time he was very thoughtful. She turned to him and held his small shoulders. "Calm down, Kristos. You've been told many times not to go exploring up there in the ancient city alone, especially after an earthquake like yesterday's. Those old walls crumble easily. Your *papa* has warned you a thousand times, too. There are still aftershocks. You could be hurt. Now go outdoors. I have to finish this section of the carpet today, or I won't get paid. This house shook so much yesterday, I lost two hours' work when my loom slipped."

"But *Mana*, you have to see it! it's a real cave!"

"Maybe when your *papa* comes back from Fira, he'll look at your cave. Now button up your jacket, and go outside and play until he comes home. Look down the mountain road and watch for him."

Kristos' father, Elias Kaldara was a guard for the ancient city of Thera where Kristos found the cave. He was very knowledgeable about the history of the ruins which dated back to 1450 B.C. The ruins, located on top of Mesa Vouno, were five hundred feet above the Kaldara's house and 1500 feet above the Aegean Sea. The Kaldara's home was isolated on a small terraced strip of land carved out of the mountainside. A quarter of a mile below their house was the small village of St. Demetrius.

Elias Kaldara enjoyed telling his son, Kristos, stories about the cultures that had populated the ancient city of Thera over the centuries. Although only ten years old, Kristos had already made up his mind to become a famous archaeologist. His father often retold stories about what Plato had described about the fall of the ancient city of Atlantis in his dialogues: Timaeus and Critias. Kristos loved those stories, and, like all schoolchildren on Santorini, he knew that some scientists thought his island could be ancient Atlantis. He had learned much about the island's ancient inhabitants.

Kristos ran outside and raced down the hill to the village below. He looked up and down the main street for someone with whom he could share his discovery.

It was a blustery, cold December day, and almost everyone was inside or at work. He spotted *Papa* Ioannis, the priest from the Orthodox Church of Saint Demetrius, riding his donkey, Sophocles. towards the church. The tall, white-bearded clergyman rode a small, spindly-legged donkey side-saddle with great dignity. His pillbox hat bobbed, and his cloak flew out behind him like the wings of Pegasus, as the donkey clip-clopped along the cobblestone street.

Kristos ran after him, calling out loudly to be heard above the howling wind, "*Papa, Papa*, wait for me!"

The priest beckoned the boy to run alongside and listened as Kristos told him of the cave he had discovered in the grotto of Hermes and Heracles. He begged the priest to come take a look. *Papa* Ioannis was fond of Kristos because the boy often served the Divine Liturgy on short notice when those assigned did not show up.

Like most natives of Santorini, *Papa* Ioannis had a keen interest in the ruins on the island. Often, on his day off, he helped at a dig known as the Kalliste site, located at the far end of the island under the city of Akrotiri. Kalliste was discovered in the 1960s when a donkey stepped into his cave stall, and the ground collapsed under him. The donkey's owner and friends put drop lights into the hole and were startled to see the donkey standing on steps thirty feet below. The local archaeologist was called to the site immediately. After digging for several days through pumice, a door and a window were discovered. After further test digs and carbon dating was done in the ruins, it became apparent that probably an ancient city had been buried, possibly since 1600 B.C. when the island was destroyed by the most devastating volcanic eruption ever recorded.

"Ah! A cave with stairs you say?" *Papa* Ioannis said. "Well, Kristos, I think I can take a little time to look at this important find of yours." he leaned over and extended his arm. "Here, swing up. Sophocles can carry the extra weight of a small one like you."

They reached the ruins on the top of Mesa Vouno. The donkey plodded through the ancient paths toward the far end of the ruins. The fierce wind burned their faces.

When they reached the grotto of Hermes and Heracles which was only four feet deep, Kristos jumped down and ran inside. *Papa* Ioannis followed him and saw the large gaping hole in the back brick wall.

"See! See! Isn't this a great discovery, *Papa*?"

"You are right, this is significant, Kristos. "But we must be very careful," the priest warned. He peered into the hole and studied the unstable limestone walls and ceiling of the grotto. "We'll just take a quick look inside the opening."

The priest and the boy crouched low and slowly went down four steps into the darkness until it was impossible to see further.

"It's too dangerous without a lamp, Kristos," the priest said. "Tonight I'll contact Nikos Konstantinou, the archaeologist and ask him to take a look with your father."

"But I found it! If he comes, then he'll get all the glory!" groaned Kristos, close to tears at the idea of an archaeologist taking over his find.

Papa Ioannis put his arm around the boy's shoulder and raised his chin in his hand. "Kristos, I promise you that I will personally see to it that you get credit for your find. I'll see that it is recorded that Kristos Kaldara was the first to lay eyes on this ancient cave on Friday, December 14, 1994. I promise."

* * * *

The next day, Dr. Nikos Konstantinou, examined the site and immediately notified the Greek Archaeological authorities in Athens that the cave appeared to be a significant find. Etched on the walls of the hand-hewn steps were reliefs of lions, the symbol of the Greek god, Apollo, who used lions to pull his chariot across the sky. And, below the fourth step was a landing that led off into two tunnels. On the wall of one tunnel, they saw a relief of an Egyptian cartouche displaying, Isis, the goddess of motherhood and fertility.

Two archaeologists from the Archaeological Society in Athens were sent to investigate the site. They had only gone a short distance into the cave when a strong aftershock shuddered through the walls. They escaped before chunks of limestone began to fall from above.

The Society concluded that the reliefs of the lions and Isis were strong clues that the cave was prehistoric, dating back to a time when early inhabitants honored both Egyptian and Greek gods. Possibly it should be explored, but financing was a problem. Their budget was earmarked for the island's other major site, the ancient city of Kalliste at the opposite end of the island. The directors voted to offer a qualified team, the opportunity to sponsor the exploration, which could be both dangerous and costly.

CHAPTER TWO

Greenwich, Connecticut, January 1995

The Lee Bradley Travel Agency was by far the most successful agency in town. Its clientele included many of the most affluent families in the area. At forty-one, Lee Bradley was chic in an understated manner. Her warm personality and captivating smile reflected both her confidence and sophistication. Her clients often wondered why someone so attractive wasn't married. She spoke little of her private life.

Ten years earlier, Lee's dream of owning her own agency had come much sooner than she'd anticipated. She'd read the Greenwich Time commercial real estate ads every Sunday, but whenever she found the perfect location, the price was always too steep.

Then one day, a friend in real estate phoned with good news. "Lee, I think I've found the ideal place for you. A Dr. McGuire, a general surgeon at Cornell Medical Center in New York just called. He owns a small, vacant office building in the most perfect location downtown, and he's anxious to sell."

That Saturday morning, Lee met Dr. Matt McGuire. When they shook hands, their eyes met and held, and for a brief instant neither spoke as they acknowledged the surge of chemistry between them. During the meeting that followed, they found it difficult to keep their minds on what the real estate agent was saying. They kept looking at each other. They signed the necessary papers for the sale, and Matt invited Lee to lunch. Within a week, they became discreet lovers. Dr. McGuire was a married man.

His wife, Sarah, had been a popular Greenwich socialite, but was now an alcoholic. Within the first few years of their marriage, she became disenchanted with Matt's medical career, complaining that he cared more for his patients than for her or their social life. When it was determined early in their marriage that Sarah could not conceive, they began adoption procedures. But each time they were close to adopting, Sarah would find something wrong with the baby or the parents. In the past ten years, her drinking problem had escalated and Matt had admitted her to several treatment clinics to be detoxified. Now she was beyond help; she was terminally ill with alcoholic cirrhosis.

Rita Burke, an R.N. with psychiatric training, cared for Sarah around the clock. Matt now spent as little time at home as necessary, because his presence always triggered Sarah's uncontrollable verbal tirades and physical abuse. But alone with Rita Burke, Sarah was calmer and less apt to display explosive behavior. Matt, in his middle fifties, was burned out and worn down. His affair with Lee was the only thing that kept him from having a breakdown.

His best friend and surgical partner, Dan Gilbert, urged him to take a leave of absence. "For God's sake, Matt, your depression is affecting your judgment," he warned. "You've even come close to botching simple surgical procedures. As your doctor, I'm prescribing a complete change of pace for you. Find some place far away, and do things that have no relation to medicine. Go to Italy! have an affair! get the hell out of here before you make a serious mistake and jeopardize your career. I'll keep an eye on Sarah."

Dan knew about Matt's ten year affair with Lee, but like other friends who knew, he was discreet.

* * * *

A few weeks later, Matt had lunch with Wade Stanton, a Cornell classmate and old friend who was a noted geologist and speleologist.

"So what exciting adventure are you involved in now, Wade?"

"Mostly research this past year, but hopefully, I'm about to embark on a fascinating project in Greece. I've been selected foreign director on the exploration of a newly discovered cave."

"That sounds like fun."

"It will be! As soon as I read about this exploration in one of the journals, I wrote for details. I couldn't believe it when I got a letter from the director of antiquities in Athens asking if I'd be interested in heading up a team, and find other qualified volunteers. The only drawback is, it's a non-paying job, and I have to raise funds for the exploration."

"Sounds like you've got some hustling to do. So you're still into cave thrills, huh? do you remember you took me caving a couple of times when we were in college, and we got lost both times? It scared the shit out of me."

"That was no big deal. We were only lost for about fifteen minutes. A real scare is when the cave you're exploring collapses around you. Remember when I was working in a tomb in the Valley of the Kings in Egypt?"

"Yeah, you were almost buried alive. I didn't think you'd ever go underground again."

"Well, this cave is limestone and lava, so a cave-in isn't very probable."

"Where is it?"

"On the Greek island of Santorini."

"Ah, Santorini. I've seen it in pictures and travel posters, I love those magnificent Aegean outlooks."

"That's it. A mountain rising from the sea, and a frequent stop for cruise ships on their way to Crete."

A fleeting thought occurred to Matt. "Would I like it?"

"You'd love it! Lots of scholars-and not all of them whacko, think Santorini is possibly part of the lost kingdom of Atlantis."

"No kidding? Hmmm, I might go with you."

"Go with me? Would you? I'd love to have you on my team."

"What do mean 'team'? I need a hiatus, not work."

"You can be my man Friday; carry my supplies."

Wade laughed as Matt glared at him. "Actually, it would be comforting to have a doctor along. All kinds of things can happen in a cave like this one."

"Then I'll take my Hippocratic oath and my all-purpose Greek-cave medical bag."

"Seriously, Matt, I'm trying to put a team together, and right now all I have is a Greek archaeologist from Santorini, who'll keep an eye on any treasures that we may find. What I really need is another archaeologist, preferably American, who can spare the time for an unpaid adventure. It's a pretty expensive proposition. Know any angels who might want to back the project?"

"Well, let me give it some thought." Matt decided the prospect of a two-month adventure might be just what he needed. He was confident that Rita Burke could keep Sarah stable; and Dan Gilbert would be available in case her condition worsened.

The next day he gave Wade a definite "yes" after discussing the trip with Lee Bradley. She encouraged him to go. "It'll do you a world of good, Matt, even though I'll miss you terribly." Suddenly a secret smile covered her face. "I just had a thought. I have a wealthy client whose husband is an ex-archaeologist and might be interested in taking part in the exploration and offering financial assistance. I'll get in touch with his wife right away!"

CHAPTER THREE

Greenwich, Connecticut, February 1995

Merit Morton-Powers suppressed a smile as she swerved her Jaguar out of the driveway onto the country road and headed in the direction of downtown Greenwich. The piercing February wind, the snow, and the lead-gray clouds shrouding the skies did not dampen her blithe mood as she contemplated her secret mission. Merit and her husband, Brant, would celebrate their fifth wedding anniversary in May; They had started a tradition of anniversary vacations and took turns surprising each other with the destination. This year the choice was hers. Merit had selected it solely for Brant's total gratification, and it undoubtedly would be their most unusual anniversary vacation yet. They always traveled in luxury, but creature comforts on this trip would be minimal.

* * * *

Merit maneuvered her car through the heavy rapidly accumulating snowdrifts and reminisced about the origins of their exciting annual anniversary tradition that began in 1990. Brant had secretly planned their honeymoon with Lee Bradley, their travel agent. He'd chosen France, as traditional and romantic a destination imaginable. After a flight on the Concorde to Paris, he'd scheduled jet hops south to the Riviera and Monaco. Next they took a three-day balloon trip over the wine country and stayed each evening in medieval castles and estates.

When they'd first arrived in France, they spent three days in Paris, staying in the most luxurious suite of the Plaza Athenee'.

Merit thought back to their first day in Paris: She had told him, "Brant, I intend to shop every afternoon for new clothes since you wouldn't tell me how to pack for our trip."

Brant had grinned. "That's exactly what I planned, darling."

While Merit shopped at her favorite salons, Chanel and Yves Saint Laurent, along with many other smaller, trendy boutiques, Brant had immersed himself in the Greek and Roman antiquities rooms of the Louvre. Like a reunion with old friends, each artifact, sculpture and carved frieze brought great joy to his soul. Always, before leaving the Louvre, he'd spend a few moments gazing lustfully at the sensuous, smooth marble body of Venus de Milo. His beloved Aphrodite actually aroused sexual feelings in him.

Dr. Brant Powers had received his PhD in archaeology at Harvard University and had pursued that profession by doing research in museums and working at digs around the world. But his career ended abruptly when his father died at age fifty-nine. Being the only son in the Powers family, Brant found himself trapped in the position of presiding over his family's worldwide multimillion dollar banking corporation, which had been in existence since the early 1800s. His aristocratic looks and demeanor added a beneficial dimension to his profession as a world famous capitalist. He had inherited his intense, angular face, high cheekbones, large nose and thick black eyebrows from his father's side. He was tall, lean and broad-shouldered, and his London-tailored suits lent an added air of sophistication. Depending on the circumstance, his steel-blue eyes could be either penetrating and serious or delightfully captivating. His black curly hair was naturally unruly.

Although Merit's easygoing personality was in direct contrast to Brant's serious nature, they'd been attracted to each other from the moment they met at a cocktail party when she was twenty-two and he thirty-three.

Merit also came from an old, established Greenwich family and had been educated at the finest Eastern schools. She was a champion equestrian, a talented artist and an avid photographer. Her style of dress was often mentioned as trend-setting in the fashion world. Her picture often appeared in glamour magazines attending fundraising events. She was a regular at New York socialite parties. Her high cheekbones were enhanced by sultry gray eyes that tilted upwards at the outer edges and were framed by long, thick, dark lashes. Her beige skin tone contrasted with her platinum blond hair, cut slightly above her shoulders and casually parted on the right-dramatic in its simplicity.

Her greatest passion was collecting antique jewelry. She possessed a treasure trove of priceless pieces, much of which had been bequeathed to her on her sixteenth birthday by her Grandmother, Merit Morton. On her eighteenth birthday, she received the first installment of her trust fund and began an obsessive buying binge of antique jewelry. Sotheby's and Christi's kept her informed if rare pieces were to be auctioned. She seldom wore her precious jewels except on special occasions. An underground vault on her family's estate was the repository for all of her treasures.

* * * *

Paris weather was delightful during their honeymoon that May in 1990, especially the evenings. On their first night, they dined in a small bistro near their hotel, then took a limousine to the Eiffel Tower. They rode the elevator to the viewing area, watched Paris flicker amid the millions of lights that illuminated the city, and exchanged wedding gifts.

Brant insisted that Merit open hers first. When she unwrapped the gold paper and opened the small, black velvet ring box, she was startled. "Brant, it's magnificent! Where in the world did you ever find it? What an incredibly preserved antique ring. Tell me about it. Who did it belong to?"

"To a woman almost as lovely as you."

"Who? Tell me who," she begged, sliding the large, sparkling dinner ring on her right hand and holding it out to admire. Diamonds and rubies were artfully enmeshed in a platinum setting. Being an avid collector of antique jewelry, she knew the approximate era of the ring because of the European cut of the stones.

Brant grinned and whispered in her ear, "It belonged to Marie Antoinette."

Merit gasped and hugged Brant tightly. "It will always be the most important piece of jewelry I've ever had in my collection." She'd had difficulty finding a gift for Brant, a man who had everything, but her gift shocked him. "Here, darling, a bit of history for you, also."

The small, silk moire' jewelry box held two coins. Brant's eyebrows flew up in surprise, then slanted in a frown. "My God, Merit, these can't be the real thing?" He ran his finger over the irregular coins. "If they're real, they'd be among the first coins ever minted in Greece, about 650 B.C. on the island of Aegina. See, this is a sea tortoise. It's the island's symbol."

He was unaware as he intently studied the coins that Merit was upset by his insinuation that the coins might not be genuine.

"Jesus, these are the real thing! Merit, where in the hell did you get them?"

She glared at him and didn't answer his question. Instead she handed him a small, velvet bag. "Here, I had Cartier design these gold cuff links so the coins can snap in and out with ease, without damaging them."

He realized by the tone of her voice that she was upset. He held her chin up in his hand and looked at her contritely. "Darling, have I said something to offend you? You know I'm thrilled with the coins. I was just concerned about how you came by them. I mean they're such valuable museum pieces. Did they come from a private collection?"

Merit blurted, "I don't like what you're suggesting! Why don't you tell me first how you acquired this ring? Is it contraband?"

Brant apologized, "Of course not, Merit. Please forgive me."

"I can't believe you would make such an outrageous insinuation about my gift. Believe me, they were not stolen! How could you think that? Have I ever questioned how you and your family acquired all your priceless ancient artifacts? Don't ever question my integrity again!" She crossed her arms over her chest and turned her back on him. Tears welled up in her eyes.

He threw his hands up in the air, turned her around, and pleaded, "Forgive me, Merit. I had no right to say what I did. I just couldn't believe that I was holding such priceless treasures in my hands." Enveloping her in his arms, he looked down into her eyes. "I promise you I'll never say anything like that again, Mrs. Morton-Powers."

She succumbed to his tight embrace. "I accept your apology, Dr. Powers."

The soft night breezes caressed them. They clung to each other without embarrassment while a small group of tourists watched. Then, like typical French lovers, they kissed passionately, and their audience chuckled and applauded the final act of the lovers' first quarrel.

Their first gifts of antiquity to each other set a precedent for future anniversaries, but they never again spoke about how they'd acquired their rare acquisitions.

* * * *

Brant was more obsessive than Merit, and this manifested itself in most everything he did. He was obsessive about success in business dealings, and in recreational activities, but most particularly in his acquisition of antiquities, much like his father and grandfather had been. In that area, he was truly addicted and usually got what he wanted. Actually, he never made the purchase himself but enjoyed hearing his buyer relate to him all the intriguing details and challenges involved in the acquisition. The possible or probable illegality of the sale of an item was a strong consideration, but his buyer was shrewd in those matters. Keeping Brant Powers name out of the deal was the most important part of his job.

The Marie Antionette ring was brought to Brant's attention by his buyer who had been looking for the perfect wedding present for Merit. Brant had known she would be thrilled with his gift.

* * * *

The storm increased in intensity, and snow accumulated rapidly on the narrow country road. It was still a few miles to Greenwich. Merit's mind drifted back to other anniversary trips. The first in 1991, was to Australia and New Zealand. She planned the trip with Lee Bradley's help. Instead of May, they celebrated their first anniversary at the end of the year by inviting a group of their friends to cruise with them and watch the America's Cup races in Freemantle.

Merit's first anniversary gift from Brant was a gold ring that had belonged to William Bligh, captain of the BOUNTY. The face of the ring was engraved with the insignia of the British Royal Navy, and the initials "W.B." were inscribed inside. She also gave Brant an Australian gift, an original chart, dated 1552, drawn by one of the British explorers of that continent, which was known at the time as Terra Australis.

Brant's surprise second anniversary trip in 1992 was to Seoul, to attend the Summer Olympics. He'd combined it with a business trip, spending time in meetings with heads of his subsidiary banking institutions in Seoul and Pusan.

Merit knew members of the U.S. Olympic equestrian team and had spent most of her free time working out with them. She had qualified for the Olympic team four years before but took a bad spill in the preliminaries and fractured her wrist; she had to drop off the team.

Merit's second anniversary gift from Brant was a beautifully carved miniature jade pagoda ring from the Ming dynasty. Her gift to him was a twelfth-century B.C. Peking opium pipe.

For their third anniversary in 1993, Lee Bradley had helped Merit arrange a one-month photo safari in Africa. They postponed the trip until October because of the intense heat in Africa in May. They traveled more then two thousand miles through Kenya and Tanzania. Brant's greatest thrill was the trip to Olduvai Gorge, where the Leakeys had unearthed the million-year-old fossil hominids, the earliest near-man skeletal remains ever discovered. Merit made arrangements for Brant to meet with Dr. Mary Leakey and view the fossil finds at the Archaeological Museum in Nairobi.

Their anniversary gifts to each other that year were very old, delicately carved ebony figurines. His was a graceful, life-sized, high-breasted young woman, and hers a tall, muscular warrior aiming a spear. Both gifts were said to have belonged to an ancient chief of the Masai tribe.

* * * *

Merit was about two miles from the town when she recognized a car coming from the opposite direction. It was her best friend, Stacy Logan. They pulled up beside each other and lowered their windows.

"What in the world are you doing out on a day like this?" Stacy yelled.

The snow was beating against Merit's face, and when she opened her mouth to reply, she caught snowflakes and laughed. "On my way to see my favorite travel agent to make plans for our 5th anniversary trip."

Stacy shouted back, "Bring me back another exotic gift like this sable hat you bought me last year in Russia."

"My god, did I buy that monstrosity for you?" Merit laughed.

Stacy pulled the fur hat down over her ears, waved goodbye, and called, "*Nostrovia.*"

Merit grinned, remembering their fourth anniversary trip. In 1994, with Gorbachev's policies of perestroika and glasnost in full swing, Brant had to make a trip to Russia to investigate some lucrative banking opportunities. He'd been a bit dubious about Merit enjoying their fourth wedding anniversary in a communist country, but once again, Lee Bradley put together an exciting itinerary that included visits to interesting sights in Moscow and St. Petersburg. The highlight of the trip for Merit was Brant's anniversary gift. He had arranged a meeting for her with an antique dealer who had just acquired a magnificent Imperial Faberge' egg, which had been presented to Czar Nicholas II by Karl Faberge' himself. It was an eight-inch, milky agate egg, mounted on a gold and lapis lazuli base, and enclosed by a golden trelliswork cage. Set at each intersection of the cage were magnificent rose diamonds, amethysts and champagne diamonds. The oval egg opened lengthwise, and the surprise inside was a black onyx stallion with golden hoofs and ruby eyes. It reared up on its hind legs when the egg was opened. It was made in St. Petersburg, authentically marked with the workman's initials in the cyrillic characters used by Faberge'. The gift enthralled Merit.

Merit's gift to Brant was a letter written in 1560 by Ivan the Terrible to his son, Theodore.

Both gifts had to be taken out of Russia secretly. A friend at the American Embassy transported them back to America in diplomatic pouches.

* * * *

Merit turned into the parking lot next to Lee Bradley's agency. She ran through the unplowed snow and entered the foyer.

The receptionist greeted her warmly, "Hello, Mrs. Powers. You're brave coming out on a day like this. Here, let me have your jacket, and I'll let Lee know you're here."

Lee came down the hall and into the reception area, extending her hand. "I guess I knew you'd show up, in spite of the storm."

"I can't wait for you to fill me in on the details on this great adventure," Merit said. "Let's get right down to work."

They settled themselves in the lounge area of Lee's office, and the travel agent opened a folder. "I'll run through what I have so far," said Lee. "First, are you sure that Dr. Powers can be away from business for May and June? Because that's the most important part of the commitment. He'll be the only American archaeologist member of the team.

My client Dr. McGuire who brought this exciting exploration to my attention, stressed that hanging in there with Dr. Stanton, the director, for two months is vital.

Merit assured her, "I checked with Brant's closest associate, and he saw no reason why Brant couldn't be away for that length of time. I think the opportunity to take part in an archaeological exploration of an ancient cave on Santorini will be the most meaningful anniversary vacation I could give him. He's always wanted to go back there. When he was in college, he worked on a dig in Santorini one summer. He speaks Greek you know. His mother who passed away a few years ago, was Greek and had taught him the language when he was a child, and he has often taken refresher courses."

"Oh, I didn't know that," Lee sounded pleased. That will come in handy, I'm sure. I have some good news for you, Mrs. Powers. You've been given permission to be an official member of the team. Dr. McGuire received a letter yesterday from Dr. Stanton stating that he'd be delighted to use your photography and art skills."

"Oh, that's great! Now I won't feel like a fifth wheel." Lee handed Merit two large books. "Dr. Stanton sent these books on archaeological photography and drawing so he can put you to work when you get to Santorini."

"I'll start studying right away."

Lee said, "The only drawback now is getting funding for the project. Dr. Stanton is still waiting to hear from sources that had seemed willing to help finance the project.

"Tell him not to worry about financing. "Merit said. "I will be happy to cover all expenses. Brant does that when he hears about an excavation being halted for lack of funds. Please inform Dr. Stanton that I would be honored to underwrite the project. You did say Dr. Stanton is doing the excavation unpaid. How generous of him."

"Yes, he is, and I'm sure he'll be thrilled to hear about your generous contribution. Why don't I give you Dr. McGuire's phone number at the hospital, and maybe you and Dr. Powers can arrange to meet with him and Dr. Stanton to get all the details? I assume you'll have to tell Dr. Powers very shortly."

"I have a wonderful idea. Why don't I set up a dinner date with the doctors, and I'll tell Brant it's to discuss our 5th anniversary vacation. You must come, too, Lee!"

"That's very nice of you, Mrs. Powers, but it's not necessary."

"Of course it is. You brought this adventure to us. And really, Lee, I wish you'd call me Merit. You've been an important friend to both Brant and me for such a long time."

Merit stood up and walked over to the window, now thickly laced with powdered snow. She murmured softly, "Imagine, Lee, exploring a cave on the ancient Greek island of Santorini. I've read that some people think it might have been Plato's Atlantis." When she turned, her face glowed with animation, and she held her hands together as if praying. "If it really were Atlantis, just think of the treasures we might find in the cave. Maybe we'll find a magnificent cache of ancient jewels, hidden for thousands of years. My God, wouldn't that be exciting?"

An uncomfortable feeling came over Lee, and a disturbing thought crossed her mind: I wonder if I made a mistake involving the Powers in this exploration, knowing their obsessiveness about antiquities. I hope their motives are honorable.

* * * *

A few weeks later at dinner with Wade Stanton, Matt McGuire and Lee Bradley present, Merit announced to Brant, the plans for their 5th wedding-anniversary trip. He was astonished.

"I'm speechless, and that doesn't happen often," he chuckled. "I can't think of anything I'd rather do! Thank you so much my darling, Merit. He hugged and kissed her. Then turned to Wade. "Wade, let's get together real soon, so you can fill me in on all the details."

"Yes, we should do that, Brant. I'll be going a month ahead of the rest of you to make sure everything is in order. And again, let me tell you and Merit how much I appreciate your financial help. This exploration would never have been possible without it.

Brant commented with a sly grin, "I think the main reason our unlikely team is being allowed to undertake this exploration is because of my darling wife's generosity."

Wade added, "I'm also sure, Brant, that because you have been the money angel behind numerous archaeological endeavors certainly helped win approval by the authorities.

Brant shrugged off Wade's remark and asked, "Who is the Greek archaeologist we'll be working with?"

His name is Dr. Nikos Konstantinou. He sounds very organized. He's lined up laborers, and he's settled all the legal necessities. He said the authorities in Athens are pessimistic about what the cave might hold, but he's optimistic and feels that it will turn out to be a significant find. He sounds like a very congenial fellow. He's arranged housing for us in the small village of St. Demetrius, about 500 feet below the cave site. We'll be in the compound where his home is located. Brant, you and Merit will have a house to yourselves, and we men will be in the main house, which will also serve as the dining and meeting area. Matt and I will sleep upstairs. The only thing that bothers me, after seeing this magnificent home of yours, is that your quarters in Santorini may not be acceptable for you. The place sounds very primitive. No private baths, but we will have maid service and a cook. Nikos says, "We'll all be like one big happy family."

"Oh, I think it will be fun roughing it for a change, Merit said.

Matt looked at Merit and frowned. "You ought to make Lee come along. She got you into this mess."

Lee frowned at Matt. "No thanks, I'm slightly claustrophobic. I don't think I'd be much help in a cave."

Matt and Lee always tried to be discrete when others were around, but she blushed when Matt casually slid his hand under the table and squeezed her knee.

A moment later, Lee placed her hand on Matt's thigh and pinched him. She loved his body, it was so solid. Although his waistline had thickened a bit and his brown short-cropped hair was sprinkled with gray, at fifty-eight, he still was an attractive man. His square-jawed Irish face was highlighted by pale blue eyes that crinkled at the edges, giving the illusion that he was smiling all the time. In fact, he did have a wonderful sense of humor. Lee would miss him greatly.

From that evening on, their anticipation grew as they all looked forward to the upcoming adventure.

CHAPTER FOUR

The Island of Santorini, April 2, 1995

Wade Stanton, a slight, wiry, soft-spoken man, was fifty-six. He was married and had four children. His hair had thinned out on top, giving him the look of a friar. His demeanor would make one think he was timid, but that was not the case. He had explored some of the deepest and most dangerous caves in the world. He was a highly respected speleologist and geologist.

He loved ancient history, and ever since he'd received word that he would be directing the Santorini cave exploration, he read everything he could about the island's history. He left a month before the others to make preparations.

Although he had read a great deal about the geology of Santorini, he was overwhelmed as the ship sailed into the horseshoe-shaped caldera of Santorini. The island had once been round until a catastrophic volcanic eruption blew out the middle of the island and left a circle of land. Then slowly, parts of the circle broke away, leaving the island in the shape it is today. The ominous stratified rock formations on the walls of the caldera were streaked with red, green, white, black and gray. He couldn't begin to judge the millions of years it had taken to build such a magnificent monument of nature.

Also dramatic was the array of whitewashed houses and blue-domed churches that seemed to grow out of the top of the thousand-foot cliff. There were also smaller islands in the caldera, and Wade easily spotted the most interesting one, Nea Kaimeni. Below it is a semi-active volcano exuding gases and steam. He had read that this oozing up from the sea had been taking place for centuries. Cinder cones of subterranean volcanoes have been growing steadily since the 1600 B.C. volcanic eruption. He thought it eerie to suddenly realize that he was sailing into a harbor over the crater of an active volcano lying a thousand feet below the ship.

Because the caldera was so deep, the ship had to tie up to a buoy and small tenders called *caiques* were standing by to ferry passengers ashore to the port of Skala, a small landing area that can only be reached by donkey or the newly built cable car system.

Dr. Nikos Konstantinou, the local archaeologist, had written Wade to say that he would meet the ship. He would be Wade's first assistant and also act as *thesaurophylax* (protector of treasures). He would be responsible for making sure that any artifacts discovered at the site were not stolen. He was curious about the unusual team that would be exploring the cave; a speleologist, a wealthy archaeologist and his wife who'd paid all the expenses for supplies and equipment, and a medical doctor.

He approached the ferry in a private *caique* and recognized Stanton immediately, sizing up all the crates spread out around the man. He yelled to a sailor who was assisting passengers. "Yo! That's my passenger. Will you help load his equipment on my *caique* down here?" He rolled up some drachma and tossed them up to the sailor, who unrolled and counted them, then grinned and said. *"Efcharisto."*

Wade waved to Nikos, thinking, he looks like a cheerful sort, thank God. He hoped that he wouldn't be stuck with a dour Greek who would challenge the team's every move. Greek archaeologists have a strong tendency to distrust foreigners who work their turf, and with good reason; so much had been stolen in the past.

Nikos shook Wade's hand as he hopped into the *caique* and said in a humorous voice, "Ah! Dr Stanton, I presume."

"Ah! Doctor, er, ah…give me a second now, Kon-stan-ti-nou. How'd I do?" Wade grinned.

"Good! To be good friends, call me Nikos."

"Okay, Nikos, and call me Wade."

The crates were loaded aboard the *caique*, and it set off for shore. When they landed at the dock at Skala, Nikos offered drachma to two dock workers who agreed to transport the crates by donkey up to his truck. He had parked it in downtown Fira which is the largest city on the island and the capital city of Santorini. Nikos and Wade rode up to the town in the newly built cable car. After the crates arrived, the drivers unloaded them from the donkeys onto Nikos' truck. The two men then drove off towards the southeastern part of the island. Although the truck was old and noisy, the main road was excellent until they came to a turnoff, where they began to climb the steep and serpentine mountainside. The road was mostly paved, but Nikos was a wild driver. Wade became more nervous at each hairpin curve. It seemed the wheels must surely be teetering on the edge of the road.

When they reached the top of the thousand foot mountain, known as Mesa Vouno. Wade took a deep breath of relief. The ride had been somewhat frightening.

They got out of the truck, and Nikos grinned at Wade. "The hill is like your roller-coaster ride, eh?"

"Worse!" Wade admitted honestly.

"You'll get use to it. Look up," Nikos said, pointing. "Five hundred feet above us are ruins of ancient city of Thera, where cave is. And see, look down below, that is my village, St. Demetrius. Let's get back in truck and drive up to ruins and unload our equipment, eh?"

THE SANTORINI ODYSSEY

When they reached the site of the ruins, Wade jumped out and ran ahead quickly up the steep path to the entrance of the ruins. He was awed by the sight of the 3,500-year-old rubble that had once been an important ancient city. "God, this is incredible, Nikos!"

"And look out to our splendorous Aegean Sea. Now you can see why ancient Thera was built up here, eh? very strategic location. You can see if enemy try to approach island." Nikos stopped. "Ah, here is your office, which as you can see once was Byzantine church, eh?"

Nikos put his arm over Wade's shoulder. "My friend, come, before we unload, we'll go inside office where it is cool, and have drink of finest wine you ever tasted. Our retsina of Santorini is gift from our gods." Nikos threw his arms up to the heavens in a gesture of thanks.

Nikos, tall for a Greek, was over six feet. His classical dark-skinned face was highlighted by a trimmed moustache that continued along the sides of his mouth to join a V-shaped goatee. His smile exposed large white teeth and a gold eye tooth on the left side of his mouth. His broad shoulders accentuated a narrow waist. A black cap with a visor was cocked jauntily on his jet-black hair. His friendly eyes caught one's attention immediately.

The office was a small shed covered by a tin roof and closed in by ancient Byzantine era walls. It contained an old kitchen table, four chairs, and a cabinet that held fragments of pottery. Along the walls, shelving had been installed that displayed potshards and fragments of stone scored with unintelligible marks, laid out like a jigsaw puzzle waiting to be solved. Picks, mattocks, shovels, and sifting screens lay scattered about.

Nikos and Wade were greeted by the guard, Elias Kaldara, who held out two glasses of wine to them.

"*Yia sas*! To your health, Dr. Wade Stanton," Elias said as they clicked the three glasses together.

"Ah, *efcharisto*," Wade muttered, stumbling over the difficult word for 'thank you'.

Elias finished his wine and excused himself.

While they drank the dark, retsina, Nikos brought Wade up to date on what had happened since Elias' young son, Kristos discovered the cave.

"We feel sure that steps leading down mean something of importance, for sure," Nikos said. Then he paused and smiled. "Don't steps always lead somewhere?"

"I hope you're right, Nikos. Could you give me a tour of the site now?" Wade didn't want to be inhospitable, but he didn't want to finish the wine, which tasted like turpentine. He placed the half-empty glass on the table.

"Of course, of course. You are anxious to see cave, eh? You'll see, I'm good guide. But don't you want more wine?" Nikos teased, knowing full well how the wine had affected Wade. Then, once again, he put his big arm around Wade's shoulder and led him out of the office into the sunlight.

The pressure of Nikos' grip on his shoulder actually hurt, and Wade was relieved when Nikos let go and walked ahead of him up a path to the ruins, narrating while he led Wade through the ancient streets of Thera.

"How big is the city?" Wade asked.

"I would say it is about 800 meters long but only about 150 meters wide," Nikos answered.

He conducted the tour with great enthusiasm. "Here is *agora*, marketplace, eh? Like, how you say? Downtown. Where action is, dude!"

Wade laughed, "You're pretty good with American slang. Where'd you pick it up?"

"American tourists love to rap with Nikos, eh? And I love it, too, especially with ladies," he said in a sexy tone, raising his eyebrows.

Wade thought with some relief, I'm glad the ladies turn him on. The shoulder hugs made him a bit nervous.

"Look here," Nikos yelled. "This is commandery, lookout garrison for army. And here, look, their gymnasium." He made a pose like an ancient discus thrower.

Nikos led him through the rubble of the sanctuary of Artemidoros of Perge, the Temple of Dionysus, the royal Stoa, the theater, the Temple of Pythian Apollo, and the sanctuary of the Egyptian gods.

"Over here, look, Wade, you see Temple of Apollo Karneios. He was male god. And here, square of *Gymnopaidiai*, a place where exciting festival took place. Maybe today, you'd say, yo! erotic happening, man!" his face burst into a mischievous smile. "I tell you about it."

He jumped up on a two-foot ancient platform that was supporting a large fragment of a Doric column. Putting his left foot on the column and laying his left hand on his knee, he leaned forward and pointed his right index finger down to Wade. It was such a dramatic pose, that for a split second, Wade visualized Nikos as an ancient philosopher who was about to expound on an important theorem.

"At full moon, here at this very place, square of *Gymnopaidiai*, which translates to 'dance of nude boys,' in this special holy place they held Karneia, it was a major festival of Dorians to honor their great god Apollo. Most important event of festival was *Gymnopaidiai*, when young nude boys danced and sang paeans to Apollo, all over square here. If you would like me to do so, I will translate for you many archaic, erotic inscriptions engraved on stones Many will tell you about how excited crowds get watching bodies of young boys swaying sensuously."

Nikos resumed his lecture, sensing that he might have offended Wade. "Very decadent era of island's history. Come now, we'll see what you came to see most, Grotto of Hermes and Heracles." Nikos led Wade under a rope and past a sign that said *Kyndinos*. "That means danger. Tourist can't go down to grotto. They have to stay behind rope. We don't want locals or tourists in our cave and steal our treasure, eh? It was big news in paper when archaeologists and I went into cave and aftershock of earthquake happen again. We didn't get hurt though." He led Wade down the steep stairs and when they reached the ancient grotto, he put one arm over Wade's shoulder and held out the other dramatically. "My friend, here it is, grotto of Hermes and Heracles." A rope had been strung across the entrance, which Nikos untied. "Come inside. Now you can see where back wall of hewn stones collapsed and made entrance to our cave, eh?"

Wade moved forward, looking around at the solid limestone walls and ceiling of the grotto, then took another step and gazed into the gaping hole in the back wall. All he could see was a huge rubble of limestone chunks piled up on the stairs. Disappointment filled him. "The earthquake, huh?"

"It's like gods didn't want us to go into cave, eh?"

"I sure hope you've hired some strong laborers, Nikos. It will take weeks to clear this rubble and uncover the stairs again."

Taking a comical stance with his feet apart, his left hand on his hip, head cocked to one side, and right hand pressed against his forehead, he said, "How you say it? Piece of cake! Three Greek men, a pulley rig and strong *moulari,* big, big mule. You'll see, no problem."

"I hope we get it cleared before my team arrives."

"Tomorrow we work. Today you are tourist. Come, my friend, let me show you Roman baths. You know they had both hot and cold. For hot, they light fires under stone floor in baths. You know, water was always scarce here, and still is. Even today, much water is brought to island by boat and piped into many homes. But every house also has its own cistern to capture rain, just like ancient times. Come up here and see private houses. You can tell that some had upstairs and down, eh? Many were built here near edge of ridge to capture glorious view of our Aegean Sea." Nikos spread out his arms to the sea, breathing in the fresh salt air.

"I can visualize from these foundations that the rooms were built around an internal courtyard," Wade said. "I'd like to build a house like that back home in Massachusetts."

"I know capital of Massachusetts is Boston. Many Greeks live there, but they come back here for visit almost every year," Nikos said with pride.

When they turned to go back to the office, Wade tripped on an uneven step and quickly reached out with his hands, flattening them against a wall to prevent falling.

Nikos heard him stumble and turned quickly. His face lit up in a big smile.

Wade frowned at Nikos, who was pointing to the spot where Wade's hands rested on the wall. Wade looked where his hands were pressed against the wall and quickly pulled them away. "Good lord, is that what I think it is?"

Graphically engraved on the bordered cornerstone of the wall of the house was a well-preserved, archaic phallic symbol encircled by a cartouche. Wade hung his head, looked away, then looked back at Nikos with a sarcastic grin.

Nikos, enjoying Wade's embarrassment, patted him on the back and winked. "So you discover House of Phallus, eh? It must have belonged to Romans, not Greeks, I'm sure," he laughed.

Wade put his hands behind his back and appraised the etching. "Tell me, Nikos, is it true that ancient Greece was the land of nymphs and satyrs?"

"And land of tragedy and comedy, too," Nikos mused.

Suddenly there was a distant clap of thunder, and rain began to fall.

Nikos looked up and held out his hands. "Our gods favor you; you bring us rain. That is good omen."

The two men ran back to the office, and Wade gathered up his personal belongings and stowed them in the truck. They drove down the hill for a short distance until they came to a level place where Nikos stopped the vehicle.

"Hurry, my friend. We must run to where you will live. My truck is too wide for village street."

They entered the village, passed the Greek Orthodox Church of St. Demetrius, then hurried through the twisting alleys.

Nikos called out to the villagers who were standing in their doorways, smiling and holding out their hands, savoring the precious rain.

The cobbled streets were clean. The houses were immaculately whitewashed cement and stucco. Most windows were arched, recessed, and decorated with lovely flowers hanging gracefully from colorful pots. Each house had pipes from the roof gutters leading to cisterns to capture the rainfall.

Many of the elderly women had few teeth and wore black from head to toe. Their skin, like that of the men, was tanned and leather-like. They were handsome people with full-featured faces. Adorable children, all neatly dressed, waved and smiled from the doorways when Wade and Nikos rushed past. The only transportation Wade saw on the narrow, winding road was a small car, a few motor scooters and several donkeys.

They entered a courtyard at a dead end. Nikos gestured for Wade to follow him toward a house with a bright blue door in the center of the semicircle of white buildings. Each of the one-two-and three-story houses had a different colored door. At the left end of the complex, set apart from the last house, was a stone windmill with a thatched roof. At the right end lay a large garden and stable.

"Welcome to your home for next few months," Nikos said, gesturing for Wade to enter.

They stood in a large room with spare furnishings and rustic lighting fixtures that hung from the walls. Nikos walked across the room, threw open the large shuttered window and pointed to the spectacular view of the Aegean. In spite of the black rolling thunderclouds, lightning and driving rain, Wade was astonished at the magnificence of the panorama that stretched out before him.

"Nikos, I've never seen anything so mesmerizing."

Nikos put his arm around Wade's shoulder. "Ah, my friend, I am glad you are happy with view because there is not much else in these quarters to impress you."

There was a knock at the front door, and a voice called out, "*Kalimera sas*, Nikos."

Two women entered the main room. The older looked to be about forty, and the other a teenager.

"Ah! Anna and Katina. And *kalimera* to you, too, my lovely ladies. This is Dr. Wade Stanton, who will be boss man on cave exploration." Nikos gave both women quick kisses on their cheeks. "Wade, meet Anna and Katina Brady. They will be our most important assistants."

Wade looked quizzically at Nikos, then stepped forward extending his hand to the older woman, Anna, who gave him a weak smile. He offered his hand to the young woman, who quickly looked to her mother as if asking for permission. Anna nodded and Katina cast her eyes down and held out her hand.

Anna, was a small-boned woman with erect posture and a full bosom. She dressed in an old-fashioned manner: a faded cotton dress, misshapen sweater, ankle socks, black oxford shoes and a kerchief tied in back on the nape of her neck. Her broad, high-cheek boned face had a majestic air, except for the soulful eyes underlined by dark circles. No doubt she had been attractive at one time.

Katina, an extraordinary beauty and tall like her mother, had a slim, voluptuous body. Her long hair fell in soft waves that turned up at the ends. Its color betrayed her mixed parenthood; it was a striking titian color. She had lovely, large dark eyes, a perfect Grecian nose and a full sensuous mouth like her mother's. Her T-shirt clung to her full, upturned breasts; the rise of her nipples and her small waist gave her torso an extremely provocative appearance. Her jeans appeared to be molded to her. Her walk, like her mother's, was a graceful, sensual stride. In spite of her obvious beauty, Katina appeared to be quite shy, or more likely, restrained by a protective mother.

"Anna and Katina will cook meals, clean houses, and do laundry. They live in house next door." Nikos smiled broadly and put his arm around the women's shoulder and squeezed it.

Anna emphatically lifted his arm away, and Katina ducked out from under his embrace.

Speaking bluntly in rather good English, Anna said, "Welcome to Santorini, Dr. Stanton. We expect prompt payment for work we do, every week, on Friday, no later. Here is your lunch basket for today. *Kalimera sas.*" The two women turned abruptly to leave, kissing their fingertips and touching the colorful icon of the Blessed Virgin and Baby Jesus on the wall next to the door.

Wade frowned at Nikos. "Well, well, do tell me, Nikos about these two women with the American surname."

"Anna is American by marriage. Seventeen years ago, she met Dr. Joe Brady, who worked on the Kalliste dig. They fell in love, married, had beautiful Katina, and then off he goes to nobody know where.

He'll never come back, and she's too proud to get divorce. She says, 'He'll come back one day.' I say she'll wait forever. She is still lovely woman who needs man. And daughter, eh? every man on Santorini has his eye on Katina, but Anna never lets her out of her sight. You'll see." Nikos began to spread out the lunch that Anna had packed in a basket.

"My, it looks delicious," Wade said.

"Maybe tonight, I'll take you out for more delicious Greek food at my cousin Spyro's taverna in Fira."

The two men stood looking out the window as they shared hard-boiled eggs, feta cheese, tomatoes and slices of crusty bread. Nikos had retsina. Wade drank beer. When they finished, Wade, who by now felt hot and sticky from his trip, asked Nikos, "Could I take a shower?"

"Ah! Come, I show you *banio*, bathroom, you call it, eh? It is two-seat *touleta* and archaic tub and shower." Nikos laughed.

They went outside to a small out-building that smelled strongly of lime and mildew. Set in the corner was a wooden two-holer *touleta* with a water box above and a chain to release water for flushing. A tin cup and a pail of lime were alongside. A cupful was to be used with each use. It supposedly kept the *banio* odor-free and disinfected. The lime and waste were carried off in a downhill culvert to a farm area, where Nikos said it was used as fertilizer. The shower over the tub was simply a piece of hose connected to a pipe which was connected to the cistern on the roof. A tattered photo of Mesa Vouno was tacked to the wall.

"A cold shower is good for you, you know, especially when you are away from your woman."

"I've heard that, Nikos," Wade chuckled. "By the way, are you married? I haven't heard you mention a wife or family."

"Ah, my friend, I came very close to marriage about seven, maybe eight times, but at last minute, I am saved. You've heard expression 'variety is spice of life,' that's me, Nikos. I fall in love with every woman I meet, and all women I meet fall in love with me. I would be very bad husband. About that, there is no doubt."

After his shower, Wade returned to the house, where Nikos was waiting and led him upstairs to his room. This is your sleeping room." He looked at his watch. "It's after one o'clock. Time for siesta, my friend."

"Siesta?" Wade asked, perplexed. "I thought we'd start working at the cave site right away, now that the storm has blown over."

"Wade, my friend, siesta is tradition that goes back to days of Homer. Would you argue with him? We will sleep now until four or five. You will see everyone stops work, all shops close, and all Greece is silent. Even birds are silent. You will learn to love siesta."

Wade smiled and closed the door to his room.

* * * *

Katina pulled back the covers on the beds for siesta. "*Mana*, don't you think Dr. Stanton looks like a nice man?"

"A nice man, yes. Nice men are not afraid to wear their wedding rings. Because he wears his ring, I know he's a good man."

"Did my father wear his wedding ring?"

"The last time I saw him, yes. How long he wore it after he left Santorini, I don't know."

"Did my father look like Dr. Stanton?"

"Not at all! your father was a big man with bright red hair. Why do you ask the same questions over and over?"

"I just wish that he would let us know if he is ever coming back," Katina said with a deep sigh.

Anna closed the shutters and looked over her shoulder at Katina. "What is all this talk about your father? Why do you keep up this useless wishing of yours? don't I take good care of you?"

"Have you given up wishing he'd come back, *Mana*? i think you have. I wish you would try to find out if he is dead or alive. Then we could get on with our lives."

Anna moved quickly to Katina's bed and glared down at her. "What do you mean, get on with our lives?"

"You don't like your life?"

Katina reached up and grabbed her mother around the waist. "*Mana, Mana*, you know I love you. I don't mean to hurt you. I just wish you didn't have to do all the hard work you do to have money. If you had a husband, your life would be so much better."

"Hah! Who would marry me? How can I marry without a divorce, which the church won't give without lots of money?"

"I bet Nikos would marry you. I know he thinks you're pretty."

"Nikos! Ha! Some husband he'd be!"

"He's nice, *Mana*. He's always nice to me."

"What do you mean nice to you. Have you ever seen him alone?"

"No, of course not. Then she added with a shy smile, my friends tell me he's a very sexy man."

"Sexy! I've never heard you talk like that before. I don't think you even know the meaning."

"*Mana*, I'm sixteen years old. I hear lots of things. and I know I'm pretty because people tell me so. I also know I must be sexy because my friends tell me men look at me, well you know, like they desire me."

Anna put her two hands up to her mouth and cried out, *"Kristo's Kai Panayia*! what now am I to do!" She knelt down at the side of Katina's bed, pulled Katina out, and made her kneel. She blessed herself, and with her eyes only, instructed Katina to start praying with her for the salvation of her soul. Katina dropped her head and suppressed a smile as she prayed aloud with her *Mana*. Katina wished that there could be a man in their house, either a husband for her *Mana*, or a husband for herself.

CHAPTER FIVE

By April 30th, the local laborers had cleared the rubble from the cave entrance and exposed the set of stairs that had been sealed off by the aftershocks of the earthquake in the previous December. Wade and Nikos anxiously looked forward to the arrival of Merit and Brant and Matt McGuire the following morning. Matt's room would be upstairs in the main house, where Wade was also staying. The Powers would have the small one room house with the yellow door located to the left of the main house. Glass doors opened out to a patio covered with white clematis and a spectacular view of the Aegean. The four Americans would share the archaic bath in the shed. The downstairs of the main house would serve as the dining and sitting room for the whole team.

The house with the pink door belonged to Anna and Katina. It was to the right of the main house. They had a sitting room, bedroom, a kitchen and an inside bath. Nikos lived next door to the Powers in the three-story house with the double green doors. There were three bedrooms, a living room, large kitchen and inside bath.

Nikos set up one of his bedrooms as a darkroom for Merit's photography. Fortunately, electric power in the village was supplied by the island's oil-fired, steam-generating plant. Both Nikos' and Anna's kitchen had electric-stove top burners along with brick ovens for baking.

* * * *

At eight o'clock in the morning on May 1, the passenger ferry from Athens sailed into the harbor of Skala.

Brant, although still skeptical about how Merit would handle the isolation of a remote island for two months, was anxious at the prospect of getting back to archaeology.

The ship's sailors were standing by to secure lines to a buoy, and *caiques* waited to take passengers ashore.

Brant, Merit and Matt were awe-struck by the spectacular view that stretched out before them when they sailed into the caldera.

"Look," Brant said, pointing to the sheer, black cliffs that rose up from the sea like an iron barricade. "And look up at the white houses and churches all along the rim."

"It's both sinister and wondrous." Merit gasped. "It looks like a make-believe village."

Matt, hung over the rail and searched for Wade in the flotilla of small boats below. He turned back to Brant and Merit and said, "I think I'm going to love this place! it looks exciting!"

"I once found it erotic!" Brant said, scanning the mountaintop. "When I was a nineteen-year-old college boy and worked here at the Kalliste dig site, it was work hard all day and play hard all night with the women."

Smiling wryly, Merit squeezed Brant's face in her hands. "You'll only be playing with one woman this time. Remember that, Dr. Powers!"

Matt spotted Wade and called out, "Wade, up here!" The large *caique* circling near the bow, beeped its horn. Wade and Nikos waved.

It took quite a bit of time to load all the luggage into the small rocking boat. They could barely introduce themselves because of the noisy engine and didn't say much until they reached shore.

Nikos never took his eyes off Merit. He was captivated by her beauty. He became unusually subdued, and even his flamboyant personality disappeared.

Wade thought, Oh God, he's pathetic. He's fallen for her already! He caught Nikos' eye, winked, nodded toward Merit, then shook his head back and forth in a "no way" gesture.

Nikos nodded at Wade and mouthed, "I know, I know."

Merit became self-conscious as Nikos continued to sneak stares at her. She had practiced saying his name, and when they arrived at the dock, she looked at him and said. "Dr. Konstantinou, we really appreciate all you have done for us. We're looking forward to working with you." Nikos stared blankly, then recovered. "Oh, me too! He reached into his pocket. "Here, I have gifts for you, husband, and Doctor. They're called *kombologia,* worry beads. Nikos demonstrated. See, you drop bead, then another, over and over, click, click."

They all took the dark amber beads that were strung on a small linked chain and tried to copy Nikos, dropping a bead at a time. "It helps you not be nervous, eh? They're like Captain Queeg's balls. Did you see CAINE MUTINY? I saw it in Athens. He was nervous and always rubbing his balls in his hand, eh?"

The three Americans suppressed laughter at his unwitting ribald statement, pretending to be laughing at their ineptness in handling the beads.

He threw his arm out expansively toward them. "We'll be good friends, I know that. Call me Nikos, please."

Merit said, "And please call me Merit, Nikos."

"Good, I'm happy about that. I thought I had to call you Mrs. Two Names, Morton-Powers?"

They all laughed.

"I'm Brant."

"And I'm Matt."

"Okay, now we're friends. The donkeys will take your luggage up to my truck, and we'll take cable car."

Nikos held Merit's elbow and directed her view up the thousand-foot zigzagging donkey trail of stairs. "See how men hold donkey's tail," he said. "It helps them to climb steep stairs and control donkey. It is believed that these donkeys contain souls of dead, and when they get big heavy tourist, they are doing their purgatory." he laughed. "The cable car is faster but not as exciting, eh?"

"I'd like to try the donkeys sometime," Merit said.

"Okay, we'll do that on our day off." Nikos answered.

They all rode to the top in the cable car.

Once the donkeys arrived with the luggage, the bags were loaded onto Nikos' truck, which he drove alone, followed by Wade and the others in a rented car.

They enjoyed the ride along the highway until they turned off and started up the switchback road to the village. Not only did the hairpin curves frighten the newcomers, but Nikos' old truck made the journey more treacherous. They were following so closely behind that the windshield of the car was continuously pelted with dust and donkey dung, almost blocking Wade's vision completely.

When they reached the village, Wade parked the car behind the truck and said to his passengers, "I bet you didn't think we'd make it."

"No shit, Wade! Sorry. pardon my language, Merit." Matt said.

Merit said to Matt. "I'll never go down that road again until we're going home." She looked back down the mountain and shivered.

"Oh, come on, it wasn't that bad. I didn't mind it!" Brant bragged almost childishly.

Merit and Matt gave him a sarcastic look.

There were six village men with donkeys waiting to unload the gear and take it through the winding alley that led to the compound. The donkey drivers doffed their caps when the newcomers approached.

Some elderly village women, with arms folded across their chests, gathered near Nikos' truck. They were anxious to get a look at the foreigners. When the newcomers approached, the women leaned into each other while muttering comments. Merit realized they were staring mostly at her. She smiled and waved. They grinned toothless smiles and said, "*Kalimera sas.*"

Nikos ran to Merit's side and whispered in her ear, "Say *kalimera sas* to them. It means good morning."

Merit smiled and nodded to the women repeating, "*kalimera sas*"

"Ah, see, you make friends easy. They like you." he said enthusiastically.

"How nice of them to welcome us so warmly," Merit said to Nikos.

The donkey drivers, although small in stature, were strong. They quickly unloaded the truck, tied the luggage onto the donkeys' backs, then led the parade up through the narrow cobblestone street. Villagers came out to see the entourage pass by.

Merit said softly to Brant, "I can see already that we're going to have a very different anniversary vacation, but I'm sure it'll be fun."

Brant put his arm over Merit's shoulder and said, "I hope you still feel that way two months from now."

When they reached the gates of the compound, the donkey drivers stopped and waited for Nikos to tell them where the luggage should go.

Anna and Katina stood inside the compound gate. They nodded to the group, and Nikos quickly brought them forward.

He put his arms on their shoulders. "Ah! Here's the lovely Anna and Katina Brady."

Wade had written a glowing report about the women to the Powers and Matt.

Merit noticed how the two women gracefully squirmed out of his hold, and she suppressed a grin. She couldn't help but notice how intently the young girl was appraising her from head to toe. "Hello, Anna and Katina." She shook their hands. "How nice to meet you."

Brant and Matt stepped forward, greeted them and shook their hands. Both men were intrigued by the womens' shy demeanor.

Brant thought, the mother reminds me of a woman who probably was once attractive but now looks tired and drawn. And that girl, like a ripe peach! A strange feeling of de'ja'vu ran through him, making him feel that somehow he had seen the young beauty before.

Matt, a man deeply in love, sensed in the older woman a suppressed ardor, but her appearance was stoic. The daughter, he thought, was like a filly waiting to break from the gate. His thoughts turned to Lee; he missed her already. He had been told that Nikos had a telephone that the team could use. He'd check on his wife and talk to Lee tonight. He hated the charade he and Lee had been playing for the past ten years. But it would end soon because his wife could not live much longer than a year. Then, their relationship could be out in the open, and he would marry again.

Wade showed Matt his bedroom upstairs in the main house and Nikos took Brant and Merit to their small house. Anna and Katina stood by the doorway.

Nikos said hopefully, "It's small, but I think you'll like the view."

Merit rushed across the room and out through the open doors to the patio. "Brant, oh come look, quick! it's the most breathtaking sight. The sea looks like miles of glittering jewels. And look, is that a beach at the bottom of the mountain?" Brant came up behind her, put his hands on her shoulders and snuggled his head against hers. "It's a black sand beach of lava, darling!" he kissed her hair and cheek.

Anna looked at Nikos and raised her eyebrows. Katina leaned out to get a better look at the romantic scene.

Merit came back into the house and in one quick glance viewed the room that would be their home for two months. Everyone studied her face, watching for her reaction. She thought to herself, My God, I expected our quarters to be small, but, the tack room in our stables is bigger than this. She didn't know what to say. "It's so quaint, Brant. It'll be just fine." she said bravely.

Relieved, everyone smiled.

"If you need more luxury, you can share my home next door,' said Nikos. "I'd be honored to have you."

Merit thanked Nikos but insisted, "We'll be fine in our own little house."

Anna approached Merit. "Look, Missus, here is small sink in wall with good mirror for you to wash and for Mister to shave. We'll keep good water in pitcher for you every day."

Merit looked at the tiny mosaic sink. It was beautiful, but not very practical.

Katina stepped forward. "*Mana* and I will help you unpack, Missus, okay?"

"Why thank you very much, Katina. I'm sure we'll never be able to fit all our clothes in that closet and the chest," Merit said, looking around.

Anna gestured towards the two corners near the front door, "We'll make more closets in corners, here and here, and put in lots of nails for you to hang clothes. I have old curtains, I'll hang on walls for closet doors. Maybe we'll get everything put away." Then smiling faintly she added, "But maybe not. You have too many clothes, I think."

"Much too many!" Merit laughed. "I think I had better ship half of them back home."

Nikos took Brant outside, presumably to show him around, but actually he was concerned they would be too uncomfortable in such small quarters. Again, Nikos offered to share his home. Their luggage alone took up most of the room.

Brant reassured Nikos they'd be fine, "It'll be a challenge for Merit. She's a very adaptable woman."

Meanwhile Merit and Katina began unpacking while Anna rigged the additional closets in the corners. Katina "oohed" and "aahed", holding each piece of clothing for inspection and running her hands gently over the material.

"Missus, I've never seen so many beautiful clothes, "Katina sighed. "I'll take very good care of them when I wash and iron."

Merit looked at the young girl and could see how entranced she was. She felt guilty about having brought so many impractical things. "Maybe we could share some of them, Katina. We look to be the same size."

Anna quickly spun around, raised her head up proudly and in a harsh voice said, "No! Katina has plenty enough clothes."

Merit and Katina were startled by the ferocity in Anna's voice. Katina stared at her mother in disbelief.

Merit realized she had offended Anna and tried to soothe the situation by saying lightly, "I'm sure she does, Anna, I always bring too many clothes when I travel."

Katina was mortified by her mother's rudeness.

Anna looked sternly at her daughter and ordered, "Go to our house, and make us some cold lemon drinks."

When Katina was gone, Anna looked at Merit, then dropped her eyes in embarrassment. "Missus, I'm sorry. I can see my Katina thinks you're like movie star. She's never seen so many pretty clothes. She has never met any rich people before. If you spoil her with such fancy things, she'll be unhappy with her life here long after you leave our small village. I try to keep her happy, but we are very poor. I cook and clean for Nikos and scientist people who live here. I sell waste from *touleta* to farmer who lives down hill. I grow most of our food. Our life is very simple, not like *Ameriki* where her father came from."

"Yes, we'd heard that you were married to an American, Anna."

Anna briefly told Merit about the desertion of her husband right after Katina's birth. Then she laughed. "Because Katina is one half *Ameriki*, she begged me to buy her jeans to dress like *Ameriki* for when you come, Missus. She is very wonderful child, eh? I try to give her best life I can." she turned away and continued working on the closets.

Merit was deeply touched by Anna's protective love and put her hand on Anna's shoulders. "I understand. I won't spoil her, but it would be easy to do so. She's a delightful girl. If you let me, I'll give her some of my clothing as pay for any extra jobs she does for me. I will need a helper with my photography. Would that be all right?"

For a moment they stared at each other in silence, each seeking understanding. Anna smiled slowly. Merit grinned and put out her hand, "Is it a deal, Anna?"

THE SANTORINI ODYSSEY

Anna gripped Merit's hand. "It's good deal, Missus, but no charity. You pay Katina for her jobs with clothes. That is deal! But no more too tight jeans like she has now, eh?"

Both women laughed and held each other's hands.

At noon, after they unpacked, and moved their luggage and many of Merit's clothes into Nikos' house, the group met in the main house for a luncheon Anna had prepared. The table was covered with a hand-woven blue tablecloth, and beautiful flowers were laid out down the middle in a long red basket. During the meal, Nikos and Wade gave a joint dissertation on the cave site, touching on the historical background of the ancient city of Thera and the ruins that remained. They discussed their plans for the exploration of the cave while the newcomers listened attentively.

"Can we go up to the site after lunch, Nikos?" Merit asked.

"Yeah! How about it, Nikos?" Matt joined in.

"Sorry to say, no," Nikos said, "But you know old saying, 'When in Rome', Well, when in Greece, after we eat midday meal, we have siesta!"

Moving away from the table, the newcomers grumbled about not being tired, but they obeyed Nikos' order and went off to their rooms for siesta.

Merit and Brant stripped to their underwear and stretched out on their double bed. "It's going to take some getting used to, sleeping in this small bed after our king-size," Brant said while they positioned themselves.

"With your annoying habit of rolling over in your sleep, I'll get dumped on the floor." Merit teased.

Brant took her in his arms and pulled her close. "Then we'll sleep like this all the time. Isn't it nice?"

"Very nice," Merit purred, seductively crawling on top of her husband. arousing him almost instantly.

* * * *

Anna and Katina finished washing the lunch dishes and went to their bedroom. Katina talked endlessly about Merit and Brant. To her, they were like Cinderella and Prince Charming. Her face flushed with excitement.

"They are very good-looking, very rich and very nice, Katina dear, but they are just human beings. Stop gawking at them as if they were the king and queen of *Ameriki*. I keep expecting you to curtsy or bow, you silly girl," Anna teased, giving Katina a hug.

"Don't you think they are the most romantic couple? And I like Dr. Matt too. Don't you? I don't think he's married; he doesn't wear a wedding band."

"You're very observant young lady, but, yes, Doctor Matt does seem like a very nice person. Nikos told me he is married, but his wife has been ill for a long time. He came here to get a rest from doing so much surgery, Nikos says. But I guess he must be a good husband because he asked Nikos if he could use his telephone to check on his wife's health." Anna paused, then added, "But it does seem strange that a man would leave his sick wife. Let's go to sleep now, Katina. No more gossiping about the visiting royalty."

"*Kalispera sas, Mana*," Katina said as she rolled on her side, hugged her pillow and began romanticizing about Merit and Brant.

Anna's head was filled with memories of long ago. She had met Joe Brady the first day he arrived on the island to work on the Kalliste dig at Akrotiri. Nikos had invited Joe to live in his compound until he found something closer to the dig site. Within a few weeks, Anna and Joe were in love. Three months later they married, and Anna became pregnant with Katina within the first month of marriage. Joe was always buying her presents. He promised they'd visit America after their baby was born. She had been so proud of her tall, handsome, husband when they walked through the village. He was very romantic and would tell her a hundred times a day how much he loved her and how beautiful she was. And I was, she cried to herself as she looked across at her lovely Katina. Oh God, why did Joe leave us? It was a question she had asked herself a thousand times. I look at Mrs. Powers, and I am jealous. My, God, I might have been rich like her. Her eyes filled with tears. If he wasn't dead and he returned, would I take him back? No, no, I have pride. I don't want him back after the way he has treated us. But I do need a man, I want a man, but not any of the men around here who have tried to seduce me into their beds. It is such a lost cause! She choked back a sob of despair.

* * * *

At three o'clock, Merit and Brant were awakened by voices outside their window and saw the three men milling about the yard. They hopped out of bed quickly, slipped on robes and headed to the banio for a shower. They laughed while splashing each other with the hose and giggling like children.

Hearing the merriment, Nikos was at once both jealous and greatly alarmed at the way they were wasting water. Wade assured him that he would have a talk with the Powers about water conservation.

Soon the five of them were together and began walking through the winding village street to the truck. When they arrived, Nikos looked around and gave a shrill whistle. The young boy, Kristos Kaldara, came from behind a cluster of trees leading a black Arabian stallion, He grinned and looked impishly at Merit.

"Ah! Here is my little friend, Kristos," Nikos said. "Everybody say hello to him. He is very famous, you know. Kristos is great archaeologist who discovered cave we'll be working in."

They shook Kristos' hand and praised him for his great discovery. He blushed in embarrassment, but he was pleased with their compliments and offered them his services in the exploration of the cave. They thanked him and turned their attention to Merit, who was patting the horse's nose. When Brant took the reins from Kristos, the men watched for her reaction when she realized it was hers. They had been told, that because of her love of horses, Brant had purchased the horse in northern Greece and had it shipped here. Actually when Wade had told him that they would be using a truck to get to the cave every day, he didn't like the idea of Merit riding in a truck.

"Merit, I'd like you to meet Zeus, named after the great Greek god who, by the way, was born in a cave. He'll be your transportation to work every day, or to go to the beaches below."

Merit was too startled to speak. Her face filled with delight. She kept looking from the horse to Brant.

"He's a hill horse, surefooted as any donkey. What do you think, darling?"

Still mesmerized by the majestic horse, she only half heard what Brant was saying. She turned to him. Her face had a startled look. "What? What did you say, Brant?"

"He's yours, darling."

She put both hands up to her face and let out a loud, quivering "He's mine?" She threw her arm around Brant's neck and kissed him while patting the horse's nose. "Oh, Brant, thank you, thank you, darling. And I'll ride him bareback. Oh, I'm thrilled beyond words. He's magnificent!"

As if to impress Merit, Zeus curved his neck toward her and brought his head down to his chest pointing his ears at her. He then stretched his neck, held his head high and neighed.

"He's showing off!" Merit laughed. She rubbed his nose to let him know she understood.

Brant held out his two hands and hoisted her onto Zeus. Now leaning forward and patting his head, she spoke softly to him, "We're going to be wonderful friends, Zeus, I can feel it." She gently nudged her heels into the horse's flank. He obeyed her command and cantered up the steep trail. The truck carrying the four men followed.

Nikos, overwhelmed by the sight of the blond beauty and the raven beast synchronized in motion, cried out loudly in Greek, "That is most glorious sight I have ever seen!"

PEG MADDOCKS

Brant understanding what he said, commented cynically in Greek "Do you mean the horse or Merit, Nikos?" He was well aware of the open admiration Nikos had for Merit from the moment they landed.

Nikos was caught off guard. He'd forgotten that Brant spoke Greek and stuttered, "Ah, yes, both woman and beast make beautiful picture, eh?"

The other men laughed good-naturedly at his obvious embarrassment.

When they reached the top of Mesa Vouno they looked up to where the ruins stretched out above them. They paused to gaze in awe at what had once been a thriving metropolis.

Nikos spoke, "Welcome to our ancient city of Thera. I'll take new team members on tour, then we'll go to work, okay, Wade?"

It was agreed that they would tour for an hour and meet Wade back at the office for an orientation.

Nikos gave them his usual dramatic tour, which completely enchanted them. They were inspired by the magnitude of the city's history, considering its remote and strategic location. On their return, they joined Wade in the makeshift out-building, that would now be their office. He asked them to take a seat on wooden boxes. A chart on the wall that had been drawn by Nikos showed a diagram of the cave entrance, stairs and the two tunnels as far as they had been cleared. It would be updated daily by Nikos as they progressed further into the tunnels. Wade and Nikos stood at the podium, actually a rickety table, to begin their orientation. "You're about to become 'cavers,' Wade began, and that's risky business, especially here because of the possibility of tremors or earthquakes about which Nikos is an expert."

"*Parakalo*, please," Nikos interrupted. "Scientists still say they don't know exactly when earthquakes will happen. But some here say when level of cistern water goes down quickly, it might be warning. Here are other warning signals. If all birds and insects are quiet, and it's not siesta or nighttime, or, if donkeys bray and won't stop, that's very good earthquake warning." He grinned and threw both hands out in a take-it- or-leave-it gesture. "But still some will tell you it's just silly island superstition, eh?"

Wade said, smiling at Nikos, "Speaking of siesta, I'd like to discuss Homer's old tradition of siesta. Could we vote on doing away with it? We have so little time to work on our project."

Nikos smiled broadly and said, "Everyone gets vote. Very democratic. Very Greek way to settle something. It's no problem for me, but you'll pay laborers more if they miss siesta, for sure."

"We'll work that out then. All in favor say aye." There was unanimous approval.

Wade continued the orientation. "I'm laying down some firm safety rules and asking that you strictly obey them. It may save your life, or at least prevent you from being scared to death. Right, Matt? He knows the feeling."

"If it happens again, Wade, our friendship is at an end," Matt said humorously. Matt then briefly proceeded to tell about the two times Wade and he were lost in caves.

They all laughed at Matt's stories, and Wade continued his talk. "By the way, Nikos, interrupt me if you think of anything I forget to mention."

Nikos smiled and nodded. He liked the way Wade always consulted with him. He enjoyed feeling important, especially now that Merit was on the scene.

I'm sure Brant, an archaeologist, knows full well that in underground explorations there is always the possibility of danger. The collapsing of walls, ceilings or floors. Our limestone cave is fairly safe, although where water has penetrated, cracks exist and have weakened that particular area, especially when there are tremors. That's the cause of so much rubble on the floors of the tunnels. Another possible problem is bacteria in the stagnant air as we go in deeper. I hate to have to mention this but we may possibly run into critters! it wouldn't be unusual to meet up with rats, bats, spiders or snakes.

Merit grimaced. "Yuck! Nobody told me about critters."

"Me neither," Matt glared at Wade who ignored him.

Nikos sought to reassure Merit. "I tell you truth, Merit. You'll be wearing your heavy suit and boots and the critters won't be able to bother you. Now, about snakes, Egyptians brought snakes here thousands of years ago for religious reasons, but we don't see them very often any more. We'll have plenty of light on our hard hats and snakes don't like light." Then he paused, put his left hand on his hip and pointed his right index finger at Merit. "I tell you this, Merit. I've only seen two vipers on this island in my whole life. You don't like snakes near you, eh? Well, remember this, they don't want you near them either. So, you will both stay away from each other. You believe me?"

"Merit gave Nikos a weak smile. "I hope you're right."

"That's another reason I'm glad Matt is with us," Wade said. "I've asked him to bring medical supplies along, just in case. We have no idea where this cave is going to lead."

"Now, the rules: Never go into the cave alone. Most rubble in both caves has been cleared quite a ways in. The laborers finished up today, and we won't need them again until we come to another large blockage. The floor of the cave seems fairly level, just a smattering of small rocks every now and then."

"We've only gone fifty feet into the tunnel that leads toward the Temple of Apollo, and one hundred feet into the one that heads in the direction of the Sanctuary of the Egyptian Gods. In that tunnel, we've begun to see small man-made recesses in the walls. Nikos tells me many caves on the island have them for shrines for icons or oil lamps. We haven't examined them closely, yet."

"Another important caver rule: Always wear your hard hat with the headlight on when you are in the cave, even when the large lamps are on. Keep extra batteries in your pockets, along with your flashlight, matches and candles. You all know you must always wear your heavy-duty coveralls, high boots and gloves. They are your most important protection. Your face will be the only part of your body exposed but with your headlight on, it's not likely the critters will bother you. If you're bitten by anything, get to Matt immediately. If the tunnel begins to split off in different directions, everyone will stay together or wear a safety line so no one gets lost."

"Always wear your knee pads," Wade continued, "because we may have to crawl sometimes if the tunnels decrease in height. This cave was formed many thousands of years ago from an accumulation of limestone and organic remains, such as shells, lava, and coral. A limestone cut can cause a nasty infection."

Nikos broke in, "This island has many caves. Up near monastery at Mount Elias, there is very deep cave you might want to explore. At the other end of island at, Oia, you find many *scaftas,* cave houses. Tourists stay in them, but they're too damp for me."

Wade continued, "And remember, if we have an earthquake and you're in the cave, put your dust mask on immediately because when limestone falls from the ceiling and breaks on floor, it creates big cloud of dust that could choke you. Always carry your compass, note paper and pencils because I'm counting on all of you to keep daily reports that we'll consolidate later. Your suits are equipped with special pockets for all these little essentials."

"Merit, that's a neat backpack you have for all your camera equipment and sketch pads."

"Yes it'll carry everything I think I will need," Merit said. "My Sony video camera is perfect for caving. It has a light strong enough for filming in total darkness," she replied. "And my Nikon F4 has incredible features."

Wade gave Merit a thumbs up and continued, "Merit's photos will always include a coded identification card so we'll have complete information on where and when the photo was taken. Her photos will be an eyewitness account of our finds in the event of a cave-in and we can't retrieve them."

I'm also going to be doing lots of line drawings," Merit added. "I learned a great deal from the books you sent me, Wade. I learned that my sketches will be more valuable than what I get on film. They will have much more accurate details."

Nikos looked at her in admiration. "We are very lucky to have such clever woman on our team, eh?"

"Hear, hear," Matt said.

Merit needed her spirits lifted. She was becoming more apprehensive of this adventure by the minute. She thought she had prepared herself, but now that they were here, she wasn't sure she would enjoy it. She accepted their compliments with an elegant bow and added with a chuckle, "I must say, caving is quite different from what I'd anticipated. I might have reconsidered, had I known about the critters. But, seriously, I'm honored and thrilled to be part of the team."

Wade smiled at her and continued. "And now, cavers, here's the last of my locker-room pep talk. This team is to be as one. Share every detail because you never know what the smallest clue could reveal. We are so fortunate to have two such fine archaeologists as Nikos and Brant to carry the ball when it comes to deciphering our finds. We all have to be keen detectives for that matter. When our finds are dated and identified in Athens, we'll try to fit them into the puzzle of this cave."

"Let me remind everyone about something very important," Brant said. "When you hit a 'hot spot'; something that looks unusual, resist the temptation to move it or pick it up. Leave it alone until Nikos or I view it and decide the best way to release it from its ancient grave. If we give you permission to remove it, do it slowly and carefully. Treat it like fragile stemware. Use your softest brushes to wipe away the dust."

"That's important, Brant," Nikos said. "And whatever we find must be carried back to our office carefully in plastic bags or boxes. I'll be locking the office every night now. If we discover very important find though, I'll keep it in my safe at home until I turn it over to authorities in Athens. I must make daily reports to them."

Wade added, "Remember we also must label, record and store each find, even the smallest shard. Well, that's enough information to get us started. Again, I want you all to know how much I appreciate your help, both physical and financial. By the way, I'm an eternal optimist, and I feel very strongly that we are going to discover something important. So, team, lets think positive, get suited up and hit the cave. We'll just spend a couple of hours there today because of our late start."

The opening to the cave at the back of the grotto of Hermes and Heracles, which had been cleared of boulders by the laborers, was only four feet high and five feet wide. But where the hand-hewn stairs descended, it is over seven feet high and six feet wide. When they reached the landing where the two tunnels merged, the height increased to eight feet. The damp, cool smell permeated their nostrils.

Brant theorized, "The opening to the cave behind the back wall of the grotto could have been made thousands of years ago. Possibly, whoever discovered it may have kept the opening small on purpose so it could have been easily hidden by a hewn stone facade. I'm hoping they concealed the entrance to hide an important secret temple or maybe a treasury."

Nikos assumed his favorite "point of information" position; one hand on his hip, and the other with his index finger pointed toward the others. "I'll tell you what I told Wade first time we went into tunnel. I've been in many caves on this island, and they don't smell good like this cave. Now, I ask you, what do you smell?"

They all sniffed the air. "It smells sweet," Merit said.

Matt sniffed deeply," You're right, Merit, it's faint, but I smell it too," Matt added. "It reminds me of High Mass."

"It certainly smells like incense," Brant said. "Incense has been in use since ancient times in churches and temples. This is interesting! Obviously the cave was used for religious rites, but there's no way the smell could last this long."

Wade motioned with his hand, "Let's go into this tunnel on the left where we saw the relief of the lion on the wall. We'll call it the Apollo Temple from now on."

They followed him into the black hole. At fifty feet they stopped where the bucket-line of laborers were on their way out.

Kalimera sas, Yannis," Nikos called out.

The foreman came forward, tipped his hard hat to the team and said, "*Kalimera sas.*"

"Everyone, say hello to Yannis Rallis, he's most important man. His father, and grandfather before him was always head man on archaeological digs on Santorini. He knows when he sees something important, eh? Yannis."

Yannis nodded to the group and handed Nikos a large chunk of limestone and left the cave.

Nikos examined it, then showed it to the others. "See, here are many fossilized remains of shells and fish. Was cave under sea once, eh?" Nikos grinned.

Wade lamented, "I'm sure there'll be so much to see in here and not enough time to explore it all. I wish I could have convinced the Society to give us more than two months. They're skeptical about us finding anything of importance. To them, it's just another Santorini cave that leads to a dead end."

"But they're wrong!" Brant said. "I just feel it! Why was the Apollo head and the cartouche of Isis carved at the entrance? Who can say this cave wasn't used before the devastating eruption that buried Kalliste."

Nikos nodded in agreement and said, "If that's true, Santorini would become world-famous, eh?"

The group now turned back, and Wade led them into the Egyptian tunnel, where they began to see numerous recesses along the wall and they explored carefully.

In a confident voice, Nikos said, "I'm sure we'll find places of worship for Apollo and Isis. Remember, I told you that ancient inhabitants worshipped Egyptian gods along with their own."

Brant cautioned them now, "Move slowly. Put your trowel in the recesses carefully, or you might break something. Don't be alarmed if you see critters, your light will probably bring them to the surface."

A chill enveloped Merit. What in God's name am I doing in this damp, dark, eerie cave, she thought. I'm getting claustrophobic, that's what. I hate spiders and snakes more than any of God's creatures. Hate them! Then what am I doing here? I'm here because I love Brant, and I wanted to give him an exciting fifth anniversary adventure. I wanted to get him away from the pressures of business that have been getting him so up tight lately. So be a good sport! Keep saying it over and over like a mantra. Be a good sport, be a good sport, she repeated to herself.

Soon they began to find shards of pottery on each side of the tunnel's floor.

Nikos advised them, "When you find one piece, look around for others in the same area. They may all be part of the same pithoi, large storage jars."

Suddenly Nikos' voice echoed off the walls. "Look, here in this niche! I've found something. I think it's a small figurine!" He began to brush off the thick dust.

The others surrounded him. Wade turned the portable lamp onto Nikos' hand so they could get a better look.

Brant said excitedly, "I know that statue from the shape of the head. It's Anubis!" He was represented as the jackal deity, a divine embalmer, the pharaohs' god of death, and later became the announcer of death for all. You find paintings of him on the walls of Egyptian tombs."

The team was excited about this first significant find, and Matt asked in an ominous voice, "Do you think old Anubis is trying to tell us something?"

They laughed lightly, but was it in fact a foreboding sign.

Nikos handed the figurine to Wade. "Here, boss man, it's only right that you get to clean it up so we all can get good look at ancient god."

Merit captured the cleaning process of the little six-inch god on both still film and with her video camera. The centuries of dust receded slowly from the terra-cotta figurine. Although the colors were quite faded, they could clearly discern the jackal head with large pointed ears and long snout. The body was human and sepia-toned. A large collar of pointed designs adorned the neck, and bands encircled its upper arms, wrists and ankles. The torso was covered with a loin cloth and a sash draped around the waist.

The thrill of this find so soon into the tunnel gave them hope that their mission might not be in vain.

Wade spoke confidently, "It may just be beginner's luck, but I'm really encouraged that finding old Anubis, in spite of his doomsday role, could be the start of exciting things to come, and not the end for us."

They laughed at his double entendre.

After an hour of exploring, Nikos looked at his watch. "It's four-thirty. And, because this is your first day in cave, maybe it's good idea to quit. Stagnant cave air makes you tired until you get used to it. Also, Anna has prepared big feast to welcome you to Santorini tonight."

They all agreed, left the tunnel and went back through the ancient city to the office, where they hung up their coveralls and put their equipment away in a locked chest. Nikos carried the Anubis figurine in a small box, which he would put in his home safe.

They were heading down the hill, Merit on Zeus and the others behind in Nikos' old truck, when a shriveled old woman in black ran out into the road in front of the horse. She was yelling and flailing her gnarled hands. Zeus reared up in fright, but Merit held on and dismounted.

Nikos slammed on the brakes, leaped out of the truck and ran to the old woman. He held both her hands firmly and tried to calm her down. Taking her to the side of the road, he sat her down on a large boulder and patted her shoulder gently. She would not look at Nikos but kept her eyes frozen on the rest of the team, now standing a few feet away.

Nikos came back to the group and explained, "Poor old woman, she's okay now. I'll tell you about her. Long ago, she predicted when her husband would die, and he did! After that she began to make other predictions before they happened, and they happened like she said. Old villagers think she is oracle, and they give her *drachmas* to tell them their future."

"Wait a minute, Nikos," Brant said, "I understood what she was yelling. Wasn't she telling us not to go into the cave because death was there?"

"Ah, she's crazy old woman." Nikos laughed and said, "Death is her best thing she likes to talk about. Talks about it always. Don't believe old woman who has no mind anymore. She just likes attention. I've warned her not to bother us again. Let's go, we have much to celebrate on our first day of exploration, eh?"

Merit remounted her horse, and the men got back in the truck. They all wanted to believe Nikos, but they had to admit that the old lady was somewhat unsettling. Brant, who was standing in the back of the truck, looked at the old lady when they passed by her. She gave him a strange, penetrating glare and without a doubt, Brant knew he had been given the "evil eye."

* * * *

The celebration dinner was memorable. Many bottles of retsina were consumed before and during dinner.

The team had insisted that Anna and Katina eat dinner with them, although Anna had protested strongly. "It is not our place, we are servants."

But the team refused to eat until mother and daughter joined them. Anna and Katina looked very pretty that evening in brightly embroidered, full-skirted dresses covered by small aprons. Katina wore light makeup, while Anna wore none, but she had arranged her hair in a softly waved style.

They ate everything Anna served, *dolmades*, *taramosalta soupa*, *kalamarakia*, *tiganita*, cheese, figs and honey cakes.

By the time the Americans were served sweet Greek coffee, they were happily intoxicated.

Nikos smiled at the merry group around the table, "I don't think it's just wine that makes you feel, how do you say it, euphoric, eh? I think it's special magic that Greece always casts over visitors. You are hypnotized and under our spell, eh?"

Matt tried to rise and lurched, spilling his *ouzo*. "I'll drink to that." He fell back onto the chair laughing.

Anna picked up her *bouzouki* and began playing. Nikos rose, raised both arms over his head, snapped his fingers and moved gracefully across the floor. He performed a series of intricate steps, stamping one foot, kicking out the other and slapping the floor. After circling a few times, he reached out and pulled Wade out of his chair. Brant and Matt needed no urging; they jumped up and joined hands with the others. Nikos led them into a circle with their outstretched arms locked. They circled one way, then the other, seldom in step. They mimicked Nikos, who whistled and yelled, "*Opa!*"

When the tempo of the music picked up, they moved faster. Nikos broke from the circle and moved into the middle, spinning frenetically while clapping his hands over his head.

Anna now strummed her *bouzouki* fiercely. Merit and Katina clapped and laughed uproariously.

When the music ended, the scarlet-faced men collapsed in their chairs, wet with perspiration and gasping for breath.

Nikos, in much better shape than the Americans for this kind of dancing, applauded them with shouts of "Bravo!" He continued dancing, pausing only momentarily to take a gulp of *ouzo* with one hand and reaching out for

Katina with the other. She rose instantly without looking to her mother for permission.

"Anna, play my favorite *syrtaki* music, *parakalo*," Nikos asked. When the slower, catchy music began, he reached out to Merit with his other hand, and she jumped up quickly.

Merit was wearing a pale blue dress with a full skirt and a low-cut halter top. When Nikos had first seen her that evening, he'd had to catch his breath. The contrast of the light material against the curvature of her full breasts filled him with lustful thoughts. During the evening he stole quick looks at the rise and fall of her bosom. Now ecstasy filled his face as his arms embraced both women around their waists and led them in unison to the beat.

Merit caught on to the steps at once. She realized that Nikos was squeezing her waist tighter than necessary. Several times his hand moved upwards and rested momentarily on the bottom of her breast, but each time it happened, he'd quickly lower his hand back to her waist. Although quite used to having women enjoy his amorous attention, he was somewhat in awe of Merit and feared he might offend her.

Merit thought that for a man his age, his actions were immature, but she was not offended. In fact, because she'd had so much to drink, she felt giddy.

Nikos didn't see the angry look Brant gave him. But when he sat down next to Anna, she clipped him on the back of his head with the palm of her hand while quietly berating him.

Looking at her in innocence, he asked, "What did I do, eh?" He gave her his most captivating smile and kissed her hand.

Anna laughed and smiled at him fondly. "You're like a little boy who steals a cookie and thinks no one saw him do it."

CHAPTER SIX

The morning after their first night on Santorini, the team, with the exception of Nikos, was badly hung over. They got a late start to the cave. At noon, Anna and Katina arrived at the grotto on donkeys with baskets of lunch and strong coffee for the Americans, and retsina for Nikos.

"We Greeks believe the best cure for retsina hangover is to drink again," Nikos told them.

Matt raised his eyebrows at Nikos, "We Irish believe that wine divulges truth, and I'd like to tell you the truth. Now don't be offended, Nikos, but your wine tastes like turpentine."

Nikos laughed, "You'll get used to it, Matt, I promise."

"I doubt it! I'm getting my hangover back just watching you drink it."

But they felt better after the hearty picnic-style lunch outside the Grotto of Hermes and Heracles.

When they finished, Anna and Katina packed up the baskets and left. Everyone but Matt went back into the cave. He stayed in the office to store the pottery fragments that they'd found the day before. When he lifted a large sifting screen from the wall, he heard someone run by the building. He went outside, looked around, then spotted Anna walking toward the grotto. He went up to see what she was doing. As he drew closer, he saw that she was sprinkling a bottle of water over the mouth of the grotto.

Hearing his footsteps, she spun around, startled.

"What are you doing, Anna?"

She hung her head and emptied the rest of the water on the ground. "I won't tell you. You'll think I'm stupid woman." She started to walk away.

"Wait. No, Anna. Come on, I'd never think that of you," Matt reassured her, putting one hand on her shoulder and lifting her chin up with the other. "Tell me why you were sprinkling water on the grotto."

Looking steadily into his friendly eyes, she told him, "It's old Greek custom for good luck. You wash daughter's christening dress. Save wash water and pour it where you want good luck." She dropped her eyes in embarrassment.

Matt chuckled, "I believe it! Listen, Anna, that's not as bad as some of the crazy things the Irish do to bring them good luck. Watch this," he said. putting both hands on her shoulders, he kissed the top of her head twice, then danced around her with his hands on his hips.

She smiled shyly.

Holding her shoulders again, he asked in an Irish brogue, "Now tell me, m' pretty lady, if that's not the most foolish thing fer a man to be doing to bring ye luck?"

Anna's smile faded. Suddenly she felt light-headed. She looked at him in a peculiar way for a moment, then quickly turned and ran down the hill.

Matt called after her, "Anna, Anna, what's wrong? Wait! Did I say something to hurt your feelings?" By now she was out of sight. "Damn it! I must have offended her." He decided to go after her.

Not one man had stirred Anna romantically since her husband disappeared. Matt's hold on her shoulders, and his kisses on her head had gone through her like electric shocks. She ran from him because she was blushing and was sure he'd see how his affectionate touching excited her. She was ashamed of her reaction. She knew that his silly antics were just an act of kindness to lessen her shame about watering the grotto. She ran faster when she heard Matt gaining on her. Her donkey was tied to a tree a short distance away. Suddenly her right foot came down on a large rock, and the earth around it broke loose. She lost her balance and twisted her ankle severely. When she fell forward, she thrust her hands out to break her fall, forgetting she still held the watering bottle. She hit the ground, and the bottle smashed on impact. the glass cut deeply into her hand, covering her palm with blood. She continued to slide down over the steep, rough ground, scraping the skin from her legs and hands. Seconds after she came to a stop, Matt was at her side. He raised her up carefully into a sitting position.

"Oh, my God, Anna. Here, let me look at you." He held out her bleeding hand and picked out a large sliver of glass, causing the wound to bleed more profusely. He took out a handkerchief and pressed it against the wound. "Hold that in place gently. You may have more glass chips in there and I don't want them to go in any deeper."

Anna moaned and bit into the knuckle of her left hand. "My ankle. I think it's broken."

Matt looked at the swollen ankle and began pressing gently in several places, asking, "Does this hurt?" After a careful examination of the ankle and foot, he said, "I'm pretty sure it's only a bad sprain, Anna."

Relief covered her face. She looked down at her bloody legs. She couldn't bring herself to look at Matt.

"I'll get your donkey."

She pointed down the hill. "He's tied to tree down there."

Matt raced down the hill untied the donkey and struggled unsuccessfully to force the reluctant animal to move. Anticipating the animal's stubbornness, Anna whistled. Instantly, the donkey broke from Matt's hold and trotted up the hill to her. Matt ran behind him.

"Anna, do you think if I lift you onto this ornery animal you'll be able to ride him home?"

Anna's eyes filled with tears. "Oh, I'm making big trouble for you. You have work to do. I'm very sorry, Dr. Matt."

THE SANTORINI ODYSSEY

"Don't worry about me, let me worry about you."

When he lifted her onto the donkey, she groaned loudly and fought back tears. Every part of her body hurt.

They went down the hill toward the village in silence. Finally Matt looked back at her with a sheepish grin. "You know what Anna, I feel like Joseph leading Mary into Bethlehem."

Anna smiled weakly. "That's sin to make joke about Holy Family."

At that precise moment, *Papa* Ioannis was riding down from his church on Sophocles. Seeing Matt in his coveralls leading Anna on her donkey, he guessed something was wrong. He rammed his heel into his donkey's rump to catch up to them.

Anna heard him coming and pleaded to Matt, "For God sake, don't tell him what I did at grotto. He'll think it was sin. He only wants us to pray to God for good luck. Maybe he's right, I sinned and God punished me, eh?"

Matt moved next to her and whispered, "Don't worry, Anna. What happened up there is just between you and me." Then he grinned and winked at her.

Papa Ioannis caught up with them. "Anna, my dear woman, what happened?" His eyes shifted quickly from her to the stranger. He leaned down and extended his hand to Matt. "*Kalimera*, sir, I'm *Papa* Ioannis, do you need help?"

Matt shook his hand. "Hello *Papa*, I'm Matt McGuire. Anna's donkey slipped when she was riding down the hill and knocked her off. She hurt her ankle and has a few scrapes. she'll be fine."

Papa Ioannis looked concerned.

Anna hung her head and covered her mouth to hide her dismay at Matt's excuse for her fall. He doesn't realize that Greek donkeys are the most surefooted of all God's creatures; they never slip or fall. Of all the explanations Matt could have given, he'd picked the most unlikely. She doubted *Papa* Ioannis would believe that story.

The priest looked suspiciously at the donkey and then at Anna. "You should get new donkey, Anna, there must be something bad about him." He looked at Matt. "I'll ride ahead and alert her daughter, Katina."

Anna cried out, "No! This man is doctor. He'll fix me up okay. Don't scare Katina."

Ignoring Anna, he turned to Matt, "Ah! you are doctor! You're working in cave up in ancient city of Thera. I know all about it. I'm one who went with Kaldara's boy, who first found cave," he said with great pride. "I help at ancient Kalliste dig site sometimes. I'll be happy to help you too, if you want."

"Thanks *Papa*. I'll have Nikos see you about that."

Matt then led Anna and her donkey up the village street.

The priest called back to Matt, "I'll be happy to come to cave to bless it for good luck."

A quick glance passed between Matt and Anna.

Matt called back to the priest, "Great! Thanks, *Papa*. We can use all the good luck we can get."

In such a small village, there are no secrets. When Matt and Anna started up the road toward the compound, a number of the village ladies were already waiting for them. They began to run alongside Anna, speaking all at once in concerned voices while gently touching her swollen ankle and cut legs. Anna assured them she would be all right because the man leading her donkey was a doctor.

"Ahh! *Yiatros*!" the women said in awed tones as they turned from Anna and began running alongside Matt, smiling and patting his arm. The women were excited about having a doctor in their village. They no longer had to worry about their friend Anna. The doctor would take good care of her.

When Matt and Anna arrived at the compound, Katina ran toward them, panic covering her face. "*Mana, Mama*!"

Papa Ioannis, riding out ahead of Katina, said to Anna in an authoritative voice, "Anna, I assured her, you have good doctor for injuries."

Obviously, in spite of Anna's request not to alarm Katina, he had frightened the child. *Papa* Ioannis had a very paternal attitude toward the villagers. Anna leaned down from the donkey and patted Katina on the head. Katina was sobbing, "*Mana*, you have blood on your legs and hands."

"Just scratches, Katina. I'll be okay," Anna reassured her. Matt lifted her off the donkey and started to carry her to the house, but she protested, "I'll walk, Dr. Matt. Please, I can walk by myself!"

"No way, Anna," Matt said in a firm voice. "I'm carrying you. That ankle is badly sprained, so let's not make it any worse."

Her heart pounded heavily at their intimacy. His nearness excited her. As a defense against having her feelings exposed, she began talking loudly, almost hysterically to Katina, "Take Artemis to stable now and come back to house quick." No man had ever been in her bedroom since her husband had left.

Matt laid Anna on the bed and examined the badly swollen ankle and the deep cut on her hand. He was concerned, because she was flushed and her breathing seemed labored.

"Anna, I'm going to get my medical supplies. I'll be back in a flash." He felt her forehead with the palm of his hand, and she jumped.

"Did you bump your head, too?" he asked.

His touch made her body taut.

"No, I'm okay. Go." She said weakly, looking at the cut on her hand.

Matt thought she was overly embarrassed because he had caught her doing the "good luck" watering of the cave. He read her reactions as normal; people were always apprehensive when they suddenly found themselves in a medical situation.

He was back within minutes and asked Katina, who was kneeling next to her mother's bed, to help him. "Come on kiddo, I need your help. Boil a pan of water and put these instruments in them so they'll be sterilized. Bring me a basin of warm water to soak your mother's hand. And get that worried look off your face. She's going to be just fine, honey." Katina was reluctant to leave, so he took her by the shoulders and steered her out of the room. "Go!"

She paused in the doorway and looked back at Matt with a shy grin, "Okay, you'll see, I'll be good nurse like my *mana*."

While unpacking his medical supplies, Matt asked, "Are you a nurse, Anna?"

Without looking at him she said, "I'm called village nurse. I help at our island hospital when we've have bad automobile accident or earthquake problems."

"Then I guess you know that I am going to have to stitch that cut on your hand. It's pretty deep." He took her hand and spread the laceration open. Pieces of dirt and small chips of glass were embedded in the wound.

"Anything you have to do is okay with me," she said looking up at him. Her intent look puzzled him, but suddenly she shifted her eyes to the door as Katina entered with a basin of warm water.

Matt poured a Betadine solution in the water and placed Anna's hand in it. "We'll have to soak out as much dirt and glass as possible before I start suturing that cut. Okay?"

Anna replied softly, "Okay."

Katina asked, "What else can I do for my *mana*?"

"Get another pan of warm water and some clean towels, and wash your mother's legs. Make sure you get all the dirt out of the scratches. When you're through, I'll put an antibiotic ointment on them."

"Anna, have you had a tetanus shot lately?" Matt asked.

"I got one last year."

"Good!"

Matt took an ice pak out of his bag and hit it on the edge of the chair. Within seconds it turned cold, and he placed it on Anna's ankle.

He scrubbed his hands, put on plastic gloves, retrieved his small instruments from the boiling water in the kitchen and set them out on sterile sponges on the small nightstand.

Suddenly the quiet was interrupted by the sound of a horse racing across the cobblestones of the compound and then stopping abruptly. Merit called out as she ran into the house, "Matt! Anna! Where are you?"

"In the bedroom, Merit," Matt called out.

"Oh, Anna dear," Merit said, leaning over her. "We were so worried about you. *Papa* Ioannis came to the cave and said you were thrown from your donkey and seriously hurt."

"First of all, Merit, Anna is not hurt seriously. *Papa* Ioannis completely exaggerated the situation," Matt assured her.

Anna gave Merit a weak smile, "I'm so sorry I've made so much trouble for everyone. That priest! He makes me so mad!"

Merit reached down and patted Anna's shoulder. From the moment she met Anna, Merit felt a warm empathy for her. "What can I do to help, Matt?"

"Why don't you just give her moral support and hold her other hand while I inject Novocain in this cut. I'm going to have to do a bit of suturing to close it."

Anna felt very weak. She hurt all over, but worse, she felt foolish for causing so much trouble.

Matt sensed her feelings. "This will hurt just for a minute, Anna. Then, after I've taken care of your cuts and bruises, I'm going to give you a sedative so you can get some rest."

He put a chair next to the bed and laid Anna's hand on a towel on the table. He injected the local anesthetic into the wound.

Katina, who had stopped wiping her mother's legs to watch, gasped and turned pale when he inserted the needle.

Hearing her, Matt glanced up. "Merit, grab Katina. Get her over on that chair, and put her head between her legs before she faints."

Anna moaned, "Oh, my poor baby, Katina."

Merit led a limp Katina across the room to the chair.

At that moment, Nikos burst into the room. His eyes flicked from Anna in the bed to Katina being dragged across the room by Merit. Then he looked to Matt who was working on Anna's bloody hand. He spread his hands out and gasped, "*Kristos Kai Panayia!* Anna! My dear Anna! *Papa* Ioannis said you are hurt bad." Glancing quickly at Katina, he asked, "Katina too? I drove fast to get here. Matt, tell me, what I can do to help?" He knelt at Anna's bedside, kissing her hand over and over and moaning dramatically while looking from Anna to Katina, who was now recovering under Merit's attention.

Suddenly Brant and Wade appeared at the bedroom door. Matt stopped working on Anna's hand, stood up, glared around the room at everyone and ordered sternly, "Out! Everyone out! Leave us alone. I will take care of Anna myself, please!"

Matt was irate. Everyone left quickly. He looked down at Anna. Tears ran down her cheeks and she choked back sobs. She looked sad and exhausted. Matt knew her ankle must be throbbing and her legs burning painfully from the cuts and bruises. He leaned down, taking her face in his hands and said softly, "Poor dear Anna. I'm sorry I had to yell at everyone, but, my God, this room was getting more crowded than a New York City emergency room. I'm going to put you to sleep for a long siesta and finish up my work on your hand. Then I'll go find *Papa* Ioannis and punch the old busybody in the nose, okay?"

Anna gave Matt a thin smile, and her sobs subsided. She shut her eyes and succumbed to the peaceful warm sensation that overtook her pain.

An hour later, Anna was sleeping soundly under the watchful eye of Katina, and the team was back at work at the cave.

Matt apologized to the others for kicking them out of the room so rudely. "I certainly didn't act very professionally."

When questioned about Anna's accident, he kept his promise. "Her donkey slipped on a loose rock and she fell off."

Nikos insisted that he personally would get rid of her donkey and buy a new one. "There must be something wrong with the animal. I'll sell it to the donkey men who take tourists up steep steps to Fira from cruise ships. That'll be good punishment for dumb animal who hurt my dear Anna."

It occurred to Merit that Anna probably meant a great deal more to Nikos than she would have guessed.

* * * *

Matt tried again that evening to place a call to Lee and to Rita Burke, his wife's nurse. Telephone service on the island was unpredictable. Because of the seven-hour time difference between Greece and Connecticut, Lee and Matt had agreed that he would call every third day around eleven o'clock in the morning, her time, on her private business line. Tonight he was successful, thanks to Nikos, who assisted him in reaching the overseas operator. Matt had given him the two numbers, telling him, "One is my home number and the other is my secretary's."

Nikos, ever the romantic, gave Matt a knowing wink that suggested the secretary might be more than that. Once Matt was connected, Nikos left him alone in the small phone closet. Matt spoke first to Rita Burke, who assured him everything was going well. She told him honestly that Sarah was quite happy that he was attending a medical conference, which was the story

Sarah had been given to explain his absence. He gave the nurse Nikos' phone number and said he would call next week.

Matt and Lee talked for thirty minutes. He filled her in on all that had happened since they arrived.

"I don't know if I like the idea of your working alongside the beautiful Merit Morton-Powers every day," Lee teased. "You're not getting infatuated I hope."

"No way! I've big competition for her from the handsome Greek god, Nikos. He fell for her the moment we landed. But, of course, there are very attractive Greek women here, too, especially the mother and daughter who live in our compound. The daughter is too young for me, but the mother, well, now, she's more my type," he kidded.

"Hey! What do you mean your type?"

"Only kidding, only kidding," Matt assured her, then thought to himself, what in hell made me say that?

After they hung up, Matt again thought of his remark about Anna. He felt a warm friendliness toward her and could not deny that she was an attractive woman. Maybe I feel a kinship with her because of our spouses. Hers walked out on her and made her life miserable. mine stayed and did the same to me.

* * * *

For the next several days, Merit insisted upon helping Katina cook the meals. It was quite a novelty for her, since she had seldom done anything more domestic in her kitchen than plan dinner parties with her cook. Katina was delighted to have Merit's help and was intrigued by stories about life in America.

Brant poked around the kitchen, too, but mostly, he was in the way. His being there so often surprised Merit because he rarely entered the kitchen at home.

Brant awed Katina. She fantasized him as her father, although her crush was a mixture of both romantic and fatherly feelings. He was the most sophisticated man she had ever met. He complimented her on her beauty to the point that Merit told him he was making the child vain. But something else about him nagged Merit; he almost seemed to be flirting with Katina.

A few days later, Anna became furious when Katina rushed into the bedroom to tell her, "*Mana*, Brant just suggested that I should think about leaving the island when I finish school here and go to the university in Athens or maybe even to America."

"What a stupid man! He must be blind, too, if he cannot see how poor we are. He has no right to put such ideas in your head." Anna vowed to speak to Brant.

"Oh, *Mana*, please don't be mad at him. He's been helping Merit and me every day while you've been laid up in bed."

"Then I think it's time I get up before he has you believing you're just as rich as they are."

Katina turned in anger and ran outside to the garden to pick vegetables for the evening meal.

It had become a nightly ritual for Merit and Katina to go to Nikos' house after dinner to develop the photos taken during the day. Brant, ever possessive of Merit, had made a few comments lately about the way Nikos was forever complimenting her. "I hope he's not going to be in the darkroom with you!"

She laughed it off, but she knew Brant resented Nikos' attention. She wondered how she could tell Nikos to cool it without hurting his feelings.

Usually, every evening after dinner, during the first week of the team's work, the men gathered around the table in the main house to recap the day's activities. By ten o'clock, everyone but Nikos was ready for bed. He always invited them to join him for a trip to the village taverna, but up to now, they were too tired. He'd been right about the dampness of the cave, which indeed made them lethargic.

* * * *

Four days after the accident, Anna appeared at breakfast, smiling and looking pretty in an embroidered white blouse and skirt covered with a lace-trimmed white apron. Her hair was piled in a loose bun and little wisps circled her face, another new hairdo for her.

"You should stay off that foot for a couple more days, Anna," Matt warned when he saw her.

"I'm okay, I'm okay, Matt," she insisted. I thank everyone for helping my Katina. Now I'll get back to work." The emphatic tone of her voice let them know that they could not change her mind.

Matt lingered after breakfast. "Anna, please try to stay off your feet as much as possible. Your ankle is still swollen and sore, I'm sure. Don't use your hand too much either; you'll split my beautiful stitches."

Anna smiled at him. "You are good doctor and good man. I'm sorry I caused so much trouble. I thank you for good care you gave me." Impulsively, she stepped close to him, she couldn't stop herself. Matt had made her body burn with a passion she had not felt since Joe. She looked into his eyes steadily and put her arms around his neck tightly, and kissed him on the lips.

Matt was stunned. His face reddened in embarrassment as a shiver ran through him. He held her waist and moved her away. His hands shook. He couldn't deny it, she aroused him. I'd better get the hell out of here quick, he thought.

Anna hung her head and dropped her hands to her sides, stepping back from him.

In a faltering voice, Matt said, "I'm glad that I was there to help, Anna." And with that succinct statement, he left the house.

Anna watched him leave, and a piercing feeling of shame and rejection enveloped her as she ran home and threw herself across her bed. He not only hadn't responded to her kiss, but she knew she had embarrassed him. She condemned herself. I acted like a fool. How can I ever face him again?

She thought about the other women in the village who were also alone. Some were widows, but there were quite a few married women whose husbands had left the island to find work elsewhere, sometimes for a year or more. Some of the absent husbands were fishermen or sponge divers, while others worked in factories on the mainland or in other countries. My Joe's been gone for sixteen years. Who knows, maybe I'm better off. I have my beautiful daughter, Katina. I own my own home. I'm a lucky woman, I guess.

Unlike other lonely island women, Anna never had sex with another man since Joe Brady left. She remained abstinent. She had opportunities, but no man had succeeded in winning her affection to the point that she went to bed with him. Her excuse was always the same: "I'm still a married woman, and it would be a sin."

But Matt McGuire lit a fire inside Anna that she found impossible to extinguish. Again she found herself the victim of unrequited love, and it hurt badly.

* * * *

Matt realized that Anna's kiss was not mere thanks for his care; it was too passionate. He felt badly about that. He was aware that this kind of situation often occurred between female patients and their doctors. This poor woman had been humiliated enough through the years by her husband's desertion. He promised himself, I'll avoid further contact with her unless others are around. He admitted that her sensuality affected him, causing him pangs of guilt. He loved Lee deeply and had no need for another woman's attention. Before meeting Lee he had been celibate for five years. I certainly can take two months of celibacy now!

* * * *

It was ten days after exploring both tunnels, and shipping samples of ancient pottery to Athens before the team finally found out what the dating results from their finds showed. The report stated that in all probability, various religious cults had used the tunnels for hundreds of years after 1600 B.C.

Disappointed by the report, Brant commented tersely, "That doesn't mean that we won't find artifacts from before 1600 B.C. once we've searched the entire cave." The report depressed him. Chances seemed remote they would find anything associated with the Plato's legendary Atlantis civilization in this cave. When they stopped for a break, Matt poured everyone a cup of the strong, hot coffee that Anna prepared daily. Usually on this break they discussed the archaeological or geological background of the island.

"Think about it," Wade said. "There are few places left on the earth where man has not walked for three thousand years. It's possible we're tracing the footsteps of some of the first settlers to come to this island after the Kalliste eruption in 1600 B.C." He paused, looked kindly at Brant and said what he knew Brant wanted to hear, "Or maybe even before Kalliste disappeared."

Nikos took his usual historical information pose of pointing his finger and putting his hand on his hip. "We know that Lacedaemonian colonists from Sparta came here around 1400 B.C. They didn't like being ruled by Sparta and did same thing first American colonists did to get away from English rule, eh? They started settlement up here on mountain because of strategic view of sea to spot enemies approaching."

"The geology of this place is incredible," Wade added. "Possibly the ground we're standing on could have been forming for well over 500,000 years. This island, and in fact, this whole area of the Aegean has been through many geological upheavals, monstrous quakes and submarine volcanic eruptions of tremendous magnitude. Some scientists even think that at one time, all the Aegean Islands were connected. And change continues today. The sulfur smell on this island is exuding from that little offshore island, Nea Kaimeni. It reminds you that the continuous sulfuric steam coming up through the top of that island is from a submerged volcano."

Matt interjected in a humorous and ominous tone, "God, I hate it when you talk about those scary things, Wade."

Wade patted Matt on the back, "Don't worry, old pal, I'm depending on your Irish luck to prevent things like that from happening while we're here."

Nikos immediately tried to relieve their fears, "Don't be alarmed. We won't have another earthquake for long time now. It's always lots of years in between them." Then without meaning to, he created more anxiety. "Earthquake that we had last December that opened up back of cave was not so bad, believe me! We have not had bad one since 1956. That was big tragedy for my island. It destroyed more than six thousand homes and killed and injured many. Half of population moved from island and never came back. You can still see ruins of homes from that quake."

"You had to bring that up, Nikos? Thanks a lot." Brant said.

"I don't like the idea of being trapped in this cave if an earthquake strikes," Merit confessed. "Now I can worry about earthquakes, along with critters."

Wade put his hand up. "All right, team, let's think positive thoughts about the ancient geology of this island. It still stands strong, considering the number of gigantic eruptions that have taken place in the past. In spite of the fact that the middle blew out and sank more than once, the volcanic activity below the sea built up the center again. This thousand foot-limestone and lava mountain we're standing on is the result of that kind of geological activity. We know that this island, as you see it today, was developed over many millennia because of the various-colored stratified layers we saw on the walls of the caldera when we sailed in. Those layers were deposited at different times and under different weather conditions. Think of it! Layer upon layer of stone being lifted up over thousands of years by a powerful force from the sea!"

Nikos added, "It's often said that my island is most important one in the Aegean when it comes to geology, eh?"

"It probably is, Nikos," Wade agreed, then said abruptly, "Coffee break is over. Time to get back to work. Let's move on."

They explored about fifty feet farther. The cave's height and width had gradually increased and had made numerous turns. It was about fifteen feet high and ten feet wide. As they reached a sharp bend, the odor of incense began to permeate the tunnel. Spreading out, they inspected the many wall recesses that were much larger than those they had previously encountered. there seemed to be a great deal more shattered pottery on the floor. Turning another sharp bend, they saw a wide, stone shelf. The incense smell was now quite strong.

While Merit filmed him, Nikos put his gloved hand into the thick dust and uncovered four small, tightly sealed clay jars, perfectly preserved. Below, on the ground, lay the remains of a fifth jar, obviously smashed by a slab of rock that had come loose from the cave ceiling. It was from the broken pottery that the strong aroma of incense came.

Nikos said, "I'll bet this jar was broken by December earthquake."

They knelt down to inhale the sweet-smelling crumbly substance that was mingled with chips of pottery.

"Can you imagine the scent lasting that long?" Matt was amazed."

"How is incense made?" Merit asked.

Nikos was quick to answer. He enjoyed showing off his knowledge to Merit. "It can be compound of sweet gums and spices or maybe good-smelling wood, bark, or flowers. It was burned to honor gods and drive out evil spirits. They say incense smoke carries prayers and souls of dead up to heaven."

"Let's pause here, it looks like a good photo-op." Merit said as she lined up the team for a photo with the jars. Then, as she focused for a close-up of the broken one on the ground, Nikos' face appeared in the lens smiling broadly up at the camera.

"You're a ham, Nikos!" Merit teased, snapping the picture.

You're a jerk, Brant thought.

"Ham? Is it good or bad thing to be?" Nikos asked, looking around at the others for their reaction.

"It's a good thing to be, Nikos," Matt assured him. "Ham means you're a fun person, besides being a handsome devil!"

"Ah! I'm ham first and now devil. I'm good and now bad? I'm confused," Nikos looked puzzled.

"It's all good, Nikos," Wade assured him. "You'd really be confused if I translated it literally."

"It's American slang, eh? Ah! It is like good curse to be handsome like Nikos," he joked.

Everyone except Brant laughed at his bravado. Instead he said, "Hey, what do you say we quit fooling around and get back to work?"

Wade nodded and said, "These incense jars remind me of when I was working in a tomb in the Valley of the Kings in Egypt. We found many jars that had held incense, unguents and other materials. But when they were opened, you'd only find the remnants of dried-out, fatty substances, not strong, recognizable odors like this. Let's set up some portable lighting in this area. I want to take a real careful look around here."

Nikos had carefully brushed all the dust off one jar. it was buff-colored pottery that had been painted and glazed. He carefully held it out for them to view. "See how elegantly they are shaped." Suddenly a startled look covered his face. "*Kristos*! This is most amazing find!" Nikos said emotion filling his voice. "These are Minoan, I'm sure! See the design on them, I've seen it many times on ancient pithoi at Kalliste."

Black-painted spirals encircled the centers of the jars and the rest of the surfaces were covered with primitively drawn sprigs of flora, also painted black.

"Are you sure, Nikos?" Brant asked excitedly. "My God! That means these jars were here before the cataclysmic volcano in 1600 BC and made by Kallisteans!"

"Could that be true?" Wade wondered aloud.

"It is true!" Nikos said emphatically. "We'll go to museum in town or dig site at Kalliste. I'll show you proof."

"We'll do that, Nikos." Wade said. "But before we get too excited, remember that it's also very possible that the first settlers who came to the island two hundred years after Kalliste was buried, could have found these jars, maybe near where Kalliste was buried and brought them in here for religious services."

Brant snapped back, "I don't like that scenario, but it's still a possibility, I suppose."

Wade ignored him and said, "Let's move ahead a little. This seems like an area where there might have been a great deal of activity in ancient times. We'll leave the incense jars here for now and pick them up on our way back. It looks like the tunnel is becoming higher and wider up ahead."

It was true, and with the enlarged height and width of the tunnel, the darkness intensified. Their headlights were no longer adequate for any distance, but the portable lamps partially illuminated the huge tunnel that faced them. They were awed by the sight of the black rugged walls now enveloping them.

In a hushed tone, Wade uttered, "In the words of Jules Verne, 'There is nothing more powerful than the attraction towards an abyss.'"

"It's claustrophobic," Merit said.

"You're right, Merit," Wade said. "The smaller tunnels were not so awesome because they were equated more to your height and size."

Matt, carrying the two portable lamps, stopped suddenly and yelled, "Look!" Instantly his voice reverberated off the walls, his echo repeating over and over, "look, look, look," until it faded away completely somewhere in the deep hollows of the cave.

Matt laughed at the eerie sounds. "Wow! Was that an unbelievable echo or what?" He stared off into the blackness where his voice disappeared.

"It's the most unreal sound. It always gives me a creepy feeling that an unknown is repeating what I said," Wade commented. "What did you want us to look at, Matt?"

"Look over here on this wall."

They followed him to the wall where the portable lights showed a six-foot high recess. At first they thought it was a room, but when they looked inside they could see it was only a deep storage area for an assortment of clay vessels laid out neatly on the shelves and covered with thick dust.

"Ah! It's closet for storing oil lamps to light up tunnel. And look, braziers for burning incense," Nikos informed them. "We find these in many archaeological sites around Aegean, and it means..."

Brant interrupted rudely, "It means that we must be close to where priests performed religious rituals."

Nikos frowned but said nothing.

They moved ahead slowly, noticing the ground was more thickly covered with small and large chunks of limestone. The number of recesses in the walls were increasing, and the team examined each carefully.

Merit was slowly moving her hands around the ancient dust in a small niche when she felt something hard. Elated, she yelled, "I've found something!" Then she let out a terrifying scream, "Ahhhhh! Help! Spiders are crawling all over my hands and arms!" Fortunately she was wearing strong skin-tight gloves.

The men raced to her. Nikos reached her first and swatted the large black spiders off her hands and arms onto the ground.

The others began stamping on them.

Nikos looked her over carefully to be sure he got them all off. "It's okay to open your eyes," he assured her, "You're okay now, Merit. They're all off you."

Chills surged through her body. She was still standing stiffly as if paralyzed, her arms outstretched, frozen. She could not bring herself to open her eyes or stop moaning and thinking, Oh, God why did I ever come here? I don't want to be a good sport anymore.

Brant shoved Nikos out of the way and took Merit into his arms, soothing her with soft words and gentle kisses. "It's all over, darling. You're fine, and they're all dead. You must have hit a nest."

Nikos looked at Wade, raised his eyebrows and threw his hands up in a gesture of defeat.

Wade grinned at Nikos, then reached into the niche and lifted an object out from the dust. He stood in front of Merit, holding the object in his cupped hands. "Hey Merit, open your eyes. Look what you found! It's another little figurine, I think."

Merit opened her eyes slowly, looked around at the dead spiders on the ground, then looked at the dark object Wade held out to her. Her fear receded somewhat.

"My God, Merit," Brant said in elation, carefully lifting the figurine from Wade's hands and brushing off the clinging dust of ages from the little figure. "I think it's a statue of Serapis. See, he looks like Pluto, the god of the underworld. See his long hair and beard. And look, he's sitting on a throne with the triple-headed dog, Cerberus, at his feet."

"Oh Brant, it's an important find, isn't it? You can even see what colors had been painted on it." Merit said, now delighted with her find, despite the spiders.

The others crowded around to get a better look as Brant continued to carefully brush off the dust. He thought to himself, Damn, I wish Merit and I had been alone when she found this. I honestly think I would have tried to talk her into keeping it for ourselves. But he was skeptical that Merit would have gone along with the theft. He knew she was more honest than he.

Merit also had a fleeting thought of how much she would love to keep the treasure for herself but dismissed the idea immediately.

"Refresh our memories, Brant," Wade said. "You're the mythology expert. I don't remember much about Serapis."

"Well, let's see," Brant said, holding out the little figurine where everyone could see it. "He was descended from the sacred bull Apis, who was a fertility god."

"That figures, a bull being a fertility god!" Matt joked.

Brant didn't smile with the others and continued, "When one bull died, another was found to take his place, and his funeral rites were fit for a king. His name was changed often but lastly to Serapis. He became god of the underworld. And here's a good omen for us: He was known particularly for being the god of the riches beneath the earth!"

"Aha!" Matt articulated in a stilted British accent while crossing his arms and nodding his head, "It's elementary, my dear Watson. If Serapis is here then a treasure must be straight ahead. Right, old chap?"

To upstage Brant, Nikos continued with more mythology. Taking his usual explanatory stance, he continued, "I think it's very interesting how mythical gods, both Greek and Egyptian, may be connected to our exploration here in cave. First, we entered tunnel through grotto of Greek gods, Hermes and Heracles. Hermes, son of Zeus, was born in cave! He was very intelligent but bad child. He stole fifty cows belonging to Apollo. His parents settled that problem with Apollo, but because Hermes is so smart, he become messenger of gods, but he's also god of thieves!"

"Who was Heracles, Nikos?" Matt asked.

"Maybe you call him Hercules, eh? He's also son of Zeus by different mother than Hermes. Gods have, how you say it, lots of extra marital affairs, eh? Heracles was very strong, a fact he proved often. He was demigod because his mother was mortal. When he was baby in cradle, enemy sent two giant serpents to kill him, but he strangled them. He had bad temper though, and always caused lots of trouble. He even stole that hell-hound,

Cerberus, dog with three heads you see with Merit's figurine of Serapis. When he visited underworld, god who lives there took on form of bull. Heracles proved his strength by breaking off god-bull's horn and gave it to Goddess of Plenty. Zeus is pleased with him and takes him up to Olympus because Zeus is strongest of all gods. Okay? We're sure from what we find, that Egyptian gods were worshipped here in cave, too. Remember Isis? we see her face on relief at entrance of cave. Well, she is Goddess of Motherhood and Fertility, and also aunt of Anubis."

"I remember you told us that Egyptians also lived in ancient Thera, Nikos." wade said.

"You've heard of Ptolemy of Egypt?" he asked and, without waiting for an answer, continued, "He was very important general whom Alexander picked to rule Egypt. He also made this island, then called Thera, into naval base and kept garrison of troops here to rule over Aegean. now I tell you most interesting fact!"

Brant yawned loudly. Merit glared at him.

Nikos gave Brant a sidelong glare. "Ptolemy had picked Serapis to be god of both Egypt and Greece because he had big plans to make both countries one. Now you see why maybe connection between Greek and Egyptian gods is important clue to what went on in this cave, eh?"

All but Brant applauded Nikos' clever summary.

"That's really fascinating, Nikos," Wade said. "This sure has been a productive day so far. It makes me feel that we must be getting closer to finding out what went on in this cave thousands of years ago." Wade looked at his watch. "Since it's four o'clock why don't we call it a day. Brant and Nikos, why don't you gather up the shards of pottery we want to keep and retrieve all the incense you can from the ground; I'm sure Athens will be interested in dating it. Matt, let's go back to the office and get some wooden boxes to transport the incense jars and those oil and incense burners. We'll have to carry them very carefully."

"What can I do, Wade?" Merit asked.

"You get to very carefully carry your little friend Serapis. You've been doing a great job with photos and identification of our finds. You're a real pro, Merit."

"I learned how important that was from one of the books you gave me. I'll also make sketches after they are cleaned."

Walking back to the office, Wade told Matt, "I'm glad Merit found that little figurine today. I think it made her feel better after her encounter with the spiders."

"Hell, those spiders would have frightened me to death!" Matt said. "I have to say, she really has surprised me. I wouldn't have bet a nickel on her staying here after that first day when she saw the size of their living quarters. I think she's terrific!"

"I agree, but what's with Brant? He seems to be getting more surly every day. He makes me feel uncomfortable."

"He's becoming a real pain in the ass. He doesn't like Nikos giving Merit any attention, that's for sure."

"Nikos should watch his affectionate attention to Merit. he goes a little too far."

"That'll be hard for him. I think he has a big crush on her."

"I think he just loves women." Wade said and laughed.

"Wade, what happens if we do find something terrific like Tut's tomb maybe?" Matt asked.

"I love your optimism, Matt! If we do, the Archaeological Society from Athens will converge on the place, and we'll be told to clear out. That would be damn frustrating!"

"Will Nikos have to report what we found today?"

"I think so. I'm not sure."

"What if he doesn't?"

"Well, if they found out he delayed informing them, about a significant find, he could lose his credentials to practice archaeology in Greece, and maybe even become persona non grata here on Santorini."

"I'd hate to see that happen. I enjoy his company. Brant should ease up on him."

"I agree. I don't want any bad feelings among my team members. And speaking of romance, and my team members, I think Anna might have a little crush on you, Matt."

Matt's face reddened. "I think you may be right. I felt shitty when I realized it. The God's honest truth is, I had no idea how she felt. I'll admit she is some sensual woman, and I'd be lying if I said she didn't stir my Gaelic libido a bit. But when I realized what was happening, I squelched it right away, honest, Wade, I'm determined to keep a professional attitude around her from now on and not be alone with her. The whole thing was probably my fault. I think she mistook my dumb Irish shenanigans and thought I was making a pass at her. She's a very vulnerable woman."

"You have to be careful, old pal, how you behave around Greek women. They are passionate individuals, and she's been alone a long time. I'm sure she's very lonely. So be careful. Remember what Zorba said, 'When a Greek woman asks a man to her bed, and he refuses to go, it's a sin."

"Aw, cut the crap. It would never get that far!" Matt said defensively, giving Wade a friendly punch on the shoulder.

"Speaking of sin, *Papa* Ioannis told Anna to invite us to attend the Divine Liturgy this Sunday," Wade said. "I guess it's a must, or the villagers will think we're heathens. They're very religious here, like the Irish, huh?"

"Aw, for God's sake, nobody's like the Irish when it comes to religion, or anything else for that matter." Both men laughed.

When they reached the office, they began piling up wooden boxes to carry back to the cave. Wade regretted having teased Matt about Anna. He was very fond of Matt and would not have blamed him if he had succumbed to her charms. He had a terrible marriage.

While making their way back to the cave with the boxes, Matt asked Wade, "What do you say, boss? Can we take this weekend off? We've been working out straight for ten days. It would be good for our health. Maybe do some sightseeing?"

"You read my thoughts, Matt. We should soak up some of the Greek sun at Perissa beach at the base of the mountain. We need to dry out after working so long in that damp cave. I think we should also take a tour of the excavation of Kalliste over at Akrotiri."

* * * *

Later that night, when Brant and Merit were alone in their house, he turned from the patio door, frowned and said, "Merit, darling, I want to ask you a question, and please give me an honest answer."

Merit looked up at Brant "What is it, dear? You look so serious."

"I'm very serious." He sat on the bed next to her and took her hand in his. "Have you had enough of the cave, of the isolation of this small island, of this tiny room we call home? Wouldn't you like to take a real shower? Aren't you sick and tired of putting up with that jerk Nikos, and a lot of other lousy things that you're subjected to every day just to be here with me?"

"Oh, Brant," Merit said, reaching out to hold his face in her hands. "Nikos is harmless, and this quaint, beautiful little island has done something magical to me." She jumped off the bed and pulled him out onto the patio. "Look out there, darling, it's paradise! I'm in a constant state of enchantment, completely captivated. I feel like I'm under a spell. This place embraces me more each day. It has given me a whole new perspective on life. I see things I never noticed before. Do you know, when I'm riding Zeus, I'm forced to stop sometimes, even to dismount, to get down on my knees and smell the sweet, fresh fragrance of the wild May flowers that carpet these hills. Before Santorini, I only smelled flowers that were artfully arranged in vases. I'm in awe of the spectacular show that occurs every evening when the church bells ring all over the island, and the setting sun becomes a breathtaking view of a thousand shades of gold, orange and red along the horizon."

"All my life I've been spoiled, pampered and waited on. I've never known what it was like to live as frugally as we are living here. I never realized how much I abused nature's gifts. At home, I'd shower for an hour and not even consider that I was wasting a precious commodity." Then she turned and looked steadily at Brant. "Do you know that I have never given a thought as to where electricity comes from until we came here? Can you believe that? It's downright shameful the way we live in Greenwich!"

Brant was startled by her emotional outburst. He took her in his arms. "Merit, Merit, my darling, you're wonderful. Here I've been dreading to face the fact that you might be fed up with this primitive place and want desperately to go home."

"No, No, No! I don't want to leave here until the very last moment, Brant! My heart will break when that time comes. It will be devastating to leave this enchanted little village with all its warm, engaging people. Every day, when I'm riding up to the cave, the most wonderful thing happens. The old ladies of the village run up to me with sprigs of basil. It's a gesture of hospitality. It's such a simple act of thoughtfulness, but it touches me deeply. No, Brant, don't take me away from paradise before our time is up. I want to savor every single moment. I may never be this blessed again."

Brant buried his head in her neck and held her tightly. His voice was emotional, "Thank you, darling. You're the most perfect wife a man could have. It just seems so selfish to have you involved in such a strange and dangerous experience." Then he looked at her with a scowl. "Are you sure your excitement about this place doesn't have something to do with your ardent admirer Nikos?"

Merit laughed. "Oh, Brant, don't be ridiculous! He's harmless, darling. I think Nikos feels it's his patriotic duty to act like a Greek lover with all women."

"Well, he better not get too patriotic with my wife."

"Brant darling, you're the only man for me. And I truly love exploring the cave. It's scary, I'll admit, but it's also exciting."

"Then we'll stay!" Brant said as he picked her up and laid her on the bed and began undressing her.

CHAPTER SEVEN

When Brant and Merit stepped out of their house Saturday morning, they saw a floral wreath of periwinkles, wallflowers, pink stock, and greenery hanging on the door.

"Well, who could have put it there, I wonder?" Merit asked in surprise.

"Maybe Anna or Katina," Brant said.

When they sat down to breakfast, Merit asked the women about the wreath.

"We got two wreaths!" Katina giggled.

"And I'll give you one guess who put them on doors," Anna said with a little laugh, nodding towards Nikos, who was concentrating excessively on the task of spreading honey on his bread.

"Nikos, did you leave that lovely wreath on our door?" Merit asked coyly.

Nikos looked up in surprise. "Who me? I did not put wreath on your door. Must be some other guy. Not me, for sure!"

Anna put her hands on her hips and stared at Nikos. she had a hard time suppressing a grin as she addressed the team, "It is custom on island in month of May for men to put wreath on sweetheart's door. Now you tell me, do you know anyone but Nikos who be such romantic fool as to put wreaths on doors for three women?"

Everyone laughed and teased Nikos as he continued to protest that he had nothing to do with the wreaths. A sheepish grin covered his face while he swore to all the saints in heaven that he was telling the truth.

"I think it's a lovely and romantic thought, even if it wasn't you, Nikos," Merit whispered and smiled at him slyly. She ignored the smirk on Brant's face.

He looked surprised. "You do? Ah, I'm glad you are pleased. I think I might know name of man who leave wreath, and next time I see him, I'll tell him he made you happy." After that remark, everyone really taunted Nikos, despite his continuous pleas of innocence.

After breakfast, the team climbed into Nikos' truck for the trip to the dig site of ancient Kalliste, which was buried thirty-feet below the town of Akrotiri at the eastern end of the island about twenty miles away. They were to be given a tour by one of the archaeology students who worked there. When they arrived at the excavation site, they were met by Helena Andronikos from Athens University. Helena spoke English and addressed them in a confident voice. "I welcome all of you to the ruins of Kalliste," she began. You are looking down Telchines Road, where most of the excavation has been done up to now. The ruins you see that have been exposed were built on the ruins of an earlier time, Middle Cycladic, maybe 1900 to 1700 B.C. We know this because we've found many remains from that era. We even unearthed remains from the Early Cycladic age, which was around 2500 to 2000 B.C. Pottery has given us positive proof. Kalliste is a 3500 year-old city settled by Kallisteans and Minoans who came from Crete and brought with them culture, architecture and art in many new forms as you will see. As of today, only one-twentieth of the city has been unearthed from its pumice grave. The present excavation is under the direction of Professor Khristos Doumas, who thinks it will take 100 years to finish. The original excavation was under the direction of Dr. Spyridon Marinatos. Unfortunately, he died from a fall here at the site and is buried here in the ruins, I will show you his grave. Actually, we're only working here about two months of year now because of money shortage. Let's walk along the street, and as we go by the houses, we'll stop, and I'll tell you about them, okay?"

The buildings and sites that had now been exposed were covered with a steel-framed, fiberglass roof that let light in but protected the fragile excavation from the weather.

"Many test sites almost a mile away have exposed many more ruins of the city. We think possibly Kalliste could have been a city of 30,000 people." Helena continued. "Kalliste had very modern plumbing system. Underneath the streets, there are clay pipes to carry off waste material from houses. This first house, known as Xeste 3, was two stories, with fourteen rooms on each floor and had many lovely wall paintings. I think you'll agree, it must have been wealthy family who lived here, eh? Many houses were built of stone and mud, and reinforced with wood. Stairs were made of both wood and stone. The larger homes were made of stone blocks. Most floors are earthen, but some homes have thin layered stone, maybe at the entrance hall or in the rooms upstairs. *Banios* are always on the ground floor, inside the houses, not outside like some homes on the island still have today, eh? Let's go into this house."

The team was astounded at what they saw. On the ground floor there were storerooms to keep food. These rooms had small windows that let in light and air which helped preserve the food stored there. Also in this area was a room set aside with a mill to grind the various grains.

"In some houses there are large window openings on the ground floor that looked out to the street," Helena explained. "They may have been shop windows where the owner sold his wares. Rooms on the upper floors also had many large windows. It was in these rooms that the interesting wall paintings were found on limestone-plastered walls. These wall paintings are like the ones found in the palaces in Crete. They depicted a wide spectrum of life on the island. Even papyrus, which was never grown here, was

THE SANTORINI ODYSSEY

depicted. That implies there was a connection with Egypt's civilization. Monkeys and antelopes also appeared in some of these frescoes. You must go to the Athens' National Archaeological Museum to see those frescoes that were removed from here and restored."

They moved a short distance down the street. "This is Building B, where they found paintings of antelopes, children with blue heads who were boxing and also blue monkeys. "For lady," she pointed to Merit, "Every home here has loom in upstairs room to make cloth. We found many loom weights that fell from the upper floors during the volcanic catastrophe of 1600 BC"

They came to the largest complex that extended down Telchines Road for a great distance. It had five entrances, and one with a roofed porch. On the east side of the complex there was a row of perfectly preserved, buff-colored, glazed pithoi painted with black spiral designs.

The team passed quick looks at each other. Nikos said, "These are interesting, eh?"

They all knew what Nikos meant: The designs were identical to those on the incense jars they had found in the cave, except in size. From the beginning, they had agreed not to discuss their finds with anyone outside the team.

In the next building, they saw a ground-floor storeroom that brought to life a scene from ancient Kalliste as it might have appeared 3,500 years before. Rows of pithoi that held olive oil or wine were set down in neatly spaced, deep holes in benches. There were also small, cone-shaped rhytons, used to scoop, measure and pour the liquid into smaller jars.

"Helena, have they ever found any human remains?" Matt asked.

"No, sir. Not so far. It's been established that, prior to the final cataclysmic eruption, pumice ash spewed for a very long time, giving people enough warnings to leave island. Ah! Here is the House of Ladies. It gets its name from the wall paintings that are also in the Athens museum. The paintings you'll see there are one of a lady of older age. We know that because she walked in a stooped position. She is bare-breasted and holds out her hands. You will often see bare-breasted Minoan women in statues and paintings. It was the fashion, I guess. Another Minoan lady stands in front of the old one, but all we see of her is her skirt because many pieces are missing. There is also a third lady, but she's not bare-breasted or stooped. Her arms are reaching out, too. These women are standing under an arch in front of a wall that is painted with stars. The women in the painting are almost life-size. They have long black hair, large loop earrings and colorful, ornate clothing, which is Minoan style. They are heavily made up with bright red lips and circles of rouge on their cheeks. It's not known what these painting are meant to depict. We have the same problem with the two boxing children I told you about earlier. Both children have their heads painted blue and wear one blue glove on the right hand. What does that mean? We don't know," She shrugged.

"But our most famous painting is of a fleet of ships that tells us a story most clearly. It came from West House. It shows some decorated ships sailing along with many passengers. It also shows a large number of people who came down to the shore to wave farewell from one shore, and on other shore, people welcome the ships. We assume that biggest ship belongs to the captain of the fleet, and men aboard the ships are his crew. You'll see spears and helmets on the warriors. You can assume the ships are off on a voyage at one end of the painting and are arriving at another destination at other side of the painting. Some scholars say these ships can go very far away, but others say that's not so, because the houses on both shores have the same architecture. You can make your own opinion when you see the painting in Athens."

Brant spoke up. "Like you, Helena, I worked here as an archaeology student many years ago, long before these houses were restored to their present shape. I remember that we found many perfectly preserved pieces of small imported pottery. are you still finding as many today?"

"We find thousands of pieces of different-shaped pottery every year, but most are not in their original shape. Some were made here in Kalliste and some imported. Imported ones are better than local pottery, and they are made of pure, red clay. They are also stronger because the firing process is better, but they are usually smaller than local pottery because of the transportation problem. Small things were traded from far off places and transported in pottery containers. The designs and floral paintings help us know where the pottery came from. We've even found something you Americans use, a barbecue! It's made of clay with little ridges to lay skewers of food on to roast. We've found ewers, jugs, three-legged cooking pots, braziers for burning incense, strainers, and many clay oil lamps for lighting homes. They're all now in the museum in Athens."

Knowing glances passed between the team.

"But you must go to Athens Archaeological Museum to see our best marble vases and chalices. You'll also see bronze cups, baking and frying pans, and stone tools. You will see superb artwork on the pottery that shows birds, dolphins, crocus, and lilies. also we've found a Mycenaean vase with Linear B script, which has been deciphered. You should visit the Herakleion Museum in Crete and see a Linear A tablet and the famous Phaistos Disc. The scripts on both have hieroglyphic-like symbols but have not yet been deciphered."

Brant commented, "I have an exquisite copy of the Phaistos Disc, and I've spent many hours trying to decipher the symbols."

"You'd become very famous, sir, if you translated what is written on that disc, eh?"

Merit asked, "A while back you mentioned that in the painting of the ladies, they were wearing earrings. Have you found any jewelry? I'm what you might call a collector."

Brant couldn't let that statement pass. "Might be called a collector! That's the biggest understatement I've ever heard."

Matt, spoke up in defense of Merit "Hey Brant, old pal, after seeing your collection of antiquities, you shouldn't pick on Merit about collections. I thought I'd died and woke up in the British Museum at your house."

"Thank you, Matt," Merit said sweetly.

Helena enjoyed the repartee, and said, "Now I'll answer lady's question. Unfortunately, we have not uncovered any jewelry yet. It's true that the women in the paintings were wearing gold earrings and bracelets and necklaces of beads. But we are sure that when the volcano started erupting, people left on ships with their small valuables like jewelry. Of course, we are only at the beginning of this ancient city."

Reaching the end where the excavation stopped, Nikos spoke with Helena, then turned back to the group, "Helena tells me she has cold drinks set out for us in one of houses where it is cool and where she will finish her tour. Okay?"

They entered a large room where a small table was set up in a corner where two ancient stone benches met. As soon as they sat down, a young man carried in a large circular tray with glasses and an ancient looking pitcher. He unloaded the tray and left.

Nikos rose, "This is good time to make toast to success of Kalliste dig, and to say *efcharisto*, thank you, to Helena, for excellent tour."

Everyone lifted their cups toward the girl and all said, "*Yassas.*"

"It was a wonderful tour," Merit said.

Helena was pleased and nodded in appreciation. "Now I'll complete my tour by telling you what people did in daily life here. I don't have to tell you what a big job it is to unearth this ancient town that has been buried and preserved for 3,500 years under millions of tons of volcanic ash. Many compare this site to Pompeii because it survived like Pompeii."

"We know that civilized people lived here because of the high standard of architecture and of the size of the houses. What did they do for living, eh? We know that they traded, so they were in the shipping business. They also were fishermen, farmers and wine makers, because we see pictures of grapes on the vases. We're sure the large pithoi held wine because of the stains on the inside. We're sure they grew olives, because we found olive branches deeply embedded in lava even below Kalliste. Olives have been here from beginning of time. We've found remains of foods like fish, shells, seeds, grain and animal bones from sheep, goats and pigs."

"We know that some Kallisteans were plumbers and built the *toileta* systems to keep sewers running. Some were pottery makers, millers, carpenters, and weavers. Weaving was a very important trade. Every house we've found had a loom. We know that cloth and yarn were dyed because of colors on ladies' clothes in paintings. We found purple murex shells all over floors. They also got dye from crocus and saffron. It makes orange and yellow dyes and is also used for spice."

"We think Kalliste was a very important place in 1,600 BC. We think it had a political system and a strong government. We have not unearthed forums and theaters like you see at Knossos, yet we think they're buried here. Although Kalliste was not a monarchy like Crete, with kings and palaces, it was just as important."

Helena stood, "Now, let's talk about the age-old subject of the lost city of Atlantis. Many scientists say that the dating of a giant eruption in 1600 BC coincides closely with end of Kalliste and the end of the Minoan civilization. We learned that from dating strata and unearthing remains of the two ancient places. Minoans on Crete lived in very majestic surroundings. People on Kalliste were tradesmen, but were wealthy, too. Plato says his lost paradise was two islands; maybe it was Crete and Kalliste, eh? Plato says Atlanteans became sinners and made gods angry, and that is why catastrophe happen. There are so very many scientific and unscientific theories about the existence of Atlantis. Everybody has their own ideas if it is a myth or truth. who knows for sure, eh? I hope you enjoyed your tour, and I wish you success on your interesting exploration of the cave in the ancient city."

They thanked her and left the site feeling euphoric.

The tour of Kalliste was mind-boggling in many ways. All kinds of new ideas filled their heads and spilled out in excitement.

"There seems to be such a direct correlation between our cave finds and those found here," said Wade. "Especially the various pithoi that are colored and decorated much the same as the incense jars we found."

Matt grinned and said, "Wow! That was quite revealing!"

"I have absolutely no doubt about it, Kallisteans used our cave!" Brant said.

Merit was embarrassed by his childishness and looked away.

"I always get strange feeling walking through streets and houses in there," Nikos said. "It's as if I was being beckoned by ghosts. Santorini has lots of ghosts, you know," he added with a sly grin. "But they're all friendly ghosts."

THE SANTORINI ODYSSEY

"Wonderful, Nikos." Matt looked askance at him. "I'm glad they're friendly. I think what we need is a quantum leap to the present, and as your attending physician, I'm ordering everyone to hit the beach." Matt said.

* * * *

Anna and Katina were invited to join them and packed a picnic lunch. They loaded up a cooler with beer and wine and took off in Nikos' truck in a festive mood. They chose the beach at Perissa which was at the bottom of the mountain because Nikos felt it would not be as crowded as Kamari. Both beaches are beautiful and covered with black, lava sand. A million Europeans vacation at the two beaches every year.

"You'll see many tourists on beach who think it's cosmopolitan to wear smallest of string bikinis," warned Nikos. "A few look very good. Others will give you good laugh, I promise!"

The bathing-suit issue had been hotly discussed between Anna and Katina. The teenager wanted to wear a bikini that Merit had given her, instead of her old, one-piece black silk jersey, which was badly faded. Anna finally relented because it was not too skimpy. Katina's breasts and buttocks were amply covered. Like Merit's, the suit was an Anne Cole design. Katina was thrilled with the brilliant colors and floral patterns and sequins. Merit's suit had geometric designs in red and white and was also adorned with sequins. It was the newest fashion in suits this year and bound to attract a great deal of attention from trendy Europeans. Neither Anna nor Katina had any idea what Merit's bathing suits cost, but they knew they were made of quality material and sewn professionally. They would have been startled beyond their comprehension had they seen the price tags.

Anna debated quite a while whether she would even wear her old-fashioned black bathing suit. Spending time on the beach was a luxury she seldom indulged in, but she looked forward to being with the Americans in a casual setting. She had not had much opportunity to get to know them. She wanted to talk about America, especially about Pasadena, California where her husband had lived. She never stopped searching for clues or reasons for his desertion.

When they reached the beach, they had to pick their way through the crowds until they found a place that could accommodate the seven of them. They spread out blankets and stripped off their outer clothing. Matt hollered, "Last one in the water is a blue monkey from Kalliste!"

Everyone but Anna and Nikos responded to the challenge. Anna kept her blouse over her shoulders. She was uncomfortable about her appearance after seeing how beautiful Katina and Merit looked. Nikos was transfixed by the magnificent semi-nudeness of the two young women racing toward the water.

"Put your lecherous eyes back in your head, old man," Anna teased.

He turned, embarrassed that she had noticed. Then an evil grin spread across his face as he walked toward her in ape-like fashion, grunting loudly. "I have desire like giant gorilla to take you into water!" Swiftly, he picked Anna up in his arms and ran with her toward the sea while she screamed and kicked.

"Put me down, you crazy fool!"

Nikos simply laughed and splashed into the water. When they were waist-deep, he tossed her into the sea. By then, the rest of the group became aware of what was happening and began swimming toward Anna and Nikos.

Matt swam underwater and came up under Anna who was now floating on the surface. He lifted her up out of the water completely, raising her dripping body into the air, calling out dramatically, "I am Poseidon, god of the sea, and this mermaid is one of my beautiful nymphs!"

Anna blushed and slapped wildly at Matt to put her down.

He set her down in the water with a flourish and spread out his arms to the amusement of the others who were enjoying his acting. Only now did it occur to him that possibly he shouldn't have done it. "Farewell! I have a luncheon date with Neptune. We're having Chicken of the Sea tuna!" With that, he dove deep into the water and disappeared.

Ever since Merit and Katina ran down to the water, the young men on the beach had focused constantly on them. When they came out of the water and started walking back to their blankets to have lunch, several young men blocked their way. The guys flirted good-naturedly and offered them a beer and asked them to sit with them.

Nikos, toweling his head, caught the mood of the young men's voices and decided to interfere. Glaring at them and putting his arms protectively on the girls' shoulders, he led them back to their blankets.

The guys called after him in taunting voices, "Sorry, *Papa*."

Merit and Katina suppressed their amusement, that Nikos would be offended by being called *Papa*. He would never think of himself in the role of their father.

Merit had not been embarrassed by the young men's attention, but Katina blushed vividly. Merit teased her. They were becoming close friends from working together every night in the darkroom.

Anna set out the lunch and they ate heartily. Then they stretched out to soak up the warm Aegean sun.

* * * *

After an hour of siesta, Brant became restless and asked Katina if she thought he could rent one of the small *caiques* he had seen being used for snorkeling.

"We'll go see, eh?" she said, jumping up and motioning Brant to follow. Draping a towel around her hips, sarong-style, and tying back her tangled hair, she walked past the young men with Brant at her side, now feeling quite sophisticated.

Her perception of Brant as a father figure was fading. She felt different lately, a delicious feeling she couldn't explain. She ran ahead and at the water's edge stepped up on a large flat-topped boulder, removed the towel and waved it toward one of the boats to get their attention. The pilot saw her and waved back. She gestured for him to come ashore. She draped the towel back on her hips again and stood looking out to the boat now heading toward shore.

Brant turned to say something to Katina. He froze in shock. Katina, standing poised with only one foot on the boulder now, was looking out to sea. Her curly titian hair was blowing back off her perfect Grecian face, and her perfectly defined torso, only slightly covered by the spangled bra, was easily imagined bare. She held her right hand over her right eye and her left arm was slightly outstretched as if suspended in a waving position.

Good God! Venus de Milo! A perfect likeness! He inhaled deeply and gasped.

Katina turned quickly to find Brant staring at her, his mouth wide open.

"Are you okay, Brant?" she asked, as she hopped off the boulder and touched his arm.

He spun away from her, raced into the water and dove under. His passion was so intense, it had triggered an erection that jerked his body with palpitating spasms. Eventually the cool water calmed him. What an unbelievable jolt, he thought. Katina, an exquisite replica of my beloved Aphrodite, but with arms now. He was euphoric and shivered in ecstasy. I remember the first time I saw her, I had a feeling of 'deja' vu. Christ almighty, it's a fantasy come true! But she's just a child, a magnificent, innocent, sixteen-year-old child Venus. I must have her, he thought.

Katina watched him as he swam toward the boat, then she ran back to the group. "Merit, I think Brant may be sick. He looked strange. Maybe he drank too much wine."

Merit and the others stood up. "Isn't that Brant climbing into the boat?" Merit asked.

Katina shaded her eyes and looked toward the boat. "Yes, that's him. He's renting the boat so we can go snorkeling."

They walked down to the water's edge as the boat reached shore.

Brant jumped out calling to the others, "Who wants to snorkel? They have all the equipment."

"Are you all right, Brant?" Merit knew he had had too much wine. Lately, she not only worried about the subtle changes in his personality, but also his drinking. He was becoming too overly anxious about finding treasure in the cave. Whenever they were alone now, that was all he talked about.

"Are you okay, Brant?" Matt asked.

"I'm okay, I'm okay," he answered gruffly. "The hot sun and wine don't mix too well. Come on, who is going to join me?" he was annoyed.

Merit, Katina and Nikos climbed aboard.

Anna said, "Not for me. I'll stay on beach and watch."

Matt and Wade were just about to climb into the boat when Matt changed his mind and said, "You guys go. I'm going to lounge on the beach. I hate snorkeling."

Wade gave Matt a quizzical look. "You sure you don't want to come?"

Matt caught his meaning. "Naw. I think I'll take a long walk down the beach. I need the exercise. Shove off. Bring me back a mermaid."

Something had been eating at Matt since that day Anna kissed him. This was the first opportunity that he'd had to be alone with her but to still have others nearby. He knew he had hurt her by rejecting her so curtly and wanted to apologize.

He and Anna waved to the group, now busy trying on flippers and adjusting masks.

"Anna, is your ankle well enough to take a little walk?"

Both surprised and pleased that Matt asked her, Anna replied, "Sure. I need to exercise it more."

They walked about a half a mile sharing small talk. The crowd thinned out when they reached the end of the beach where the foot of the mountains met the seashore.

"Anna, I'd like to talk to you about something that has been bothering me. Let's sit down here for a few minutes."

They leaned their backs against the flat surface of the steep mountainside. Anna was both nervous and curious.

"First, I want to be absolutely honest about my feelings for you. God, I hope I say this right. I don't want you to misunderstand what I'm trying to say. I think you are a very lovely, special woman. At another time, in another place, if you and I had met, I know I would have been very attracted to you."

Anna sat stoically, her hands folded in her lap. She had no idea what he was getting at. Was he going to tell her he wanted her in spite of being married?

"But there's something that few people know about me, but I want you to know. I know you'll keep what I'm about to tell you a secret. I'm telling you because I want you to understand why I rejected your kiss. I know Nikos told you my wife is very ill. In fact, my wife will probably die soon, six months to a year. She's dying of alcoholism. I know it must seem cruel to you that I'd desert her at a time like this, but the truth is, she doesn't want me around. I tried for years to help her stop drinking, but she resisted. We never had a good marriage."

Anna was stunned. Her heart ached for him.

Then he told her about Lee and their secret affair for the past ten years.

A surge of jealousy raced through her that she couldn't dismiss.

"Like you, Anna, I'm Catholic. I don't believe in divorce, but I sin by having an affair. It's the only way I could have hung in with this marriage all these years. I won't deny that it'll be a great relief when Sarah dies. It'll be like a release from prison. I intend to marry Lee. She's been a wonderful, supportive friend and lover for me, and deserves better than I've given her."

Anna was flattered that Matt thought enough of her to share such a personal part of his life. She envied Lee. "Why are you telling me all this, Matt?" Anna asked. "I will never tell anyone your secret, but I don't understand why you tell me, unless you maybe know that I, too, like your Lee, would like you for my lover. Now I tell you the truth, eh?"

"Yes, Anna, I felt that, and I was complimented that you were attracted to me. And as I said, at another time, another place, and if I didn't have Lee, I'm sure we would have become involved romantically." He took her hand and kissed it. "You and I, Anna, have a lot in common. Because of your religion, you've hung in there these past sixteen years, honoring your marriage vows. You've been a prisoner, just like me. You've got many good years of your life left. I wish I could help you not to waste them like I have."

"No one can help me unless they are best detective in world and can solve puzzle of my disappearing husband. Nikos and I tried everything we could to try to find out what happened to him. I know there's an answer, but I guess I'll never know."

"Wait a minute! I have an idea. I think there might be a way of finding out what happened to your husband. I think I know a way we can find out if he's dead or alive!"

"How could you do that?"

"I'll bet my brother could do it!"

"Your brother? How would he know what happened to my Joe?"

"My brother, Danny, is an agent with the FBI in Los Angeles, in California. It's like an international police organization. They're great at finding missing people."

Anna was astonished. "How much will it cost?"

PEG MADDOCKS

"Don't worry about that."

"I'll not take charity!"

"It won't be charity. It won't cost you or me any money." Matt was excited. "Just tell me all you can about your Joe Brady, and I'll phone the information to my brother, Danny, tonight and maybe, before too long, Anna Brady can begin a new life."

Anna was stunned. The implications of what Matt said suddenly sank in. "No more wishing and hoping. It is that easy? I don't believe it! Oh, Matt, if you do that for me, I'll be happiest woman in world." She let out a boisterous "*OPA!*" to punctuate her joy, stood up and threw her hands into the air.

"Now, I'm going to give you biggest kiss on lips you ever have, even if you don't want it!" With that, she pulled him up to her and hugged and kissed him vigorously until they had to break apart from laughing.

On the walk back, Anna told Matt about the last time she saw Joe Brady. "Katina was only three days old. Joe was asked to go to big important meeting in England about what was going on at the Kalliste exploration. He called it symposium. I remember that word because Joe spelled it. I wrote it down; that's how I learn English. He taught me many new English words. He was to be speaker there. He did not want to leave me and our baby daughter, but I told him go and hurry back. He gave us so many kisses goodbye, I was sure he'd miss his plane. He said he would buy us wonderful presents from big store in London called, Arods, I think." Anna wiped tears away as the memory came alive and tore at her.

"I think he probably said Harrods. It's a wonderful store that carries everything you could ever want to buy. Even the royal family shops there."

"He told me he'd be back in three days."

"When was this Anna?"

"Katina was born on Tuesday, 26th day of Iounios. How do you say month six in English?

The sixth month is June, so she was born on Tuesday, June 26th. What year?"

"It was 1979. Okay, then Joe left on June 29th, Thursday, on eight o'clock plane from Santorini. I know he was on that plane. I was worried he wouldn't make it, so I asked taxi friend who took him to plane. He saw him get on plane.

Then he didn't come back on Sunday plane, and not on Monday or Tuesday plane. I felt inside that he got sick or something bad happened. I talked to Nikos, and he talked to *astynomos*, the police. I didn't know where he was in London, or where symposium place was. When three weeks went by, I didn't know what to do.

Nikos was good friend to me. He tried to help, and he made many telephone calls to London and place in California called Pasadena, where Joe told me he lived. But no Joe Brady lived there. At Kalliste where Joe worked, no one knew where he went. He told me that he could not tell them he went to symposium in London. Why? I asked Nikos. Why did he not tell his friends at the dig in Kalliste that he would be making big talk in London about how many important things they found at Kalliste?"

Nikos said, "I checked with friend who was working on the Kalliste site. He said he thought Joe didn't tell them, because the boss man of dig would be jealous that he was not asked to be speaker at symposium instead of foreigner." Nikos also was sure that boss man would be so jealous of him, he would not let him work on dig any more when he came back.

Nikos telephoned friends of archaeology in Athens. They didn't know about any symposium about Kalliste in London. They'd never heard of Joe Brady. I told Nikos not to spend any more of his money to find Joe. I know Joe loved Katina and me very much. I know he didn't come back for good reason, so I have waited sixteen years. Do you think I am fool, Matt?"

"Oh no, Anna, you're a loyal wife. I'll get all this information to my brother by phone tonight, but I want you to prepare yourself for bad news. He may be dead or married to another woman and may not want to ever see or hear about you and Katina, although I find that hard to believe. I think probably he may have been involved in an accident or became ill, and somehow his passport and identification was lost. And of course there's the possibility that my brother may not be able to find any trace of him."

"I will pray hard that he does, Matt. I just thought of something else; my Joe always carried what he called, briefcase. He kept all his papers, passport, clean shirts and all his money in it. I know that because when he gave me money, he always got it from his briefcase. It had lock, and he had to push in numbers to make it open. And, I almost forgot, he always wore his gold wedding ring and carried picture of me and him, too."

"Do you have a picture of him?"

"No," Anna said sadly. "I wish I did so Katina could see what her *papa* looked like. But I can tell you what he looked like sixteen years ago." She gave Matt a full description.

"Well, I'll get this information off to Danny. I'm sure, with all the resources the FBI has, along with their contacts at Scotland Yard in London, we'll get the mystery of the missing Joe Brady solved before too long."

"Oh, I pray you're right, Matt." Anna replied hopefully, her eyes swelling with tears and a faraway look spreading across her face.

When they got back to the blankets, the snorkelers were just coming ashore. Matt and Anna agreed not to tell anyone about their conversation. If they did get news, it would be up to Anna to decide whether she would tell Katina and the others.

The snorkelers enjoyed their trip, particularly viewing what Nikos claimed were underwater ruins; they did resemble the large building stones they had seen at Kalliste that morning. They also saw large volcanic bombs that had been blown out of the volcano and into the sea during one of the many eruptions on the island. They were all suffering from sunburns by the time they packed up and headed home.

* * * *

When Matt and Wade were alone, Matt felt compelled to break his promise to Anna, because he knew he owed Wade an explanation as to why he had stayed behind with her.

"This is confidential, Wade. Ever since you told me about Anna's husband walking out on her, I keep thinking that there must be some way to find out why he disappeared. It's bizarre. And today it suddenly came to me how, maybe, I could help her locate him, dead or alive. We discussed it. She really appreciated the offer of help and gave me all the details about when and how he disappeared. it seems like he just vanished."

"How do you hope to accomplish that, Matt?" Wade's tone was skeptical.

"You remember my brother, Danny, he's with the FBI in Los Angeles now, and I'm going to ask him to do some investigating."

"Backtracking all those years won't be easy, Matt. Aren't you afraid of giving Anna false hopes and hurting her again if you're not successful?"

"Hey, you know how lucky we Irish are!"

"You're also dreamers! Are you sure that she doesn't think you're encouraging a romance with her; taking all this interest in her private life?"

"I can assure you, Wade, that I was able to convince Anna that any further romantic interest in me was a waste of her time."

"How in the world did you do that?"

"It's a professional secret between patient and doctor. Can't break my Hippocratic oath, can I?" he grinned.

That evening, Anna astounded Matt. In spite of the excitement that certainly must be boiling inside her, she acted no different than usual.

She was a strong-willed woman, Matt thought. God, I hope my brother finds him. He had asked Anna if she thought Nikos could give him any input, but she was adamant about not involving him.

She had told Matt, "Nikos is wonderful, kind man, but he is gossiper, and everyone on island, including Katina, would know about what you were trying to do within hours."

Later that evening Matt telephoned his brother from Nikos' house after Nikos had gone to the village. He related all the details Anna had given him: Joe Brady's age, height, weight, the color of his eyes and hair and his archaeology background at UCLA (Anna did not know when he graduated). his mother had died at childbirth. His father and a maiden aunt, who lived next door to them in Pasadena, raised him. His father died two years before Joe came to Santorini. Joe had told Anna he had had an unhappy childhood and never talked about any close friends. He seldom received mail and only wrote to people about archaeological subjects. He seemed to have money, but Anna did not know its source.

Matt's brother, Danny, concluded that Joe had been a rather secretive fellow about a lot of things. "You say he bought the house for Anna from Nikos' parents and paid cash from his briefcase? And, he went to Athens about every three weeks to get money from a bank, even took Anna sometimes, huh? Sounds fishy to me."

"I agree, but she remembers that the first thing he did on those trips was go to a bank for *drachmas*. She always stayed in the lobby while he did his banking transactions, so she had no idea what transpired. He was a consulting archaeologist on the dig at Kalliste and seemed to love his work, but the pay was very low."

"It's not a great deal to go on, Matt, but I think we'll come up with something. I'll get on it right away."

* * * *

Sunday morning the tolling bells called the villagers to church. Everyone met in the courtyard to walk together to the small church of St. Demetrius. The men all wore shirts and ties, and the women wore dresses and scarves over their heads.

Before leaving the courtyard, Anna said to the team, "I need favor from everybody. Would you all say prayers today for secret special thing I need many prayers for?"

A glance passed quickly between Matt and Wade. Anna put her arm around Katina's shoulders and led the group out to the street. Katina wondered why her mother needed everyone to pray. Should she ask? She decided against it.

When they reached the road, they joined the villagers who were in a procession to the church on the hill. Friendly greetings were exchanged.

Kristos pulled his father and mother out of line so they could talk to Merit when she passed by. He had become very attached to her and loved Zeus. He followed all her grooming instructions about the horse's care meticulously. He mucked the stall every day and fed Zeus. Merit knew that

Kristos and Zeus had developed a close relationship because every time Merit mounted Zeus, he'd turn his head back to look at Kristos. Kristos had asked Merit if he could ride Zeus sometimes. Merit told him she would need his parents' permission before he could ride the horse.

"Missus Powers, Missus Powers," Kristos called out with a grin, pointing to his parents. "My *Mama* and *Papa* want to talk to you to tell you it's okay for me to ride Zeus."

His parents approached Merit. His father, Elias, the guard at the ancient city of Thera, knew Merit from her work in the cave, but his wife, Dora, had never met her. Dora did not understand English.

Brant shook Elias' hand and smiled at his wife. He asked them in Greek if they would allow Kristos to ride Zeus. He said Merit would teach him to ride properly without a saddle. The Kaldaras quickly agreed, although concerned that Kristos was bothering Merit too much. Brant assured them that he was a charming young man, always polite and hard working, and they enjoyed his company. Elias bragged about how Kristos was the smartest in his class and had learned to speak good English. Kristos' smile became broader and broader as the conversation progressed.

Brant told Merit, "They say it's okay with them."

Merit winked at Kristos. "Okay, groom, you can ride Zeus but only when I say so. And you must never ride him without telling me exactly where you're going. Tomorrow I'll give you more rules that you must obey. Okay?"

"Sure! Rules I know about. I have lots of rules to remember. I'll be best groom you ever have." With that he waved goodbye and wiggled his way through the crowd to catch up with his parents.

Merit enjoyed Kristos tremendously. He was always smiling and so willing to please her. "Wouldn't you like to have a wonderful son like him someday, Brant?"

Brant teased, "I thought children were not in your agenda for a number of years, young lady."

"I think I've changed my mind, okay?"

"Absolutely! Maybe we should work on it after church," he said, giving her a lecherous look, then he changed his expression to admiration. Her face was beautiful, framed by the white lace scarf that Anna loaned her. "And after our first son is born, I suppose you'll want a girl?"

"And what if we have a girl first?" Merit teased, knowing what his answer would be.

"Darling, you know the Powers always have sons first!"

Reaching the church, they joined the villagers already inside. *Papa* Ioannis, standing in front of the royal doors, gestured emphatically for the

THE SANTORINI ODYSSEY

team to come and sit in the front row, which he had reserved for them. All eyes followed the team members coming down the aisle.

The nave of the church was small and could seat only about a hundred people. The walls were ornately decorated with white arches that framed colorful icon paintings of saints, the Holy Family, the Crucifixion and other religious events of Christianity. A proscenium-type structure with many recessed arches and the two royal doors faced the congregation. Each of the royal doors displayed a large icon painting. One of an angel on a cloud, and the other, the Virgin Mary. The subtle message of the paintings was that the angel was about to inform Mary that she would become the Mother of Christ.

Above the doors, set in a long narrow niche, was a small icon of The Last Supper. Below, on each side of the royal doors, were four large recessed icons: St. Demetrius, the namesake of the church; the Prophet Elias, (Mount Elias, the highest peak on the island was named for him); the martyred St. Irene of Thessaloniki, for whom Santorini was named; and St. Catherine, the most popular namesake of Greek women.

Nikos had told them that all the icons were painted by a special artist who prayed as he painted. What makes the paintings unique, is that no matter where you are in the church, the eyes of the saints follow you.

On either side of the two steps leading to the royal doors were gigantic pedestals topped with beautiful bouquets of native flowers. The two royal doors, which only the priest could enter, opened onto the altar area. The altar boys and deacons who assisted at mass entered the altar area via other doors on either side of the wall. As the Divine Liturgy began, the royal doors opened, and the congregation could view the Holy of Holies, where the altar table was located. On that table sat the Gospel, a cross, and an ornate tabernacle, which held the body of Christ; the communion of bread and wine.

The profusion of brilliantly colored icons, flowers and candlelight was a stirring sight.

Merit and Brant were intrigued with the contrast between this small, elaborately decorated church and the sedate ambience of the enormous Episcopal church they attended in Greenwich. But they agreed that the atmosphere of this small church felt much more religious.

Although St. Demetrius was a poor village, each family generously supported the church according to their means.

Nikos had told them that Greeks are extremely religious people and their church is the focal point of their lives, especially in a small village.

Papa Ioannis walked through the royal doors and the service began.

At collection time, Elias Kaldaras approached the first pew with a basket and handed to Wade who was sitting at the end of the pew. Wade put in some drachma and passed it on to Matt, who did the same. When he passed over to Brant, everyone in the church stretched up from their seats to see what the rich American couple would give. They were not disappointed. Brant and Merit both put a large amount of American dollars in the basket. Pleased murmurs filled the church.

When the Divine Liturgy concluded, the congregation filed out of the church and each was greeted by *Papa* Ioannis. He patted Nikos on the back and shook hands with Wade and Matt. He smiled broadly at Merit and Brant and thanked them for coming.

The priest handed Brant and Merit brightly colored holy cards with pictures on the front and prayers on the back. Merit's card was a beautiful icon painting of the Virgin Mary.

Nikos told her, "On back is prayer to Mary."

He explained Brant's card, "That is painting of Weeping Icon Of St. Nicholas, and on back is prayer to banish punishment cast by evil eye. It asks that God send down angel to rebuke and banish evil sorcery and evil eye of threatening person and protect those who invoke God's help."

Brant was startled since he had not mentioned anything about the old lady giving him the evil eye that first day. His furrowed brow caught the attention of *Papa* Ioannis.

"Not to worry, Mister Powers. If you get evil eye, you have prayer to ward it off now, eh?" The priest said with a smile.

Had the old lady confessed her sorcery? Brant wondered.

When they returned to the compound, Anna said, "Katina and I invite you to be guests for big meal out here in courtyard today. Everything will be ready in one hour. It'll be your breakfast and lunch together. Okay?"

"In America, we call that a brunch, Anna," Merit said.

"Okay, we have brunch," Anna laughed. Clearly, she was in a rare mood. All night, romantic scenes from her life with Joe had kept her awake; they were so real.

Anna pointed to the various dishes she had prepared: "My homemade *psomi* and *arni*, bread and lamb, deep fried *ktopodi* is octopus, *dolmades* are stuffed grape leaves with yellow sauce, *fasolakia* are beans from my garden, *baklava*, you know that is my sweet pastry. And we'll have cafe, retsina and bira.

They devoured the wonderful meal while enjoying the camaraderie, the warm sun, and the mild, constant breeze from the Aegean. They talked at the table for hours. Music from Nikos' tape collection, which was piped outside through speakers, played softly in the background. although they had only known each other for a short time, they had become closely united, like an extended family.

Brant said, "You're in unusually high spirits today, Anna."

"Yes. Today I'm happy because I'm with my good friends," she answered, smiling coyly.

Nikos looked thoughtful, "I think Anna has secret that she won't tell anybody."

Anna looked embarrassed.

Merit suddenly jumped up. "A wonderful idea just came to me! Brant, what would you think about celebrating our fifth anniversary with a big party right here in the courtyard. We could invite the whole village!"

"Great idea, Merit! Let's do it!," Brant answered in delight. "As you all know, my wonderful wife planned this year's anniversary trip to Santorini, and I love her for it!" He put his arms around her and kissed her tenderly on the cheek.

Lately, Katina felt envious whenever Brant was affectionate with Merit. Then she felt shame for feeling that way. To appease her conscience, she quickly offered, "I'll decorate whole courtyard with flowers."

"I'll borrow *souvlas*, spits, from my friends and cook big, spring lambs, eh?" Anna said, giving Merit a friendly hug.

Nikos, had gone into the house to change the tapes, and when he came out, he found everyone talking at once. "*Po, po, po,* what's happening here?"

"We're going to have a big party to celebrate the Powers' fifth wedding anniversary," Wade said.

"*Opa!*" Nikos said raising his hands over his head and snapping his fingers. "I'll hire best *syrtaki* band on island!"

Matt said, "And I'll do the Greek dancing, seeing as how I do it better than anyone else on this island." He took a handkerchief out of his pocket with his right hand, held it out, and began to do crossover steps. Tripping purposely, and dancing in one direction, then the other.

Laughter and applause followed his brief performance.

"What's the date of this grand affair?" Wade asked.

"Well, our anniversary is on Saturday, May 25th." Merit said.

"That's only a few weeks off, we'd better get busy planning." Brant said.

"Oh, I have another thought!" Merit interjected. "I've been taking video movies of scenes around the village. The people are not shy and seem to enjoy posing. Maybe I should make a point of getting all the villagers on video, and, we could show it the night of the party on a big screen. Anna, you could help make sure I don't miss anyone."

"The villagers would love that!" Nikos said. "They would be like movie stars, eh? But I don't think we have very big screen on island."

"Don't worry about that." Brant said. "I'll take care of all the video and sound equipment. I'll get on the phone tomorrow to Athens."

PEG MADDOCKS

For the next hour, exciting anticipation saturated the compound. Everyone talked at once as ideas crisscrossed the table.

"Should I send out written invitations to all the villagers?" Merit asked.

Anna and Nikos burst out laughing. "Just tell one person walking by, and within few minutes everyone knows." Nikos said.

Anna added, "Faster than telephone!"

Merit was convinced.

A taxi turned into the driveway with the horn beeping. Nikos called out, "*Kalimera sas*, Dimi. What are you doing here with your *amoxi*?"

The driver got out and tipped his hat to the women. "*Kalimera*, Nikos. Who's man named Powers?"

"I'm Powers, Brant called out. "Thanks for being so obliging and renting your taxi on short notice." He turned to the group. "A little surprise. I thought we'd enjoy a tour of the island this afternoon, and I'll take you all out to dinner."

"I'll be your guide! I'm maybe best guide on island for sure!" Nikos said unashamedly.

"Okay then, everyone get in. I'm sorry there won't be enough room for you, Anna, but maybe we could squeeze you in, Katina," Brant said in an almost lascivious voice.

Katina said, "No thank you, It's okay. We've seen island many times, and besides, we have to clean up our brunch plates before the cats do it for us."

"I'll drive," Nikos volunteered. "But first, we'll take Dimi back to his business."

After letting Dimi out at Hellenic Taxi-Rentals, Nikos began narrating about the bustling town of Fira. Because the team had been so secluded for so long, the sight of hotels, tourists, shops and large cruise ships anchored below at the port of Skala rejuvenated them. They rode the cable car down to Skala, passing the cruise passengers going up. Merit insisted that they all ride the donkeys back up, which they did reluctantly. They visited the museum, the Frankish Quarter and admired the beautiful architecture of the many churches' bell towers. In the winding alleys, Merit couldn't resist buying locally-made items of clothing, pottery and souvenirs on display outside the shops. They then drove northwest along the rim of the caldera until they reached Oia, a picturesque village carved out of the steep mountainside. Their first stop was at Zorba's Pub for cold drinks and then walked down the town's narrow street of whitewashed houses.

Nikos gave an interesting narration about the spectacular view of the caldera and its islands. "See that big island, it's called Therasia and is quite primitive. There you will also find many fishermen's hamlets and pozzolana quarry. When they were building the Suez Canal in 1859, they needed pozzolana; it's like cement, which is vital material for underwater construction. They also found first traces of prehistoric civilization buried under thick layers of ash there. They found stone tools, decorated pottery, millstones and utensils made of lava, with the remains of barley, lentils and peas." Nikos promised to arrange a boat ride to the islands soon.

They came across several skaftas (natural cave houses) that were for rent.

"How about renting one of these next weekend, Merit?" Brant joked.

Merit grimaced. "No way! I don't do caves on weekends. but I might seriously consider one of the lovely homes on the top of the hill if I decide to give up caving with you guys."

Matt looked shocked. "Glory be to God, you can't desert us! Our morale would be crushed!"

"Well, I'll stick around for a while, I guess unless we meet up with more critters."

Nikos, hearing the word critters, remembered the phone call he received last night from Yannis the foreman. He had told Nikos that his men no longer would work in the cave, because they had seen a large snake. Knowing that it would be the end of the exploration, Nikos had quickly called his friend, Dr. Manolis Makrakis, a herpetologist in Athens who was usually willing to snake hunt because of the venom shortage. Fortunately, the doctor agreed to fly over to Santorini on Monday morning. Nikos would tell just Brant and Wade. Merit and Matt would be given work to do outside the cave.

They returned to Fira for dinner at Nikos' cousin Spyro's taverna. Nikos was in a state of delight, because at last, all his friends would see the beautiful American woman he was always talking about. He knew the regulars at Spyro's were skeptical, because he was always bragging about the women in his life.

All eyes turned towards the door when the team entered. Heads leaned toward each other whispering about the new arrivals.

Spyro came from behind the bar, dancing in time to *syrtaki* music, balancing a glass of ouzo on his head. He held his arm out in welcome. "*Kalispera sas* and *yia sas*! I have prepared wonderful feast for Nikos' American friends." He handed the glass of ouzo to Merit and bowed gallantly.

After they had been served drinks and appetizers, Nikos held out his hand to Merit, saying, "I would like some of my friends to meet you."

Before he was through, he had introduced her to most of the men in the place. Meanwhile, Brant, who was drinking heavily, was becoming quite irritated while watching the men flirting good-naturedly with Merit.

Merit picked up on Brant's annoyance immediately when she sat back down at the table. She could also see that he had had too much to drink.

"Well it's about time you came back to join your husband. I thought you were going to spend the evening with Nikos and his friends!" Brant challenged her sarcastically.

Nikos, smiling broadly, said innocently, "I tell you, Brant, my friends were so happy to meet Merit."

She quickly leaned over and kissed Brant, whispering softly, "I'm sorry, darling. I should have come back sooner." She knew she should pacify him to prevent him from making a scene. Niko had embarrassed her with his outrageous introductions; "Meet my lovely co-worker." She knew he was showing off and didn't mean any harm, but knew it would make Brant angry. In spite of Brant's foul mood and his sarcastic remarks to Nikos, who pretended not to notice them, they all enjoyed the wonderful meal. Leaving Spyro's about eleven, they drove to Dimi's taxi stand. He took over the wheel, giving them a wild ride back up the mountain to the village. Dimi, it seems, was a newlywed and had left his bride of four days waiting in bed for his return. Nikos had whispered this important information to Matt, who passed it on to the others.

CHAPTER EIGHT

Before breakfast on Monday morning, Nikos took Brant and Wade aside and told them about the snake situation. "I'm sure Dr. Makrakis will capture the snake."

"Don't you dare tell Merit. I'm sure it would frighten her enough to want to go home, and I don't want to leave!" Brant warned Nikos.

"Let's not say anything about snakes until we know what Nikos' friend can do." Wade said. "And I don't think Matt has to know, either. I'll give them something to do outside the cave this morning."

Wade told Merit and Matt that the team would be doing different jobs this morning. "Nikos, Brant and I will be working below and above ground, measuring around the temple of Apollo. I want an estimate of where we are in the Apollo tunnel in relation to the Temple above. We think there might have been an entrance from the tunnel up to the temple. But I've got a fun job for you two to do out in the ancient ruins."

"What are we going to do, Wade?" Merit looked forward to working outdoors.

"My wife had asked me to get her some stone rubbings for her collection, and, I haven't had the time to do it yet. She collects rubbings of gravestones and prehistoric drawings on canyon and cave walls, and I was wondering if you two would be willing to do some rubbings from the ruins."

"Sure, we'd be glad to, Wade," Matt said. "What about the erotic graffiti all around here? Do you want that, too?" He raised his eyebrows up and down.

"Sure, why not. It'll be Greek to my wife. I'll give you a list of the ones I'd like to have, especially the two tablets with the laws."

Merit was enthusiastic. "I'm an old hand at this, Wade. I've done many rubbings of our family's gravestones."

"Great. The transfer paper and the special crayons are up at the office."

"I'd also would like to get some black-and-white photos of those petroglyphs around the Sanctuary of Artemidoros that are too large for rubbing," Merit said.

"Don't forget the eagle that's nearby," Wade reminded her. "That's the symbol of Zeus, your horse's namesake. Why don't you take some of Anna's sandwiches that she packed for lunch. We'll catch up with you when we're through."

* * * *

Dr. Manolis Makrakis, the herpetologist, was due to arrive in Santorini on the early morning flight and would take a taxi to the village, where Elias would meet him and take him up to the site.

Nikos explained to Wade and Brant as they walked through the ancient city, "My friend, Mak, is always interested in capturing poisonous snakes to milk their venom for antivenin. Did you know that antivenin is made by injecting venom into horses?"

"My, aren't you brilliant this morning." Brant's tone of voice jarred Nikos.

Nikos ignored his sarcasm. "Because they're so big, they can withstand poisonous doses without suffering any ill effects. Then they use horse's blood once…"

Brant rudely interrupted Nikos in a sing song voice, "Once the venom circulates in the horse's bloodstream, blood is withdrawn and plasma is spun off and concentrated for later inoculation of snake bite victims. Isn't that interesting?"

Wade gave Brant an angry look. His attitude was annoying. He assumed Brant was angry at Nikos because of his behavior last night with Merit at the restaurant.

Brant ignored Wade's warning and continued his surly attitude. "And I suppose your friend expects to just go in the cave and find the snake?" He asked cynically.

"Oh no, he'll need our help to do that," Nikos answered.

"No thank you, I'm not interested in doing that at all!" Brant said tersely.

Now, Wade was angry. "Hey, Brant, you don't have much choice if you want to continue with the cave exploration."

Brant felt trapped. "I don't know anything about snake hunting."

"Dr. Makrakis will tell you all you need to know, you can be sure of that," said Nikos. He'll have us use our portable lights while we pound on ground and walls with shovels. Snakes don't have ears and can't hear, but they are very sensitive to vibrations."

Although skeptical, Brant knew there was nothing he could do but take Nikos' word that this method of flushing out the snakes would work.

Wade quickly changed the subject. Come on, let's get over to the temple of Apollo.

On the way, Wade said, "Nikos and I did some measuring when I first got here and have figured out that the temple of Apollo is one hundred and ten feet from the entrance of the cave."

Nikos added, "It could be that tunnels will lead to temple of Apollo and sanctuary of Egyptian Gods.

"Well, if your calculations are correct, we'd have only another ninety feet to go to be under the temple," Brant said.

The men continued trekking silently through the weather-beaten ruins of the ancient city until they arrived at what had once been a large edifice dedicated to the god apollo Karneios. Nikos spread out a plan of how the original building was thought to have looked. Part of the temple was carved from native rock; and the rest built on a limestone base. It was built during the sixth or seventh century B.C. next to the square of the *Gymnopaidiai*. The square was by far the most sacred and important part of the ancient city and was the religious center of the Dorian cults of Thera, which the island was called at that time.

Led by Nikos, the team entered the remains of an oblong courtyard of which, like most of the ruins, only the outer shell remained.

"You see back there against wall, that was where underground cistern to hold rainwater was located." Nikos explained. Water was always used for religious rites in Greece. And here to our right was priest's room, we think. Now we go to other end of building over there, where large temple room was, but first we walk through this small area here, called *pronaos*. you say porch, eh?"

They followed Nikos, and when they reached the *cella*, the large chamber of the temple, he stopped them by holding his hand up and assuming his lecturer pose. "This was very holy place for Dorians, and others too. Probably, it once had large statue of god, Apollo Karneios on pedestal for people to pray to. Now come over here," he said, striding across the room and beckoning the men to follow. "Here you see two doorways and steps leading down to what was once two rooms, eh? We think one room was treasury and other was *adyton*, a holy shrine that only priest can enter, just like one they had at temple of Apollo at Delphi, eh, Brant?"

Brant smirked and aped Nikos lecture stance., "You're not comparing this small, insignificant temple to the magnificent temple of Apollo at Delphi, are you, Nikos?"

Nikos hesitated, "No. But yes, in layout it's like Delphi, much smaller of course." Nikos was getting annoyed.

Brant's blatant imitation of Nikos upset Wade. He'd have to have a private talk with Brant before it went any further. "Exactly what's the point, Brant?" Wade's voice was testy.

"Nothing special. I just didn't want Nikos to insult my intelligence by suggesting that this temple was anywhere near as important as the one at Delphi."

Nikos looked confused. He knew he was being chided and felt that Brant was insinuating that he was stupid. He wondered why Brant was acting this way toward him. "I wasn't going to suggest that." Nikos said emphatically. "I'm quite familiar with temple at Delphi."

Brant ignored Nikos and turned to Wade. "You see, Wade, the temple of Apollo at Delphi, which is still standing somewhat, was the most important temple in the world. It also had an *adyton* below the main floor. That's the room where the Pythia, the old priestess, through whom Apollo spoke, delivered her oracles. You see, whatever advice the Pithia gave was believed to be the right solution to a problem. Few great leaders of that era would never go into battle without consulting the oracle first. They paid great sums of money to the priests before they could present their question to the oracle. The treasuries here would not have been as rich as those at Delphi, but I suppose there could be a treasure trove of coins stashed someplace here."

"So, now if you're through with your lecture, Brant, let's get to work." Nikos said curtly.

Brant glared at Nikos, "Since when are you giving the orders around here?"

Holding back his temper, Nikos said to Wade, "I'm going back to office to see if my friend, Mak, has arrived yet. He should be here by now." He strode away, fists tightly clenched at his side.

"Screw him," Brant uttered under his breath. Then he shrugged and jumped down into the room below. "You know, Wade, this very well could have been an oracle's room. I think we ought to look for signs of a doorway to the tunnel."

Wade was furious. He jumped down into the room and in a seething voice asked, "What the hell is going on, Brant? Why are you badgering Nikos? I don't like dissension on my team, and I don't like the way you're acting toward him. let's talk about it!"

"Why not? You're a happily married man, right? How would you have felt last night if Nikos had paraded your wife around his cousin's taverna, introducing her to every man there, like she was his property to put on display. God knows what he tells them about his relationship with Merit. Probably has her sleeping with him! Yes, I'm pissed off at him!"

"Well, I can assure you, Brant, Nikos would never do anything intentional to offend either you or Merit. He's just overly exuberant at times and doesn't always use good judgment. Remember, my friend, if you want to continue to work here, you better lay off Nikos. If he decides he doesn't want us here anymore, we're as good as out. So don't blow it, please. He's really a nice person."

"You and Merit seem to be in accord about that!"

* * * *

THE SANTORINI ODYSSEY

Merit and Matt who were doing rubbings on the tablets of the laws, saw Nikos walking briskly toward the office and called out to him. He stopped but didn't turn around. They both went to him.

"What's up, pal?" Matt was puzzled.

Merit could see he was upset. "What's the matter Nikos?" She hoped that Brant didn't say anything to Nikos about last night. When they had gone to bed, he had persisted in accusing Merit of enjoying her tour of the taverna and relishing Nikos' constant attention. He had hardly spoken to her this morning.

Nikos looked at Merit in distress. "Your husband is angry at me for maybe something I did or said that I don't know about."

"We know you wouldn't offend anyone on purpose, Nikos. You have too much integrity," Matt said.

Merit looked apologetically at Nikos. "Nikos, I'm so sorry if Brant was rude to you. I think I should tell you why Brant acted that way, and I hope you'll try to understand. But, I beg you not to let him know I spoke to you about it. He'd be angry with me, also."

"I want to know. What did I do?"

"He was upset about last evening because you introduced me to all your friends at the taverna. He's very possessive of me and gets jealous easily." Merit looked kindly at Nikos, hoping to show him she was not upset, and he hadn't offended her.

"Oh!" Nikos said in surprise. Okay, now I understand! A jealous husband, eh?" Nikos was secretly pleased with this news. "I'll ask him, Are you angry with me? Please tell me why." I will not tell him what you told me. Okay?" Nikos walked away with a sheepish grine.

Merit now wondered if maybe she made a mistake in mentioning Brant's jealousy. She hoped Nikos wouldn't make a big deal out of it. Brant would be furious if he knew what Merit told Nikos.

Matt decided to run a little interference for Merit. He caught up with Nikos. "Nikos, old pal, don't mention anything about last night. Jealousy often makes a man suspicious without reason. I suggest you just drop the whole thing." He lightly jabbed Nikos' shoulder and grinned mischievously. "Hey, I bet a handsome dude like you is always making husbands jealous, huh?"

Matt's compliment worked. Nikos smiled broadly at Matt. "You've got that right, friend!"

When he again turned to leave, Merit reached out, touched his arm and looked up at him in admiration. "You're a real gentleman, Nikos. Thank you for being so understanding."

The pleasure her words gave him showed on his face. He literally pranced away.

After Wade's warning, Brant realized reluctantly that he had better apologize. He knew he had taunted Nikos much more than he had intended to. He just couldn't stop himself. This churlish attitude began to happen more frequently as he became successful in the business world. The more his self-confidence increased, the more often he exhibited moments of unrestrained arrogance. He'd verbally abuse subordinates, especially in front of others. He had even become unnecessarily sarcastic to his peers. Although sometimes his actions embarrassed him, he admitted that it also gave him a strange pleasure. He usually could have almost anything in the world he wanted. Damn! I'll have to apologize to that idiot. Much as it irritated him, he had to admit, this time Nikos held the ace in the hole.

The two men came face to face at the entrance to the courtyard.

Nikos smiled broadly and extended his hand. "Brant, you seem to be angry with me today, eh?"

A surprised look covered Brant's face, and he said, "No, not really. I think the idea of facing a snake has upset me. I hate them."

"I'm glad that's all it was. It's not good to have ill feelings between team members, eh?"

"Let's get to work." He gestured for Nikos to follow him and cursed under his breath, "Son of a bitch."

* * * *

At ten-thirty, Dr. Manolis Makrakis arrived by taxi, and Elias escorted him to the temple of Apollo. He was a giant man; at least six feet, four inches tall, with hunched shoulders and a broad frame. His small eyes were framed by black bushy eyebrow; his mouth outlined by a drooping moustache that curled around his lower lip. Elias carried his large wooden box and leather suitcase.

Nikos greeted him warmly, "Welcome, Mak, and thank you for offering to help us." He introduced Wade and Brant.

Dr. Makrakis spoke perfect English. "It's a pleasure to meet all of you. Just call me Mak, an American nickname, eh? Let's hope we're successful so you can go on with your exploration, and I get a viper."

When they reached the grotto, Mak stopped and opened the leather suitcase that contained his protective snakebite clothing and an assortment of snake-snaring devices that he described to the team as he laid them out on the ground. These are my strap sticks, snake tongs with rubber-padded jaws, my four-foot telescoping pole with a retractable leather strap for long or short range capture. This is an angle iron to hold the snake down, and this little medicine kit has some basic medical supplies and antivenin for snakebite treatment. Hope we won't need them! This wooden box is divided into eight sections. each compartment has a lid made of tightly woven screen that can be locked by a latch. I use one of these long cloth sacks when I capture the snake. It goes in head first into the bottom of the bag and then the lock is clasped tightly. I tell you all this so you will understand how I catch snakes. I hope it makes you feel confident when we are working together."

Brant asked, "Do you think there may be more than one?"

"Like all God's creatures, there can never be just one."

"Oh, great," Brant moaned.

"Nikos, we'll need some damp moss to put in the bottom of the bags to keep the snakes from drying out when I transport them back to my laboratory in Athens."

"There's plenty of moss on big boulders around here, Mak," Nikos assured him. "I'll get some right away."

"Snakes have been around since the Garden of Eden, Mak, but how long has man known how to get the venom out?" Wade asked.

"Ancient Greek physicians didn't use venom, but they had remedies for snakebite since the second century B.C. Of course, most of them were not too effective, but today you'll still find people using those same old remedies."

"What kinds of remedies?" Wade asked.

"Oh, crazy things like eating snake brains, snake stones to draw out the venom, chewing tobacco. Some even drink kerosene or alcohol. But in this century they have used snake venom to treat leprosy, epilepsy, cancer, and other ailments."

"What about this snake? Would his bite be lethal?" Brant asked.

"Lethal? Could be, if the bite is not treated immediately. I think we'll find a mountain adder or a Levantine viper. The venom of these snakes poisons both the blood and tissues. Death usually results when the blood leaks out of the normal vessels. Vipers are large snakes and their colorations vary. But their color usually closely matches their environment, in this case, black and gray cave colors. Their average length is thirty to forty-five inches. The biggest I know about is a little over five feet. Their fangs are long and their bite is extremely painful. Vipers in Greece are getting harder to come by because of the tremendous population increase and building boom of the last fifty years. Snakes have been driven into remote areas around the country. Levantine vipers like high altitudes. I know they love dark caves."

"How much venom do you get from a snake?" Wade asked.

"Not much. Depends, of course, on the size of the snake. I may have to milk between two hundred to four hundred snakes in my laboratory to accumulate one gram of venom."

Wade was astounded "Wow! I imagine that makes the cost of antivenin quite high."

"You're right, Wade! Antivenin can cost from $40 to $5000 per gram depending on the rarity of the snake."

Looking down into the opening at the back of the cave, Mak commented, "So this is where we'll be working, eh? Isn't this the Grotto of Hermes and Heracles?"

"It is, Mak! How do you remember that? You haven't been here for a long time." Nikos said.

"I remember this grotto because Hermes, who was a messenger of the gods, was also a fertility spirit who was depicted as a snake. I always remember things connected to snakes," he chuckled. "I also remember about the symbol of Hermes. It is a *kerykeion*. It looks like a staff with snakes on top, eh?"

"You're right!" Nikos said. "I think we'd better get going. Mak has to catch that one o'clock plane back to Athens."

"Nikos, get everything together while I get into my coveralls."

When they were ready to enter the cave, Mak, who was at least fifteen years older and taller than the others, led the way down the low-ceilinged stairs backwards because of his height. Then within a short distance into the Apollo tunnel, he resumed his normal upright posture. Nikos carried the big wooden snake box and suitcase. Wade carried the two big powerful lamps. Brant carried the shovels, which would be used to draw the snake out into the open. Mak told them, "Although snakes can't hear, they sense vibrations. So you men will continuously bang the shovels against the limestone walls to draw them out in the open."

When they reached the place where the snake was last seen by Yannis, they stopped. Mak said, "I'm sure vibrations from the worker's shovels drew the snake out of its nest." He made his way into the tunnel. He stopped and opened up the wooden box and suitcase and explained how every item was to be used. We will be working closely, and I want you to remember that although our timing will be critical when I spot a snake. Don't panic and get sloppy. You'd put all of us in jeopardy. Each of our actions must be synchronized. If you see a snake, alert me. The snake will probably be on the move away from us because they hate light. Try not to lose sight of it. we want to keep the snake in front of us. It won't want contact with us until it senses that it's trapped. They're very timid until challenged. I'll use whichever of the snake sticks I feel is appropriate for the situation. I will only immobilize it and not hurt it."

He turned to Nikos. "When I catch one, you will drop your shovel and hold the bag open. I'll put the snake in the bag head first, and once I have it in far enough, I'll simultaneously release the noose around its neck and let go of its body. Then you will squeeze the top of the bag shut and engage the clasp. This entire procedure will be done quickly."

"My equipment is not as fancy as some that's on the market today but it works! Here's the order of the hunt: When I say 'go,' Nikos and Brant stand by with your shovels, ready to move forward to commence banging on the walls of the cave. Wade, you'll precede them, with the two portable lights, and I'll carry my equipment on my back. I'll be the spotter, but all of you must be on the lookout, too. Don't worry about my small, squinty eyes. I have twenty-twenty vision."

He concluded his remarks with, "Move forward slowly, very slowly. If the snake is still around, I'm sure it'll sense the vibrations from the shovels and be drawn out into the open to begin its retreat from us. Let's hope it didn't decide since then to take up residence in the other tunnel. Ready?"

The men nodded anxiously. Nikos gave Brant a high five, who passed it on to Wade, who wasn't sure Mak knew the significance, but he reached down, slapping Wade's palm.

Good hunting, men. Let's go!" Mak called out as the portable lights came on and the deafening clamor of metal against hard rock reverberated off the walls and floor as the men moved slowly forward into the abyss.

Each step they took increased the danger and anticipation. The claustrophobic tunnel added another ominous dimension to their snake hunt. Wade imagined himself as Harrison Ford in an INDIANA JONES movie; those films were his favorites. He smiled when the cavernous scene was illuminated, and the cacophonous sound effects created by the rhythmic percussion of shovel against rock echoed off the walls. It conjured up instant apprehension and set the mood for danger.

The team had only gone a few feet when suddenly an eerie sound penetrated the clashing shovel racket.

Mak turned to Wade, cupped his ear and yelled, "What the hell is that?"

"It's coming closer and fast!" Wade yelled.

High-pitched squealing and thunderous tapping on the limestone and flapping on the ceiling swelled to a deafening level as swarms of black creatures, on the ground and in the air, charged into the spotlighted area. Rats and bats! Turn your back on them!" Brant screamed as hundreds of speeding rodents stampeded toward them.

"Jesus!" Wade yelled.

Nikos yelled out an ejaculation in Greek and blessed himself.

Mak called out loudly, "Don't panic! Stand still. They won't stop running until they drop, hopefully, outside the cave."

The team, protected by sturdy boots and coveralls, stood frozen in terror as the repulsive army of rodents and bats drew down on them. The rats ran over their feet, sometimes piling as high as their knees in their scramble to escape. The bats' flight was erratic and terrifying. The exodus took only a few minutes.

"All clear," Mak called out matter-of-factly. "Everyone okay? Let's move ahead!"

Their advance was slower than before. They were still in a slight state of shock but resumed their former shovel-banging cadence, although the clanging sound effects had greater force it seemed. The tunnel curved slightly, then more sharply with each step, until any view beyond was cut off. Negotiating a sharp turn, they discovered that the tunnel opened up abruptly into a large area at least thirty feet wide.

"There's something large on the ground ahead," Mak yelled loudly. Slow down."

Wade turned both lights toward a large block of stone in the middle of the chamber.

"It looks like an altar!" Brant yelled above the clamor.

Mak held up his hand to halt the shovel racket. Suddenly, a row of seven vipers sprang up behind the altar. Their mottled bodies were erect in a defiant stance. Their large triangular heads swayed sensuously from side to side and their eyes focused steadily on the intruders. Continuous hissing emitted through their open mouths displaying two large fangs and smaller hooked teeth. It was a terrifying sight!

Mak and Nikos rapidly made the sign of the cross.

Mak spoke sotto voce to the men, "Don't move. These are poisonous Levantine vipers. I can only take one at a time, and there are seven of them. We've hit their nest, which must have been under the altar. I wish to hell I knew what was beyond here. How many more feet of tunnel? Someone give me an estimate."

"Forty feet more should bring us under the Apollo temple unless the tunnel curves off drastically. In that case, I'm not sure. The silence was broken only by reptile hissing and heavy human breathing.

Then, in a soft monotone, Mak presented his plan, "I'm going for the one on the right with my pole. I should tell you, in all honesty, that I have never before been confronted by seven snakes in an attack position, so I can't predict what will happen. I suspect when I make my move, they'll disperse immediately. Brant, be ready to bang your shovel as hard and fast as you can the minute I drop the noose on the snake. We have to hope that the noise and the light will drive them away from us. Nikos, stand ready with a bag. Wade, put one lamp down and hold my other three sticks. When we see another snake, I'll ask Wade for the stick I want. and Nikos will be ready with an open bag. A silent prayer would be appropriate, gentlemen." Like a ballet dancer in slow motion, Mak moved smoothly toward the snakes, which remained upright and poised for battle. They were at least three feet long. Seven pairs of eyes, with vertical elliptic pupils narrowed to slits, peered steadily at the intruder as he slowly closed in on them. The hissing rose to a terrifying pitch, their mouths opened wider, and tongues flashed in and out. The venomous fangs, their ultimate weapons, were now poised to strike a fatal bite into the approaching enemy. "GO!" Mak bellowed, snaring the snake on the right with a single precise pass. The others disappeared. Pandemonium reigned. Confusion, elation, terror, hysteria and disorganization seized the team as they fought to control their emotions and to carry out their vital assignments.

With more force than he knew he possessed, Brant growled like an animal and slammed his shovel on the floor and wall. Wade swept the floodlight back and forth across the width of the tunnel to prevent any of the vipers from moving towards them.

Nikos stood ready with the open bag. While the viper thrashed violently, Mak grasped its tail and stretched its body tightly along the stick. The viper's head was immobilized by the leather noose, but the snake continued to hiss. Mak nodded to Nikos, the signal that he would now put the snake in the bag. He shortened the telescoping stick that held the viper's head down, guiding it slowly into the bag. when he felt the viper touch the moss at the bottom, he simultaneously released his hold on the viper's body and loosened the leather strap to release the viper's head from the noose. He jerked the stick out of the bag, and Nikos quickly squeezed the top tightly, securing it with the metal clasp. Holding the bag away from his body, he put it into one of the compartments in the wooden snake box. He gently nudged the bag down with a stick, and closed the screened cover. Mak smiled at Nikos, shook his hand and said, "*Opa*! One down, six to go." He looked at Brant and Wade, and gestured for them to move forward.

Brant had never been so frightened and suddenly wondered why he was risking his life, his valuable life, but he knew the answer: a hidden treasure. In a trembling voice he asked, "Mak, could we just take a minute to examine the engraving on the front of the altar? It might be an important clue for us, don't you agree, Nikos?"

"Yes, but let's give Wade and Mak our shovels so they can keep our defenses up."

Wade set the light in front of the altar and began banging the shovel while Brant and Nikos knelt to read the engraving encircled with wavy lines. Both men said in unison, "Apollo Karneios."

"This is encouraging!" Brant smiled and said to Nikos, "Look at the dark stain that flows from the top of the altar down the front, blood from an animal sacrifice, maybe?"

Nikos and Brant moved the light quickly behind the altar from where the vipers had risen. There on the floor lay a large pile of snake skins. Nikos gently brushed his hand at the pile of weightless, gossamer skins that slowly floated back down to the floor. He also felt something hard that seemed to break apart on contact. Small, dark discs rolled across the floor. Both men quickly picked up several of the dust-coated pieces whose weight identified them as stone or metal.

"Jesus!" Brant sputtered at Nikos, "They're ancient coins!" Wiping off as much loose dirt as they could by running the coins between their thumb and index fingers, they could see markings on the discs.

"See they're irregular shaped. I think maybe they're *colts* from Corinth or *dekadrachmas* from Athens." Nikos said and grinned broadly.

"Fantastic!" Brant yelled while scurrying to pick up more from the floor.

Mak moved in close to them, yelling while continuing to bang his shovel, "Sorry to interrupt your treasure hunt, but we have a more critical hunt to complete. Hurry! Take over your shovel, Brant."

The two men slipped the coins into their pockets and resumed their jobs. Brant was giddy with elation. His insatiable passion for treasures triggered his imagination, filling him with irrational thoughts of making a discovery worth a fortune. He envisioned chests filled with coins and jewels that had been offered up to Apollo Karneios. His adrenaline surged so rapidly, he was almost breathless. He couldn't stifle the jubilant grin that spread across his face.

Wade noticed that Brant's face was wet with perspiration and covered by a strange, almost crazed expression. Damn him! Should he mention it to Mak? They were in such a hazardous situation; their teamwork had to be perfectly coordinated.

Brant caught Wade looking at him and understood what Wade was mouthing, "Are you okay?" That brought him rapidly back to reality, Brant nodded yes.

They were only about fifteen feet past the altar when they spotted another viper on the floor of an alcove. They stopped, and Mak gave the command to halt the banging. The viper lay semi-coiled, its pointed head extended flat on the floor. It seemed to be "playing possum."

Without wasting a moment, Mak took his putter-like stick from Wade and whispered jokingly, "Okay, caddy, watch me make a perfect putt, if in this case, my opponent keeps his head down." He moved forward slowly, holding the putter in his left hand away from his body as if gauging his line. suddenly, with incredible speed, he pinned the viper's head to the floor by pressing on its neck. He stepped on the snake's middle section to stop it from squirming. Reaching down with his right hand, he put his thumb and middle finger on each side of the snake's skull, and his index finger on the top of the head, then cast aside the putter. His left hand took a firm hold of the thrashing reptile, and he was out of harm's way within seconds. He dropped the snake into the bag held open by Nikos.

He held his hands in front of him, looked at the amazed team and said in a gleeful voice, "Couldn't have made par on that hole if I weren't ambidextrous, eh?"

They were spellbound by his skill.

Advancing again, they noticed the rubble on the floor increasing, making it extremely difficult to walk. They picked their way slowly and carefully, wanting to be sure that the remaining vipers weren't underfoot Now the walls were notched by large, arched alcoves and smaller niches. The large ones were recessed from the ground up, while the small niches were carved out at eye level. No doubt this section had been used in religious rites, and the alcoves probably held statues and smaller figurines of the gods. They'd have to examine this area carefully later.

Within the next thirty minutes, in the same area, Mak captured four more vipers; only one remained. They proceeded at a snail's pace while Mak poked his tall stick into the niches and alcoves, but the viper did not reappear. He held up his hand for the hammering to cease. looking at his watch, he said, "Gentlemen, I can only stay for another few minutes. My taxi will be here shortly, and I don't want to miss my plane."

Brant's heart sank. "But...but you can't leave without capturing the last snake. It would be too dangerous for us to work here!"

"I know, young man, but I have appointments to keep this afternoon," he answered sympathetically. And I must get back to Athens on that one o'clock plane. I'm sorry."

Wade apologized and gave Brant a dirty look. "We understand, Mak, and we deeply appreciate all that you have done for us today. Hopefully the last one got past us and left the cave."

"Could be. You think we may be near the end of the cave, so let's give one last try. Let's go!"

A few feet farther along, the tunnel made an "S" curve and ended abruptly at stone stairs going down and covered with large chunks of limestone debris, making it impossible to proceed.

Shining the lamp down over the stairs, Wade said grimly, "Well, we'd never find him in that rubble."

The men looked around slowly.

Nikos pointed up to a section of flat ceiling. "That's unusual," he said. "We haven't seen any flat man-made ceiling before. Could be that adyton room in temple is right above us, eh? And I'll bet there's secret opening in floor to get into tunnel."

"Yes! Of course! Undoubtedly," Brant sputtered, "These stairs lead down to the hidden treasury of priests. Give me that light, Wade!" he commanded brusquely. "I'll try to climb down over the rubble to see what's at the bottom of the stairs."

They looked at him in astonishment.

"Young man," Mak said, "You could be killed by a landslide of those boulders or more likely by the viper!"

Brant, frantic that they would call it quits, "Maybe, maybe not. I'll take that risk. I've come a long way at great expense, and I have no intention of turning back just when we're steps away from an important discovery."

"Brant! For God's sake, that's stupid." Wade was outraged. "I'm in charge of this exploration, and I forbid you to try such a foolhardy stunt."

Brant gave Wade a contemptuous glance, stepped down on the pile of limestone rocks that carpeted the stairs and tried to balance himself with outstretched arms. "Just cover me with your light," he ordered.

Mak and Nikos, looked at each other and spoke softly in Greek. "I think your Mr. Powers is a very foolish man, Nikos. Unfortunately, that is a lesson he may soon learn."

"I think he's too obsessed with finding treasure," Nikos said. "He already is very wealthy man. He's crazy to risk his life."

"Obsession is a terrible addiction, Nikos. It can overpower a person's sanity. I think your Mr. Powers is crazy at this moment."

"Brant, wait!" Wade yelled. "Don't go a step further. I'm going to insist that you at least tie this rope around your waist. God only knows how far it is to the bottom. Caves can be bottomless."

Brant reluctantly accepted the rope, tied it around his waist, then gave Wade a cocky look and a thumbs up as he began his descent.

The men watched Brant maneuver slowly over the large chunks of limestone that wobbled precariously. Suddenly, as he straddled two boulders, the rocks around him began to move, cascading downward with a deafening and frightening roar. The men held tightly to Brant's lifeline while he struggled for a foothold. The rocks at the top of the stairs joined the downward slide, striking Brant's feet and legs with considerable force. He turned his back to the onslaught and hopped up and down.

Suddenly, out of the sliding rubble, the last viper emerged, dodging the rocks by slithering over the top. Almost as suddenly as it began, the avalanche stopped, and the viper and Brant were virtually back to back, no more than three feet apart, easy striking distance for the viper. But neither of them were aware of that. Brant was still facing down the stairs while the viper was peering up at the men at the top who viewed Brant's situation with alarm.

Mak signaled for silence by putting his finger to his lips. He feared that alerting Brant to the proximity of the snake would panic him. In a calm, but emphatic voice he said, "Brant, do not move or turn around. The enemy is

THE SANTORINI ODYSSEY

out of hiding and close to you but has not discovered that you are behind him." Mak used the word enemy, hoping to keep Brant's fear level in control.

They could see Brant's body stiffen in terror as he followed the order.

"You have the advantage, Brant. The enemy's attention is solely on us. I am going to try and capture it with my telescoping stick. We must not spook it, Brant, because its impulse will be to turn and slither away, which means it'll head right into you."

Brant's heavy breathing and the snake's hissing were perfectly synchronized.

Mak carefully took the stick from Wade's hand. He loosened the noose and extended the pole fully toward the viper, which was now poised erect for a strike, its eyes focused on the advancing stick.

Suddenly, a large nearby rock began to move. Brant and the viper turned their heads simultaneously. Brant gasped and the viper opened his treacherous mouth with fangs brandished for a strike. Brant's face drained of blood and turned ash gray.

At that same moment, Mak lunged for the snake, but his reach was an inch too short.

The snake, sensing the diversion behind it, spun its head back toward the stick, but only for an instant. It turned back to Brant, arched for a strike and lunged.

Brant dropped his head. The viper impacted with his steel helmet and was momentarily stunned. He recovered quickly and rose up again to attack.

Nikos yelled as he ran down the first two steps that were now partially cleared of rubble, "I'll distract it with shovel. Try again, Mak."

The enraged snake swung its head back and forth between its tormentors, Brant and Nikos. It chose Brant and lunged at him while Nikos swung his shovel forcefully across the outstretched body of the snake just as it made contact with Brant's upper arm.

Brant shrieked, fell and curled in a fetal position.

The snake, felled by Nikos' crushing blows, laid dazed on the rocks next to Brant.

Nikos continued striking fiercely at the snake. Mak, now at his side, halted Nikos' attack and picked up the limp snake and examined him. Wade stood ready with an open bag.

Nikos climbed down to Brant. he pulled his hand away from the now bloody puncture mark on Brant's sleeve. Quickly, he took out his knife and cut away the sleeve, exposing the wound. "Mak! Come quickly. Brant's been bitten."

Mak quickly put the limp viper in the bag. "He's dead," he said sadly, "Let's take a look at his opponent, who undoubtedly will survive the battle."

Brant was close to being in shock, not so much from the bite as from fear. His skin was cold and clammy, his pulse and respiration rapid.

Mak knelt next to him, opened his medical kit and examined the wound. "A good place to be bitten, Mr. Powers, because the muscle is thick on the bicep. The fang glanced your arm and has not penetrated deeply." He cracked open an ammonia inhaler and held it under Brant's nose. The reaction was swift. Brant's eyes opened wide, and he began to cough. "Take it easy. Lie still. I want to raise up your arm to slow the spread of the venom. Only one fang hit you, thanks to Nikos, who probably saved your life. Actually, you're very lucky because it's not a deep penetration, which means it didn't get too much venom into you. I'd call it just a surface bite. I'm putting a gel ice pack on the wound and wrapping it with a bandage. That'll slow down your lymphatic draining system."

Brant looked up at Mak and asked in a quivering voice, "Shouldn't you cut my arm where he bit me and suck out the venom?"

"That's only done in the movies, Mr. Powers. You'll be fine. We'll get that doctor member of your team to keep an eye on it. He'll put you on an antibiotic, probably."

"It hurts like hell!" Brant cried childishly.

"That's normal. Most snake bites do. Come on now, let Nikos and me help you up, and we'll get you above ground. Wade, why don't you go ahead and get that doctor. I'll have a quick word with him before I leave for the airport." Wade hurried on ahead, carrying the snake box and sticks.

Brant shrugged off the offered support and walked away from them. Both surprised and annoyed at Brant's surliness, Mak spoke authoritatively, "Young man, you are in a weakened condition and behaving rather badly again. You disregarded the proper procedures in the cave, risking your life and the lives of the rest of us! I think you owe everyone an apology and a large debt of gratitude to your teammate, Nikos. He performed bravely when I failed to snare the viper. He put his life at risk for you, against a very dangerous, angry snake."

Without turning, Brant called back to Nikos, "The good doctor is right, of course. I got carried away with the idea that we just had to know what was at the bottom of the stairs. Thank you, Nikos. You were really right on the ball! I'm sure Merit will be eternally grateful to you." Then he thought, *That ought to really make his day!* "Thanks to you too, Doctor. Sure glad you were with us. I'll send you a donation for your laboratory in Athens."

Mak had come to dislike Brant Powers immensely. Although he could always use funds to support his work, he refused the offer, feeling it was not sincere, but rather a bribe to make up for the man's arrogant behavior. Thank you for your offer, Mr. Powers, but our laboratory is well financed," he lied.

"Really? I'm surprised. It's not often people refuse donations for their research work," Brant retorted. He sensed the man's dislike for him but thought him stupid to refuse a contribution.

When they passed the altar where they first discovered the vipers and the coins, Brant stopped. "Nikos, why don't you dig around in there a little more, see if there are more coins?"

"We'll see later. Not now. Now we get Matt to take care of you."

When they came out of the tunnel, Merit, Matt and Wade were running toward them. Merit and Matt were stunned when Wade told them about the snake hunt and that Brant had been bitten.

Merit threw her arms out to Brant, "Darling, are you all right? Quick, Matt, look at the bite," she cried.

Wade wondered if he should tell Merit the truth about Brant's stupidity. He was concerned about Brant's behavior. It was becoming more erratic each day.

Mak and Matt discussed treatment, and Merit kept her arm around Brant's waist as they walked back to the office to see Mak off in the taxi, which had now arrived and stood ready to take him down the mountain.

Mak got in and leaned out the window. "A bit of advice, Mr. Powers," he said sternly. "Let the scar of the viper's bite serve to remind you of the very high price you almost paid for your foolish obsession for treasures." With that, he ordered the driver to leave.

It was an awkward moment for those in the group, and they felt uncomfortable, everyone that is, except, Brant.

"Kind of a moralistic type, isn't he?" Brant sneered.

Staring sharply at Brant, Wade said, "I think he summed up your actions rather well, Brant."

Merit looked from Wade to Brant and frowned. "Okay team, we're going to call it a day. Let's head back to the compound." Wade said.

"Good idea," Matt added. "I want to get some antibiotics into Brant right away."

Merit was concerned by Dr. Makrakis' remark. It was evident that both he and Wade were angry with Brant. What had Brant done? She knew she hadn't heard the whole story. Once they were alone, back at their house, and she had made Brant comfortable in bed, she asked him.

Brant looked up with a sly smile. "Darling, nobody in the world understands obsessions for treasures more than you and I. You know that! I just took a risk because, well, we were so close to finding a treasure. I just knew it! I could feel it. You know that feeling." He pulled her down on the bed and began kissing her.

She fought him off gently, explaining that he was still in some shock and his legs were badly bruised from the rocks that pounded him in the rockslide. she knew he hadn't told her the whole truth, and she wasn't sure she really wanted to hear it from the others. Ever since they arrived on Santorini, Brant was a different man. She had thought about it quite a bit lately. Somehow, she was seeing him in a different light here. She felt uncomfortable about his mood shifts: cross and arrogant one minute, cheerful and loving the next. Unfortunately, he had always seemed to get what he wanted without delay. She had wondered more than once since they arrived if this had been such a good idea for their anniversary trip after all.

* * * *

Katina fawned over Brant so much at dinner that Anna finally told her to sit down and leave the poor man alone.

"But I love it, Anna," Brant said, winking at Katina who blushed.

Wade had told Matt what happened, and of his concern about Brant's mental stability. Wade was still angry about Brant's impetuous actions.

Matt said, "I think Merit should also know the truth, and I'll try to find an opportunity to speak with her about it."

During the next several days, Brant remained in the care of Anna and Katina. He continuously engaged the young girl in conversation about her life and friends on Santorini. Anna had to constantly remind her daughter to get back to her chores.

Anna wondered, Why is he interested in such small talk about a teenager's life? Why would a man his age pay so much attention to a sixteen year old girl? She decided she didn't like Brant Powers. On the third morning, after the team had left for work and Anna and Katina were cleaning the *banio*, they heard Brant calling from his house.

"Anyone around?" he yelled.

"I'll see what he wants, *Mana*," Katina said.

"Come right back!" her mother said emphatically.

Katina knocked at the Powers' door.

"Come in, I'm in bed," Brant called out.

Katina opened the door and stepped inside. Brant was propped up in the bed wearing only khaki shorts. Magazines and papers were scattered about. "Ah, the beautiful Katina. I didn't know if anyone was around, and I'd like to have these letters get in the mail as soon as possible. Can you find someone who might be going into town right away?"

"I will find someone for you," Katina said, moving close to the bed and reaching for the letters.

Brant swung his legs over the side of the bed, dropped the letters on the floor and said, "Oops."

Katina reached down to retrieve them.

Brant took both her hands in his and pulled her towards him.

A sensation raced through her body as Brant grasped her hands tightly and gazed into her eyes lovingly. She was transfixed. Blood rushed to her face and burned her cheeks.

Brant felt a strong surge of passion., stood up, and as he pulled her toward him, footsteps approached the house. He quickly let go of her and bent down to pick up the letters, then thrusting them wildly at Katina as Anna appeared in the doorway.

With a mother's instinct, Anna realized that she had arrived just in time to prevent something from happening between her daughter and Brant. The telltale signs were visible on their faces. Katina was totally flustered and her face flushed.

Brant did not acknowledge Anna's presence. He quickly turned his back to the women, thrust both hands deep into the pockets of his shorts, and casually walked out the open door to the patio. looking up at the sky, he faked a yawn. "It's a beautiful day, isn't it? I've asked Katina to get those letters in the mail as soon as possible."

Anna could only guess why he had to turn his back on them and make the hasty exit to the patio. She was furious. She snatched the letters from Katina's shaking hands. "I will mail letters," she said icily. "Come, Katina, we have much work to do." She led Katina out of the room and into the courtyard, leaving no doubt in Brant's mind that she was aware of what his motives had been.

Unfortunately, Katina's immaturity in such matters did not provide her with the sophisticated nonchalance that Brant had displayed. Her whole being was still reacting to the titillating moment of passion that was now turning to guilt. She cast her eyes down and wrung her hands as her mother spoke.

"Katina, I forbid you to ever be alone with Brant Powers again! Do you understand? I know you have illusions about him as a father, but I'm sure you now know that his feelings toward you are not fatherly. I don't trust him alone with you. Never let him get you alone again!"

Katina's eyes were darting everywhere except toward her mother. She was so confused. She became defensive and sobbed "I didn't do anything wrong! I don't have romantic illusions about him either! He's just a nice man who is friendly to me. What's wrong with that? I'm not a child! I'm sixteen!"

"And he's almost forty, an old man compared to you! Stay away from him, or I'll tell Nikos what I think he wanted to do to you today." Anna's face was livid.

"You think all men are bad! You hate all men just because my father walked out on you!" Katina ran to their house and slammed the door.

Anna was shocked. What Katina said had hurt her deeply. *I don't hate all men! How I wish there was a man for me to love, to come to my bed, to fill the yearning that never leaves me.* She thought of the first time Joe had made her feel passion. *What a wonderful emotion, but oh, what a dangerous feeling for one so young and unworldly as Katina. I must protect her reputation. Maybe the time has now come for "the talk."* Ha, I have to laugh when I think back to how embarrassed my mother was when she tried to tell me the facts of life. I must do a better job.

* * * *

On Friday, Brant insisted he was well enough to go back to work in the cave. The team had been exploring the area below the stairs, where Brant and the viper had their encounter. Thanks to the rock slide, they were able to get down the ten steps that ended at the doorway to a room about thirty by fifteen feet, but they had to move much debris to gain access. When the room was illuminated, they found an assortment of empty limestone sarcophagi with the covers lying alongside. Nikos informed them that the Greeks had used limestone for coffins, believing that the limestone disintegrated the body. To prove that belief true, not one trace of human remains or any other debris were found. They did find smaller, empty caskets with their covers scattered about all over the floor that were ornately decorated with floral designs and letters that again spelled out Apollo Karneios.

Nikos, looking around the room with his hands on his hips, said glumly, "I'm sure this room was treasury, and that caskets were used to store offerings of money and jewels to priests of temple of Apollo. But treasures were probably moved aeons ago by priests or robbers, eh?"

It was discouraging to them all, but particularly to Brant, now standing in the doorway with one hand on his sore arm and the other pulling roughly at the scraggly beard that had now grown a few inches. Consumed with stinging disappointment, he hissed, "Shit!"

Wade frowned at him, "We're all disappointed, Brant"

Nikos put his hand on Brant's shoulder, causing him to stiffen.

"Brant, my friend," Nikos said, ignoring Brant's reaction to his touch, "I have to send the coins we found under Apollo's altar to Athens right away."

Brant was stunned. He had hoped that Nikos would forget that he had put some of the coins in his pocket. He had had no intentions of turning the coins over to Nikos. He planned to tell him they were lost somehow in his battle with the viper, but he said, "Oh, yes the coins. I forgot about them. I'll get them for you later."

Suddenly, the ground shook slightly and specks of stone and dust fell on their heads and clothing. They froze momentarily, but even before Nikos yelled, "Clear out!" they began running. By the time they reached the cave entrance the tremors had stopped. Wade came up the stairs last and when he emerged, he saw the others nervously dusting off their clothes.

"That was just a little aftershock," Nikos assured them. "It happens from time to time. No big deal! But it's good idea to get out of cave to be sure," Nikos smiled, trying to put the team at ease. "It's true that my island has tremors occasionally. You know that dormant volcano under our island and in surrounding waters, expands periodically because of heat buildup, it stretches, eh?"

"Will it be safe to go back in the cave, Nikos?" Merit asked, hoping he'd say no. With each passing day, she was becoming more concerned about their safety. Her mantra of 'Be a good sport' wasn't working any more.

"Sure, it's safe. We can go back!" Nikos assured them.

"Good," Wade said. "I'd really like to get to work in the Egyptian tunnel, now that we've explored the Apollo tunnel. Merit has taken photos of everything we found, and I'll get Yannis and his men to take out the Apollo altar and the sarcophagi and coffins. We'll transport them to Athens for carbon dating. let's go back into the cave."

"Saved!" Matt said. "I see Anna and Katina coming with our lunch."

* * * *

When lunch was over, they picked up their gear and followed Wade back through the small grotto opening. Matt caught Nikos surreptitiously making the sign of the cross and followed his example.

The Egyptian tunnel did not have as much rubble as the Apollo tunnel. And it certainly had turned up a great many ancient artifacts. They walked carefully over small pieces of limestone, still leery that a viper might crawl out. They continued to investigate the many recesses and collected numerous pottery shards. When the tunnel narrowed, the geology changed noticeably. Playing the lamps on the ground and walls, they discovered they were traces of lava on both areas.

It didn't take Wade long to discover how the volcanic matter penetrated the limestone tunnel in that area. Pointing to a large fissure in the ceiling, they saw a cone-like formation covered with the residue of molten lava, its mouth narrowing as it spiraled downward.

"I'd guess that during an eruption, a volcanic bomb opened up the ground above us, creating the fissure and allowing the lava to flow down here," Wade theorized.

They continued forward, and within a short distance the tunnel widened again, and the trail of lava disappeared. They encountered another geological change within forty feet, when the ground suddenly sloped steeply. Stopping abruptly, they were unable to see far enough down the rock-strewn covered slope to see where it leveled off.

Wade said, "I think Nikos and I will put on ropes and survey the incline first. Many times, a steep pitch like this will suddenly become completely vertical without much warning."

Nikos suggested, "I'll drill holes for ring bolts into wall for our ropes. It'll make it easy for Brant and Matt to keep tight hold on our ropes."

Merit began filming the men's preparations.

Wade and Nikos secured the ropes around their waists while Brant and Matt ran the other ends through the rings, now secured into the wall. They got into position, leaned back, and slowly began descending the slope walking backwards while Brant and Matt let the rope out slowly.

Merit gave them a thumbs up sign and said, "Be careful, guys."

Although backing down slowly, the limestone fragments under their feet began to give way and started tumbling down, creating a deafening roar. Wade and Nikos came back up to the top. After several minutes the rockslide stopped, but suddenly, a familiar sound of fluttering wings and racing feet came rushing toward them. Brant grabbed Merit and held her head close to his chest. They all turned their backs, covered their faces and froze in place when the invasion of rats raced over them and bats flew past their heads.

Merit screamed, "Oh, my God, Brant! What's happening?"

Brant held her tight and uttered above the din, "Just hang on. It'll be over in a minute."

When the last of the cave dwellers disappeared, everyone but Merit relaxed and looked at each other with sly smiles.

Merit looked at Brant in anger. "Has this happened before, and you never told me about it? Is it going to happen again?"

"I'm sorry, darling. Yes, it did, but I didn't think it would happen again." He hugged her and kissed her gently.

"Everyone make sure you didn't get bitten," Wade said.

He played the large lamp over them to see if their suits were torn.

Merit shivered and said a little hysterically, "Are you sure it's all over? I hate it! I hate it!"

Brant put his hand under her chin and said, "You're wonderful and brave, darling. would you like me to take you out of the cave."

In a choked voice, she said, "No. If you guys are going to stay, I'll stay. I wish I had had my camera on. That would have been a scene to remember, although I'll never forget it. I think I'll leave it on from now on."

"A rats and bats Hollywood horror movie." Matt said and patted her shoulder.

Wade and Nikos scanned the incline, then resumed their descent. At about thirty feet, Wade called up, "You won't believe this, we're now on wide stairs, but we still can't see the bottom."

Brant and Matt continued to play the rope out carefully.

Wade's and Nikos' voices sounded hollow when they called back and forth to the others. "The steps are carved out of limestone, just like the ones at the entrance. Whoa!" Wade yelled.

"We're at the bottom!" Nikos called out. "Can't see very far, though. someone bring down big lamp, eh?"

"I'll bring it down," Brant volunteered. "Untie your rope, Wade, and I'll pull it up."

He pulled the rope up and tied the lamp on his back and the rope around his waist and began the descent. Immediately, a sharp pain radiated in his upper arm when he gripped the rope tightly. He realized that his snakebite had not healed completely. Reaching the two men, he turned on the lamp. Merit and Matt heard shouts of astonishment echo from below.

"Oh, my God!"

"It's unbelievable!"

"*Kristos kai Panayia*!" I only see this wonder of nature in caves on mainland!" Then Nikos gave a long whistle.

Matt yelled down, "What in God's name did you find?"

"What is it, what is it?" Merit shouted excitedly. "Can we come down and see?"

Wade's voice echoed up to them "Yes!" You won't believe it! Pull the two ropes up and secure them tightly to the rings, and bring the other lamp down." Wade said. "Stay next to Merit all the way, although it's a relatively easy descent on the stairs. We'll keep our lamp on you. Move slowly."

The moment Merit and Matt reached the bottom, Wade turned off his lamp, casting them into semi-darkness. He immediately untied the second lamp from Matt's back.

"Hey, what in the hell are you doing, Wade?" Matt demanded. Now only the beams from their headlights crisscrossed their faces.

"Trust me," Wade answered. It's for dramatic effect! When I turn on both lights simultaneously, you'll witness an incredible sight, one I never expected to see in this cave or on the island. Get ready. Now! everybody, look straight ahead."

When the lamps illuminated the scene in front of them, startled gasps echoed throughout at the spectacular wonder of nature that appeared before their eyes.

Ancient limestone deposits grew downward from the ceiling. Small stalagmites on the floor were scattered in orderly divisions that had been building up for eons by dripping calcareous water from the ceiling. They looked like ancient minarets. The stalactites that hung from roof of the cavern were much larger; some seemed deformed like enormous growths frozen in time."

They all stared up in wonder.

Wade said, "It's not only these complex designs of nature that are astonishing, but the vast expanse that we see before us. Caverns this large dwarf you. This magnificent setting seems not to have been disturbed by human presence for thousands of years. Yet I can see that others before us shared this wonder of nature. Do you see what I see?"

Everyone peered steadily into the darkness.

Brant said excitedly, "Yes, yes, you're right, Wade. I see what you mean. Everyone look toward the back and center of the cavern. See that huge towering mass of rock and look what is encircling it on the floor."

They focused their big lamps on the giant boulder.

"Look at that!" Matt said in a hushed tone. "They're seats, stone slab seats, around it."

"That mass of rock is at least one hundred feet wide in circumference at the bottom," Brant said.

Wade looked up toward the top. "Yes, but see how it gradually narrows and becomes dome-shaped where it meets the ceiling. It looks like the top is partially covered with a layer of lava that poured onto the top and ran down the sides; like frosting on a bundt cake."

The team moved forward carefully, dodging the delicate stalactites. Expressions of delight and wonder were uttered continuously. Merit followed the four men, alternately taking movies and photos. They stopped when they reached the circle of stone seats and scanned the huge mound that rose high above them.

Nikos walked toward the mound speaking rapidly in Greek. He ran his hands over the roughly carved reliefs that were scattered on the surfaces of the mound where lava had not spread. "Look, look! See, here are many reliefs of *scarabaei* beetles!"

Brant ran his hands over the figures. "My God! Yes" he exclaimed. "These are the types of beetles used in ancient Egypt as ornaments, talismans, and symbols of resurrection."

Wade moved back a short distance to get a better look at this wonder of nature. "Geologically, I'm sure this gigantic mound of limestone was here hundreds of thousands of years before the cataclysmic volcano of 1600 B.C. I think there's a good possibility that it may even date back before the Early Cycladic or Middle Cycladic era. You know, rocks get stronger with age.

Therefore older formations are more likely to survive a strong quake. We'll do lots of testing around here. It looks like the lava poured down onto the mound during a volcano through a fissure that opened up in the ground above, like the one we saw back there in the tunnel. I guess the lava could have poured in during the 1600 B.C. eruption."

"It's a strange-looking form," Merit said while snapping photos from all angles. "It's shaped like half of a giant egg."

Nikos abruptly stopped examining the scarabs and stood back to scan the oval-topped formation. He looked puzzled "*Po, po, po!* What did you say, Merit? Half of egg?" Suddenly he let out a loud, "*Opa!*" that reverberated off the cavern walls. "I know why beetles are carved on mound. You gave me good clue, Merit. I'm sure this giant mound represents giant omphalos. It's shaped just like one, only it's biggest one I've ever seen."

"What's an omphalos?" Matt asked.

"Omphalos means the center of earth," Brant said. "Scarabs are always carved on an omphalos, right, Nikos.?"

"You're right, Brant! The naval of our world. It was important religious symbol for both Egyptians and Greeks. Usually, ancient temples had marble ones. There is still one at Delphi." In an awed voice he said, "A giant omphalos created by nature!"

Matt looked curious, "So obviously, this was a place where people came to worship and honor their gods. I wonder who they were?"

"Good question, Matt," Wade answered. "We'll have to do some keen detective work and look for more clues to get to the bottom of this puzzle."

Concerned that this important find might have to be reported to the authorities before they had a chance to fully investigate the cavern, Brant asked Nikos, "Will you have to report the omphalos to Athens?"

"Not yet. We'll wait until we complete full exploration of cavern. Then I'll notify them, and then they will come to look at what we've found."

"We've certainly seen some reliable evidence that civilizations of different eras used the cave," Wade said. "I keep thinking about those incense jars. They were a perfect match to those found at Kalliste. It certainly seems likely Kallisteans and Minoans must have used this cavern, too."

Brant added, "And the coins and the miniature figurines could probably have been brought into the cave by Romans, Dorians or even Egyptians." Nikos was elated and added, "Yes! Now we have excellent clues to prove that cave was used before and after 1600 B.C. by different civilizations, eh?"

Wade smiled and said, "I have a request that may seem silly to you, but I want all of us to walk around the omphalos eight times for good luck. I'll tell you why. When I was in Luxor prior to my going to work in the Valley of the Kings, I was told by a very old man that if I walked eight times around an ancient stone omphalos covered with scarabs, I would get my wish. I made the eight turns feeling a bit foolish. It must have been one hundred degrees in the shade that day, and I longed for, wished for, a cold drink of water. When I left the area, a *caleche* came racing down the dirt road behind me. I heard the driver yelling, but I couldn't understand what he was saying. He reigned in his horse and came alongside of me, raising up a huge cloud of dust that clogged my parched throat. He smiled at me and pointed to an old tub in the back seat of his *caleche*. He threw back the carpet that was covering the tub, revealing bottles of water lying on chunks of ice. I thought it was a mirage! My wish had come true! So, team, let's assume that a scarab covered omphalos will bring us luck."

Wade led the march, carrying one of the lamps. Merit followed, continuing to snap photos and take movies. Matt locked arms with Nikos and sang, "We're off to see the wizard, the wonderful Wizard of Oz. "Brant, unable to get into the spirit, reluctantly brought up the rear, carrying the other lamp. He was not good at silly group activities like this. Actually, he was embarrassed and thought it stupid.

After the eighth time around, Wade led the team to the limestone seats that circled the mound, and they sat down, laughing. Brant's sullen attitude went unnoticed by all except Merit.

Wade stood up, leaned back against the mound, folded his arms across his chest and grinned broadly at his teammates. Merit quickly snapped a photo of him at that moment. "I suppose I'll have to buy that one," he joked. Then his face became serious. "I feel positive that this magnificent omphalos, this incredible creation of nature, has been the site of worship for many ancient people. I think this cavern is a very significant find, and there is much more here yet to be discovered."

For one moment, there was dead silence as Wade's provocative statement sank in.

He continued, "This is a small island, but it has always been an important one it seems. I think it's reasonable to assume that this ancient cave was rediscovered many times. Look how many ancient people we know about who lived up here in the Ancient City of Thera after 1600 B.C. Just as many may have lived here before also. Who knows! Let's get to work, team, and chip some samples out for carbon dating."

For the next hour, they pried off small samples of the various layers of the omphalos along with other specimens of limestone, lava and the stalactites and stalagmites. At four-thirty, they left the cave for the day. It was Friday and Anna was preparing a special fish dinner that evening. They also were having a Powers Anniversary Party Committee Meeting.

There were many unanswered questions mulling around in the minds of the team members that day. They all sensed that they had uncovered something very important, and that there would be many more exciting discoveries to be made.

CHAPTER NINE

Despite the exciting discovery of the cavern and omphalos on Friday, the team looked forward to the weekend to get out in the sunshine and away from the dampness of the deep cave. Saturday and Sunday promised to be busy days preparing for the upcoming anniversary party. Large crates containing the big television screen and the other audiovisual equipment that Brant had ordered from Athens arrived Friday afternoon. A young man named Aristotle, son of the owner of the TV company, traveled with the crates. He was the technician who would set up the equipment. Brant had been advised to get it set up for a dry run a week in advance, in the event additional supplies were needed.

Aristotle, who would stay with Nikos for the week, was invited to join the team for dinner.

On their way to the dining room, Nikos asked the young man, "Don't you think Aristotle is too formal a name for such a young man? We'll call you Ari, eh?"

"Thank you. Yes, I'd prefer that."

When Nikos and the young man walked into the large room at dinnertime, everyone stopped talking. They were quite taken by the young man's good looks and casual demeanor. His facial features, though typically Greek, were highlighted by large black eyes, looking intensely as they darted around the table and resting momentarily on Katina. He was tall and lean with broad shoulders. The sleeves of his casual white shirt were rolled up below his elbows, and the unbuttoned front exposed a gold cross on a heavy chain. He sat down between Nikos and Katina. His English was fairly good, but he often turned to Nikos to translate for him. He had a hard time keeping his eyes from Katina. His nearness had her in a frenzy. She had never seen or spoken with a young man this handsome and sophisticated. Island boys never dressed or talked like Ari.

Anna pushed more food toward the boy.

"I don't eat much usually," he apologized. "But this is wonderful meal. It's good food, like my *mana's* cooking.

Anna was pleased by the compliment. "That's nice thing to say to me, Ari."

After dinner, they discussed the various preparations for the anniversary party until almost midnight. When the evening ended, Ari shook hands with everyone and squeezed Katina's hand tightly. She blushed.

When Katina got home, she threw herself across the bed and moaned, "Oh, *Mana* isn't he the most beautiful Adonis you've ever seen!"

"He's very handsome and very well-mannered, too. But maybe a bit old for you, though."

"Ughhh! *Mana, Mana,*" Katina cried in exasperation, making fists of her hands and shaking them violently. "Are you ever going to let me have a man?"

Anna raised her eyebrows. "Of course. When a proper man wants to court you, then we'll discuss a relationship. It'll have to be a man who is not years older than you. Don't go falling in love with this Ari; he probably has many girlfriends in Athens. Get to bed now. We have much to do in the morning."

Anna had not let Katina out of her sight since that day she walked into Brant's house. That night she had tried to have "the talk about sex" with Katina but she was rebuffed.

"I know all about it! Did you forget that you told me everything when I got my first period?"

"Well, there are lots of things I didn't tell you that you should know."

"I don't want to talk about it. You'll make it sound dirty and scary." Katina was frightened already by the strange sexual feelings she had experienced with Brant. It was nothing she could discuss with her mother.

* * * *

After breakfast on Saturday, Merit, Anna and Katina borrowed Nikos' truck to go to Fira to purchase supplies for the party.

After arriving in town, they began shopping. Anna and Katina were stunned that Merit never asked the price of the items she bought. When they got the chance, they slipped away from Merit for a few minutes and purchased a beautiful silver icon of the Blessed Virgin holding the Baby Jesus. Anna talked the saleslady into allowing her to buy the icon on credit. It would be their anniversary gift to Brant and Merit.

After lunch, Merit insisted that they all buy traditional island costumes to wear at the party as part of a surprise Merit was planning. Despite Anna's protests, Merit finally talked them into allowing her to pay for the costumes. The blouses were soft white cotton with intricate, brightly colored embroidery on the neckline and sleeves. The black velvet vests were also richly embroidered. The colorful skirts were lined with stiff white petticoats. Small white aprons, long white stockings, black flat shoes and brightly colored kerchiefs, adorned with spangles, beads and ribbons completed the costumes. The three women had a wonderful time being outfitted.

They continued to shop, wandering through the busy, winding streets of Fira, stopping frequently to enjoy the antics of gregarious tourists. One loud-mouthed, pot-bellied European put his arm on Merit's shoulder when she passed by and asked her to have a drink with him.

Anna pushed him away and put her face next to his, threatening him with bodily harm in Greek. He did not understand, but nearby Greeks laughed heartily at her reprimand of the huge man. Then in English, she said, "She does not speak to foreigners, only Greeks. Now you go away, or I'll call police!"

While Anna was putting the foreigner in his place, Merit and Katina locked arms and walked away quickly, unable to suppress their laughter any longer. The man retreated in the opposite direction, yelling back gruff, guttural profanities at them.

When Anna caught up with them, they all sat on a wall and laughed until tears streamed down their faces.

Their merriment was interrupted by a man's voice calling to Anna.

"Anna! Anna!"

Anna beckoned him to come sit with them. "It's the man from t*ahethro Mos*, ah, Post Office," she said.

When he reached them, he waved a thick envelope., and spoke in Greek, "Anna, this is important letter for man in your village. It just came by Air Express. I'm supposed to see that he gets it right away, but my lumbago is so bad today. Will you take it to him?"

Anna froze and her face drained of color when she saw that it was addressed to: Dr. Matthew McGuire, c/o Nikos Konstantinou St. Demetrius Village, Santorini, Greece. The return address read: Agent Daniel McGuire, FBI Regional Office, Los Angeles, California.

Feeling faint, she sat back down on the wall clutching the thick envelope tightly to her breast. She hung her head, silently chastising herself for her sudden show of weakness in front of Merit and Katina and thinking, I've been able to bear the suspense of not knowing about Joe for many years. Now I must not be a coward about facing the truth. Her heart pounded furiously. her mouth was dry.

"*Mana*, what is it? What's wrong?" Katina begged. putting her arms around her mother.

Merit lifted up Anna's face, "Anna, dear, why has that mail package upset you so?"

"We must get home right away. This is very important information for Matt. He has waited for it for long time. Please don't ask me anymore questions."

"It might be bad news for Matt. Maybe something has happened to his wife." Merit said solemnly.

"I don't know. We must get home right away." Anna stood up and walked swiftly toward the truck.

Katina and Merit looked at each other, puzzled, but they refrained from questioning Anna again. When Anna stopped the truck outside the village, she jumped out and went quickly to the compound. Matt was standing in the courtyard with a mass of electrical wires in his hand. She waved the bulky envelope at him. Her face now masked in panic. "It's here, Matt! It's here!" she cried in a hysterical voice.

Matt dropped the wires, ran to her and took the envelope. He put his arm around Anna's waist and led her to her house.

All the men working in the compound looked curiously at the drama that just occurred. Wade yelled, "What's the matter, Matt?"

"I'll let you know shortly, Wade." He and Anna went into her house and shut the door.

Wade guessed that it must be news from Matt's brother. Merit and Katina walked over to where Brant was working on the TV setup with Nikos and Ari.

"What's going on?" Brant asked.

"We don't know," Merit replied.

Nikos was concerned, "What is mail all about, Merit?"

"Really, Nikos, we don't have any idea. The postman gave it to Anna in town, saying it was very important and should be delivered to Matt immediately. Anna became very upset when she saw it, but she didn't let us look at it."

Katina added, "My *Mana* said Matt was expecting it."

* * * *

Reaching across the kitchen table, Matt squeezed Anna's hand, then tore open the heavy envelope. He pulled out a sheaf of papers and a small faded green plastic bag secured with a rubber band. He held the bag in his hands for a second, then set it aside on the table.

Looking at Anna with tenderness, he hesitated, "Anna, I hope I did the right thing. I don't want you hurt anymore than you have been. Are you prepared for bad news? Would you like me to read it first, then tell you what it says?"

"No!" She answered emphatically. "I've been ready for sixteen years for news of my Joe, good or bad. Read it to me, please."

Matt began reading the top sheet:

"Dear Matt:

Just a quick hello, and good to hear from you, kiddo. I can't believe my big brother, the surgeon, is doing what you say you're doing in Greece, exploring an ancient cave? Why don't you write once in a while? I saw the folks last week. Dad wants you to give him a physical. Ma says he needs it!

Your request for information on the disappearance of Joseph Brady turned out to be a piece of cake. Actually, it took less than a week with a little help from our friends in England. Is this Anna Brady someone special to you?"

Matt looked at Anna and nodded his head up and down. Anna was wringing her hands and hung her head.

"I can keep a secret you know; it's my business. I'll tell you up front that she's a…"

Matt stopped short as he read the word "widow" and looked compassionately at Anna.

"She is what?, Anna asked. What word did he say I am? Tell me, Matt!"

Matt laid the letter down. His heart ached for Anna. He reached across the table and held her hands tightly. "Danny says that you're a…widow, Anna. Your husband, Joe, is dead."

Anna's reaction was swift. Pulling her hands away from Matt, she rose quickly. Her face reddened and tears ran down her cheeks. She began speaking rapidly in Greek and paced back and forth across the kitchen floor. She kept clapping and folding her hands together. Matt felt helpless. He tried to comfort her, but she thrust him aside. Suddenly she stopped, took out a hanky, wiped her eyes, blew her nose and sat back down at the table while gesturing for Matt to do the same. Her breathing was labored. but she blurted out, "So, I am widow, eh? How do they know my Joe is dead?"

"Let me continue with the report, and we'll see. Oh, Anna, I'm so sorry."

"Be glad for me. Now I know at last. Okay, okay, you read more, please. What happened to my Joe?"

Matt laid the cover letter down and picked up several sheets that were stapled together and read the first page of the FBI report.

"Re: Bartholomew Joseph Brady, missing for past sixteen years. Last seen alive on June 29, 1979.

Anna interrupted him, "Why do they call my Joe by other name?

"I guess we'll find that out later in the report, Anna," Matt assured her and continued.

"Age - At time of disappearance thirty-two years.
Nationality - U.S. Citizen. birthplace-Pasadena, California
Physical Description (as provided by widow):
Weight - approx. 170 lbs.
Height - six ft. one-inch
Hair - red/brown.

Eyes - blue.
Complexion - ruddy.
Teeth - minor dental work.
Scars or disfigurations - large scar on right knee. No known disfigurations.

"Information by widow: Victim last seen alive on June 29th, 1979 Took a plane from Santorini to Athens to London to attend a symposium. Expected back in few days. He was to be speaker re archaeological dig at Akrotiri, where he worked. Disappearance investigated by both local and London authorities.

"FBI requested Scotland Yard to check for information on any John Does in files around date of Brady's disappearance. Their records showed no one fitting his description expired in that time frame. (Official report from Scotland Yard enclosed.)

"FBI contacted Greek Archaeological Society in Athens for information regarding archaeological symposium held at that time. No record of that event in London area. Brady not known to them.

"UCLA, Brady's alma mater, contacted next. Records showed Brady's last known address. Agent McGuire visited Pasadena address and found a Miss Emma Brady lived next door. She was elderly aunt of Joseph Brady and maiden sister of Brady's father."

"Matt! That is my Joe's aunt." Anna was stunned.

"That was luck finding her." Matt read on.

"Aunt unaware that Brady was missing, although hadn't seen him in past sixteen years. Receives mail addressed to him once or twice yearly from banks in Los Angeles and Greece. Does not remember names of banks. Admits that in past several years, she's thrown out his mail without opening it. Brady's marriage to a Greek woman surprised her. Genuinely upset about his disappearance, in spite of fact her last contact with him was Christmas card in 1973. She saved postcard and showed it to agent. At that time, he was in England taking courses at Oxford University. Obviously hurt because Bartholomew, whom she had raised from infancy (his mother died at childbirth,) cut off their relationship. Brady, baptized Bartholomew Joseph Brady, after father. Was teased so much as child by his first name, asked to be called Joseph."

"I agree with Joe, Bartholomew is a strange name, for a kid." Matt smiled and continued. "Brady's father was senior vice president of a large aircraft company in Los Angeles. Spent very little time with son but was very generous with financial support for boy and aunt. He died in 1970, leaving substantial sum of money to son but considerably less to Miss Emma Brady. She expressed desire to hear from Brady's wife and child."

"Oh, Matt, I would like to see her, too."

"Maybe that can be worked out, Anna." Matt continued, Scotland Yard contacted Oxford Police Inspector Thomas from Oxford P.D. He telexed FBI and offered his services. All pertinent information telexed to him. Two days later FBI received the enclosed report from Inspector Thomas."

Matt read a note that was attached to the report from his brother. "Matt, I've condensed the report from Inspector Thomas, but I'll also send along the complete official report. It might be needed."

Matt read the condensed report: "The borough of Oxford is the capital of Oxfordshire and the seat of the University. It's fifty-two miles, west north west of London. Inspector Thomas examined missing persons files, and John Does in morgue file for that area, concentrating on deaths that occurred close to date of Brady's disappearance. He came up with positive match from widow's description and forensic report. Coincidentally, this Inspector Thomas had been assigned to that murder," Matt's voice dropped…"case."

Anna gasped. Matt reached across the table and held her hand again.

"Oh, my Joe, murdered!" she sobbed. "That's why he didn't come back to us." She buried her head in her hands, then looked up at Matt. "That is why Nikos didn't find him. He was not speaker in London; he must have been speaker in Oxford. Who murdered my Joe?"

Matt looked back at the report. "Anna, why don't I read this over first. It'll be very upsetting for you to hear the details."

"No! I want to hear it all. I've lived for sixteen years with all kinds of stories in my head. Now I want to hear true story."

Matt reluctantly continued, "The case was closed and placed in an unsolved murder folder, a few sheets of yellowed paper stuffed in a dusty police morgue file (Inspector's own words.) The corpse was found in a densely wooded area about fifty feet from road along river bank at confluence of Cherwell and Isis Rivers, tributaries of the Thames.

Coroner's report stated that deceased had been murdered at close range by single .353 magnum bullet that entered heart and exited through victim's back."

Matt paused again. "Anna…I don't…"

"Go on, Matt. I have to know everything if I want to close book on that part of my life."

Matt continued. "Severe bruises and lacerations covered victim's body. From decomposed state of body, coroner's report fixed time of death on or about June 29th, 1979. Body was discovered approximately three weeks after murder by group of hikers. Victim's body was in flexed position. No personal belongings found except for gold wedding band on victim's finger."

"Oh Matt, he wore his ring! He loved me! I knew it! Maybe I could get his ring? Hurry, read on."

"It was determined that robbery was motive for murder. His nude body had been beaten severely. Large green plastic Harrod's bag found under body. Because of large size of bag, it was felt that it had probably contained several items. Murderer obviously missed smaller Harrod's bag, found rolled up in bottom of large bag. It contained silver baby's spoon engraved with name, "Katina."

Anna's mouth, which had been pressed tightly in horror now exploded, "*Panagnia Mou*! (Mother of God) Oh my poor Joe. Oh, Matt, he did love us," she wailed.

Matt jumped up and ran to her side to hold the sobbing, pitiful woman in his arms. "Of course he loved you. You've known that all along. That's why you saved yourself for him all these years."

He sat back down and removed another note attached to the small, green plastic package and read it as he handed the parcel to Anna. "It says, Inspector Thomas sent spoon, ring and a key in diplomatic pouch along with this report. He thought they would be valuable keepsakes for victim's daughter and wife. He hoped it would soften their sorrow when they were notified that their loved one had been murdered. Inspector Thomas said that this murder has always haunted him because of the baby spoon that was never delivered."

Anna spoke softly, clutching the precious package in her hands, "I won't open it. I'll let Katina. Oh, Matt, it will make her so happy to know her father loved her so much, eh? I think all these years she never believed he loved us. It makes me want to cry for joy that my Joe wore his wedding ring. It belonged to his father. I think maybe murderer couldn't get ring off Joe's finger because it was too tight. I always joked with Joe that tight ring was good because it made him remember that he has wife, eh?" she smiled faintly.

Matt smiled back. "Anna, there's more. Do you want me to continue reading?"

She nodded assent. Then a pensive look spread across her face as Matt started to read on.

Anna interrupted him, "You know, key, Inspector sent is probably safe deposit box key."

Matt said, "Inspector Thomas said it was found near body, but may not have necessarily belonged to the victim."

Anna looked puzzled. "I just now remember, Joe always wore little key on gold chain on his neck. He told me it was his key to bank in Athens. Maybe it is his key, eh?"

"Do you remember which bank Joe used in Athens, Anna?"

"I only remember that bank have American name. It's near Constitution Square."

"Anna, if that key is to a safe deposit box, well, sixteen years have gone by and, if the rental fees were not paid...we'll have to see about that."

"What would be in bank box?"

"I honestly don't know, Anna, but I think you should find out if it still exists. I'm sure it has personal belongings of your Joe."

"Is that end of your brother's report?" She was anxious to tell Katina the news.

Matt scanned the page. "Not quite, just a few more paragraphs." he read on, "Inspector Thomas checked with the Archaeology School at Oxford and discovered that there had been an all-day symposium on June 13th, 1975. Joseph Brady was a guest speaker. His subject was the Kalliste dig at Akrotiri. Brady had been invited to speak by Professor Ashley Browning. Thomas contacted Prof. Browning, who indeed remembered Brady. He had invited Brady to speak, in spite of fact he was an American working on a Greek dig. Brady had been a favorite student of Browning's, and he was glad to give him the prestigious opportunity to speak at Oxford. The professor vividly recalled how angry he had been when Brady failed to show up, leaving an hour's gap in the program. He claimed he never heard from the young American again. Inspector Thomas informed the professor of the American's demise. He was unable to offer any clues, but asked the Inspector to offer his sympathy to widow and child."

"That was good of professor to send sympathy, eh? Now he's not mad at Joe. Now we know why my Joe didn't tell people at Kalliste why he is going to Oxford, eh? They would not like an American to give talk, I think." Anna kept looking toward the door. Matt knew she was anxious to speak with Katina.

"There is just one more thing, Anna. Inspector Thomas has very graciously offered to make arrangements to have the remains of your husband sent to Greece if you so desire. I have his telephone number here. The body was interred in a pauper's grave in a public cemetery on the outskirts of Oxford."

"Oh, yes, yes." Anna cried, putting both hands to the sides of her face. She then quickly covered her mouth to hold in uncontrollable sobs. Striving to get control of herself. she wailed, "I'll bring my Joe back home, and we'll have proper funeral. Matt, I must bring Katina in house right now and tell her about her *papa* and give her his gift. I can't wait any longer." Anna was shaking with excitement.

Matt got up, kissed the top of Anna's head and patted her gently on the back. "I'll get her, Anna, and leave you two alone. May I tell the others? I'm sure they're concerned. By the way, Anna, I think you should try to remember the name of that bank in Athens and find out if his account is still active. Remember, his aunt said she received mail from a bank in Greece once or twice a year."

"Yes. I must think about doing that. She looked up at Matt in gratitude, grabbed his hands tightly, and kissed them. "Yes, tell my friends my news and thank you, thank you, my dearest friend. You have given me great happiness today in spite of my great sorrow. Now, like Katina says, I can get on with my life because shadow for past sixteen years has been lifted."

Matt smiled and left to get Katina.

The moment he walked out the door, Katina ran to him. "Matt, is everything okay with my *Mana*?"

"Yes dear, everything is fine now, and she wants to see you."

Katina raced frantically into the house. Matt then joined the others and explained about the package from America. They were both sad and happy for Anna and Katina, especially Nikos, who reacted with smiles through his tears.

He hugged Matt. "Thank you, Matt. You gave my friend Anna her life back." Then looking woefully at the others he said, "Oh, poor Anna, all these years she's been most loyal woman I've ever known. I'm so glad she is released! I will take care of bringing Joe's body home for burial here, and I'll take her to Athens to see about safe deposit box. Greeks believe that our soul survives when our body dies, and it is very important to have proper funeral rites for our dead, or they will not have peace in life hereafter." Nikos solemnly bowed his head and blessed himself.

Matt put his arm around Nikos' shoulder and led him away from the others. "You're a good man, Nikos, and Anna is a good woman. Know what I think, old pal? You ought to start courting her right away before the other men on the island find out she's a widow."

Nikos broke quickly from Matt's hold and looked indignant. "Who, me? I'm just good friend. Nothing more! I'm glad to help arrange for her husband's proper funeral and take her to Athens to see about bank box. Nothing more!"

Matt laughed good-naturedly at Nikos' bravado. "Okay, Nikos, whatever you say. But about that box at the bank, I doubt the bank would hold the box in Joe Brady's name all these years if the rental fees weren't paid."

"That could be true, except in Greece." Nikos informed him. "Greeks are very honest and also never do anything in hurry."

Anna and Katina came out of the house later with their arms around each other's waists. It was obvious that they had been crying hard; their faces were blotchy and red, but both were smiling faintly.

Katina broke from her mother and rushed forward. "Look, look everybody. Look at what my *papa* bought for me in London many years ago. It's real silver and has my name engraved." Katina gently removed the small silver spoon from the faded Harrod's green felt pouch. It had obviously been recently polished, probably by Inspector Thomas before it was shipped.

Both Anna and Katina were hugged and kissed by each of the team. Even Brant offered kind words.

It was sad to think of all the years the two women had suffered by not knowing the truth, but there was great joy now that they were freed from the emotional limbo that had enveloped them for so long.

The news of the letter spread rapidly, and villagers appeared at the compound with food and flowers. The elderly widows, as was the custom, gathered together and wailed for a considerable time to mourn Joe's death. *Papa* Ioannis, who heard the news while in Fira, hired a taxi to get back as quickly as possible. He felt it was important that he be there to offer spiritual comfort to the widow.

When he arrived at the compound, he eased through the villagers and found Anna surrounded by women all talking at once. He moved them aside and reached out to Anna. "Anna, Anna, my dear, dear friend. I came immediately from Fira when I heard the news. You must let me help you through this sad time. Let's go inside where we can talk privately and seek God's mercy to ease your suffering."

Anna knew it would be disrespectful not to accept the priest's kind offer. She excused herself from the women and went inside.

Katina, surrounded by her school friends, caught Ari looking at her. She waved to him, excused herself from the group and went to him.

Ari took her hand and squeezed it tightly, saying with genuine sincerity, "I'm sad to hear about what happened to your papa, but you must find comfort in the truth. May I see the beautiful silver spoon?"

Katina could not bring herself to look at him directly. A hot blush spread over her face. She thought he surely must hear her heart beating loudly. She held out the spoon and Ari placed his hand under hers.

"This memento of your papa must bring you much happiness, Katina." Then with his other hand, he lifted up her face to his. "I also hope that you will give me the opportunity to share in your new-found happiness from time to time."

Brant saw what Ari did and immediately walked over to them and put his arm around Katina's shoulders, "So my dear Katina, what a wonderful gift your father left to you. Ari, did you know that Katina is thinking seriously about going to college in America? You know we've learned to love this beautiful child and want so much for her to have a proper education in the States."

Katina was startled by Brant's remark. She wanted to deny it but was unable to do so. His dominating personality always made her yield to him.

"What good luck for Katina," was all Ari could think to say upon hearing this disappointing news. It seemed strange to him that this man was so overtly possessive of Katina. He sensed Brant was making her uncomfortable. Ari had disliked him from the moment they met. The others were friendly, but Brant treated him like an intruder.

Katina wanted desperately to break away from Brant's hold, yet she could not deny that his attention flattered her. Her admiration for him had grown into infatuation, especially since their brief encounter in the bedroom a few days ago. She had relived those few moments over and over in her mind; each time feeling a titillating thrill, yet overshadowed by strong feelings of guilt. She was confused by the rush of new emotions she had experienced in the past few days and was having trouble trying to sort them out At the same time she was very much attracted to Ari.

Her dilemma at this moment was quickly resolved when Anna frowned at Brant, who still had his arm around Katina. In a curt voice, she called across the courtyard, "Katina. Come immediately. *Papa* Ioannis is going to have a service for us to remember the soul of your *Papa*."

Relief enveloped Katina as she quickly broke from Brant's hold and ran to her mother's side.

* * * *

Nikos and Anna were taking the morning plane to Athens on Monday and planned to return that evening if they could complete Anna's business with the bank.

Anna asked Merit to keep a close eye on Katina. "I think my daughter and Ari have romantic feelings about each other. Please don't leave her alone at any time." Actually she was much more concerned about Brant, but she could not say that to Merit. She knew that if Katina were with Merit, she would be safe.

Nikos asked the team to spend the day outside the cave while he was gone. He explained, "It's unfortunate, but my orders from Archaeological Society are to be with team members at all times when in cave. Maybe you can work in office or catch up on cleaning and labeling pottery we found, eh?"

When Anna and Nikos walked toward the taxi that would take them to the airport, Anna looked back and her eyes met Brant's momentarily. A

PEG MADDOCKS

feeling of panic caught in her throat. She shifted her gaze to Merit, who noticed her worried expression.

Merit grinned at her and called out, "Don't worry, Anna." Merit admired the way Anna protected Katina.

But Anna couldn't shake the fearful premonition she felt. She couldn't take Katina with her because there was cleaning to do and meals to get for the team.

To relieve Anna's anxiety, Merit and Katina made silly faces and placed their arms protectively around each other as they waved Anna off. Then they ran after the taxi, comically throwing kisses at Anna until the taxi was out of sight.

To keep her promise to Anna, Merit decided Katina should join the team and help with the work at the office. Katina would not see much more of Ari because he had gone into Fira for supplies and was not expected back until late evening.

The team worked at labeling pottery shards throughout the morning, and at noontime Merit and Katina rode Zeus back to the compound to pack a lunch. When they returned, they spread out the picnic food on a grassy knoll. Then after lunch, they stretched out for a brief siesta in the sun.

Merit and Katina lay side by side. Katina whispered to Merit, "Don't you think Ari is very handsome?"

"Very," Merit answered lazily.

"How do you know if you are in love?" Katina asked as she rolled over on her stomach and looked at Merit in anticipation, hoping for a helpful answer.

Merit laughed, turned on to her stomach, propped her head on her hands and grinned at Katina. "So you think you are in love with a young man you just met?"

"No, no, I don't know if what I feel is love, or what it is. My mind is all mixed up with new feelings that run through my body lately. My *Mana* says I'm not ready yet for relationship, but what do I do with exciting feelings that go through my heart…and other places? I'm confused."

"Ah, youth and love." Merit laughed softly. "My dear Katina you are too young to think about any man seriously. Lots of men will fall in love with you, and I'm sure you'll be attracted to many of them also. But the important thing is to save yourself for the right man."

"But how will I know who is right man?"

"That's not always easy. The right man is someone whom you trust completely. He will respect you as much as he loves you. You must both want the same things out of life. You'll find that out as your relationship grows. Don't rush into marriage. You want to be sure that the man you marry will love you forever and will always be faithful to you." Then, smiling slyly, she said dramatically, "You want a marriage that will last 'til death do you part."

Katina looked anxiously at Merit. "You and Brant will stay together until death do you part, won't you?" She realized she had made it a question.

Merit surprised herself by giving Katina an honest answer, "I'm planning on it, but it's hard to know for sure, Katina. Sometimes people change. If you really care, you work hard at making the marriage a success."

She looked over at Katina, who was sitting up and clutching her knees tightly to her chest. She looked wistful as she heaved a huge sigh. Merit smiled to herself, recalling how she had reacted to the first sweet pangs of adolescent love.

Katina had learned to love Merit. She could never hurt her, but she was confused and ashamed of her recent feelings toward Brant. A tragic thought crossed her mind, Maybe Brant doesn't love Merit anymore, and that's why he flirts with me. Oh, that couldn't be true. How could he not love his beautiful and wonderful Merit? I will have to stop him if he ever tries to flirt with me again.

"Dear little sister," Merit teased, breaking into Katina's reverie, "Let's get off this serious subject. I have a great idea for tonight, but I'll need your help."

"I'll do anything I can to help you, Merit?" Katina responded enthusiastically.

"Well there's going to be a full moon tonight, and I've been wanting to get some photos and movies of ancient Thera on a bright night. I think it'll be spectacular with the ruins lit by moonlight and the silver sea in the background. Will you help?"

Katina looked shocked. "Go to ancient Thera at night? Oh no! it's too dangerous up there at night. We'd have to ride by ancient cemetery of Salada that's haunted by spirits. I've heard stories about how ancient ghosts float through ruins. Oh, we should never go there at night, Merit."

"Katina Brady, I'm surprised at you. You don't honestly believe those stories, do you? There are no such things as ghosts! And even if there were, just think of the spectacular photos we could get!"

"How can you be so sure? Many people on Santorini have seen them and felt their presence. And what about vampires who come out at night up there? They say sulfur fumes from caldera are so strong at night in ancient city, that only vampires can survive there because they are already dead. It's their final resting place." Katina's face paled; she looked genuinely upset.

"Well okay, if you don't want to go with me, I guess I'll have to leave you in Brant's care," Merit teased. "Some assistant you turned out to be."

"No," Katina answered more forcefully than she intended, realizing the possible danger she might find herself in if left alone with Brant. "Okay, okay, I'll go with you, but if we see ghost or vampire, I'll die of fright, I'm warning you!"

"Don't worry, we'll be riding Zeus, and if ghosts or vampires try to bother us, he'll throw thunderbolts at them."

"And I'll take an icon of the Blessed Mother for protection, just in case."

Brant wandered over and looked down at them. "And what are you two beautiful nymphs conspiring about?"

"We're planning a moonlight photo session up here in the ruins tonight," Merit answered, accepting Brant's hand to help her to her feet.

"Alone?" he frowned, offering his hand to Katina and holding it longer than necessary.

"We'll be riding Zeus and won't be out that long," Merit answered.

Brant looked at them skeptically. "I assume, then, that you two are not believers in the spooks that supposedly inhabit the ruins at night."

Katina, trying to act sophisticated in front of Brant, said, "I'm afraid, but Merit convinced me we'll be safe riding Zeus. He'll protect us." A tone of apprehension hung in her voice.

"Really?" Brant raised his eyebrows. "Blind faith, huh? Merit, maybe I should go with you two on this adventure, although we boys had planned to continue our high-stakes cribbage game tonight. I'm down two bucks."

"We don't need any male protection," Merit said emphatically and smiled. "My plan is to work for an hour or two after dinner developing and printing the photos I took on Friday and then come up here when the moon is high."

Wade and Matt joined them. "Come on team, it's back to work."

* * * *

Anna and Nikos did not return on the last plane of the day. Anna called and told Wade that their business at the bank could not be done until Tuesday.

After dinner, Merit helped Katina with the dishes and then they went to Nikos' house to work in the photo lab.

Looking at a negative, Katina remarked, "I think this beautiful cavern must be most exciting find yet, eh? I would like so much to see giant icicles that hang from ceiling and grow up from floor."

"When Nikos gets back, we'll see if he'll allow you and your mother to look at them. It's a spectacular sight. It will be hard for you to keep it a secret, but you know you must."

"*Mana* and I never tell anyone anything about cave exploration."

Katina held a strip of film up to the red darkroom light. "Look at this negative, Merit. It's strange. I think it's Wade. He looks like teacher standing at blackboard with writing on it. See, his arms are folded across his chest, and team looks like students sitting in class."

Merit looked closely at the negative hanging by a clip on the drying line. Even in the low red light, she could tell it would be an interesting photo. "In fact he was lecturing us. I also took a close-up of him in that same pose. I promised him an enlargement. Here. See, it's this one," Merit said as she pointed to one at the bottom of the strip.

"Is he standing in an arched doorway?" Katina asked.

Merit squinted at the negative. "No. There's no door." But she was puzzled. "That's strange, I don't remember seeing that. Hmmm...it does look like an arch above his head. What looks like writing is actually scarabs. They are carved all over the omphalos; that's what that huge mountain of stone is called. It never ceases to amaze me how often the camera sees things that the eye misses completely. You often get a totally different perspective from what you thought you saw. I'm anxious to see a print of this one."

"Maybe we should wait until tomorrow to make prints. It's ten o'clock, Merit." The later it got, the more nervous Katina became about their moonlight escapade.

"Okay, let's call it quits and get going up to the site. I've got all our equipment near the front door."

They closed the lab and started across the compound to the stable. passing the dining hall, Merit stuck her head in the door and called out, "We're off to ancient Thera by moonlight. See you in about an hour."

The men scarcely looked up from their game but called out, "Good ghost hunting!"

A chill ran down Katina's back. She wished desperately there was a way to get out of this trip.

The women slung the equipment on their backs and mounted Zeus, who was frisky in the cool night air. Merit felt confident; she had ridden him at night before, and he was familiar with the road up to the site.

Katina, filled with trepidation, held both arms tightly around Merit's waist during the ascent.

The higher they went, the brighter the night became. The heavens were crowded with twinkling diamonds, and the glow of the moon on the ruins and the Aegean was spectacular. The only sound was the clip-clopping of Zeus' hoofs on the hard-packed ground. They spoke very little and when they did, it was in whispers. They safely passed the ancient Salada Cemetery. Then the Kaldaras' house loomed up in front of them. To Katina, it seemed like a lifeboat. At least other humans would be nearby. The rickety gate to the ancient city was open. They passed the office, slowly wending their way up through the weathered fragments of the *agora*. The starkness of the moonlight on the ragged ruins reminded Merit of a ghost town she'd seen in California. Strangely, that thought now sent a shiver through her, in spite of the fact that she had no fear of this place at night. The air was heavy with the sweet scent of spring flowers but tainted by the faint odor of sulfur fumes rising up from the caldera. They approached the hill above the theater, which had been built in the Ptolemaic period and later revised during the Roman occupation of the island. The only clues left that still identified it as a theater were the semi-circular stones that outlined the stage area, and the broken rows of stone seats scattered up the hillside. The rise overlooking the theater was a perfect spot to get a view of the ruins.

Zeus halted when Merit gave him a gentle command with the reins, and they dismounted. Merit threw her arms out expansively, as if trying to gather the entire panorama to herself while Katina set up the two tripods, one for the still shots, and the other for the video camera.

"Oh, Katina, I was right! I'm going to get some wonderful photos up here."

"Yes, it's pretty sight." She loaded the cameras and urged Merit, "Let's get right to work." She wanted to get it over with as quickly as possible and return to the safety of the village.

They shot four rolls of film and videotaped for ten minutes. Then Merit removed the Nikon and the video camera from the tripods.

"Before we pack it in, Katina, I want to get a little more footage of the ruins with the moonlit sea in the background. You use the Nikon and go east, and I'll go west with the video."

"No, I'm staying right beside you, Merit. Please don't leave me alone!" Katina begged.

"Okay, come on, little chicken sister," Merit teased. Speaking softly into the camera's microphone, Merit identified each ancient ruin, the buildings now starkly outlined on the rim of the mountaintop. Katina, walking close behind her, snapped pictures without any thought of focusing.

A far off sound reached their ears. Neither of them spoke as they strained to identify the noise. Zeus whinnied.

Katina spoke first, "Do you hear something?"

"Yes. it's strange. It's coming from the west."

"No, it isn't, Merit. It's over this way."

Suddenly they both turned sharply toward the theater where the muffled sounds now became more pronounced.

Katina slung the camera over her shoulder, pulled the icon out of her pocket, closed her eyes and prayed.

Merit tried to fight off the fright that began to seize her as the eerie sounds came closer.

The weird din sounded like a large group, all talking at once, although it was not distinct enough to understand the mumblings. What could it be? Merit wondered. then they heard other discernible sounds like shuffling feet and the rustling and swishing of long stiff garments.

Zeus neighed and sidestepped nervously in a circle. His nostrils flared, and he snorted loudly and jerked his head in the air.

Merit and Katina moved close to Zeus. Merit put the video camera on her back and quickly brought the straps over her shoulders. She grabbed Zeus' reins and spoke softly to calm him, "It's okay, Zeus, it's okay, good boy. Stand still." he became so skittish, she almost lost the reins.

Katina screamed and grabbed Merit. "It's ancients or vampires! They're coming up hill for us! I told you they were here! Hurry! They've taken island people before!"

Merit strained with all her might to steady Zeus so they could mount him. But his panic was so intense, he broke from Merit's hold and raced down the hill toward the approaching apparition. Now terror-stricken, Merit and Katina froze as the moving mass, camouflaged by a fog-like cloud, came closer to Zeus; their only hope of escape.

When he met up with the specters, he reared and clawed fiercely with his front hoofs, challenging the ghostly vision. He seemed to be momentarily engulfed in the moving mass. Then he reappeared as if he had passed through them. He paused as if stunned, then raced up the hill to the girls who were now screaming hysterically.

"*Christos kai Panayia!* We are going to be taken," Katina shrieked.

"No! No we're not, Katina. Quick, run, take my hand." Frantically, they raced over the rough grounds of the ruins, stumbling and screaming.

"It's moving too fast!" Katina screeched. "It's right behind us, Merit!"

"Oh God," Merit moaned. "If only we could get up on Zeus."

Zeus, running on the perimeter of the hill above them, was parallel with the women but twenty feet away.

Suddenly the cold, eerie fog closed in and enveloped them. Their bodies became rigid. Ghostly voices all talking at once pierced their ears and flimsy apparitions passed through their bodies generating sensations of freezing, penetrating chills. They tried to scream but were powerless. They clutched each other fiercely. Merit forced her eyes open for a split second at the moment of contact with the apparition and saw the grayish, non-discernible shapes that passed through them. Seconds later, the phantom phenomenon of sound and sensation moved away. Merit opened her eyes fully in time to see the apparition fade in the distance. She wasn't dreaming; she saw it happen.

Katina had fainted, slipped out of Merit's hold and now lay slumped on the ground at her feet. She dropped down next to her and for a moment feared the spirits might have frightened Katina to death. She was terrified as she pulled Katina's limp body into her arms. She removed the Nikon that was hanging from her neck. "Katina! Katina! Are you all right?" she screamed, feeling for a pulse. She slapped Katina's gray cheeks. Movement! She was alive! Katina's body suddenly began shivering and her breathing came in gasps. she screamed and began beating on Merit with her fists.

"Katina, darling, it's me, Merit. You're okay. They've gone!"

Katina opened her eyes slowly, looking around suspiciously. Color returned to her face. Sobbing uncontrollably, she stood up and lashed out at Merit, "See! I told you, but you wouldn't believe there were ghosts. Hurry, we must leave before they come back and take us away."

She held the icon of the Virgin Mary in front of them like a shield, praying as they ran.

Merit whistled for Zeus, who was waiting ahead of them, but he wouldn't come to her. He neighed two or three times, shook his head as if saying no, then slowly obeyed her command and trotted to them. Merit patted his nose, and they quickly stood up on large, ancient block and mounted him, then sped through the ruins. Merit could feel Katina's body shivering as the young girl held tightly to her waist. Her own heart was pounding rapidly, She must get control of herself. She tried to analyze what happened, but what they experienced was beyond her comprehension. Trying to convince herself, she thought, I don't believe in ghosts and yet I saw gray, shadowy figures passing through us. I did see them. I heard them. I can't deny that. They were there! I didn't really feel them go through me but they did, and I was so cold! I can't even describe what they looked like. They floated more than walked. They were human-like, but nothing about them was distinct. I can't even describe what their faces looked like, or even if they had faces. Yet they were not hallucinations!

As they neared the gate to the ancient city, a terrifying scream pierced the stillness. They both shrieked in panic, and Zeus reared up, almost dumping them. Merit fought to control him. Katina almost forced the wind out of her, she was holding on with such force. Merit dug her heels into Zeus' flank, urging him into a gallop. Again, a shriek filled the air. Zeus stopped abruptly, neighed and reared again. They strained to stay on but slid off landing in a heap. Merit quickly jumped up, trying to grab the reins, but he was completely spooked and out of control, kicking up his hind legs like a wild bronco.

Katina lay curled on the ground in hysterics.

Suddenly a third scream wailed, but this time it sounded like, "Katinaaaaaa."

"Oh, my God, it's coming after us!" Katina screamed and clung to Merit.

Emerging from the ancient ruin of a building they saw a black form coming slowly toward them. They backed away in terror. Merit, struggling to keep her last thread of sanity, bravely picked up a rock, threw it and screamed at the approaching specter, "Get away from us!"

The figure stopped and flailed its arms. In a crackling voice, it spoke in Greek.

Katina cried in great relief, "Oh, thank God, it's only Helena, our village oracle!"

Merit was so distraught, she screamed fiercely at the old woman. "You frightened us half to death, you stupid woman!"

Katina spoke to Helena in Greek. "Why did you scream at us? What are you doing up here at night? There are ghosts all around here. We must get out of here right away!"

The old woman moved her toothless mouth, but nothing came out. Katina put her arms on the sagging shoulders and the old one began screaming again. Merit now joined Katina in trying to soothe the old woman and make her walk.

"What is she doing up here, Katina? Is she all right?"

"She seems to be dazed. she's trying to talk."

Finally the old woman looked at them with frightened eyes and mumbled. Katina translated. "She says death is up here at night. We must leave right away. She says she saw many ancient spirits coming for us, but she was able to drive them off with her powers." The old woman was now gesturing frantically for them to leave. She started shuffling down the hill, continuously turning to look back at them, calling out the same word over and over.

Katina translated. "She keeps saying, death"

Merit called Zeus, who now watched from a safe distance away. Slowly he came to Merit.

Merit and Zeus walked behind. The old woman. They passed the Kaldaras' house, which was in darkness, and began the descent down the hill. When they came to the place where the old woman had tied her donkey, they stopped. With amazing agility, Helena boosted herself up on the donkey and rode sidesaddle in front of the girls who were now on Zeus. They were so emotionally drained, they didn't speak. Merit sensed that Katina was also very angry with her.

Just before they reached the village, the old woman turned and spoke to Merit.

"What did she say, Katina?"

Katina frowned. "She says you should not have married in month of May."

"What! Ask her why she says that, Katina."

"She said May is month when donkeys mate, not people."

The humor of the superstition relieved Merit's anxiety a bit. She'd have to ask Anna about it.

When they arrived in the village, the old woman crossed herself, mumbled words that Katina could not understand, and disappeared into an alley.

They went together to stable Zeus but did not speak. Merit fed her horse some treats and spoke softly to him to let him know that everything was all right now. They crossed the courtyard together and went into the main room where the men were playing cards. Their faces told the men that something was very wrong.

The men stood up and Brant questioned them, "What happened, Merit? Katina?" Brant asked putting his arms around both women.

"Come sit down," Matt urged and pulled out chairs. "You look like you really saw ghosts up there."

A furtive glance passed between Merit and Katina.

Merit spoke first, reluctant to tell them that she'd indeed seen ghosts. She was sure they would scoff at the idea. She thought, Maybe I'll just tell them about meeting the old oracle in the ruins. "The old oracle frightened us."

Katina, unable to contain her terror any longer, began to sob. "We met oracle after ancient demons tried to capture us. They were much more frightening than old oracle. There were many of them, all talking. They passed through us, making us freeze. Our old oracle drove them off or they would have killed us. I warned Merit we never should have gone up there at night!" Tears streamed down her face, and her body shook uncontrollably. Brant held her in his arms and consoled her.

The men looked to Merit for confirmation, but she just stared at them, a strange look on her face. She reached over and tried to take Katina's hand, but the girl pulled away from her. "Katina is telling the truth. she's angry at me for taking her up there. She did tell me that there were ghosts, but I didn't believe her. We have just been through a terrible, frightening experience that I don't understand. Nor can I give you an intelligent explanation of what occurred. You probably won't believe our story anyway. I wish I could say I have doubts about what happened, but I can't. The horror of it will stay with me forever."

"Let me get you both a bit of brandy," Matt said. "Obviously, you've had a very traumatic experience." Then he thought to himself, They're telling the truth. Something terrible must have happened up there. If only

Katina had experienced it, I'd have doubts because she's young and superstitious like most people on this island, but Merit is a sensible person.

Merit proceeded to tell the men what happened, choking up when she tried to describe the moment when the specters passed through them. Katina sat completely still, her hands holding the icon in her lap and her head down.

Brant, although sympathetic, was skeptical about their story. "I can't believe Elias or his wife, or at least his dog, didn't hear all that commotion."

Merit said, "Their house was in darkness."

Wade spoke up, "I've studied supernatural phenomena and for that reason maybe I'm more inclined to believe their story. I'll even consider the possibility that the old oracle had the power to drive off the specters. She must have seen you two going up to the site and followed you. I believe your story. It's one thing to read about such a happening, but it must be terrifying to experience it firsthand."

Matt and Brant seemed startled by Wade's statement. He was a learned man, not one whom they would expect to believe in superstitions. but they could see he was not simply humoring the two women; he believed them.

Brant couldn't resist asking facetiously, "Did you get any pictures of them?"

At first Merit answered angrily, "NO. Of course not." Then she looked thoughtful. "But come to think of it, I never did shut my video camera off. When we started running I slung the straps over my shoulders." she picked up her video camera. "It's still on!"

"Maybe we should have a look," Brant said.

"NO," Matt said emphatically. "The girls are already too distraught. I suggest they get to bed. I'll give you both a sleeping pill, but don't take it right now on top of the brandy. just keep it at your bedside in the event you can't get to sleep."

Merit remembering that Anna was still in Athens, asked Katina, "Would you like me to sleep with you?"

"No, thank you," Katina answered curtly. She was still angry at Merit for talking her into going up to the ancient city. "I'll be okay. My Virgin icon saved me once tonight; she will again."

Matt walked her across the courtyard to her house. She assured him that she would be fine. She felt safe in her own home. Not used to alcohol, she already felt dizzy.

Brant and Merit went to bed quickly. It was a warm night and they left their patio door open. Merit slept fitfully, tossing and turning so much that Brant couldn't get to sleep. At midnight, he got her a drink of water and suggested she take the sleeping pill. It must have been potent, for she fell into a deep sleep very shortly thereafter.

After trying unsuccessfully to get back to sleep, Brant gave up and went out onto the patio with a bottle of wine. He sat down, put his feet up on the wall and consumed the entire bottle. He was fascinated by what had happened to Merit and Katina but didn't believe it was anything more than their imaginations playing havoc with them. But he couldn't help wondering what the old oracle was doing up in the ancient city at that time of night. Maybe she does have supernatural powers. Then he laughed to himself. He felt lightheaded and giggled, I think you're drunk, old boy, he thought as he tilted his chair back and began drifting off to sleep. But a strange muffled sound startled him. The curious noise sounded like whimpering. Is it an animal? Is it the ghosts? No, the sound is human and is coming from Katina's house! Clad only in bikini briefs and barefoot, he jumped over the patio wall and made his way quietly toward the sound. When he reached the wall of her patio, he realized it was Katina sobbing. The plaintive sound tugged at him. He thought, Maybe I should go get Merit. I hate to wake her. But, I should see if little Katina is okay, shouldn't I?

He leaned over the wall, and speaking Greek, called quietly, "Katina, it's Brant. Are you all right, dear child?"

The sobbing stopped instantly. He heard bare feet hurriedly padding across the tile floor toward the patio. She flung open the doors fully and stood in the arch.

Brant was stunned. She was a vision of loveliness in the moonlight! He had to catch his breath, and his heart skipped a beat.

"Oh, thank God, it's you, Brant. For minute, I thought it was more ghosts coming. I've been so terrified." Katina sighed.

"Didn't you take the sleeping pill, dear?"

"I was afraid to take it. I thought if I slept, ghosts would try to carry me off."

Her hair was pulled back in a ponytail, and damp tendrils framed her magnificent sculptured face. She was wearing a thin, loose-fitting nightgown.

"I heard you crying, and I was concerned," he said as he hopped over the patio wall.

She was startled. He wore only extremely brief black underwear. Embarrassed, she looked away and blurted out pathetically, "Oh, Brant, I'm so frightened. Ghosts seem to be flying all around my room." Tears spilled down her cheeks. "You probably think I'm a baby. I'm not! At least Merit has you to protect her."

"You poor darling, come here." He held out his arms. She flew into his embrace.

Brant was ecstatic. A rush of passion seized him. My God, a dream come true! He picked her up and carried her back into the room and thought,

I'll never get another chance like this, but I must not frighten her. God, she's so naive. "You're safe now, darling." He set her down. Her lovely young body, silhouetted through her nightgown by the moonlight, elated Brant. He shut the patio doors. He began comforting her in softly spoken Greek. He patted her hair. Slowly, he ran his hands down her neck, eased the straps of her nightgown off her shoulders and gently kissed them. "My poor dearest Katina, you've had a terrible fright. I'll make you forget all about the ghosts." He felt giddy. This was so easy. He managed to lower the top of her nightgown to just above her breasts, while softly kissing her beautiful neck and shoulders.

Katina suddenly realized what he was doing and was stunned. I must stop him, she thought. but she couldn't. Just a moment before, she was filled with ghostly dreams. Now, sensations she had never experienced before surged through her. Her heart pounded. She was completely incapable of stopping Brant as he moved her nightgown down lower. Her gaze locked on his face. Both were breathing in short gasps. His eyes were glassy and wild-looking. He mesmerized her. She shivered with passion and whispered, "Oh, Brant, no, no. stop, please."

He opened his mouth over hers, his tongue teased hers. Then he moved his mouth down to her taut, high breasts, kissing them gently and encircling her erect nipples with his tongue. "You're making my fantasy come true, my darling," he whispered.

She was ecstatic! She couldn't stop him. She had never felt anything so wonderful in her life. Her whole body vibrated.

He dropped her nightgown down to her hips, pulled the gown to one side and twisted it into a knot to hold it in place. Now it hung loosely from her hips down to her feet. "Everything must be perfect, you know," he said. "You must appear to me exactly like you always have. I always visited you in Paris every chance I got; you know that! I sat and adored your beautiful body! I lusted for you!"

Katina was bewildered. Why have I let him undress me? Am I powerless to stop him? Dear God, it's sinful. Why is he saying such strange things? She was frightened. What is this about being in Paris with me? I've never been off the island. She tried to push him away. He grabbed her tightly. She tried to cross her arms over her breasts. "Stop! You're drunk, Brant," she pleaded.

A foolish grin spread across Brant's face. "Now, now, my little Aphrodite, stay close to me. You must do what I tell you." He slowly let go of her, stood back and ordered, "Hold your arms out like this." He showed her how he wanted her to extend her arms towards him. "Do it now!" he commanded abruptly. he envisioned her now as the statue of Venus de Milo in the Louvre. His angry voice terrified Katina, but she slowly held out her shaking arms.

"That's it! Now turn your palms up. Make your hands beckon me to you. I know what you want me to do to you."

"What?" she gasped in fright. His menacing voice almost paralyzed her. "I don't want you to do anything to me! Let me go!" Her body trembled in terror. I must escape from him. Should I scream for help. NO! I'd be disgraced forever. She began to lower her hands and back away from him.

"DON'T MOVE! Keep your arms out to me." he growled. Then a raptured expression covered his face and his eyes grew wide. "Oh, God, what an incredible moment! Your lost arms restored, Venus! You are mine now, sweet Venus from Milo. All men have adored you for centuries but now you belong to me, my beautiful virgin. You're about to become a woman." He began to tug his briefs down sensously. "Wait until you see what I have for you."

It was then that she saw the huge pointed bulge in his underwear as he moved closer. She pounded both her fists against his chest. Terrified, she realized what he was about to do. She had never seen a real male's private part. Only from postcards of ancient statues had she known what it looked like. Bile rose in her throat as he closed in on her.

Horror propelled her into action. She pulled her nightgown up, clutched it over her breasts and made a sudden movement away from him. Then in a warning tone, she said, "You stay away from me! She lifted her head up and prayed, *Panagnia Mou* save me!" she looked at Brant in horror when he stopped, and a crazed look covered his face.

"You wanted to do this, didn't you? You were enjoying our fantasy! This is the second time you've let me get all worked up. You can't stop now! Come back to me this moment," he demanded. "Don't you dare try to deny me! You can't escape me." He pulled his briefs off and sprung towards her.

Katina dropped to the floor and buried her head in her hands.

At that moment a car pulled into the compound. the sound of an engine running and voices reached their ears. A car door slammed, and a male voice said "*Kalinikta.*" as the car drove off.

"Christ! They're back!" Brant raced across the room pulling his briefs on. Fled out the patio door and leaped over the wall. The noise of footsteps on the cobblestones crossing the compound sent shock waves through him. Realizing if he were caught, he'd be kicked off the island. I'm not ready for that yet, not until I get my treasure. I'll bet she won't let her *mana* know what happened. I'm safe there." He moved stealthily, hunched over, along the back of the houses until he reached his own. The footsteps stopped, then started again. They were going to Nikos' house. A door opened and closed.

Shit! It must have been that God damn kid, Ari. He waited a moment, then silently climbed over the wall onto his patio and eased himself into the safety zone of his bed, where Merit still slept soundly.

Katina crawled across the floor and huddled under the icon of the Blessed Mother at the front door. She could not look at it, her shame was so great. Pangs of guilt and grief racked her body. She was unable to squelch the sobs that burst from her lungs. She prayed to the icon, begging the Blessed Mother to forgive her. She could never confess the sin to *Papa* Ioannis for she feared he would tell her mother. She raced to her bedroom, burying her face in the pillow so no one would hear her. "What disgrace I have brought to myself. How can I ever be forgiven? How could I have been so stupid to trust him? My *Mana* knew he was not honorable, but I was so fascinated by him, such a rich and handsome man to pay attention to me, a poor peasant girl. His arms felt so protective around me; it was a good feeling! Oh God, and worse, I have deceived dear Merit in the worst way possible. I'm dirty and cheap. But worst of all, I have been disloyal to my *mana's* trust in me. There is only one thing left for me to do."

She went to the kitchen, got a large glass of wine and brought it back to her room. She picked up the sleeping pill, swallowed it, then drank the entire glass of wine without stopping. She opened the patio doors wide and spoke, "Now, ghosts, vampires, evil spirits, come, take me away, for I'm an evil sinner and do not deserve to live." She laid on the bed and offered herself up to the ancient spirits.

* * * *

Katina did not come into the dining room at breakfast time. Concerned, Merit went to her house and knocked gently on the door. There was no answer. She opened the door quietly and looked in the bedroom. Katina was asleep. The bedding was totally disheveled and the patio doors were wide open. Her face was blotched and tear-stained. Merit felt badly. She knew Katina had been frightened, and she should not have left her alone. She shut the bedroom door quietly and went into the kitchen, where she gathered up the dishes and food for breakfast. She explained to the men that Katina was sleeping so soundly, she didn't want to wake her. "I think her sleep must have been filled with nightmares. Mine sure was!"

"I'll bet that sleeping pill knocked her for a loop!" Matt said. "Anna told me Katina has never been sick. I'll bet she never has had so much as an aspirin before."

"I'm glad you gave me one," Merit said, "I couldn't get to sleep. I still get chills, thinking of what happened up there last night. I can't push it out

PEG MADDOCKS

of my mind. I'll go over to Nikos' house to fix breakfast. I don't want to wake Katina with kitchen noises."

Merit met Ari when she walked into Nikos' home.

"*Kalimera*, Missus Powers."

"Kalimera, Ari. I'm getting breakfast this morning since Katina is not feeling too well."

A concerned look covered his face. "I am sorry to hear that. Can I help?"

"No, thanks. join the others in the dining room, and I'll be right along."

He was just about to shut the door when he said, "Oh, Mrs. Powers, Nikos just telephoned. He and Katina's *Mana* will be back this afternoon."

"Good. Go tell the others, Ari."

When Merit arrived with a large tray, she announced, "Breakfast is served." It wasn't the usual elaborate meal that Anna normally served.

"Ari, Mrs. Powers has a video we would like to see, "Brant said. I'd like you to set up the VCR so we can view it before we go up to the site this morning."

"Oh, sure. I'll set it up after breakfast in Nikos' house, Mr. Powers."

"Oh, I almost forgot!" Merit said in an excited voice. "I have another piece of my photography you'll want to see. When we were developing Friday's photos last night, Katina pointed out something I hadn't noticed. Wade, do you remember that picture I took of you standing in front of the mound?" She intentionally did not say omphalos in front of Ari. "You had your arms folded, and you were talking to us?"

"Sure, you were going to charge me ten bucks for it, as I recall." Wade laughed.

"I haven't made a print of it yet, but I will this morning. it's very interesting!"

"For God's sakes, what is it, Merit?" Brant asked in a gruff voice. He had been surly since he woke up.

She resented his tone. "Maybe nothing, but it looks like the outline of an arch right behind you, Wade."

Wade quickly looked to the team, surreptitiously putting his finger up to his mouth for silence and pointed toward Ari who, at that moment, had his head down, spooning up his cereal. They were not sure whether they could trust the young man.

"Did you have a nice evening in town last night?" Matt asked Ari, changing the subject.

"Yes. I met some old friends from school. I got home near midnight, and I heard strange noise in back of houses. I'm sure I saw something like shadow of figure, too. But then it disappeared. It scared me."

They all looked at each other. "Probably just one of the ghosts from Mesa Vouno," Brant laughed Ari looked at him in confusion.

Wade spoke up. "Merit and Katina went up there last night, Ari, to do some photography and had a bad experience with something supernatural that frightened them. Maybe it wasn't so unusual, though. Before I came here, I read quite a bit about the island, and I remember what one author, Lawrence Durrell, said about how spooky this place is: 'That it's no surprise that the modern folklore of Greek peasant superstition has picked on the island (Santorini) as a specially favored home of the vampire. Vampires in retirement, vampires that have shot their bolt, vampires wanting to get away from it all. They find their haven here.'" He further stated, "And I remember this because it struck me funny."

"In fact, in the demonic there is a saying that closely parallels our own proverb about taking coals to Newcastle. It is: 'He who takes vampires to Santorini is performing a particularly redundant function.'"

All laughed except Merit and Ari.

Ari called the team to Nikos' house when he had the VCR set up. Merit gave him the tape, and they settled down in the living room to watch.

They complimented her on how incredibly beautiful the site looked in the moonlight, although they agreed it was eerie.

"Here's the part when we first heard the noise." I remember, I had just zoomed in on the stage area of the theater. Hear that! Shuffling feet and that swishing sound!"

They all leaned forward. They heard it! They could hear them screaming. They saw Zeus racing down to the theater floor, where a foggy cloud began moving up the hill. He kept rearing up and clawing his hoofs, trying to strike at the cloud, which passed through him and continued up the hill, coming closer and closer to the camera. One moment the theater seats were clearly outlined, a second later they became fuzzy as a mist obscured them. There was movement in the fog; dark, shadow-like figures, but nothing clearly discernible. The sounds became louder. Strange sounds, swishing movement, mumbling like many voices. The picture was shaking as vague outlines came closer. seeming to come right at the camera, to pass through it.

"The camera is on my back. We're running now." Merit didn't have to explain. They could see the scenery in back of the girls shaking violently each time the camera hit her back.

"Incredible!" Wade exclaimed.

Matt noticed Ari blessing himself over and over.

Tears flowed down Merit's cheeks, and she buried her head in her hands. Brant rushed to her side. "Poor darling. What a terrible experience for you. Turn it off, Ari!" he commanded.

The room fell silent for a moment. Each of them tried to grasp what they had just seen.

"Merit," Wade said, "You've captured a rare sight on film. congratulations. I'm sure there are many who would pay a fortune to see what we have just seen." He was desperately trying to make her feel that what had happened was not all bad.

She wiped her eyes and tried to smile. "Thanks, Wade. I don't want anone to tell Katina about this film. Last evening's experience will haunt the poor child forever. We must all help her forget last night."

They agreed, especially Brant. A devious thought ran through his mind. If she ever accuses me of trying to seduce her last night, I'll say she was so distraught, she was hallucinating, that she must have had a fantasy about me. I'll even say she often flirts with me. Little bitch, little holier-than-thou bitch. She seemed to enjoy being undressed by me, he mused.

"Let's get our gear together and get up to the office," Wade said.

"I'm going to stick around here," Merit said. "I want to be here when Katina wakes up. I'll make prints of those negs I was talking about. I'll bring lunch up to you around noon. I know Katina and her mother will have a great deal to talk about."

That sent a nervous jolt through Brant, but in his arrogance, he was convinced that Katina would not dare tell her mother. "I know her mother doesn't trust me and probably warned her to stay away from me. I think she'll keep her pretty little mouth shut."

CHAPTER TEN

At*hens, Greece*

When Nikos and Anna arrived in Athens on Monday morning, the sun was bright and the sky a vivid blue. Anna was excited about being back in the big city after so many years, and to see the city that had grown so rapidly in the past sixteen years. So many people were hurrying about their business. There were endless lines of traffic, yet Athens had kept its old-world charm. Probably the city remained fresh in her memory because she thought about it so often and the wonderful times she had here with Joe.

They had reservations at the elegant old Grande Bretagne Hotel, located downtown in Constitution Square. Anna had argued with Nikos about the expense of flying to Athens and staying at such a fancy hotel. "It's money spent foolishly, and I intend to pay you back. What if we are able to complete our business right away and don't have to stay overnight?"

"Then we will just use the rooms for siesta." Nikos said.

They were shown to adjacent rooms on the fifth floor, each with a balcony and a spectacular view of the city. To the right on a hill stood the Acropolis and the magnificent Parthenon. To the left they could watch the changing of the Evzone soldiers who guard the Tomb of The Unknown Warrior at the palace once occupied by King Constantine.

When they were settled in their rooms, Nikos had Anna look through the telephone directory of banks to see if she recognized any of the names. All she could remember was that Joe had told her it was a branch of an American bank.

Running her finger down the list she stopped suddenly. "Ah! Nikos! I found it! I'm certain. See it says it's a Bank of America."

Nikos looked at the page. "It is Bank of America at 39 St. I know where that is. Okay, Anna, let's go see what we can find out."

Walking through the elegant old hotel lobby, Anna felt out of place in her plain black dress. Stylish women were coming and going in the lobby. Although always poor, she was a proud woman with much dignity. She was glad she was wearing the pearl necklace Merit insisted she borrow, saying, "It's just costume jewelry."

Nikos looked distinguished in his black, summer-weight suit, Anna thought. He carried a black leather briefcase with all the documents Matt's brother had sent. Anna had also brought along her birth and marriage certificates, Katina's birth certificate, the affidavit from *Papa* Ioannis certifying that all the documents were authentic, and a statement that Anna Brady was a person of outstanding respectability on the island of Santorini.

The doorman bid them *"Kalimera"* as they emerged from the hotel. Nikos suggested they walk to the bank since it was very close by.

"Good! I'm very nervous. Walking will help me calm down."

"You have nothing to be nervous about. I will tell them all they have to know. Just say a prayer that they have not destroyed Joe Brady's box, and maybe another little prayer that it will contain things to make you happy, dear Anna."

Anna suddenly stopped. "There!" She pointed to a building. "I think that is where my Joe always did his business. See, it says, Bank of America, I'm right!"

Inside the bank, Anna stopped. She looked puzzled. "Maybe this isn't Joe's bank. It looks different."

"Of course it does. Sixteen years have gone by, Anna. They probably remodeled it since then."

Nikos went to the information desk and smiled at the young girl. "Excuse me, could you please tell me who I should speak with to see if a safe deposit box is still here in Mr. Joseph Brady's name? This is Mrs. Brady."

The girl looked from Nikos to Anna. "Er, ah, doesn't Mrs. Brady know?"

"No. It's a rather complicated situation," Nikos said and smiled.

The girl looked confused. "I think maybe our vice-president, Mr. Kanellopoulos, would have to handle this matter, but unfortunately he's out of town for the day. Could you come back tomorrow?"

"Isn't there someone else who can see if Mr. Brady's box is still here?" Nikos asked.

"Ah, well, why don't you go down to that last door on the right. I think Miss Economides might be able to help you."

"Thank you." Nikos smiled.

He held Anna's elbow and led her through the lobby to the office of Miss Economides, a rather heavy, stern looking matron.

"Good morning, Miss Economides. I am Dr. Konstantinou and this is Mrs. Anna Brady, the widow of Mr. Joseph Brady, who did all his banking here and had a safe deposit box when he died."

Miss Economides furrowed her brow and looked from Nikos to Anna and back again at Nikos. "I assume that Mrs. Brady would like to open her husband's box. You have a key? What is the box number? May I have the official death documents from the municipal record's department?"

"I have the key. It says number one hundred and seventeen." Anna's hand shook as she took the key from her pocketbook and handed it to the woman who checked the number.

The woman scrutinized the key, turning it over several times. "I hope it works. Why is it so scratched?"

Anna had polished the key with steel wool because it was quite rusty.

"It is a long story, Miss Economides," Nikos answered. "Please look at these papers and see if you need to have anything else." He handed her the thick envelope.

She put on small reading glasses and removed the contents of the envelope. The letter from Father Ioannis, written on St. Demetrius stationary, was the first item she scanned quickly, then laid it aside. She glanced hastily at the various certificates but stopped when she came to the death certificate of Joseph Brady. A perplexed expression crossed her face. "This death certificate is from Oxfordshire, England? Was he English?"

"No. You see he died in England," Nikos said.

"When?"

"Sixteen years ago, Miss."

"Sixteen years ago!" She took her glasses off, startled. Then she looked at Anna. "Why haven't you come here before this?"

Anna gulped then said in a soft voice, "I didn't know he was dead, or that he had a box here until..." Anna's nervousness made her appear guilty.

Miss Economides looked skeptically at both Anna and Nikos. "This is most unusual. I never heard of a wife who didn't know her husband had died or had a safe deposit box. Most unusual! Most unusual! How did he die?"

Anna and Nikos looked at each other. "It's in the reports from the United States FBI and from Scotland Yard. He was murdered," Nikos said softly.

That news seemed to be too much for Miss Economides. She put both hands up to her mouth in astonishment and whispered, "Oh my, oh my. excuse me, I want to get one of the bank officers."

Nikos blocked her way when she started to leave the room, and in his most charming, irresistible voice said, "Dear Miss Economides, you seem like such a caring person. I can see that you have great sympathy for Mrs. Brady and her tragedy. Could I ask for a very small favor on her behalf before you get the officer?" With that he placed his hands on Miss Economides' shoulders and looked serenely down into her eyes, saying softly, "Could you just take a second to see if box 117 is still in Joseph Brady's name?"

Anna could see his charm working on the woman. her eyes were fixed on his and she mumbled, "I, I, really shouldn't. I mean I think it would be improper for me. Well, I suppose it couldn't hurt to just look here in the file, but I rather doubt it if he's been dead for sixteen years." with that she put her glasses back on and opened a long file box on her desk. "Let me see. b-r-a-d-y, YES!" she was startled.

"J-o-s-e-p-h and A-n-n-a. Box number one-one-seven. Why yes, it is still in his and your name, Madam. Very unusual, I mean still being in your names, and no one having asked to open the box since, let me see...June 29th, 1979."

Anna and Nikos looked at each other, sharing the same thought. The day he died.

Miss Economides said, "Please sit down, I will bring an officer right back."

The moment she left the office Nikos grabbed Anna and hugged her tightly. "I didn't tell you before Anna, but I had a dream last night that you'll open the box and find a treasure. When you dream about finding a treasure you know it always comes true."

"You're a great dreamer, Nikos," Anna said with a laugh. "I think you have always made your dreams come true. Maybe you just change them around so they fit what happens, eh?"

Both were nervous, Nikos because he didn't want Anna to have more disappointments in her life; Anna because she was uncomfortable about banks and legal papers. Both her parents had died when she was young, and she'd attended school for only six years. She was naive about worldly matters. She had taught herself to speak English so she could get a job in a tourist shop.

A young, blond man of about thirty returned to the office with Miss Economides. He smiled pleasantly, extended his hand to Nikos and nodded at Anna. "*Kalimera.*" He turned to Miss Economides and told her to ask them if they understood English.

Nikos smiled at the young man saying, "Yes, we both do. This lovely lady is my very good friend, Anna Brady, and I am Dr. Konstantinou."

"Well that's going to make things easier for me, for sure," he smiled. "I'm Jack Woods. I'm just learning the ropes and to speak Greek, so I hope I can help you. The man who knows all about these things, Mr. Dimitri Kanellopoulos is not here today, but maybe I can answer some of your questions. Want to tell me what you folks need to know?"

Nikos and Anna spent the next five minutes trying to explain briefly all the pertinent facts.

"Gee, Mrs. Brady, you didn't know what happened to your husband for sixteen years. Gosh, that must have been rough. From what Miss Economides told me, the box in your husband's and your name is still here. That's pretty unusual, although maybe they do things differently here in Greece. Back in the States, if the bank hadn't heard from the owner and the annual charges hadn't been paid, they'd advertise in the newspapers that the contents of the box would be confiscated if the owner or relatives were not found. Then they drill the box open. Well, we're not going to have that problem here, are we? Looking at your card here, credits have been made every year for the rental charge. Hummm, that's interesting."

Nikos and Anna looked at each other, bewildered.

"Well, if you just leave all the documents here, I'll have Mr. Kanellopoulos look them over and meet with you tomorrow because I really don't feel qualified to let you open the box today. How about meeting with him, say about ten o'clock. would that be convenient?"

"Mr. Woods," Anna asked timidly, I would like to ask favor of you."

"Sure, Mrs. Brady. What is it?"

"Could I just see box with number one hundred seventeen. not open it. Just look at it. Please?" she begged.

"Just look at it? Sure. I don't see why not. After all, your signature is here on the card."

"It is?"

He held the card up for Anna to see.

"That's my handwriting. Maybe I remember now. Joe made me sign some things for bank."

"Well, just so that everything will be on the up-and-up, let's follow the regular procedure when a person opens their box. Just sign here on this line, and we can compare the signatures?"

Anna wrote out her name.

Mr. Woods held the card up for Nikos and Miss Economides to see. "That's the real thing, wouldn't you say?"

Everyone agreed, smiling at Anna.

"Follow me, Mrs. Brady, and I'll show you your box, which I'm sure you'll be able to open tomorrow." He led the way down a flight of stairs. Miss Economides unlocked the door to the vault and stepped aside to let them enter.

There were hundreds of metal boxes in all the walls. Mr. Woods began scanning and said, "Ah, here we are in the one hundred block. Come here, Mrs. Brady. You can find it yourself now."

Pointing her index finger, Anna began to read the numbers, moving faster as she got closer to her number. She stopped suddenly, pressing her finger firmly against one hundred seventeen. Bending her head, she fought back tears.

Nikos rushed forward, putting his arm around her. "I feel Joe's presence, Nikos. it's so strong."

"Yes, yes, of course, dear Anna. It's because he has left some wonderful things in that box for you."

Not knowing what to say or whether to say anything, Mr. Woods uttered softly, "I bet he did, too."

Nikos offered Anna his handkerchief, and she dabbed at her eyes before turning around.

"So," Nikos said. "We'll go now and be back tomorrow at ten o'clock for grand opening of box 117! Eh?"

"Gee, I'm sure sorry you have to wait another day," Mr. Woods said with great sincerity, "But I hope you understand."

"It's not problem. I will take Mrs. Brady to Archaeological Museum. We'll have wonderful lunch at my favorite restaurant, Bajazzo's, and then have siesta. And tonight we'll dine at our hotel and then go dancing. I'll keep her so busy, it'll be tomorrow before she knows it."

Anna gave Nikos one of her sidelong glances and smiled weakly at Mr. Woods.

When they were outside, Anna frowned at Nikos. "I wonder what that Mr. Woods thinks about our relationship. You made it sound like I was your woman...'then we siesta,' you say, like we would be doing it together!"

Looking impish, Nikos raised his eyebrows. "Is that completely out of the question?"

"Just try it, and you'll find out!"

Nikos laughed, took her arm and hailed a taxi for their trip to the museum.

The next morning at ten o'clock, Anna and Nikos walked into the Bank of America. Nikos told the young receptionist that they had an appointment with Mr. Dimitri Kanellopoulos.

"One moment please, let me ring his office."

Almost instantly, John Woods appeared and shook both their hands enthusiastically. "We've got good news folks. It seems Mr. Kanellopoulos is familiar with your account, but I'd better let him tell you all about it. I'll take you to his office."

Mr. Kanellopoulos rose from his chair when they entered, bowed graciously to Anna and shook Nikos' hand rather limply. He was an older man with stark, white hair. His dark pin-striped suit was elegant. His refined demeanor matched his soft-spoken articulate voice. "How nice to meet you, Mrs. Brady, and you too, Doctor," he said in a soft voice. "Please sit down. Would you like some coffee?"

They both said "Yes" simultaneously.

"I must say, Mrs. Brady," he continued after he rang for the coffee. "I am very, very pleased to meet you. Your account here has been an enigma to us. Am I to understand that you had no knowledge of the account or of the safe-deposit box until recently?"

"I only learned a few days ago about the box. I didn't know anything about an account," she answered softly. "My husband took care of all the money matters. I did come here with him a few times, but I didn't know anything about his bank business. I thought he had a bank in America that sent him money here."

"That's true, his bank in America did send him money here. That was a correct assumption. This bank is a branch of one of the largest banks in America. You see, he had the bulk of his savings account in the Bank of America in Los Angeles. They have a written order from him directing them to deposit $25,000 annually in our bank here in Athens until otherwise notified. the last time he made a withdrawal was in June of 1975. Then the only activity on his account, ah, I should say your joint account, it's in both your names…"

Anna gasped. "My account, too?"

"Why yes. Didn't you know that?"

"No. My Joe never told me."

"But, my dear lady, you did sign the signature card. Maybe you forgot. It certainly was a long time ago. The problem seems to have been that we didn't have a home address for your account in Greece…" His voice dropped off as he scanned the lengthy report on his desk. "Ah, I see that the annual bank statements were mailed, not to you, but rather to a Miss Emma Brady at 27 Elm Street in Pasadena, California. That seems strange, but it was the only address we had, you know, and the statements were never returned, so we assumed the proper person was receiving them. Ah, yes, now I remember…the report from the FBI…that would be the aunt of Mr. Brady, and I assume you did not know about her either."

"No. And she did not know about me, until recently." Anna hung her head in embarrassment. "You see, I did not know what happened to my husband. I thought after some time that maybe he just deserted my daughter and me, maybe for another woman." She looked up at the banker as if wondering what his reaction would be. "I didn't want to believe that, so I kept waiting for him to come back. I also did not think it would be proper for me to go to his bank here if he had deserted us. He never told me anything about his money, and I think it would have been dishonest to pry into his affairs with the bank without his permission."

Nikos interrupted, "She is a most loyal and honorable woman, eh? She considered herself married for all these years. She is greatly admired in our village. Her husband was very generous to her. He bought her a house with cash. I know that, because he bought the house from my parents. When he disappeared, I tried to find him. At that time Anna didn't tell me about this bank. She is a very private and proud person, a trait which you don't find in women too often." He was embarrassing Anna. He smiled and patted her hand.

"A remarkable story, and you are a remarkable woman. Your honesty and candor are admirable, Mrs. Brady. You have my deepest sympathy for the loss of your husband. How tragic not to have known what happened to him for all those years. I have read over the papers you left here yesterday. It was astounding that the American FBI and Scotland Yard were able to piece together the background of your husband's disappearance. I'm sure it must have been a great relief for you to finally know the truth."

"A great relief, yes."

"Well let's get right down to business. I have here a sixteen year record from our microfilm files of all the activity on your account. From June 1975, the only items that appeared on the account were the automatic transfers of funds from the Los Angeles branch to our bank. That amount was always $25,000 per year, as per your husband's written instructions. And, let's see, service charges for the annual fee for the safe-deposit box was automatically deducted each year, and the interest, a substantial amount that has been added to the account through the years."

Confusion crept across Anna's face. Nikos looked startled.

Mr. Kanellopoulos continued, "The balance of the account as of this date is substantial. In American dollars, let's see..." He began running figures into his small calculator.

"There," he said looking up and smiling. It is about 145,350,000 drachmas. That would be about half a million in American dollars.

Anna's mouth fell open and her eyes widened in shock.

Nikos stood up and leaned close to the banker, a look of utter astonishment on his face. "How much did you say Anna has in her account?"

The banker smiled, "145,350,000 drachmas, Doctor."

Nikos turned back to Anna. She leaned back in the chair, gasping deeply as if she was choking. Her face went gray. She put both her hands up to her head and cried out, "Holy Mother of God!"

Nikos began fanning her face. He was sure she was going to faint. He felt quite faint himself.

Mr. Kanellopoulos looked concerned as he poured a glass of water from a carafe behind his desk and rushed forward with it.

Anna just kept rocking back and forth, moaning.

"Anna, dear Anna! Are you all right? Shall we call a doctor? Say something, Anna!" Nikos begged. Then to the banker, "I have never seen her like this. She is such a strong woman, but for her to suddenly find that she is no longer poor...she is suddenly rich...this is a terrible shock to her, I can tell you!"

Both the men hovered over her. Mr. Kanellopoulos dipped his handkerchief in the glass of water and patted her forehead. She stopped rocking, slowly took her hands from her face and focused on the two men.

She took a deep breath and looked at Nikos. "That is too much money, Nikos. It frightens me." She reached out for his hand and held it tightly.

Mr. Kanellopoulos leaned down to her. "Are you all right now, Mrs. Brady?"

"I'll be okay in a minute. It's such a shock, so much money coming here every year, and I didn't know about it."

With a coy smile on his face, Mr. Kanellopoulos said, "Maybe it will ease your concern to know that it was only recently, a few months ago, that we received a final deposit on this account from our Los Angeles bank in the amount of $2004.88, and also a notice that the account was now closed out."

"Whew! "Yes, that's good news!" She began laughing, almost hysterically.

Both men joined her hilarity.

"Mrs. Brady, I want you to know that our bank will be happy to assist you in any way we can. Naturally we hope you will consider keeping your account here and drawing on it as needed. We have good interest rates. Possibly, once you've had time to think about it, you might want to use one of our financial advisors to help you invest some of your money. We're at your service. Would you like to open your safe deposit box now?"

"My box! I completely forgot all about it. Oh, yes, I would like to open it right now. Oh, Nikos, I can't believe all this is happening to me. I have been so poor, and now I am rich! You must help me with so many decisions, my good friend."

Nikos was swelling with pride and happiness for Anna. "I will always be ready to help you, you know that."

She stood up, clasped his face in her hands and looked at him with great affection. "You have always been my best friend, eh?" They stood looking at each other.

Mr. Kanellopoulos coughed politely. "Allow me to take you to your safe-deposit box now."

Once they were in the vault, Mr. Kanellopoulos took Anna's key and the bank's key and put them in the door. He turned them simultaneously, and the door opened the drawer that held the box. He gestured for Anna to take it out. "There's a private room right outside the vault that you may use to go through the contents of the box. Stay as long as you want. I will see you before you leave the bank. You probably would like to make a withdrawal, take some money out, I'm sure." he left the vault.

Anna's hands shook as she slid the box from the metal drawer that had held it for sixteen years. a thousand thoughts raced through her head. Turning, she walked out of the vault, spellbound by all that was happening to her. Her heart was pounding. Nikos stood outside the private room and gestured for her to enter, then began to shut the door to leave her in privacy.

"NO!" she screamed. "You must be with me when I open the box. I need you to be here with me. Please, Nikos. I may not understand things that are in the box."

Nikos consented and took a chair across the table from Anna.

Very slowly, she lifted up the lid. The first things she saw were photographs. She picked up one of Joe and a man. It had to be his father. They were both the same height with bright red hair and looked very much alike. They had their arms around each other's shoulders and were smiling at each other. "Look, look, Nikos. My Joe, with his father." She kissed the photo and pressed it to her heart. Tears of joy streamed down her cheeks.

"Oh, Nikos, I was beginning to forget what my Joe looked like. now I have this, and Katina will see what her papa looked like. this is more thrilling than the money!"

"Now she will have pictures of her grandfather and maybe even her grandmother! Look through the other pictures." Nikos was caught up in her excitement.

There were black and white photos identified as Joe's mother and father on their wedding day and colored school pictures of Joe at different ages. there was a photo of Joe and a handsome young man, taken in London with the Westminster Abbey in the background. The men had their arms around each other's waists, and were looking at each other affectionately. It was signed, "All my love always, Your Neil." The photo had obviously been crumbled and then flattened out again.

"I wonder who Neil was?" Anna frowned at Nikos. It looks like someone tried to destroy the picture and then changed his mind, eh?" A vague suspicion crossed Anna's mind because of the romantic way the men held and looked at each other. She dismissed the troublesome thought and laid the picture aside.

The same thought had crossed Nikos' mind. Had Anna noticed? probably just college chums fooling around. They looked to be in their twenties.

There were black-bordered death remembrance cards for Joe's mother and father, and a dark blue leather case that held Joe's father's medals from World War II: a purple heart, an Air medal, and a Bronze Star. In a small, velvet box lay a beautiful ring, a pear-shaped diamond in a gold setting, enhanced by diamond baguettes on each side.

"Oh, look Nikos. Isn't this the most beautiful ring you have ever seen? I wonder who it belonged to."

"I don't know, but it's yours now! Try it on."

"Oh, no I couldn't, I…"

"Anna, you must understand that everything in this box now belongs to you."

"But somehow it doesn't seem right. I feel like I'm going through someone's personal belongings."

"You are, dear Anna, but that someone is you now."

Nikos reached out for the ring. "Here, let me see if there are initials inside." He held the ring under the light." Ah, it says B.J.B.-K.M.B. two, eight, forty-two. B.J.B. could be Joe's father, Bartholomew Joseph Brady, and K.M.B. would be his mother. Two, eight, forty two could be their engagement or marriage date, eh? Do you know what Joe's mother's name was, Anna?"

"I think it was like our Greek Katerina. Remember, his mother died with the birth of my Joe. When I said I wanted to name our baby girl Katina, after my childhood friend who was killed in the earthquake in 1956, Joe said okay, because it was like his mother's name." Anna placed the ring back in the box and closed it. Then she picked up a small felt bag that had coins in it. She spread them out on the table. The coins were gold American pieces and Greek coins.

Nikos picked them up to examine them. "My God, Anna! These Greek coins are worth a fortune. I wonder how he ever got them. they are usually only found in museums." Nikos frowned as he turned one of the coins over in his hand. "See this one, Anna. It's a silver tetradrachma, sixth century B.C. See, that's the head of the goddess Pallas Athena. She was famous in mythology and called the Goddess of Wisdom. And here, look on this side. It's her favorite sacred thing, an owl. You've heard the expression 'wise old owl' eh? Now you know where it comes from. See here." He held his finger under three letters. "AOE, that means it was struck in Athens. In that era, coins always had the name of their city printed on them."

"You think he got them illegally, Nikos?"

"I wouldn't want to say that, but I don't know of any legal way he could have such rare coins in his possession."

"If that's the truth, we should give them to our Santorini museum." She looked upset when she put them back in the bag. She picked up a thick envelope and spilled the contents out on the table.

"Look Anna, his will!" Nikos said. "I think if you read it, you will see that everything that belonged to Joe is now yours."

She looked at him skeptically. "You think so? You read it."

Nikos unfolded the document. "It says LAST WILL AND TESTAMENT OF BARTHOLOMEW JOSEPH BRADY, JUNIOR."

'I, Bartholomew Joseph Brady, Jr., a resident of and legally domiciled in Pasadena, California, do hereby declare this to be my last will and testament. I leave all my worldly personal possessions, monies and properties to my wife, Anna Brady and in the event of her death to my daughter, Katina Brady.'

"It is signed by him and two witnesses and dated June 29, 1979."

"Oh, Nikos, that means that he made it out and put it in his box here the day before he was killed! Do you think maybe he had a premonition that he was going to die?"

Nikos patted her hand. "No, no dear Anna. He did it because he just had a new baby daughter and wanted to make sure she was included in his will."

"Look! An envelope with Katina's name on it. It's not sealed. Should I open it, Nikos?"

"Of course. Remember she was only a few days old when he wrote it to her, so he expected you to read it, I'm sure. here, I'll read it for you.

Athens, June 12, 1975
'My dear, baby daughter Katina:

I am writing this letter to you today from my bank in Athens. (In case, God forbid, anything should happen to me before I return to you and your mother.) I have just gone through my papers and personal belongings in my safe-deposit box, and there are some things I want you to have when you grow up. When you are old enough to understand, your mana or I will read this letter to you. I am leaving my mother's, your grandmother's, diamond engagement ring to you. She did not have much time to wear it before she died, but I hope you will wear it in her memory often during your life.

Because you were born on the Island of Santorini, one of the most important archaeological sites in Greece, I want you to have my rare collection of ancient Greek coins. They were given to me by my grandfather, who received them from his grandfather (my great-great-grandfather, and your great-great-great grandfather). My great-great-grandfather was a civil engineer who was hired by a French company to work on the construction of the Suez Canal in 1859. A quarry on the little island of Therasia, which you can see from our village, had an abundant supply of pozzuolana, used in underwater construction. My great-great grandfather was sent there to assist in the purchase of this vital material.

Shortly after he arrived on Therasia, there was a serious cave-in in the quarry, and two men were buried under the ash-like substance. He was responsible for saving the men's lives by sinking pipes down to them, so they could breathe until they could be dug out. The owner of the quarry wanted to reward my great, great grandfather, who did not feel he should be rewarded for what he did. But one of the men whose life he saved insisted that he take a gift of some ancient coins that had been in his family for years. The man claimed that if he did not accept the gift, the man would have bad luck for the rest of his life. The man and his family were so superstitious about repaying him, that my great-great-grandfather felt he must oblige them.

He was not aware of the rarity or the value of the coins and put them away in a box. My grandfather found the coins, and this story in that box after the death of his father. He put them in a small safe he kept at home. He, too, had no idea of the value of the coins. On my sixteenth birthday, my grandfather gave them to me. I was curious about their age so I went to the library to see if I could get some information about them. I was stunned when I found out how old they were, and when I asked a coin dealer in town what the value might be, I was shocked! On that day I decided I wanted to be an archaeologist.

I've been cowardly about donating them to a museum. I've found it very difficult to part with them. Maybe you will be more courageous and less selfish than I, and give them to a Greek museum. I think that is where they belong.

I love and miss you and your mana so much already, although we have only been apart a few hours. I am looking forward to our happy years together. I hope you will always be proud of your papa.

I will be in London this afternoon and will buy keepsakes from Harrods for you and your mana. Tonight I will be with an old school chum, who will drive me to Oxford University tomorrow. I will tell him all about my new life with my wife and new baby. Tomorrow I'll speak at Oxford on the archaeological site at Kalliste. It is a great honor for me.

Your loving Papa

Anna put the letter back in the envelope. "Katina will be so happy to have this letter from her *papa*. Nikos, if we knew who my Joe stayed with in London that night and drove him to Oxford…"

"I thought the same thing, Anna. Could it have been that Neil in the photo? could he have been the mur…"

Anna put her hand over Nikos' mouth. "I don't want to talk about that person anymore! I am going to tear up this picture right now." Fiercely, she tore the photo into tiny pieces. "We will never talk about him or the picture again, Nikos, you understand?"

Nikos realized that Anna probably had the same suspicions that he had about Joe's relationship with the young man, Neil.

PEG MADDOCKS

"Let's not look at anymore papers now. I want to go home, Nikos. We'll stop upstairs, and I'll take some money out of the bank, so I can pay you back for this trip."

"I will not let you!" he was indignant. "I was happy to do this for you before you became the richest widow on Santorini, you know that!"

"I know that. You are a wonderful friend, Nikos, and I have an important favor to ask of you. I'm still in a state of shock because I have so much money, but I don't want anyone else to know about it yet. I need time to think about it. Too much money can sometimes ruin a person's life." She was thinking about Brant and Merit. "I want to make sure that Katina and I don't suffer from having too much money. I know you are the worst person on Santorini to keep a secret, but you must do this for me. Please. promise me."

Nikos put his arms on her shoulders and looked down at her. "Of course, my dear Anna. You're right, I am not good at keeping secrets, but I will not tell anyone, I swear to God and all the saints."

She smiled up at him. "You are such a good man, Nikos. I don't know what I would do without you. Please take me home."

When they got back to the hotel, Anna said she had an errand to do and would meet him in half an hour. Nikos wondered what she was going to do. but he did not question her.

When he was out of sight she went down to the lobby shop and into the jewelry shop of Ilias LALAoUNIS, the world-renowned international jeweler who has shops in most major cities.

The salesman bowed slightly and asked, "Good morning, how may I help you?"

Anna's heart was pounding with both fright and fascination. She couldn't believe she was now able to make a purchase in such an expensive shop. "I want a special-gold gift for four men who have done me a great service." she thought that sounded elegant enough to convince the man she could afford whatever she wanted.

He startled her by saying, "Those are beautiful pearls you are wearing."

She reached up and held the pearls out. "These? They are just costume jewelry."

The man came around the counter and looked at them carefully. "Madam, these are an extremely expensive strand of perfectly matched pearls. You cannot fool me," he chuckled.

"You can tell, eh?"

"Absolutely!"

"Well, I'll be honest with you. They were loaned to me by a friend." Then she did the most impulsive act of her life. "I was hoping that you might have a strand like these that I could buy for myself?" Anna was

156

shocked at what she was doing. She would chastise Merit later for not telling her the truth about the pearls.

"Why yes, I think I can show you a strand that is quite similar." He was curious about this woman, dressed so poorly and carrying a plastic pocketbook while wearing a fortune in pearls. He returned back in a moment with a strand of pearls laid out on a velvet tray. "They are quite expensive, Madam."

"Expensive, eh? Then it's a good investment. I'll take them!" Anna said emphatically without even asking the price. "Now, what about the gifts I want for the four men?'

The man pulled at his chin and frowned as he thought for a moment, then reached into the display case. "Might I suggest this handsome gold money clip with a magnificent carved relief of Apollo, or maybe this one of Hermes, the messenger of the gods." He slipped a folded drachma into each of the clips to demonstrate how they were used and held them out to her.

She picked up the Hermes. "This is perfect for the three men who brought me a wonderful message. And the Apollo will be fine for my other friend, who is not unlike a Greek god in many ways."

She asked if they could be engraved with a short message right away, explaining that she had to catch a plane at noon.

"Yes, I can have them ready. Will this be a charge, madam?"

"No, I will pay for them with a check from my bank." When she withdrew cash from her account, Mr. Kanellopoulos had presented her with a checkbook with her name at the top of each check. She was thrilled. Nikos explained how she could now pay for things with the checks instead of cash.

The clerk presented her with a sales slip. Her heart stopped for a second when she saw the total, but she didn't flinch. Her hand shook when she wrote out the check and the inscriptions she wanted engraved on the gifts. She took a deep breath as she handed the check to the man, saying, "Thank you, sir, you've been most helpful."

"I will have your gifts wrapped and delivered to your room by eleven." He saw her to the door, bowed and said, "Thank you very much, Mrs. Brady, and do come back and see us again."

She smiled, thinking to herself as she walked across the lobby, so this is how the rich feel all the time, eh? It is wonderful! I like it!

* * * *

The Olympic Airlines Shorts 330 touched down on the narrow runway on Santorini at 2:55 p.m. As he had promised, Dimi was waiting with his taxi, and soon they were heading up the steep mountain road toward their village. Anna had given Nikos his gift on their flight home. He was so touched by her thoughtfulness, that much to her embarrassment, he had hugged and kissed her until she blushed vividly. When she regained her composure, she told him she also bought money clips with the god Hermes on them for Matt, his brother, and the kind policeman in Oxford.

"Ah! Does my getting the Apollo clip mean that I'm special, like the god Apollo, the god of manliness?"

She gave him a flirtatious look. "Could be. I might describe you like that."

"Hmmm," He took Anna's hand in his, winked at her, closed his eyes, leaned his head back against the seat and murmured, "Manliness, yes, that does describe me, eh?"

Anna grinned. She had never felt so at peace.

* * * *

By noon, Katina still had not awakened and Merit was concerned, although she had checked on her continuously. She went to the stable and asked Kristos to ride Zeus up to the office with lunch for the team. She wanted to be at the house when Katina woke. He was thrilled with the responsibility and the opportunity to ride Zeus such a distance.

The kitchen activity finally woke Katina. She slipped into jeans and a T-shirt. She was so filled with shame, she felt ill. She dreaded facing Merit, whom she had deceived so terribly. She glanced in the mirror and was shocked by her ghastly appearance. She walked into the kitchen with her head down.

Merit was startled by Katina's face. Her eyes were almost swollen shut, her face was blotched, her hair was tangled and damp with perspiration. "Oh, my poor dear Katina, you look dreadful, and it's all my fault."

Katina couldn't look at Merit but mumbled, I wish I never woke up. Then I wouldn't have to remember last night." Her stomach tightened in a knot as flashes of her encounter with Brant and the ghosts filled her mind.

"Let's not talk about what happened last night for a while. Matt thinks we should try to put it out of our minds until we can discuss it without reliving the full horror. Fortunately, we were not hurt, just shocked. Are you still angry with me, Katina?"

"No." She walked over to the window and looked out to the courtyard. "I wonder, when my *Mana* will be home?"

"She'll be here soon."

"Go take a shower, and I'll fix you some breakfast. I don't want your *mana* to see you looking like this, or she'll think I didn't take very good care of you. And I guess that's true. I feel guilty about taking you up to the ruins last night. Can you forgive me?"

A sharp pain seized Katina's head. can I forgive her? Could she ever forgive me? She looked at Merit, sobbed and said, 'Oh, Merit, I love you, and I'm sorry. I...I mean, I can't believe what happened last night, I..."

Merit took her in her arms. "Don't say another word! We'll forget about everything that happened last night. Hurry, get into the shower before Ari sees you looking like this. He's asked about you at least ten times this morning."

"Where is everyone else?" She had made up her mind to never look at or speak to Brant again.

"They're up at the office working on pottery. Oh, and by the way, you were right about an arch over Wade's head. Here, look at this photo I developed this morning. See it's a perfect arch."

Katina stared at the photo. "Usually arch is over door."

"A door?" Merit was puzzled. "We didn't see a door I'm sure. See this photo of the omphalos, that's where this arch is located."

"Greek buildings often have arch-shaped doors and windows. It's better than square-shape when earthquake comes."

Merit looked closely at the photo again. "A door? Hummm," she mused. "An interesting observation, Katina! A large portion of the omphalos is covered with lava, but see, it looks like lava probably has chipped off and exposed that section of the arch. You can tell because of the different colors. Well, enough speculation. You hurry and get showered and dressed. We're going to have a busy afternoon!, Katina. Go get yourself fixed up."

Katina spent twenty minutes under the shower, scrubbing fiercely, trying to cleanse herself of her sins. She suddenly realized how much water she was using. She never had used that much water in her life. She was ashamed of it. she dressed quickly and brushed her hair. She had to keep pushing last night's sin out of her mind.

When she came back into the kitchen she glanced shyly at Merit and asked, "Do I look okay now?"

"You look as beautiful as ever!" Merit said, but she noticed that dark circles had replaced the puffiness under Katina's eyes. Katina didn't eat much breakfast. She apologized repeatedly to Merit for not waking up sooner and doing her chores.

Merit gave her a hug. "That's what big sisters are for!"

A pang of guilt seared Katina. Oh, God how could I have betrayed her. She is such a wonderful person. She's been so good to me. She would hate me for what I did with her husband last night! Why did I let it happen? Was I to blame? Yes, of course I was. I didn't try to stop him until...

Hearing Zeus' hoofs coming across the compound, they went out to help Kristos lift the food baskets off the horse's back.

"Mrs. Powers, bossman tell me to tell you that they'll be down soon. Do you want me to take Zeus back to stable?"

"Would you like to ride him around the village for a little while?"

His answer was a wide grin.

Ari came out of Nikos' house and hurried toward the women. He put his hand gently on Katina's shoulder. "Are you okay?"

She jerked away from him and kept her head down as she answered, "Yes, thank you."

"Would you like to walk down to the village with me? I have to borrow more staples for the gun that Papa Ioannis loaned me."

Katina answered, "Okay." Merit said sternly, "Listen, little sister, I am ordering you to go. A walk would be good for you. It'll put some roses back in your cheeks. Just don't be gone too long, and remember you two, not a word to anyone about what happened to us last night."

Merit watched them as they walked out of the compound. Ari tried to hold Katina's hand, but she pulled it away. Merit was surprised She thought Katina would have been delighted by the gesture. *I think she's suffering quite a bit more from last night than I am.*

* * * *

At two o'clock, the men came down from the office. Merit and Katina were busy preparing vegetables for the evening meal. Katina panicked at the thought of facing Brant. *Would he say anything about last night? Of course not!*

Actually, he avoided looking at Katina. Matt and Wade asked how she was feeling, but Brant acted as if she wasn't even in the room. He gave all his attention to Merit and was openly affectionate with her, suggesting, "You're working too hard. Let's go to the house for a little siesta. Leave the chores for her." He gestured toward Katina.

"We're almost finished," Merit said. She was surprised by his terse words. Usually, he treated Katina so gently. "Oh, by the way, let me show everyone the photos of the arch that Katina pointed out. I have them over at the dining room."

Brant was the last to leave the kitchen. At the door, he turned back and when he was out of earshot of the others, he sneered at Katina contemptuously and said, "Katina, you know what you are, you're a whore! Don't ever come on to me like that again. If there's one thing a man hates, it's a tease, and you're good at that!" He turned and left.

Stunned, by his biting words, Katina had to swallow the bile that surged into her throat. She clasped her hand over her mouth, holding back the vomit until she reached the *banio*. She knew the American word meant "prostitute." He was blaming her completely. Was it all my fault? Did I tease him? Yes! Yes! I didn't stop him from exposing my breasts. He must have thought...Oh, God, I've ruined my reputation. Shame and guilt racked her whole being and she dropped to the floor in a heap, sobbing hysterically. She heard a car pull up out front. "Holy Mother of God, It's my mana and Nikos." She quickly splashed water on her face, smoothed down her hair and raced out sobbing as she flew into her mother's outstretched arms.

"Oh, my baby, what's wrong? You look terrible." Anna was visibly shaken by her daughter's appearance. She hugged her fiercely.

The others, hearing the car stop, also came out to greet them. Merit, overhearing what Anna said, went directly to her. "It's all my fault, Anna. Please come in the dining room, and we'll tell you all about it.

"Anna momentarily stared hard at Brant, who responded with a raised eyebrow. "The girls ran into evil ghosts last night, poor things," he said in a taunting voice.

Startled, Nikos and Anna both said, "Ghosts!" Where?"

Merit led Anna and Katina into the dining room and the men followed. Briefly, Matt told Anna and Nikos what happened, and suggested that they all drop the subject for now. "It's still too frightening for the girls to talk about. Give them a few days, and they'll be able to discuss it more rationally."

"I've heard stories about ghosts up there since I was little boy," Nikos said, "But I never really believed them! Okay, let's take doctor's advice and listen to happy subject: what Anna found in her safe deposit box!"

Everyone turned toward Anna, urging her to tell them her good news.

Katina looked to her mother in anticipation. "*Mana*, did you find my *papa's* things?"

"Yes! And so many things your *papa* wanted you to have. Oh, how he loved you! When I show you, you will change that frown on your face to big smile, eh, Nikos?"

"That's for sure! I know for sure, too, that if your *papa* had lived, you would have had best *papa* in world."

Katina thought momentarily how idiotic she had been to look upon Brant as a father. Then a strange sense of security she had never known filled her. My father truly loved me. How sad that I never knew him or his love.

Anna interrupted her thoughts. "Katina. Wait until you see how many surprises I have for you. First and most important, now you can see what your dear *papa* looked like, and here are pictures of your grandparents!"

Katina's face lit up in astonishment while flipping through the photos that Anna identified. "Look, look," she said to the others, passing them around the table. "My *papa*! At last I know what my *papa* looks like. Oh, he was so handsome."

Comments went back and forth across the table about how much Katina resembled her father. Everyone, was touched by her excitement. Brant alone passed the photos on, showing little interest.

"Now for big, big surprise, Katina. Here is letter your *papa* wrote to you one day before he died. You will read that he has left you some of his family's treasures, like your grandfather's war medals. I think it would be nice to share your *papa*'s letter with all our good friends here, eh?"

Katina's hands were shaking, and her voice was unsteady, "My dear, beautiful baby daughter Katina…When she read the words, "your grandmother's diamond engagement ring," she looked up at Anna, her mouth wide open. "*Mana*?"

Anna smiled broadly, handing her the velvet ring box. Katina opened the box slowly, an expression of wonderment covered her face. "Ohhhhh!" she moaned in pleasure.

"It's absolutely exquisite, Katina," Merit said excitedly. "It must be at least two karats, and the baguettes, the diamonds on each side, are beautifully cut. You have a real treasure there, dear. Try it on."

Katina slowly slid the ring on her trembling finger and held it out for all to see.

"Read on, Katina," Anna said elatedly. "Read about real Greek treasure your *papa* left you."

Those words caught Brant's attention. When the story of the coins unfolded, he had difficulty resisting the urge to reach out for the bag that Anna handed Katina. When Katina spilled out the coins on the table, he couldn't contain himself. "Don't mishandle them like that! they scratch so easily!"

Everyone looked at him in annoyance.

Nikos spoke kindly to Katina, "They should be handled carefully, Katina dear. I know these coins, and they are very valuable. They are sixth-century silver tetradrachmas from Athens. I hope you want to give them to Greek museum like your *papa* suggested."

Brant lost control again, blurting out, "That would be stupid! I'll pay you a fortune for them! Then you and your mother won't be so pitifully poor anymore."

His words stunned everyone. Merit glared at him. "Brant! How dare you say such a thing! How rude of you! Apologize to them immediately." Merit had never spoken to Brant like that before.

Anna put her hand up to halt Merit from saying more. Then she looked pointedly at Brant. "Mr. Powers, I'm sure Katina would not sell her coins for any amount of money, and we don't need any of your money. My husband left us well provided for."

Brant shrugged and thought to himself, peasants! But he offered no apology and left the room.

Anna turned to Katina. "Continue your father's letter, dear."

Merit was distraught. She wanted to go after him and ask him to apologize to Anna and Katina. Lately, he seemed to be more arrogant and short tempered with all the team members. In the last few weeks, when they were alone, he'd constantly complain about petty things. His favorite gripes were about Nikos.

Katina finished the letter, and Matt, hoping to ease the tension, led the applause while he came around the table to kiss Katina's cheek. Wade and Merit both gave her a hug.

"I think this calls for toast," Nikos said. He went to the side table and brought back glasses and a bottle of champagne he had purchased in Athens for the occasion.

He toasted, "To new, exciting life for Anna and Katina Brady, *yiasou*!"

"*Yiasou*!" the others cheered.

Brant re-entered the room. Merit had never spoken so harshly to him in public like that before. He didn't like it one bit, but if he wanted to get those coins, he'd better mend a few fences. It galled him to think that this peasant girl, with whom he was now totally disenchanted, still had something he wanted badly. Holding his glass in a toast position, he said casually, "Forgive me, Anna, if what I said was rude. I get carried away sometimes with my obsession for antiquities. I didn't mean to offend. I just meant if you wanted to sell them, I'd love to be the buyer." He then smiled.

She ignored him completely and looked at Merit. "Merit, you lied to me."

Merit and the others were stunned by Anna's tone. "What do you mean, Anna? I..."

Anna interrupted her. She took the pearls off her neck, trying hard not to smile. "Here are what you called your costume jewelry pearls, eh? You tried to fool me, eh?" She pinched Merit's cheek gently with one hand and held the pearls out to the group with the other. "Here are what you called your costume jewelry pearls, eh? You tried to fool me, eh? See these, they are very expensive strand of perfectly matched pearls that Merit told me were only costume jewelry."

"But how did you find out?" Merit asked.

"Oh, they were admired by my salesman at Ilias LALAoUNIS jewelry shop at Grande Bretagne.

Merit grinned, "You went shopping there? They just happen to be one of the most expensive jewelers in the world?"

Anna did not reveal that she now owned valuable pearls also. "Yes, I know. But I had to buy best presents for good friends of mine. I already gave my good friend, Nikos, his gift. Now I want to give to you, Matt, these three gifts. One is for you, one is for your FBI brother and third one is for policeman in Oxford. It is my way of saying thanks to you for what you did for me. please open yours."

Matt unwrapped the small box, taking out the handsome, gold money clip. "Oh, Anna it's beautiful. You did not need to get me a gift. but I thank you, and I'll treasure it forever." he kissed her cheek.

"Read what is inscribed on back." Anna said.

He read, "To Matt, who gave me a new life. My deep appreciation, Anna." he smiled warmly at her. "Who is the ancient Greek on the front?" Matt asked.

"That is great god, Hermes, messenger of gods. You know, Grotto was named for him. You three men brought me messages that gave me new life."

Nikos couldn't resist boasting and displaying his clip. "But see, Matt, I got most important god. I got Apollo, god of manliness, eh?"

Matt shook his head and laughed with the others. "You are right, Nikos, my friend, you are the height of manliness."

"I know that. Anna told me same thing."

Anna blushed at his insinuation, then grinned and shrugged her shoulders at the others.

Brant looked at his watch. "Wade, I suppose it's too late to go back to the tunnel and take a good look at this arch in the photo."

"Yes it is. When we go up there tomorrow, we'll bring some chipping tools to see what's under the lava."

Anxious to be alone, Anna and Katina excused themselves and went home. Merit also left, saying she wanted to get a little rest.

"I have some good reports from my friend in Athens who has been doing some carbon testing for us," Nikos said. "It looks like we've found some very old artifacts."

The men sat back down at the table. Nikos said in a hushed voice, "But before we look at the report, you must tell me about ghosts, now that the women are gone. Do you men really believe it?"

"How would you like some proof?" Wade asked. "We all saw it this morning."

"Saw what?" Nikos asked excitedly. "You're telling me someone captured ghost!"

"Actually, Merit did, on film." Brant said.

Nikos looked around the table in disbelief. "Ghosts on film?"

"Come on, pal. We'll show you the spookiest movie you've ever seen," Matt said.

Ari was working on the video equipment. He offered to set up the film for them. "I want to see it again, too."

They all watched Nikos' face when the ghostly scenes appeared. He stood up, blessed himself and uttered in a hushed tone, *"Thee mou*! (my God)" He was visibly shaken as he dropped back down in the chair.

When the film ended, they told Nikos about the old oracle and how she claimed to have saved the girls.

"I still think that old gal knows a lot more than she tells," Brant said dryly.

"By the way, Nikos, I'm sure you agree that it would be best if we kept the ghost incident to ourselves," Wade said. There is no need to alarm the village people."

"They must never know! You are right," Nikos said firmly. "I cannot believe what I have just seen. I would never want our villagers to see it or ever know about it. I will ask Merit never to identify location of ghost film, if she shows it in America. Our little island would never be same. We must keep it secret."

There was a knock on the door. Nikos opened the door to Elias Kaldara. "Ah, Elias, what brings you down from mountain?"

Elias took off his cap and held it to his chest when he noticed the others in the living room. "Could I have a word with you privately?" he whispered in Greek.

"Of course. come, we'll go out into the courtyard."

When they were out of earshot, Elias spoke. "Nikos, something unlawful happened last night up at Thera. You were away, so I didn't say anything until I talked to you first. It was a little after ten o'clock. My wife and Kristos were asleep, and I was reading. Suddenly my watchdog, Pluto, started growling. I put his leash on and we went outside. In the bright moonlight, I saw two women on horseback going up to the ancient site. Thank God, Pluto calmed down, because like me, he recognized who they were. Otherwise he would have broken from my hold and attacked them. I thought about following them and making them come back, but I knew they were honest people and wouldn't steal anything. you know who it was, eh?"

Nikos grinned at Elias. "Ah! I know who it was. It was Mrs. Powers and Katina, eh?"

"I couldn't believe that two women would go up there alone, what with the ghosts and vampires that are said to prowl up there at night. It was a stupid thing to do. I hope you'll talk to them. Please let them know that they are not allowed up there at night, that it's against the law. I could lose my job if the authorities found out."

"I'm very sorry about this. When I got home today they told me they were doing night photography up there. I warned them never to go up there at night again, that it was against the law," Nikos lied. "I did not tell them that they might have been frightened to death by evil spirits."

Nikos thought to himself, I won't have to warn the women after what happened to them, but I'll have to tell them about the law.

"I'm relieved that they didn't meet up with any demons. I'll tell you why I say that and don't think I'm crazy, eh?"

Nikos laughed. "Why would I think that?"

Elias leaned in close to Nikos and said in a whispered tone, "I have seen strange things up there at night, like a low, small cloud moving through the ruins. I hear sounds, like voices; not real voices but noise like voices. I sometimes hear shuffling feet. I've never gone up to investigate. Naturally I'm too frightened to go alone, and my Pluto refuses to move when this happens. His hairs stand straight up on his back, and he whines and scratches to get back into the house. It's the only time he's ever cowardly. Of course when someone besides the ancient spirits trespasses up there, I can't restrain him from attacking them. I have to give him big chunks of lamb to make him let go of the intruder."

"I'm sure the women didn't see ghosts, Elias. They would tell us that, eh? Did you see them come back down the hill?" Nikos was very surprised that Elias did not hear them screaming and racing down the hill, or hear the old oracle screaming.

"I'm ashamed to say that my intention was to leave my window open and listen for them to come back down safely..."

"But what happened?"

"I poured a little 150-proof raki, well, maybe a little too much to help me stay awake. I forgot to open the window, and I fell asleep. The biggest catastrophe was that Pluto knocked the bottle off the table, trying to wake me I guess, and he lapped up so much, he got drunk and passed out!"

The men laughed loudly.

"My wife, Dora didn't think it was funny when she woke me up this morning. The raki stained her rug badly, and Pluto got sick on top of the stain. Holy shit, was I in trouble!"

"I'm sorry you had so many problems because of the Americans, Elias. Don't worry, none of my team will go up there at night again, of that you can be sure."

"And you won't tell anyone about the ghosts, eh?"

"Of course not! the Americans would not believe it."

Elias got back on his donkey. "I'm sure they wouldn't!"

Nikos waved him off and went back into the house. He had already made up his mind not to tell the team about Elias' ghost stories. He felt they didn't need to be frightened any more. But Elias' stories now convinced him that the ghosts must exist. He was still stunned by the movie.

He did tell the team that Elias had seen the girls going up and was upset. "I think it's my fault because I never told you that it was against law to go up there at night. Elias' dog, Pluto, is vicious with strangers who trespass, and if he attacks, Elias can only get his teeth out of the intruder by bribing him with chunks of lamb. I never thought any of you would go up there at night, especially the women—they were lucky that the dog didn't go after them."

They laughed when he told them about Elias and the dog drinking raki and passing out.

The men left Nikos' house and went back to the dining room to go over the reports on their finds that Nikos brought back from Athens. The Athens archaeologists were delighted with the figurines and the other finds, but they did not feel a visit to the site had to be done immediately. Their dating tests coincided closely with the team's estimates of the time periods. The figurines would be cleaned by professionals and then placed on display in the Archaeological Museum in Athens one day.

The team was relieved that no one from Athens was going to visit the site as yet. Finding the omphalos had raised the team's expectations for an important discovery. Nikos had not yet surrendered the buff-colored incense jars that were decorated with the same designs as those found at Kalliste. He would eventually turn them over to the authorities, but hoped that they would find other Minoan artifacts to prove it true. He also hoped that the authorities would allow him to keep them on Santorini and display them in their own museum. He felt that there was no need to have them tested to be certain that they were made prior to the eruption in 1600 BC. In his judgment they were Minoan, without a doubt.

* * * *

When Anna and Katina finally were alone in their house, Anna grabbed Katina's hands and yelled, "Opa! Opa!" as she began to dance in a circle with her daughter, singing an old Greek song of joy.

Katina had never seen her mother act like this before. "Mana, Mana, you are so happy to have papa's things. I have never seen you act so silly before."

They both laughed as they danced.

"I'm excited, my darling daughter, because wonderful things are going to happen to us."

"More things than we already have? I'm so thrilled about the pictures of my papa and my beautiful ring. What else do we need?" Then her tone of voice changed dramatically. "But I'm going to give the coins to our museum here on Santorini. I wouldn't sell them to Brant Powers for all the money in the world," she blurted out with vengeance.

Anna stopped dancing and looked intently at Katina. "Did he do something to you while I was gone? Why have you change your mind about him?" she asked in an accusing voice.

Too late, Katina realized she shouldn't have said anything. She must now lie to her mother, for she could never tell her what happened. It would break her heart. She kept her head down while she tried to think of what to say. "I...I don't like him anymore. He said something to Ari about me that was not true, and he called us peasants!"

Anna wondered why Katina would not look at her. Her intuition told her that Katina was not telling the truth. She lifted the girl's chin and forced her to look into her mother's eyes. "What was the terrible lie Mr. Powers told Ari?"

Katina could not fight back the tears, and in run-on sentences, she blurted out, "He told Ari that I was going to go to college in America, and Ari believed him. When I went for a walk with Ari today, he was very upset that I would leave Greece. He wouldn't believe me when I told him that Brant had lied and that I never would leave Greece. Oh, *Mana*, I like Ari very much! He calls me Tina."

"Wait a minute, wait a minute, what is this? You went walking with Ari today? Where? For how long? Where was Merit? She promised me she would not leave you alone with Ari."

More run-on sentences: "Oh, Mana she made me go because I was so upset by the ghosts last night. Matt gave us sleeping pills so we could sleep, and I didn't wake up until noon. I looked awful so she said a walk to the church with Ari would put some roses back in my cheeks. I didn't let him hold my hand when he tried, honest!" Then she sobbed uncontrollably.

Anna took her in her arms and said soothingly, "My poor baby. Your sadness is because you are going from childhood to womanhood so quickly, and you are confused. I know what has happened to you."

Katina's mind raced in panic, thinking, Oh, my God, what does she know?

Again, Anna forced Katina to look up at her. "I think Mr. Brant Powers' attention went to your head, and you were infatuated with him until Ari came along. am I right?"

With enormous relief, Katina took a deep breath and said, "Yes."

"Good! I'm glad you've come to your senses. Mr. Powers is not a good person. Now that I know how you feel, I will not have to worry anymore about him taking advantage of my daughter. What a relief!" Anna smiled broadly and kissed Katina all over her face. They hugged each other.

Katina had to try to put the encounter with Brant out of her mind, although she knew the guilt would always be there, like a deformity that could never be corrected.

A sly smile crept across Anna's face as she said,

"Katina, sit down at the table. We have to have a serious talk about money." Very slowly, she went over the events at the bank. "Oh, you should have seen me when Mr. Kanellopoulos told me we had money in an account, I almost fainted for the first time in my life."

"How much money, Mana? How much? Can I get some new clothes or maybe a bicycle?" Katina asked excitedly.

Anna's face brightened into a gleeful smile. "Ha! anything you want my darling, Katina. We are Rich! Rich like maybe the Powers." The amount was so great, Anna thought that might actually be true.

Anna took both Katina's hands in hers. Her smiling eyes brimmed with tears. "We have more money than we could ever spend."

Katina broke away from her mother's hold, threw herself back onto a chair and flung her arms into the air. "My God! My God! Is that the truth, Mana?"

Anna smiled again. "Well, I did spend some money for the presents for the men and for myself." She reached into her pocketbook, took the pearls out of the case and put them around her neck. "There now, aren't I as fancy as Mrs. Merit Morton Powers?" She posed in an elegant manner.

"Oh, Mana, they're beautiful." Katina said, fingering the silky pearls. "I'm so happy that for once in your life you're doing something nice for yourself."

"I will leave them to you in my will, and maybe I'll let you borrow them on special occasions, eh?"

Katina let out a yelp of joy but Anna shushed her quickly. "You must not tell anyone about the money your papa left us. Only Nikos knows, although I may tell Matt. I trust him completely. I may need his advice about what we should do with so much money. Oh, to have such a terrible problem, eh?" Then, with feigned seriousness, she asked Katina, "Do you think Ari would be upset if you went for a short visit with me to America to visit my Joe's aunt in Pasadena?"

"Visit America?" Katina's face lit up in amazement. Then in a la-de-da voice she said, "Oh, I don't think he would mind too much as long as we did not stay too long." She blushed and giggled in embarrassment.

"My God, what two incredible days we've had, child, eh? We should go to church and say a prayer of thanks for all our blessings."

They clung to each other silently for a few minutes, digesting the enormity of what had happened to them and how their lives would now change.

Although their lives would never be the same again, Anna would insist that they continue with their commitment to care for the team's needs until they leave.

* * * *

When Brant came back from the meeting with the men, he found Merit lying on the bed, looking up at the ceiling. He knew she was angry. "Are you feeling all right, dear?"

She did not look at him when she answered. "No, I'm upset, very upset."

"About last night's encounter with the ghosts?"

"The ghosts frightened me, but they didn't hurt me as much as you have lately." She sat up and looked at him intently. "Brant, something serious is happening to you, to us. You're so uptight most of the time, now, and you've been acting in such an arrogant manner. It frightens me that we'll be celebrating our fifth anniversary this Saturday, and I'm having misgivings about our marriage." She stood up abruptly and placed her hands on his arms as if trying to hold his attention. "Can we talk about it?"

"You mean because I yelled at that stupid girl for throwing those priceless coins across the table? Come on, how would you feel if you saw someone dump some of your precious jewels on a hard surface?"

"Brant, I'm not talking about coins! Those coins are not yours. She can chop them to pieces if she wants to, and there's not a damn thing you can do about it!"

"Oh, really?" He thought to himself, I could threaten her with scandal, the little slut. He looked at Merit with a sly smile.

Merit looked puzzled. "Maybe the old oracle was right," she said softly, getting up from the bed and looking intently at Brant.

Brant snapped, "Oh, and what amazing prediction did the old bat come up with this time?"

Sadness darkened Merit's face. "She said it's unlucky to marry in the month of May."

A look of amusement spread over Brant's face. "Why is May a bad month to marry?"

Merit anticipated his reaction and headed toward the door. then she stopped, looked back and said, "Because May is when donkeys breed."

His uproarious laughter jarred her as she left the house and strode across the compound to the stable. Once inside, where she could no longer hear his maddening jeer, she gave relief to her unhappiness, letting a flood of tears flow down her cheeks. Merit seldom cried, but this was different. She stood between her black thoroughbred stallion and Anna's humble dapple-gray jackass. Merit laid her head against Zeus' neck, stroked his nose and thought, I wonder if our May marriage was doomed from the beginning for lots of reasons other than the breeding habits of donkeys.

She thought back over their life so far. Were there signs I didn't see? Did I overlook them because I was so in love? But Brant has changed so much. He's not the same man I married at all. Maybe I should go home. A separation might be good for us. But I don't want a scene before the anniversary party. So many plans have been made and the villagers have been looking forward to it. Afterward though, I think I will leave. I know he won't go with me. He won't leave until he's found his damn treasure, and if he doesn't find one, God only knows what will happen to him. His obsession is making him neurotic. Maybe I'll talk this over with Matt, after our anniversary party Saturday night.

Merit heard Anna coming into the stable, humming happily. Quickly wiping her eyes, she pretended she was checking Zeus' hoof. "Hello Anna. How wonderful to see you so cheerful. I'm so glad life has turned around for you and Katina."

Anna set down her bucket of vegetable peelings for the animals and walked toward Merit. Although there was not much light in the stable, Anna could see Merit had been crying. She looked at her compassionately, "You know, Merit, one woman knows when another woman is suffering. I see it happening to you more every day. I'd like to help you, but it wouldn't be polite to interfere in your personal affairs."

Merit put Zeus' hoof down, straightened up and looked directly at Anna. "Dear Anna, you're right. I am suffering." She couldn't hold back the tears.

Anna took her in her arms.

"Oh, Anna, I see my husband turning into someone other than the man I married, and I don't know what to do about it. I'm so sorry for the unkind statement he made to you today."

Anna wiped Merit's eyes with her hanky. "I think maybe he's sick, Merit. I know when person is sick, they sometimes get cranky, especially men. They don't like to admit they're sick, eh?"

"I don't think his sickness is physical, Anna. He had a complete medical checkup before we left. I'm afraid he's becoming mentally ill. I think it's his irrational, obsessive desire to find a treasure here that's making him act so strangely."

"I wish there was something I could do to help."

Merit looked at Anna and forced a smile. "Just knowing you care helps a great deal. I think I should discuss it with Matt, though."

"I think you should, too. He's good man."

"Speaking of good men, you should start thinking seriously about finding yourself a good man now. What about Nikos? I think he's a fine person and a real gentleman."

Anna scoffed, "Good man, eh? Yes, I suppose I have to admit that, but he's woman chaser! You know that! What kind of husband would he make?"

"I think he loves all women but none seriously enough to marry. But maybe he's been waiting for you to be free all these years."

Something crashed behind them. Anna's donkey had backed out of his stall, put his foot into the pail of vegetable skins and was trying to get his foot out.

The women laughed at his antics. "Shoo, shoo!" Anna yelled, swatting him. He kicked up his hind legs, tossing the pail into the air. Anna lost her balance trying to avoid it and landed on her bottom. A shower of peelings floated down on her while she cursed the donkey in Greek.

Merit helped Anna to her feet and giggled as she picked the peelings out of Anna's hair. "Oh, how I wish I had my camera!"

"Stupid animal!" Anna shook her fist at the donkey, who stared at her. She glared back at him. "I just might get rid of you! You haven't even bred this spring. I'll buy automobile for transportation."

"That reminds me, Anna, did Katina tell you that the old oracle told her to tell me it was unlucky to marry in the month of May because, she said it's the month the donkeys breed? Is that a Greek superstition?"

Anna laughed. "I've heard that. Oracle never forgets old island superstitions. You see, Merit, before we had automobiles here, donkeys were only way to get around to get water and food. Everyone puts yearly breeding of donkeys before everything else, May is best month for donkey breeding because foal will come following spring in good weather and have plenty of greens in fields to eat. So, nothing else of importance, even weddings, takes place. If you have wedding in May, who would come? No one, because everyone stays home to watch to make sure that their donkey breeds. It would be very bad luck for bride and groom to marry without friends around, eh?"

Walking back to the house, Merit said, "Anna, I hope you forgive me for taking Katina up to the ruins last night. It was a stupid thing to do. I never believed there was any danger there. It frightened her half to death—both of us, for that matter."

Anna put her arm tightly around Merit's shoulder. "It's all over now, and it's not good to keep thinking about it, like Matt said. Besides, with all wonderful things I found in my Joe's box for Katina, I think she'll get over her fright quickly. And I think that nice young man, Ari, is helping too, eh? He wants to call her Tina and write to her when he gets back to Athens."

"That's exciting news for her, I'm sure."

"Yes, I think so too. He is kind of man I would like for my daughter."

"Anna, can I help with the cooking for the anniversary party? I won't be working in the cave tomorrow."

"Sure. I'll give you jobs to do. How is your movie of our village coming along?"

"I'm going to finish editing it today. I have some wonderful footage. I think the stars of the movie are cats! I've never seen so many cats in my life, Anna. And another star is, Kristos. Every time that child sees me with the camera, he finds some excuse to walk in front of it, waving and smiling. He's such a darling. How I would love to have a son like him," she added in a melancholy tone.

"Maybe that's what your marriage needs, if you don't mind me saying so."

"Yes, I thought so too, until recently, but now I'm not sure, Anna. Brant is not the man I married."

"Yes, you want to be sure, because I know that it's not easy to bring child up without father."

"Or to raise a child with a father who is not loving and caring."

CHAPTER ELEVEN

Since the discovery of the arch, and now, the possibility of a door below it, Nikos felt obliged to start sending daily reports to the authorities in Athens. He knew he should have their permission to proceed, but decided not to tell the others, especially, Brant. He didn't want to discourage their enthusiasm. Although the authorities encouraged him to continue the gratis exploration, they seemed to be skeptical about the team finding anything significant.

* * * *

Wednesday morning the team went back to work in the cavern of the omphalos.

They set up a makeshift platform to stand on so they could reach the eight-foot high lava-covered arch. It was slow, tedious work with the chipping hammers and chisels, but soon they began to dislodge large chunks of the half-inch thick, reddish-colored lava. The chipping caused sharp flakes to scatter in all directions. In spite of safety glasses, they found they couldn't work too closely together without the flying chips nicking each other's face. Matt suggested they wrap their scarves over their faces for protection. After three hours, they had managed to clear only about a foot below the keystone of the arch, but they now exposed a horizontal slab of limestone that lay over four separate vertical slabs, fitted so precisely, it was difficult to see where the seams met. It now was obvious that the vertical piers of the arch continued downward on both sides. The space between the two piers of the arch measured about four feet.

Their hands grew stiff from the labor. Matt suggested a coffee break so he could inspect the cuts on their faces and treat them with an antibiotic ointment.

Wade stood back and looked up at the area where they had been working. "I'm encouraged!" he exclaimed. Now if we can pry open those vertical slabs…"

Brant, massaging his sore fingers, groaned, "This job would be much easier with power tools."

"Ah! Maybe I know where I can get some battery-powered drills," Nikos said.

"Well for God's sake, why didn't you speak up sooner!" Brant snapped at him.

Matt threw Brant a dirty look. "Why didn't you think of it sooner, Brant? Power tools would be great, Nikos. It might save my career. Look at my poor surgeon's hands. They're battered, bruised and stiff. I couldn't take out a splinter right now if I had to."

"Could you get the drills today, Nikos?" Wade asked.

"I'll try. I'm almost positive that Elias has some power tools in his workshop."

Wade looked at his watch. "I'll tell you what we'll do if it's okay with you, Nikos. Matt and Brant will stay here and explore the outer perimeter of the cavern, and I'll go with you to see what tools Elias has that we can use."

Nikos was reluctant to leave Brant and Matt in the cave alone; it was against the rules, but he trusted Matt, at least.

After the two men left, Matt began to walk slowly around the cavern, inspecting the walls. Brant chose to continue to chip away at the lava.

Suddenly Matt called out to him from across the cavern, his voice vibrated off the walls. "Hey Brant, there's weird writing carved on the wall here. You can just barely see it. It looks like hieroglyphs!"

Brant tossed off his safety glasses and walked carefully through the stalagmites to where Matt was standing. He focused his headlamp on the ancient script. "Nice find, Matt! But it's not hieroglyphs, they're pictorial. This looks like syllabic writing, like Linear-type script. Linear script!" In an excited voice he said, "Matt, guess who used Linear script? MINOANS! This is fantastic. Jesus, nice going, Matt!"

"Ya-hoo!" Matt yelled, and his echo blared throughout the cavern.

"Let's see if we can find more." Brant urged excitedly.

The two men scanned the walls closely with the large portable lamp. They found many crudely carved recesses that held clay oil lamps, heavily concealed by eons of accumulated dust.

"They must have used these to light the cavern when religious services were held," Brant said.

"Boy, what a sight that must have been, with the oil lamps flickering on the walls." Matt shivered. "I can picture them sitting on those stone seats."."

"Here come Nikos and Wade, Brant. I see their light."

When Matt and Brant showed them the ancient writing on the wall, Nikos was elated. "This looks like Linear B. This could be more proof that Minoans used cavern!"

"I really don't think we need any more proof!" Brant said emphatically.

"And more good news," Wade said. "We have some great battery-powered tools."

They went to work, and within an hour they drilled off another foot of the lava with comparative ease. They stopped for lunch and shared a bottle of retsina that Nikos brought back. It was a gift from Elias. By now the men had developed a taste for the strange-tasting wine and enjoyed the treat.

By four o'clock, they had removed another two feet of lava and began to expose an ancient carving on the limestone slabs. Brant and Nikos recognized it immediately. It was the double axe, sacred emblem of Minoans.

"My God, more proof!" Brant exclaimed jubilantly.

Nikos explained, "Double axe played very important role in Minoan religion!"

"Maybe we're about to uncover an entrance to a temple or something." Matt said.

"And, they sealed it with these limestone slabs to protect treasures that they couldn't take with them when the volcano erupted." Brant added.

"Could it be hollow inside omphalos, Wade?" Nikos asked.

"I doubt it," Wade said. "It would have crumbled eons ago."

Nikos put his arm over Matt's shoulder. "My friend, this is what archaeology is all about. You are now having thrill of discovery that archaeologists hope for all their lives, and I have very big feeling in here," he said as he punched his fist against his stomach. "We are going to become very famous team, eh?"

"I agree, Nikos, but I think we'd better quit for today because if we don't give our hands a rest, we'll be useless tomorrow. Am I right, Boss?" Matt looked to Wade for support.

"Definitely."

"God, I hate to stop," Brant groaned, joining the others as they began to pack up the supplies.

The men were filled with anticipation as they left the cave and made their way back to the office where they locked up their gear, then drove back to the village.

* * * *

When the men arrived at the compound, music was coming from the dining area. Merit, Katina and Anna, along with another woman and some of Katina's girlfriends, were dancing, holding each other's hands with crossed arms. The women wore brightly decorated, native costumes. Their heads swayed from side to side while their feet performed intricate steps. Dancing past the doorway, they spotted the approaching men and stopped immediately.

The men applauded.

Merit went forward to greet them. "Now you've ruined our surprise! We didn't expect you back so soon. Say hello to Irene Gavalas. This wonderful lady has come from Fira to teach us this old folk dance called the Salamis Dance. We're going to perform it Saturday night at our party."

The men greeted the teacher.

Anna said with pride, "Irene danced with famous Dora Stratou Company all around the world.".

"That was long time ago," the woman laughed.

"You all look beautiful in your costumes. This will be great treat for everyone," Nikos said with a broad smile.

Matt, with an impish grin on his face, asked, "You mean," then he paused dramatically, "I'm not going to be the big dance attraction at the party?"

Irene Gavalas picked up on his joke. "You would like to join us, eh? Come on!" She gestured for Matt to take her hand, and all the girls reached out for him.

He fended them off. "Oh, I'm so sorry, but as you can see, my poor old hands are very sore from today's work. And I don't know that particular folk dance anyway."

Irene looked at him mischievously. "It's dance just for women, but maybe when your hands are better, you'd like to come to my studio in Fira, and I give you private lesson."

Matt kept the joke going. "Well, thank you very much, but actually, I'm also a professional dancer, and I really don't need any lessons."

Everyone laughed and Matt looked at them indignantly.

"Good!" Irene Gavalas said with a smile. "I will look forward to your performance Saturday night."

"Oh, oh," Matt said, burying his face in his hands. "Now I'm in trouble." He saluted them and did a "shuffle off to Buffalo" step out the door amid peals of laughter.

"Now gentlemen," Irene Gavalas said, smiling. "I will call end to rehearsals today, and you men can have your house back. It was pleasure meeting you, and I'll look forward to seeing all of you on Saturday evening, especially Fred Astaire." She grinned, gesturing with her thumb toward the door.

After she left, Brant quickly changed the subject. "Merit, you'll have to come with us tomorrow to take photos because we made some very exciting finds today. We've found ancient writing that I'm sure is Minoan because it's syllabic like other Minoan writing I've seen. and, there is a double axe carved on the limestone slabs under the arch, which proves that the cavern was used by Minoans!"

"Oh, how exciting!"

"Now I'm positive we'll find our treasure!"

Merit looked to Wade for confirmation of Brant's claims.

"Well, we don't know for certain what's there yet."

Turning back to her husband, Merit said with a sly smile, "And, Brant, it won't be OUR treasure. It'll be Greece's treasure."

He looked at her dourly. "Well, you knew what I meant!"

The others felt uncomfortable with the obvious tension between the couple.

"Are you coming back to the house, Merit?" Brant asked curtly.

"Ah, no. I have to pick some more wild flowers for decorations and do more work on my movie." She obviously didn't want to be with him at that moment.

During dinner that evening, a series of small tremors occurred and everyone stopped eating and went outside until the vibrations ended.

"Aren't these tremors happening a little too often, Nikos?" Brant asked in concern.

Nikos smiled, trying to reassure them. "You get used to it when you live here long enough. Our island is not sitting on most stable parts of world. What's under our island has to stretch every now and then. You know, like your stiff hands. You have to move them for relief, eh?"

Everyone tried to share his optimism.

* * * *

On Thursday morning the team resumed work while Merit took photos and movies of their recent discoveries.

By noon, they were within a foot of the bottom of what they were sure had once been an entrance into the omphalos. They chipped furiously at the final foot, stopping only when the last of the lava was removed at ground level. They took off their scarves, goggles and gloves and sat down on the stone seats and kneaded their stiff hands. After a short breather, they began to examine what they hoped was a limestone entrance into the omphalos. It was over eight feet tall. The keystone of the horseshoe-shaped arch was a foot above the horizontal slab below it. The left and right piers of the arch continued downward along both sides of the four vertical slabs, all the way to the ground. The vertical slabs, lateral to the piers, were eight feet long and one foot wide. Now that the lava had been completely removed, they faced the herculean task of trying to gain entrance to the omphalos. The outer edges of the slabs had been chiseled and aligned so perfectly, it made it difficult to see where the seams met.

Wade took out a credit card and tried to slip it between one of the seams. "These slabs have been put together as tight as the blocks of stone on the pyramids at Giza. It's perfect alignment. We sure have our work cut out for us. Let's stop and take our lunch break," Wade suggested.

THE SANTORINI ODYSSEY

They were all keyed up, both from hard labor and anticipation. They consumed Anna's lunch with gusto.

"Well, we've finished the easy part," Wade said, standing up and contemplating the limestone barrier.

"What's next, boss?" Matt asked.

"How to remove the two middle slabs." Wade answered.

Brant leaned forward and twirled his index finger through his scraggly beard. "What we need is a 'come along,' you know, a ratchet, but I'm sure we'll never find one of those on this island. What about a good old fashioned block and tackle? Surely they must use those here."

Nikos answered quickly, "We used block and tackle when we put up our windmill. It's big four-wheeler, too. My father used it to hoist wheel for sails up to top of our mill house."

"Well, let's go get it," Brant shouted eagerly.

"Hold it. Hold it," Wade said. "There's a lot more chiseling to do before we need the block and tackle."

Matt glared at Wade, an agonized look covering his face. "No, No," He put up his right hand as if taking an oath. "I swore to God that I would never again chisel anything, or anyone. Please, please boss, have mercy on my poor surgeon's hands. Do you want me to be out of a job?"

"Don't panic, pal. We'll let you off easy. We're probably going to need supplies to use with the block and tackle, so we'll send you to town while we slave away here, okay?"

"Oh, thank you, kind boss, thank you, thank you." Then he looked at the others with a weak smile. "And thank you, too, fellow chiselers. You'll never regret this. I will do any future surgical operations you may need for free."

They all laughed except Brant, who ignored Matt's antics and pressed Wade. "What's your plan?"

"I think we should try to chisel out about one-inch where the seams on the bottoms and tops of the two middle vertical slabs meet. By leaving the two end vertical slabs in place, we still leave enough support for the horizontal beam. We'll also have to loosen the two center slabs by chiseling between them and the outer slabs. I'm almost positive the slabs on the entrance are the same thickness as those on these seats. I'd say about six inches thick."

"Brant said. "We'll also have to chip out the lava around the bottom and under the two middle slabs. That ought to loosen them enough so we can pull them forward with the block and tackle."

"And when the entrance is opened, what do you think we'll find, Nikos?" Matt asked in a sinister tone.

Nikos spread his hands out as if displaying something large and said dramatically, "We'll see 3,500-year-old secret Minoan chamber materialize before our eyes, eh?"

Suddenly they heard rocks falling near the incline that led down into the cavern. Everyone froze.

"What's happening?" Merit asked in a frightened voice.

"It's not earthquake, I'm sure," Nikos said. "Something at top of incline must have made rocks fall. Could be rats again."

They still saw rats and bats every once in a while but not in droves.

"Oh, God, No! I don't want to be trapped down here with rats." Merit shivered.

The men moved slowly toward the incline. They had secured two ropes at the top so it would be easy to pull themselves back up. They flashed their two big lamps directly at the incline, and standing at the top, was Kristos, his face hidden in his hands.

"Oh, thank God, it's only Kristos," Merit said.

"What are you doing here, Kristos?" Nikos yelled in an angry voice. "You know you are forbidden to ever come into cave."

"Where in the hell is Mrs. Powers' horse that you are supposed to be watching?" Brant was unnecessarily provoked.

Kristos, terrified at being caught, could hardly talk. In a whisper, he said, "I have him safely stalled in my *papa's* barn. Since few days ago he will not ride with me in ruins. I told you that, Mrs. Powers."

"Yes, you did, Kristos," Merit answered and scowled at Brant. The day after the ghost happening, Zeus would not go any farther than the Kaldaras' house. She had told Kristos not to try to take him through the ruins anymore.

Wade called up to him. "Have you ever come into the cave before, Kristos? Could you hear us talking just now?"

The boy hung his head and sobbed, "Yes, I came before, and I heard what you said today about finding 3,500-year-old Minoan treasure. This was my cave! I'm one who found it!" he cried out in a resentful voice. Then he slumped down in a heap, burying his head in his hands and sobbed.

Nikos and Merit both made their way up the ropes to him. Merit took him in her arms, and Nikos quieted him with soothing Greek words.

Nikos called down to Wade. "He has promised me faithfully that, even though he has known what we have been finding, he never told anyone, not even his *papa* or *mana*. I believe him."

"Why would you believe a kid who sneaks around spying on us?" Brant asked sarcastically.

Wade gave Brant an annoyed look. "Lay off the kid, Brant." Then he pulled himself up to the top of the incline. "Nikos, why don't you take Kristos out of the cave and get the block and tackle from your house. Matt,

I'll give you a list of the hardware I think we'll need from Fira. And check to see if the block and tackle needs new rope."

"Okay, Wade," Nikos responded. "And I'll be back as quickly as possible."

Wade wrote down the type of lead anchors, eye bolts, screws and other items he thought they might need. Then, smiling slyly at Matt he asked, "Do you think you can drive Nikos' truck down that steep mountain road and find your way into Fira?"

Matt threw him a look of disdain. "A piece of cake! I'll just close my eyes, like I always do every time I come to those hairpin curves. I'd walk to Fira just to get out of chipping, old buddy."

Merit asked, "If you don't need me here any more, Wade, I'll go into town with Matt, I need to get a few more things for the party." She saw the trip to town as a golden opportunity to discuss Brant's behavior with Matt.

"That's fine with me, Merit. We'll just be chipping. I don't see any reason for you to stay."

Walking back to the office, Nikos peered down at Kristos with a fake mean look. Shaking his finger at the boy, he said, "I want a promise from you that you will never go into the cave again unless we are with you."

Kristos looking chagrined, blessed himself and said, "I promise the Blessed Virgin and you, too, Nikos, Mrs. Powers and Dr. Matt, I'll never go into cave again without you!"

Nikos made a fist and shook it at him. "You better not!"

Matt tousled Kristos' hair. "I think you're a real brave kid to go into that cave alone. I'd never have the courage to do that!"

Kristos looked up at Matt in amazement. "A man would be afraid to go into cave?"

"This man would," Matt said, shaking his head, a look of fear covering his face.

When they reached the office, Matt and Merit took off their dusty suits and put away their equipment. Then they all went to Kaldaras' house. Matt and Nikos drove down the hill in the truck. Merit and Kristos went into the Kaldaras' barn and Merit mounted Zeus.

"Kristos, please don't go back in the cave alone again. My heart would break if anything ever happened to you." She smiled down at him and rode away.

He kept waving to her as she rode down the steep hill until she was out of sight.

Back at the compound, Merit stabled her horse, then went to her house and changed into a sleeveless cotton dress. It was a hot day and there was no air conditioning in the truck.

Matt and Nikos took the block and tackle back up to the office and unloaded it.

Matt drove back down to the village and picked up Merit. He then began the slow descent down the serpentine mountain road. He admitted to Merit that he was nervous. The trip could be extremely perilous if the driver did not give his full attention to the continuous curves that twisted all the way down the thousand or more feet. There were no guard rails and the road was not well paved. For that reason, Merit and Matt said very little to each other. When they reached the bottom of the mountain and began to drive along the main highway to Fira, they finally relaxed.

"Matt, I asked to come with you because I have to talk to you about Brant. I'm very frightened that something is wrong with him. I'm so distressed by the rude way he has treated everyone here, including me."

Matt looked over at Merit. "He's on a dangerous course, Merit. We're all worried about him. I'm glad you want to talk to me about it. As a physician, I've felt guilty about not taking Brant aside to discuss it with him, but I know he'd be furious if I told him he was heading toward a serious problem. If we were back home, I'd risk our friendship by telling him he'd better get help quickly."

Merit wasn't surprised by Matt's words. Actually, they just confirmed her own suspicions about Brant's condition, and it frightened her.

"You've got a tough road ahead of you, Merit. Believe me. I'm an expert on compulsive behavior. I don't know if you're aware of it, but my wife is a chronic alcoholic. At this moment, she's dying of alcoholic cirrhosis of the liver."

Merit looked sympathetically at Matt. "I had heard rumors at the club, Matt."

"She's been mentally ill for years with an alcohol addiction I couldn't cure. God knows, I tried. Brant also has an addiction problem, Merit. It's his obsession with finding a treasure. I'm not a psychiatrist, but I think I can tell you what's happening to him and what has to be done to help him."

"Oh, Matt I'd appreciate any advice you can give me. I'm seriously considering going home right after the anniversary party Saturday night, but I'd feel guilty about leaving him here for you and the others to contend with."

"Did you ever see any signs of this behavior before you married him?"

"Obsessiveness? Yes. But I couldn't very well condemn him for that. We both come from well-to-do families who have the money that allowed us to become obsessive collectors as you well know."

"When I first met Brant, he had just taken over the family's business conglomerate after his father's death. He resented the burden, but he was the only son and heir. His dream to spend the rest of his life as an archaeologist was over and that clearly bothered him."

"I can understand that," Matt said.

"Occasionally, in the first few years of our marriage, I noticed an attitude of arrogance from time to time. I thought he was probably just trying to show off, acting like a big shot, now that he was such an important international entrepreneur. It was such a new role for him. But I loved him very much and would forgive almost anything he did. He was a wonderful husband; considerate, caring, thoughtful and he treated me with such warmth and love."

"In the last couple of years though, I noticed some changes in his personality. I thought maybe this trip might bring him back to be the man I married. Quite the contrary has happened, as you well know."

"Yes. His obsession with finding a treasure, which by the way, I truly feel he's beginning to think is his. It's getting worse by the day. That shows you how serious his problem is becoming. Frankly, Merit, I dread opening the door to the omphalos. If we find a treasure, he could go off the deep end when the Athens crew takes it away. And, if we don't find one, the same thing might happen."

"Oh, Matt, what should I do?"

"I'm not sure, Merit. A mental disorder of the thought processes like this is usually due to unresolved internal conflicts. Those make living a normal life difficult. I think we both know what his conflict is: he wants to be an archaeologist, but he's been forced to be a business tycoon. He maintains his contact with reality, unlike people with a psychosis. His uncontrollable obsession with finding a treasure that he wants desperately is dominating his behavior. What can be done? I'm sure he should have psychotherapy and soon, Merit."

"What's the prognosis if he does get help?"

"I have to be honest. Generally, Merit, it's much more difficult to cure a neurotic disorder than an organic one. I can show my surgical patients a cancerous growth on an X-ray or CAT scan, and I usually have no problem convincing them it must be removed. But problems of the mind, not connected to an organic disease, cannot be seen by the patient. It's a very difficult road back to recovery. Brant is an intelligent individual. I suspect he's aware of his personality change but probably makes excuses for himself, the pressures of his job, and now the anticipation of finding his treasure. I wish I had an easy answer for you, but I don't."

They pulled up in the center of town, and Matt shut off the motor. "I could offer him tranquilizers, if he would accept them, but that's just a Band-Aid, Merit."

Matt looked at her beautiful face, now stricken with worry. "Come on, kiddo, I'll buy you a nice cold beer in the shade. It's hot here!"

After being refreshed by the cold beer and the air conditioning in the small taverna, they began to look for the hardware store tucked away on a narrow alley at the bottom of a hill. Matt was fascinated with the items on display. The proprietor was very helpful, for Matt knew nothing about how the items he was buying were going to be used.

"I tell you what I think you should do. You buy three, maybe four different sizes of anchors and bolts. When you get back to work, see which one your boss thinks works best, eh? You bring back what you don't use, and I give you back your drachma. Okay?"

"Okay!" Matt smiled and shook the man's hand, and they selected a large assortment.

Leaving the store, the proprietor tipped his cap to Merit and grinned broadly. He followed them out onto the street and waved.

CHAPTER TWELVE

By seven o'clock on Friday morning, the team had already eaten breakfast and was eager to get up to the cave. Filled with anticipation, they gathered up the equipment. Merit slung her video on her back and said to Matt, "I'm so excited, I've got butterflies in my stomach."

"Take two Alka Seltzer and call me in the morning if you don't burp them up," he quipped.

Wade picked up his pack and addressed the group. "We're at the ten-yard line, team, and I have a gut feeling that we're really going to score!"

Brant, especially euphoric this morning, joked. "All that's left to be done this morning is pound those anchor and ring bolts into the slabs and also into that wall. Then, hook up the block and tackle and…TOUCHDOWN!"

The day before, Wade, Brant and Nikos had finished chiseling the tops and bottoms of the tightly wedged slabs and had chipped away the residual lava around the bottom. By the time Matt and Merit had returned from Fira, the men were already back at the compound soaking their swollen hands in ice water and sipping beers.

Anna handed Matt the large thermos of coffee. She had been serving breakfast alone for the past few days, allowing Katina to sleep in. Ever since the night Brant tried to seduce her, Katina avoided being in the same room with him as often as possible. Anna had no doubt that the nightmares that continued to plague Katina were caused by her terrifying experience with the ghosts in the ancient city.

When the team was leaving the compound, Katina stood at her window and watched them leave, all except Brant; she could not look at him without feeling sick.

Anna waved goodbye, wished them luck and reminded them, "Don't forget you promised to let Katina and me see cavern of omphalos before authorities come. We'll say special prayers for you this morning."

Kristos, who had been waiting, beamed as he led Zeus to Merit. She hugged the boy and whispered in his ear. "Promise me, you won't go into the cave, Kristos."

He whispered back, "I promise I won't." Then impulsively, he kissed her cheek and blushed.

Merit smiled at him. The sweet kiss pleased her. She thought, that must be the wonderful feeling a mother gets from her child's kiss. Looking down at Kristos, she asked, "Aren't you going to ride up with me today?"

He was so embarrassed about the kiss, he forgot that he always rode up with her and returned with Zeus once they reached the site. He loved riding with her up to the ruins every day. He'd hold her waist tightly and inhale the sweet smell of her hair as it brushed against his nose.

Riding through the village, Merit said, "Everyone seems to be in high spirits today, Kristos."

He told her, "Everyone is excited about your big party tomorrow night, Mrs. Powers. We've never had such big party!"

On the truck ride up to the ruins, each member of the team had private thoughts about how the discovery of a great archaeological find might affect them.

Nikos, the romantic, saw himself being honored by his peers, maybe even given a medal by his government. It would certainly give him status in the realm of Greek archaeology and bring honor to his island.

Wade, always the scientist, was ambivalent about what excited him the most. Was it because what they found could bring greater historical understanding of events in the pre-eruption period? It wasn't one of the more exciting explorations of his career as a speleologist. Actually it was dull in comparison to the deep caves he had explored. He'd gained new geological information, hunted down poisonous snakes, but most of all, it was the island itself that captivated him. He'd miss it immensely.

Brant's every thought for the past couple of days had been about ancient, golden finds from the Lost City of Atlantis. He'd envision how Heinrich Schlemein must have felt when he finally uncovered ancient Troy. He visualized himself as Howard Carter, peering through a crack at the golden treasures in the tomb of Tutankhamen. He had completely blocked out any possibility that there may not be a treasure. But the most prominent thought crowding his mind concerned the ingenious plan he had devised to pilfer the artifacts that delighted him most. He would make the theft appear as if it had been done by a robber who had somehow learned of their discovery. He had already decided where he would hide the loot-inside Nikos' windmill until he could get it off the island. He had gone inside the small thatched building and found several old dusty barrels half-filled with rotting grain. If it was discovered there, who would get the blame? That jackass, Nikos, of course. He was pleased with his plan. When any small sense of guilt crept into his mind, he rationalized that the treasure never would have been discovered if he hadn't financed the exploration. Greece certainly owed him a great deal!

Most of Merit's thoughts were concerned about Brant's reaction if they did or did not discover a treasure. Either way, she feared Brant would be seriously affected. For the past week, at night in bed, he talked incessantly about the possibility of the Greek government certainly awarding them some of the antiquities.

She could not convince him that was not a possibility. Greece no longer had any interest in sharing its treasures with foreigners. Too much had been stolen in the past.

Matt had called Lee last night and shared his excitement with her. His prospect of finding a treasure was quite different from the others. He visualized how he'd describe the expedition later to a captive audience. He'd hold a pre-surgical orientation for the doctors and nurses and intentionally get on the subject of his archaeological trip and the daily dangers he faced; rats, bats, snakes, spiders, tremors and ghosts. And like a true Irishman, he'd embellish the story with exaggerations because of the religious duty of Irishmen; never tell a story like it happened, but make it better! He'd time his tale, so they'd be called into surgery just as he had them spellbound, and was about to reveal what they found inside the omphalos. They'd be so tantalized to know what was discovered that their eyes would be bugging out at him above their surgical masks as they operated.

He missed Lee so much and had telephoned her more often than they had planned. It would be some telephone bill!

* * * *

When the team reached the cavern floor, they went to work immediately. Merit set her video camera on a tripod in a position where she could capture the installation of the block and tackle and, hopefully, the opening of the entrance into the omphalos.

The men drilled holes in the center of the two middle slabs of the doorway for the lead anchors. They repeated the same procedure on the floor of the cavern directly across from the slabs. Then they threaded large steel ring screws into the lead anchors. The rope on the block and tackle, which had been put into position the previous day, was rigged and stretched out on the ground. They fastened the rope to the ring bolts now securely fastened in place.

"The moment of truth is near," Wade said. "But, before we go any further, both Nikos and I want to discuss a few things with everyone."

"Oh, for God's sake, Wade," Brant growled. "What are you trying to do, torment us?"

"No, Brant. What I have to say deals with the safety of the team. What Nikos has to say deals with the professional discipline we all must use if there are ancient antiquities inside. As an archaeologist, I'm sure you know we just can't storm in there. We have protocols to follow."

In a childish reaction, Brant folded his arms across his chest and looked up at the ceiling, bored.

This so irritated Wade he was tempted to tell Brant to leave if he didn't want to play by the rules.

Matt did it for him. He walked over to Brant and looked up at him defiantly. "Hey Brant, COOL IT!" The two men matched angry glares. Matt's face looked fierce. He had never reacted this way before, and it stunned everyone, including Brant.

Brant let out a strong puff of breath. He turned quickly to Wade, "Okay, okay, okay. Let's hear it."

"We can assume that the inside of the omphalos has been tightly sealed by the limestone slabs and lava for thousands of years," Wade began. In all probability since the devastating volcanic eruption in 1600 B.C. there doesn't seem to be any visible signs of openings anywhere on the omphalos. For that reason, we have to assume that once we pull those two slabs away, we could be overcome by foul gases that have accumulated inside through the centuries. We'll want to use our gas masks today. Let's put them on when the slabs are almost loose and keep them on until I do a chemical analysis test. When I'm sure that there are no signs of toxic or combustible gases, we'll remove the slabs. But, if the air is unsafe, we'll leave the cave until the level of toxicity has evaporated. Here's a pleasant thought for you, Merit. If it's sealed up as tightly as I presume it is, we won't encounter any critters."

"Yeah!" Merit cheered. "That's great news!"

"Once it's safe to enter, Nikos and I will go in first and take a quick look around to make sure a trap wasn't set for intruders. I realize we're all filled with great anticipation, but we must also prepare ourselves for disappointment. There may not be an inside. It might only be a recess for a statue or a room of rubble."

They heard Brant's groan.

"Okay, Nikos, your turn," Wade said.

Nikos took his lecture pose. "Here are important rules we must follow. Number one, everything will be left in situ until I say to move it. Number two, you all know that I must bring all important finds to attention of director of antiquities in Athens immediately. Maybe they'll tell me to close off cave and put security around it until they arrive."

Merit interrupted, "But Nikos, does that mean that I won't have time to do sketches and take measurements like I've been doing? That takes a great deal of time."

"No, of course not, Merit," Nikos said hesitantly. He still had not told the team that he was in daily contact with Athens. "I'll try to give you time to do your work. It's important that you do that." Nikos put his fingers to his forehead as if thinking deeply. "I will have to see about that. Let me make that decision when we see what is inside." But as he said that, he thought about how strongly he had been warned by the authorities in Athens. "Remember you are *thesaurophylax* of treasures and must immediately report important finds. You are accountable for their security. And, it is your responsibility to make sure that anything you find is not damaged or stolen."

"Ah, I just thought of something else," Nikos said. "If we make important discovery, it must be kept secret. It will be up to Athens to make announcement to press. They'll want to keep public away until all treasures are removed from cavern. I'm sure they'll close down Ancient Thera to public for long time, maybe."

"Nikos, Merit and I would be grateful if you don't make your report until Monday. We're going to be so busy all day tomorrow with our anniversary party. We should probably go home early today."

"Ah! Of course. How could I forget that! I'll think about it." He didn't want to commit himself in the event they found something spectacular.

Wade also hoped Nikos would wait until Monday and told Nikos, "I'd hate to have to rush through the investigation if there are many important things in there. We have to make a complete inventory of what we find for the authorities. That's something that must be done carefully and accurately. I'm sure you agree, Nikos?"

"Ah, yes, the inventory. That is most important. Wade and I will make plan so if there are many articles in there, we must record them in orderly way." Again, he did not commit himself to Wade's request to wait until Monday.

"The initial inventory is always very important," Wade said. "I'm reminded of what happened when Carter and Lord Carnarvon were about to open the sealed door to King Tut's tomb. Of course, they had already peeked and had leaked some of what they saw to the press. That was a big mistake. People and companies from all over the world came and wanted samples of the seeds, food and cloth. The city of Luxor was overwhelmed with journalists and the curious. They even got offers from movie companies. And there were insinuations that some of the treasures had been stolen before the authorities arrived. Actually, the outer tomb had been plundered many times over the centuries before they discovered the inner tomb of treasures."

"Can we get to work?" Brant asked curtly.

"Yes, of course," Nikos said.

Brant said emphatically. "Then let's get going." He rubbed his hands together rapidly and kept shifting his feet.

They went to work, stretching the end of the rope on the block and tackle until it was taut, then took up their positions along the rope. "One, two, three, PULL!" Nikos called out.

Merit zoomed her video camera in on each of the men's faces, capturing the various grimaces as they exerted raw strength to loosen the ancient slabs from their wedged hold.

Then they felt just the slightest bit of movement on their first try. "IT MOVED!" Wade yelled.

"Again!" Nikos yelled, "One, two, three!"

This time they all felt the slabs move more easily and cheered. "We've moved them half an inch!" Wade reported jubilantly.

It was the kind of encouragement they needed to increase their adrenaline and to pull harder. "Pretend you're Heracles, men!" Matt urged.

They grunted and groaned and pulled with great might until the slabs came forward about two inches. Merit was so excited, she jumped up and down, urging them on and frantically photographing their every move.

"Hold it, men," Wade ordered. "I think it's time to put on the gas masks. You too, Merit. And, I think it'll help if we dig out a little more lava in front of the slabs."

With their small pickaxes and shovels, they cleared a foot-long, inch-deep trench in front of the slabs.

"That's enough." Wade held up his hands to stop them.

The men went back to their positions on the rope line, and Nikos called out the pulling orders. They could feel the slabs had loosened and were almost three quarters of the way out. Wade called another halt.

"Okay, team, listen up. When we get to the point where we have only an inch or so to go, we must be careful. Remember, once we move the slabs from beneath that horizontal beam that's keeping them from coming forward, they'll fall right at us. And when they hit the floor, thick dust and chips will fly."

A few minutes later, Wade stopped them again. "We've reached the point where the slabs and the horizontal beam are about to separate. Move back."

The men dropped the rope, moved, and gathered in a circle as they watched Wade place the toxic fumes indicator on the ground next to the opening.

He stared intently at the needle but saw no signs of irregular fluctuations on the dial. He gave them an "okay" signal with his thumb and index finger and waved them closer to him.

"This is it, team, we're going for the touchdown. I want everyone to keep alert. Resist the temptation to rush forward once the slabs have fallen." He thought only Brant might be that aggressive. "I'll want to test again, so wait until I give you the signal to move. Nikos and I will look first with the lamps to see what's there. I'll indicate when you should follow." He raised his arms up for a high five, which they all passed to each other. Their hearts were beating rapidly in response to both the physical exertion and their expectations.

Merit hugged each of the men.

They went back to their positions on the line. Nikos gave the order, "Now! One, two, three!"

With their first tug, the two slabs came loose, fell forward, crashed to the cavern floor with a roar that sent ear-piercing echoes bouncing off the walls. Chips flew in all directions and clouds of dust filled the cavern. When the air cleared, Wade and Nikos went forward with the lamps, and the others waited in breathless anticipation. Brant fought to get control of himself. The gas mask was making him claustrophobic.

Wade shone his light into the dark narrow opening and placed the meter just inside. The needle remained steady. His heart pounded in excitement when he saw that the opening led to a chamber. He turned to the team, took off his mask and gestured for them to do the same. He beamed as he beckoned them forward and announced joyously, "Incredible news, team! There are no toxic fumes and, it's not a recess, it's a CHAMBER!"

They were all jumping around for joy, hugging and congratulating themselves when all of a sudden, the floor began to shake. They heard chunks of limestone crashing on the floor of the cavern.

"SHIT!" Brant yelled.

"We better get out of here quickly," Nikos warned as he led them across the cavern floor. It probably is just another tremor."

But as they were pulling themselves up on the ropes, another jolt threw Wade and Brant back down to the ground. Wade yelled to the others, "Keep going, we're okay."

Matt and Nikos held Merit's hands as they ran.

They all made it safely outside, and no one was hurt.

Brant went into a childish tantrum. He squeezed his fists and shook them violently, "GOD DAMNIT, We were there! All we had to do was to walk through the opening. Are we cursed? How many more earthquakes are we going to have, Dr. "know it all" Konstantinou. Why don't you level with us about your earthquakes? Maybe you'd be happy if we all got killed!"

"Brant!," Merit looked at him in anger.

"Brant," Wade said in a calmer voice "That's enough. Don't blame Nikos. You know this island is prone to earthquakes." He looked at his watch. "It's been almost a minute since the first tremor. Let's wait a few more minutes, and if it doesn't start again, maybe we can go back in. What do you think, Nikos?"

"I think it will be okay, too, Wade. It was just a couple of tremors.

A few minutes later, they slowly made their way back into the cave and down into the cavern.

"Nikos and I will take a quick check of the interior to be sure it's safe to walk in."

When Wade and Nikos edged their way through the doorway, they smelled a moldy odor, not unpleasant, but quite different from the earthy smell that permeated the cave. The illumination from their lamps revealed a small room crowded with a large number of objects.

Nikos, astonished by the sight, gasped loudly and squeezed Wade's shoulder.

"Oh, my God! Wade uttered as they backed out and turned to the others, waiting in frozen expectation.

Wade's face broke into an enormous grin, threw his arms up over his head and yelled "YES!"

Tears welled in Nikos' eyes, and he shrieked, "It's most incredible sight you'll ever see!"

Brant, unable to stop himself, rushed forward, pushing past Wade and Nikos.

Wade grabbed him and yelled abruptly, "STOP! Brant! Wait a minute. We're going to enter slowly. The room is filled with ancient artifacts. We must step very carefully." The expression on Brant's face worried Wade.

"Get your cameras ready, Merit. Okay everyone, let's go in slowly. There is not a lot of room to move around."

Nikos and Wade held the big lamps in position as they edged through the narrow opening and were followed closely by the others. The team's anticipation had reached such a peak that only their heavy breathing could be heard in the rapt silence. The brilliant lamps penetrated the darkness, but it took a few moments for their eyes to adjust to the sudden illumination of such a small area. When the interior came into focus, hushed cries of amazement filled the air. The scene before them was startling. The small square room's walls and ceiling were plastered in a light tone. The floor was littered with objects and the walls had paintings. They were dumbfounded and consumed with thrilling sensations when the realization hit them that they were standing in a sanctuary that had been sealed for possibly thousands of years. The brightness of the room was a stunning sight, because it was in such direct contrast to the dark and rough scenery of the cave. Their eyes flashed in every direction, as they tried to take in what lay before them. There was so much to see! Many objects were recognizable; others were mysterious.

Nodding his head up and down, Wade spoke reverently, "Oh, dear God, look at what we've discovered!"

Nikos blessed himself and uttered, *"panagnia mou!"* Tears ran down his cheeks.

A mesmerized Brant stood stark still behind Merit. He gasped between sobs, "My dream has come true, Merit. More so than I ever hoped for. This is the greatest moment of my life!"

Merit put her arm around his waist and said soothingly, "Yes, it's incredible, Brant. I'm so happy for you."

Matt, at a loss for words, had a large lump in his throat and couldn't speak but thought, now I've really got a story to tell.

"Look at the walls!" Nikos said as he pointed. "These wall paintings are much like those found at kalliste ruins, eh?"

Although badly faded, houses and people were discernible.

Matt commented., "Our discovery will solve many puzzles about what life was like in 1600 B.C. It's like ancient Kallisteans and Minoans have come back to life!"

Brant moved forward as if in a daze. Merit stayed by his side. He stopped and looked up at a deep niche in the wall. Putting both hands over his mouth, he murmured, "Oh, Christ, look up here, Merit. A beautiful golden statue of a female deity. I can't believe what I'm seeing." He stared at the foot-high figure in ecstatic admiration, making strange, almost animal-like sounds.

A quick glance passed between Merit and Matt, who put his arm around Brant's visibly shaking shoulders. He said calmly, "Hey Brant, pull yourself together."

Brant looked at Matt with anger. "There is nothing wrong with me getting excited. You couldn't possibly appreciate this! What do you know about archaeology? This is an incredible find! A find that will make news all over the world! This is a dream come true!" He moved in closer to the beautifully carved statue and again began staring up at it in adoration, unashamedly wiping away tears that streamed down his face. He reached for the statue.

Wade, aware that Brant was precariously close to hysteria, said softly, "Please don't take it down yet, Brant. We have to organize a plan to inventory all these priceless objects. Okay?"

Brant paused, pulled at his scraggly beard and said reluctantly, "Okay."

Merit was now both embarrassed and frightened by his bizarre behavior. Wanting to exclude Brant's actions from the video, she had stopped filming.

But Wade said, "Turn the camera back on, Merit. I want to record this memorable moment of history, for posterity."

She focused on Wade's face as he spoke.

"Our hopes and dreams of finding something significant have come true today with the discovery of this ancient room! We're the happiest team of cavers in the world!"

Matt, thinking that a bit of levity might give Brant a chance to get a grip on himself, he nudged Wade out of the way and stood directly in front of the camera. "Give me the microphone, Wade." Pretending to hold a mike in front of his mouth, he spoke in a serious tone. "We interrupt regular programming at this time to bring you this special news bulletin. Today, Friday, May 24th, 1995 at..." He looked at his watch. "Two o'clock, Greek time, deep in the bowels of an ancient cave on Mesa Vouno on the volcanic island of Santorini in the Aegean Sea, a team of brilliant scientists have uncovered an ancient Minoan room dating back to around 1600 B.C. Could this room that you see behind me be a clue that will help to prove that Plato's kingdom of Atlantis existed here? Let me ask this famous Greek archaeologist, Dr Nikos Konstantinou how he feels at this incredible moment in history." He placed the invisible mike up to Nikos' mouth. "Doctor, do you have a statement to make to the world?"

Nikos looked embarrassed and grinned sheepishly. "I don't know what to say. Ah, this is happiest day of my life without doubt, eh?"

Wade grabbed Matt's imaginary mike and said with a wide grin, "We will now return to regular programming." Everyone laughed. "We need a plan, team. Let's go outside, eat lunch and discuss how we are going to proceed with the inventory in such tight quarters."

They left the room and sat down on the stone seats. Merit unpacked the lunch basket.

Wade said. "We have to develop a sensible system for sorting out and recording what's here. We'll have to work rather fast if we want to see, touch, feel and record everything that is jammed into the room before nightfall. We won't have much time tomorrow because of the party, and if we discover something tremendously important, Nikos will want to notify Athens right away, I'm sure."

"That is true," Nikos added. "And when big shots come from Athens, they'll take over this place like it's their own. Well it is I guess. We may not get back in again."

They ate quickly while Wade laid out his plan. "Here's what I think we must do. I'll want all kinds of stills and movies of the objects and the frescoes, Merit. We'll make our way slowly through the room. Nikos, you'll select an item, pick it up, identify it, if you can, and I'll assign it a number and write a brief description of it. Then pass it on to Brant, and he'll hold it up for Merit to photograph. Brant will then hand it to Matt who will very carefully lay it back on the floor over on the back side of the room where there is more empty space."

Ten minutes later they were back in the chamber and began the systematic inventory of the room's treasures.

THE SANTORINI ODYSSEY

Because the beautiful gold female deity statue that Brant had discovered in the niche was closest to the door, Nikos removed it first and described it. When it finally reached Brant's hands, he became so enraptured he clutched it tightly, forgetting to hand it to Matt.

Matt nudged Brant and said humorously, "Okay, buddy, turn the doll over to me, or I'll report you for molesting the lady."

Brant looked up with a guilty smile and gently laid the statue in Matt's hands. "Sorry."

Wade said firmly, "Brant, we have to move faster than that, or we'll be here all night, okay?"

"Right," Brant said. "I'm sorry." He thought I may never get to hold her again.

Next they carefully catalogued seven four-foot tall clay pithoi, which were beautifully decorated with a variety of colored motifs. Each had molded handles that facilitated the lifting. Some of them had sediment in the bottoms.

Nikos suggested what they might have held, "These pithoi are just like those we see in Akrotiri, eh? They hold grain, oil or other food items. I know they were made right here on island. They would be too big and fragile to transport on ships of those days. The laboratory in Athens will test what's inside." Again, the word, Athens, gave Nikos a sinking feeling that he may have used poor judgment in allowing the team to open the room without first getting permission from the authorities. But he could hardly stop them now.

Once the pithoi had been moved, Nikos played his lamp around the room. He stopped the beam abruptly at the corner of the far wall. "Look! Over there!" he pointed. "See, it looks like it might be sarcophagus. We'll have to clear away everything that's piled up in front of it to get good look. Whether it's here because it was used for burial or for storing treasure will be mystery until we get to that side of room."

Next they examined a row of large clay tablets emblazoned with etchings of birds, animals, flowers and the same Linear script they had seen on the cavern wall. Neither Nikos nor Brant knew the significance of the tablets.

Next they found a large group of ceremonial vessels, both small and large. Beside them, there were several beautifully carved stone figurines of male and female deities, some of which were broken. They carefully placed them and the fragments in plastic bags, knowing how important it was to save even the tiniest pieces for restoration.

Up to this point, everything they found was probably made locally except possibly the gold deity. Then they found three magnificently carved white marble chalices, each a different size. Both Nikos and Brant were sure they had been imported since their quality was quite different from the other finds.

Under a pile of broken pithoi, they found an extraordinary artifact. It was a large oblong bronze box with a double axe engraved on the cover.

"Open it, Nikos!" Wade shouted.

Nikos grinned broadly. "I'm very nervous. I've never seen anything like this before." His hands shook as he carefully pried off the top. When he saw what the box contained, his eyes widened and his jaw dropped. He held it out for the others to see. "Look at this!"

"My God, weapons!" Brant exclaimed in awe. "Look at them! A dagger with a gold handle, a sword with an ivory hilt, arrowheads and small spears." He picked the dagger up in one hand and the sword in the other. A hideous grin covered his face. "I love these. They're masterpieces!" He put the dagger in his belt and pretended to duel with the ancient sword.

"Minoans were not militaristic people, Brant," Nikos said. "These weapons must have been used to hunt for animal sacrifices."

Matt held Brant's arm steady so Merit could photograph the sword. He then slid the dagger from Brant's belt and placed it in his hand so Merit could get a photo. Matt ignored Brant's glare and said, "You know what the boss said, Brant, we have to keep moving."

Wade was having a tough time trying to write accurate descriptions of all the artifacts, they were so astounding. His tape recorder was also recording all conversations.

Now they were getting closer to the sarcophagus, they could see that it was made of cement with glazed terra cotta floral decorations on the side. It was shaped like a bathtub with two handles on each end for carrying. Its cover was flat and decorated with the now familiar double axe and bull horns. On the wall above, niches held oil lamps and incense burners, similar to those they had previously found in the tunnel. Some were quite ornate.

Although they were now almost next to the sarcophagus, their way was still impeded by more large pithoi. Some were standing, but many others had fallen over, and in some cases the small objects they had held were strewn across the floor. There were ewers, cups, rhytons, vases and other kinds of utensils. Many were decorated in black and red. Some were imported as indicated by their splendid shapes and decorations. The team had to step very carefully to avoid crushing them. They also found carbonized food, animal bones, shells and some stone-like beads. It took some time to sort out and package up the shards that belonged to the broken pithoi and move them to the other side of the room.

Wade reminded them, "It's getting late. I think we'll have to speed it up."

THE SANTORINI ODYSSEY

Finally the way was cleared enough that they could inspect the sarcophagus.

"It's smaller than the ones we saw in that room below the Temple of Apollo," Wade commented and asked, "Were Minoans small people, Nikos?"

"Not at all," Nikos said. "They had sturdy bodies. But I must explain to you that when people died then, they were buried immediately after death while their body was still flexible enough to bend head and shoulders forward and double up arms and legs. In some ancient cemeteries, you'll find many bodies buried in large funeral jars."

"Well, let's get to work and remove the lid." Brant said anxiously.

They all looked to Wade for instructions. "I honestly don't know what to do." He said pointing to the sarcophagus. "I'm against disturbing the dead."

"Oh, come on!" Brant grumbled. "Are you suggesting that we don't open it?"

Merit agreed with Wade. "It's strange you should say that, Wade. I don't think it's right to open up tombs either."

"Oh, for Christ's sake! I can't believe you two! We've come all this way and you're both actually suggesting that we don't open it? Archaeologists open tombs all the time. It's our job, and if you don't want to do it, I'll be very happy to do the dirty work."

Wade frowned and spoke, "Well I guess we've come this far, we might as well go all the way," he said, looking down at the cover of the sarcophagus and feeling around the edges.

Actually, everyone but Brant had misgivings about opening up the sarcophagus. It was obvious from the expressions on their faces, they were reluctant.

Brant gestured to Nikos, to go to the opposite end of the sarcophagus. "Matt, you stand over that side and Wade, you get on the other side. When we lift the ends up, get your hands under the cover." Brant and Nikos began prying the lid up.

Brant's heart was pounding erratically. His mouth was dry and his breathing was labored. When they felt the lid give, Brant shouted, "Quick! Quick! God damn it! Wade, Matt, get your hands under it! Lift it! Lift it off!"

Merit, filming the procedure, moved the camera away from Brant's face that was covered with a bizarre look.

Wade glared at Brant and warned, "Take it easy, Brant. We don't want to break it."

Brant ignored him and bent down to look under the lid, now suspended about three inches above the sarcophagus. "For Christ's sake, move it off completely! Lay it on the floor!"

Wade shouted, "Hold it right there, men."

Brant looked at Wade with a fierce glassy stare and snarled, "And I said, take it off!"

"Listen to me carefully, Brant!" Wade cautioned him. "Get control of yourself, or I'll escort you out of here and take you off the project. I have that privilege. I'm the boss here, and the team does what I say, not what you say. Do you understand that?"

Brant gave Wade a disgusted look. "Well, pardon me all to hell! Aren't I allowed to get excited about this or what?" His voice was contemptuous.

"Put the cover back down, guys." Wade ordered. Nikos, Matt and Wade lowered their sides, but Brant held his up.

Tension filled the room. A grim standoff between Wade and Brant now took place.

Wade, furious and out of patience with Brant, said, "Brant. I'm damn sick and tired of your attitude. You get your act together or get out!" Wade's face was scarlet. The veins on his neck pulsated. His lips and fists were clenched so tightly, they were white.

Dead Silence followed. The two men glared at each other. Wade knew that the time had come for him to make a decision. He was extremely concerned because Brant looked dazed and out of control. He thought, what if he goes berserk in this small room with all the precious artifacts on the floor. He quickly looked to Matt for help.

Matt nodded to Wade in the affirmative and stepped in front of Brant.

In a slow and deliberate manner, Matt asked Brant, "Do you understand what Wade is saying? Do you understand how Wade expects you to act from now on? He's waiting for an answer, and it had better be the right one, or you're out of here."

Wade stared intently into Brant's eyes, waiting for a reply.

Brant slowly put down his end of the cover. His eyes squinted, and a wrinkled frown formed on his forehead. He was confused and unnerved by Wade's tongue lashing. No one had ever spoken to him like that before. He could feel his blood pounding in his ears. He looked at Wade with false remorse. Although his impulse was to continue being confrontational, he knew he had to make his apology meaningful. "Wade, I...ah, I'm sorry if you thought I was trying to usurp your authority. I...ah, guess I was out of line. I now realize that." He chuckled lightly. "Just a little enthusiastic I guess." He put his hand out to Wade. "Please accept my apology."

While reluctantly shaking Brant's hand, Wade gave him a final warning, "Don't ever do that again, Brant. I mean it. Let's get back to work, team."

Merit was so distraught, she was close to tears. She was certain that this was probably the first time Brant had ever allowed anyone to speak to him like that. She was frightened by his actions. *Oh, God, he's really becoming mentally ill. I should get him home, but he'd never leave now.* She looked to Matt.

He shrugged his shoulders, then mouthed, "He'll be okay." He hoped.

The men went back to their previous positions. They avoided making eye contact with Brant as they slowly lifted the lid from the ancient casket and placed it alongside on the floor. Immediately, all eyes peered into the sarcophagus. Enthusiastic gasps filled the air as they stared at the amazing sight. A considerable trove of artifacts lay scattered over the skeletal remains that lay anatomically correct on the bottom of the casket. The skull was fully exposed and strands of white long hair lay about the neck bones. The rest of the bones were blanketed with an incredible array of objects: ancient figurines, beaded and gold jewelry, libation vessels shaped like birds and bulls, a variety of amulets, a gold and ivory square that looked like a game board, the bones of a small animal, a terra cotta snake with carnelian eyes, a magnificently carved griffin of glazed terra cotta, and other items not immediately identifiable.

For a few seconds, not a word was spoken. Then Nikos said in a hushed tone, "Objects placed over remains are funerary items put there as offerings to deceased to honor him in death. I'm sure he was beloved priest."

Wade spoke hesitantly. "Because we've invaded the privacy of this person's grave, I think it would be fitting if we bowed our heads and offered a few moments of silence in respect for him in the event we have offended his spirit."

They all bowed their heads.

Brant was able to successfully resist reaching into the casket to touch the treasures by stuffing both hands tightly into his pockets. His stomach was in knots.

Wade spoke quietly, "Brant and Nikos, I'm not sure what the protocol is in a find like this, so I'll defer to you archaeologists. Tell us how we should proceed."

Brant took a big breath and looked as if he were going to say something, but instead he looked at Nikos and gestured for him to be the spokesperson. "I'm in shock, but wonderfully so, eh? I'm not sure what to do. I know we must take inventory, but I think we can't do that properly without moving some of treasures on top of the ancient priest. There are so many things, eh?"

Matt said, "I think the remains are a man. If I could get a better look at the skeleton's pelvic area, I could confirm that. Men have smaller pelvises than women."

"Brant, how do you feel about moving some things off the skeleton?" Wade asked.

Brant was thrilled that Wade didn't seem to be angry with him any more. He would love to touch each of the objects and examine them. A few, he was positive, would end up being his. A thrill ran through him. "I agree with Nikos that this is undoubtedly the tomb of a priest, and I feel we must make an inventory of everything that's in the sarcophagus. I don't think we can do that without taking out at least some of the things that are lying on top of the remains. For instance, if you look very carefully, you can see parts of his right hand under those ancient figurines and some of his finger bones have ornate rings on them."

Merit who had returned to filming, now stopped and leaned in to see what Brant was talking about. Strangely, she did not feel the usual sensation of excitement when she was about to see priceless jewelry. That's a healthy sign for me she thought.

The arms of the skeleton were crossed, and the hands lay in such a position over the clavicle and sternum that the fingertips were facing toward the head.

"Well, Nikos where shall we begin? Wade asked.

Nikos wiped his forehead with the back of his hand, then threw his hands outward. I don't know. I don't know what to do. Something up here in my head says, call Athens right away. But then I think, will they fly to Santorini this late in the day? I think we should take inventory so we are all witnesses to what we find, eh? It's important.

I don't see how we can seal up room again to keep treasures safe. But I know that authorities would not want us to take them out of cave. That I know for sure. They will want to be ones to do that!" Then he took his usual thinking position. He pressed his fingers to his forehead and placed his other hand on his hip. "Okay! We must take complete inventory! When we leave, we'll put cover back on sarcophagus. And I think we should cover the entrance into the tomb to keep rats and bats out. There is plywood in the office. Wade and I will come back and do that. Today, our treasure is safe here because only we know about it, but I will have to tell Elias. Tonight he will keep his watch dog, Pluto, outside. No one can get past him. Maybe Elias will put barbed wire inside entrance to grotto to block it." Nikos looked at his watch. "It's almost four o'clock, we better get back to work."

Brant wondered what he'd do if barbed wire was placed in the grotto. He'd have to use wire cutters, he supposed. He wasn't worried about Pluto, because he had stolen quite a few sleeping pills from Matt's medical supplies over the last few days. If he had to face the dog, he'd put him to sleep by lacing chunks of the lamb they'd be cooking for the anniversary party. His biggest worry was that Nikos might call the authorities, and they'd come before tomorrow.

The team now began the task of carefully lifting out each object, numbering it, recording its description, photographing it and placing it carefully on the floor nearby.

Merit, despondent over Brant's behavior, wished she could somehow escape from her responsibilities here. She sighed, "Wade, I'll never have time to do sketches of all these things today, and I'll be too busy tomorrow."

"I know, Merit. We'll try to work something out. And speaking of artwork, I'm anxious to take a good look at the wall paintings."

"Me, too!" Matt joined their conversation. "I noticed the back wall has a painting that looks like a volcano erupting, I wonder if it could be the volcanic eruption of 1600 B.C.?"

"We'll get to the walls somehow." Wade promised.

They began the inventory of the sarcophagus and removed fifteen small figurines of mythological gods, goddesses and animals. They appeared to be made of terra cotta, painted, then glazed. The Minoan goddesses were wearing long dresses with open bodices, exposing their breasts.

Nikos held up a figurine, "We know this Egyptian God, Annubis, the divine embalmer. We find smaller one before, eh?"

"He's an appropriate god," Matt remarked.

A large pile of jewelry, nested in the torso cavity of the body, was difficult to sort out since many of the pieces seemed tangled together. Nikos slowly lifted out a particularly exotic gold necklace with diamond-shaped beads separated by small teardrop-shaped beads. The focal point of the necklace was a large circle of gold engraved with the eagle that represented Zeus.

Brant and Nikos both agreed, it probably had been imported from Crete. Several strands of beads, made of lapis lazuli and other colorful glass-like stones were tangled together, and Nikos left them that way. Next, he lifted out an ivory cartouche with a cuttlefish ink inscription in hieroglyphics that was hanging from a gold wire. The last piece, a magnificent scarab necklace, was made of artistically carved blue and orange beetles. At the bottom, an interesting collection of smaller items in bronze and gold lay in a pile.

When Nikos handed the life-like spiders, scorpions and other unidentifiable insects to Wade, he commented, "These are put in tomb to protect priest from being bitten by snakes."

Next, he handed Wade an assortment of amulets, which Brant recognized as charms that supposedly protected the body against evil.

The last items, scattered about at the foot bones, were wide-banded rings of gold and ivory with carved depictions of bulls, griffins, lions, cows, goats and sheep.

Laying in a slack position across the skeleton's groin area, Nikos pointed to a wide gold belt. "I presume this is belt that originally circled priest's waist when he was laid in sarcophagus."

They all leaned in for a closer look. At the center of the belt, on a buckle-type block of gold, the sacred horns of the bull were carved.

"We cannot take this off," Nikos warned.

Now that the priest's upper body was cleared. Matt said, "Can we pause for a minute? I'd like to take a look at the bones." He leaned in for a closer look but did not touch them for fear they would disintegrate.

"They seem to have survived rather well. I was afraid they might crumble when you started to remove things from his chest area."

Matt looked closely at the skull, which was bent forward slightly. "When I first looked at his head, I thought it was flexed, but I can see now that our priest friend here probably died of a broken neck." He pointed to the neck area. "You can see the wedge-like compressions here, where the vertebrae were forced against each other. I suspect that the anterior spinal ligament was also ruptured, which would have allowed sufficient subluxation to sever the spinal cord. See how the vertebral bodies are out of alignment. I also see quite a bit of spurring on the vertebrae. Those are characteristic changes in an older person because of his osteoarthritic disease. His true age would have to be determined by carbon dating the bones. He was not a young man. It doesn't look like he made regular visits to his dentist either, because of the obvious bone shrinkage. He probably stood about five feet tall, maybe taller."

Matt carefully examined the finger bones. "They are solid, but deformed at several joints. You can see that he had severe arthritis in his fingers. Arthritis is often worse in the hands. That's all I can tell you about our friend here, except that he must have been revered by his family and friends to have been given such priceless gifts to take on his death journey."

"Thank you, Doctor. I'm sure glad I asked you along." Wade smiled at Matt.

"You'll get the bill in the mail."

Next they lifted out the square gold and ivory piece that looked like a game board. There were several smaller round pieces on top of it, which obviously were used by the players.

"His favorite game, no doubt," Brant said, holding it out for Merit to photograph.

Next, from along the sides, they carefully removed several delicate libation vessels shaped like birds and bulls.

They were hesitant about picking up the small cluster of animal bones that lay between the priest's upper leg bones. "Matt, what do you think about these? Any idea what kind of animal it was?" Wade asked.

"Don't try to move them," Matt warned. "The head, as you can see, is similar to the human skull, but smaller. If I have to make a guess, I'd say it was a monkey. Is that possible, Nikos?"

"Absolutely, Matt. Many Minoans had monkeys as pets. You see them in wall paintings from Kalliste, eh?"

A coiled reptile made of terra cotta had green eyes. It brought back a flood of memories of their encounter with the Levantine vipers. It looked like the real ones they had captured.

Nikos picked up the carved, terra cotta griffin, whose head, fore parts and wings were that of an eagle, while its body, hind legs and tail resembled a lion. "The griffin had been engraved and painted before being glazed," Nikos said, "The workmanship is superb."

The last items to be recorded were the rings from the priest's fingers. Matt said, "Do not try to remove them. I'm sure the bones will break apart."

His right hand held three rings and his left hand, one. The three rings had small oval bezels set at right angles to the ring.

"This type of ring was often used as a seal," Brant said. "And sometimes as a pendant."

The birds, flowers and animal engravings on the rings represented nature. The elaborate gold ring on his left index finger had its bezel set with a magnificently carved golden serpent's head. Its eyes looked like red jasper. The open serpent's mouth revealed two long, sharp fangs of blue violet amethyst.

"That's a most unusual ring. It's beautiful!" Merit whispered, photographing it from several angles.

"And I bet you'd love to add it to your collection of rings," said Brant.

She shook her head slowly. "I think we've had enough of snakes, but it certainly is unique."

"Well, that about does it," Wade said, closing his notebook. "Let's put everything carefully back in the sarcophagus and put the top back on."

Once everything was back in place, the men lifted the heavy lid, but before they placed it over the sarcophagus, they paused briefly for a last look at the treasures. They knew they might not get another look at them until years from now when they were displayed in the Archaeological Museum in Athens.

"Now let's take a quick look at the wall paintings," Wade suggested.

Nikos said, "I'm sure this room was used by old priest when he had religious services around omphalos."

"It's amazing to me how they leveled the limestone walls flat enough to be able to plaster them," Matt said.

"These walls are like plastered walls found at Kalliste." Nikos explained. "They had many different-sized basalt anvils they used to shape hammers, grinders and polishers. Once surface of wall was level, they plastered with local clay, smoothing it out with flat beach stones."

"I would have loved to have seen these wall paintings when the colors were vivid," Merit said.

For the next ten minutes, the team moved slowly along the walls, each pointing out small and large details, elaborating on them, and exchanging opinions on their meanings. They tried to imagine how the inhabitants of the island must have felt at this moment in time, when their world was about to be destroyed. That was the story told in the paintings.

The wall nearest the door depicted houses, one and two stories high. Quite a few seemed to have been damaged. Many individuals were in the streets. The men's bodies were tan-colored and scantily clad while the women were white skinned, and wore various colored clothes. From the position of their bodies and legs, they seemed to be moving rapidly. Many of the women carried bundles on their heads, and the men led yoked-oxen-type animals pulling carts filled with household items.

"These wall paintings are not as artistic as those recovered from Kalliste." Nikos commented.

"These seem to be amateurish." Merit added, "And, I can tell that each section was done by different artists, they're done in varied styles."

The adjoining wall was startling. The team concluded the mural portrayed the initial eruption of a volcano. It showed a darkened sky over a mountainous, round island surrounded by an angry, dark green sea. Houses like the ones they saw at the Kalliste excavation, and larger buildings lined the narrow streets. Vegetation and various animals in motion were part of the scene. There were crowds of people on the shoreline looking skyward. Standing out prominently among them was an elderly man with a blue monkey on his shoulder.

"A monkey!," Matt said, pointing to the small animal. "I'll bet that old man is our friend over there in the sarcophagus and the small skeleton buried with him must be this little primate."

"What a story these paintings are telling!" Merit was surprised at the details. "Look. See how the old man's head is in a slack position and two men seem to be supporting him under his arms. He's wearing a decorated loin cloth. And look!" Merit pointed out, "He's wearing that same gold belt we just saw on the skeleton. His hair is long and white. Most of the other men in the picture have black hair. That must be this priest!"

Next they saw a high peak in the center of the island, fire and smoke spewed upward in black and red columns. It sprayed outward and fell back to earth like heavy rain.

The third wall contained a scene of activity on a rocky shore lined with crowds of people. Many boats of various sizes were jammed with passengers and rowers. Others had their sails unfurled and were under way. The painting depicted an obvious exodus.

The fourth wall painting was divided into two parts. The first panel showed a parade of people climbing up a steep mountain road in the black rain. A team of oxen pulled a cart containing a sarcophagus. The second panel showed the inside of a cave with a giant mound in the center, which the team instantly recognized as the omphalos. Oil lamps burned on the walls. A large number of human figures sat on slab seats with their heads bowed.

The team felt certain that the wall paintings depicted a pictorial account of the burial of the priest and evacuation of the city of Kalliste. Also the beginning of the devastating volcanic eruption of 1600 BC that buried the city. These historic events were quite familiar to them, since they'd recently viewed the ruins of the ancient city. They fell silent, each trying to grasp the importance and magnitude of what they had uncovered today.

"The people must have loved the old priest dearly to risk their lives, bringing him way up this mountain when everyone else was escaping," said Matt.

"And I wonder what prompted them to take the time to do the wall paintings, considering what was happening in their town," Merit added. "Their lives were obviously in danger."

"Maybe there was some person or prophet among them who realized their island was facing total devastation," Nikos suggested. "Someone who thought it would be good to let future generations know what happened. They must have felt that this cavern and the omphalos, would likely survive that calamity as well. So they painted their story here, eh?"

"It's very likely that what we've seen on these four walls could have been the beginning of the end of Atlantis," said Brant.

"The archaeologists working on the Kalliste dig will be thrilled when they see these wall paintings." Nikos commented. "I'm sure there are many clues in these paintings here that will help in their explorations."

Suddenly they heard a strange noise outside and anxious looks were exchanged. It sounded like a muffled roar. Wade went to the door. Nikos and Matt followed right behind him. Brant stayed inside with Merit until Wade, fearing the temptation to take something might be too much for Brant, told them to come outside.

The men slowly moved the lamp around the cavern, but saw nothing. Suddenly, the noise came again. It was a frightening noise and was coming closer.

Merit cried out, "Oh, God, ghosts!"

CHAPTER THIRTEEN

By six o'clock, Anna was worried because the team had not returned. Thirty minutes later, when the sun began to set, she decided she should ride up to the site and talk to Elias. Katina refused to go with her, saying she would die of fright if she had to be in the ruins in the dark.

Ari, overhearing this conversation and sensing Anna's concern, offered to go with her. There were still quite a few villagers in the compound putting up lights and hanging the aromatic bunches of flowers and herbs between the lights, so Katina would stay and help. To save time, Anna and Ari rode donkeys up to Mesa Vouno.

When they neared Elias' house, they saw that he and Kristos were just starting up to the ancient city.

Anna called to them, "Elias, Elias! Wait for us."

He turned and walked back. Pluto leaped ahead to check out the intruders. He stopped, sniffed at Anna and wagged his tail, but then turned to Ari and snarled until Elias whistled to him.

"*Kalispera*, Anna. You too are worried, eh?"

"Yes, very much so. The team is always home by now. They've never stayed this late. This is our friend, Ari."

"Well, if the boy wants to help, let me get him a kerosene torch to carry."

"Get two," Anna said. "I'm going with you."

Elias looked at her in surprise. "A woman your age wants to go into that black cave? That is foolish!"

Anna glared at him. "I'm not an OLD woman! And foolish or not, I'm going with you," she said firmly.

Elias threw his hands in the air in resignation and softly swore to himself. He noticed that at least she wore a wool sweater and sturdy shoes. The boy was also dressed warmly.

When they reached the grotto, he commanded Pluto to stay, and told Kristos to stay outside.

Kristos begged his father, "Please, *Papa*, I want to go, too."

Elias ignored Kristos and led them into the grotto. He lit their torches and flashed his large light through the opening at the back wall.

He stepped down one step and called out loudly, "Nikos! Nikos! Answer me."

There was no response.

Kristos yelled into the grotto, "*Papa*, I have something to tell you. I know you'll be very angry at me, but I can tell you how to find them."

"What are you saying, Kristos? How can you find them?" A puzzled look wrinkled Elias' face.

Kristos hung his head, then slowly looked up at his father. "I've been in the tunnel before, *Papa*. I know where they are working today."

Elias was furious. "You disobeyed me! You have gone into tunnels? Kristos, you will be punished severely for this! Go home immediately!"

Anna laid her hand on Elias' arm and spoke softly to him, "Elias, from what I know about the tunnel, and from what I hear from the team, it could be difficult and dangerous to try to find them without a guide. Maybe you should let Kristos lead us, eh?"

Elias shook his head in exasperation, "Ah! I guess I have no choice. Get back in here, Kristos," he called.

Kristos turned on his flashlight, ran into the grotto and went right past his father and down the steps. "Follow me," he yelled excitedly as he shined his light along the floor of the Egyptian tunnel.

Anna and Ari exchanged looks of relief. Kristos obviously knew exactly where to go, thank God.

The three adults followed the boy through the winding tunnel. Their torches casting eerie shadows on the black walls. They continued to call out Nikos' name. The deeper they went the more nervous the three adults became.

Elias now stopped abruptly. "I think maybe something bad has happened. I'd better go get the police for help."

"Noooo!" Kristos cried out. "You can't do that, *Papa*. We are almost there."

"Why should I believe a young boy who disobeys his father? Why shouldn't we call the police? They know how to handle this kind of problem. People are always getting lost in the caves here on Santorini. The police have good equipment for searching."

Kristos put his hands against his father's chest. "No, *Papa*, don't call the police. Nikos made me swear not to tell anyone what they've found, but I must tell you now. You see, *Papa*, they didn't want anyone else to know. They think they have found a great treasure. Maybe that is where they are now."

Elias was puzzled, "What treasure? How can you, a little boy, know all this? Why don't I know about it? I'm the guard here!"

"Because, *Papa*, the tunnels were my discovery, so I followed them sometimes. They caught me and were angry. But I promised to keep their secret, and now all of you have to keep the secret, too. I'll take you to them now, okay?"

Elias was stunned and angry. "Why didn't they tell me or your *mana* that you were following them into the cave all the time? They borrowed tools from me because they said they had to chip through some stone to continue their work in the tunnel. They tell me nothing. They don't trust me, but they trust my son?"

"Oh no, *Papa*. I'm sure they were going to tell you tonight so you and Pluto could be on guard, that is, if they make an important find. That's your job. They told me that. They know that for a fact." He lied to ease his father's hurt feelings.

Elias was only slightly appeased. They resumed following Kristos and calling out Nikos' name. Their voices echoed off the walls. The farther in they went, the more concerned Elias became, knowing full well the hazards of a cave: the snakes, bats, rats, spiders, even ghosts, maybe. When they neared the area where the steep slope led into the cavern, Kristos held up his hand to stop them.

"We are almost there, just a few more turns. I think I should warn you about what you are going to see. I don't want you to be frightened to death like I was the first time I saw the cavern. It has icicles hanging from the ceiling and growing up from the floor. It's very scary at first, but you will get used to it," he said cheerfully.

They looked skeptically at the boy.

Elias put his hand on Kristos' shoulder and said, "If you made it, I guess we can too. Lead on."

They moved forward slowly. Suddenly, a loud roar stopped them in their tracks. It took a moment for them to realize it was human voices echoing off the cavern walls. "Who's out there?"

Kristos ran ahead of the others and called out, "It's us! Me, Kristos, my *papa*, Mrs. Brady and Ari!"

They were standing at the top of the slope above the floor of the cavern. The team's bright lamps and the torches illuminated the cavern area below.

Elias, Anna and Ari looked down in stunned silence. They were fascinated by the magnificent sight below them.

Wade yelled to them while moving toward the slope. "We were just getting ready to leave. I'm sorry if we worried you."

Nikos chimed in cheerfully, "You came to us, and we were just going to go to see you, Elias."

Kristos took his father's hand, smiled up at him, and said, "See, *Papa*, didn't I tell you they were coming to see you about guarding the cave?"

Merit scolded Anna, "What are you doing in the cave, Anna?"

Nikos then quickly scaled the slope and was at Anna's side within seconds. "You should not have come in cave without proper clothing. It's dangerous!"

Speaking loudly so everyone could hear, Anna said sarcastically, "If some people came home when they should because they know what time I serve dinner every night, then I wouldn't have to come into cave to tell them dinner is ready and getting cold, eh?"

Her scolding brought chuckles from those at the bottom of the slope.

"We apologize, dear Anna!" Matt yelled up to her.

Elias spoke out in an authoritative voice, "So, what is happening here? My son knows all about this cavern, but I'm told nothing. It's me who has responsibility for ancient city of Thera, you know." His tone of voice let them know he was upset.

"We apologize, Elias," Wade said, pulling himself up to the top. "Until today, we really didn't know if there would be anything inside that giant mound you can see down there. We discovered there was a doorway but it was blocked by huge pieces of limestone that had to be removed. That's why we borrowed your tools."

"Why didn't you tell me about what you were doing?" Elias asked in annoyance.

Nikos quickly put his hand on Elias' shoulder. "Until we removed limestone away from entrance, we didn't know what was inside. Maybe nothing we thought. But now we have good news! We have made momentous find, my friend, and we'd like you to see inside room because we have uncovered an incredible amount of ancient artifacts worth a fortune. And now, Elias, it will be your responsibility to protect the treasures until the Archaeological Society comes from Athens to remove them. You will be very important man on island now. Come we'll show you what we have found."

"Can I see inside, too? Please?" Kristos asked, tugging at Nikos' arm.

Nikos looked from Elias to Kristos to Anna, then to Ari where he paused briefly.

Ari sensed that Nikos wasn't sure that he should see the room and said, "Nikos, I will understand if you feel I should wait here."

"No, you come too Ari. The four of you risked danger to make sure we were okay, so all of you deserve to see room of treasures. But remember, what you see here must not be discussed with anyone until it is all safely in hands of Archaeological Society. Maybe they come tomorrow, or maybe not until Monday if I can't get in touch with them tonight."

Slowly the four newcomers made their way down the slope. Nikos came down with Anna and whispered, "You should not have worried about me and risked your life to come here to find me."

"Ha!" she said loudly. Then in a quieter voice she said, "I only came because I thought if someone were hurt, I could help. I didn't come just because of you!"

THE SANTORINI ODYSSEY

Nikos slipped his arm tightly around her waist. She let go of the rope with one hand to slap his hand that was holding the rope above hers. She lost her hold and began to slide rapidly. He embraced her tightly to help her regain her balance. When they reached the floor, she glared at him. "I will get back up by myself, for sure!"

The newcomers became frightened when they made their way across the enormous cavern filled with stalactites and stalagmites.

Elias could scarcely speak. "To think that all this was always here, right under my feet, when I made my rounds of the ruins."

When they gathered at the omphalos, Wade led them inside the chamber. They were awe struck and stood frozen in place.

Nikos pointed out the sarcophagus at the back of the room and told them that it contained an ancient skeleton, Elias and Anna, superstitious about disturbing the dead, turned and hurried out pulling Kristos and Ari behind them.

Wade told Elias, "Nikos and I have to pick up some plywood tonight at our office and bring it back here to seal up the chamber. We're afraid if we don't close it up, rats will steal some of the small treasures."

Elias now spoke in a very officious voice, "I will allow you to do that, but I must come with you, because everything here is now my responsibility."

"That'll be fine, Elias," Wade said. "We have taken a complete inventory along with photos of everything inside the chamber."

"That is good." Elias held out his hand. "I will take that list and the film now, please. You will not be allowed back in here again after you block up the door."

The team was stunned by Elias' order.

"But Elias," Nikos said, "Wade wrote the inventory in great haste."

Wade added, "Actually, I scribbled. I don't think anyone would understand what I wrote. I hoped I could make the list look more professional."

Merit looked at Elias with a pained expression, "Elias, I'll be heartbroken if you don't let me develop my film."

Elias flailed his hands in the air, "Okay, okay. You and Wade make your list and photos look, how you say it, professional. Just remember, until the authorities get here, they are my property."

They made their way up the incline and through the tunnel with Kristos in the lead.

Elias told Nikos, "I hope my wife, Dora hasn't called the police." When they stepped through the hole of the back wall of the grotto, Pluto leaped at them, wagging his tail furiously and barked a welcome.

Elias patted the dog's head saying, "Good boy, Pluto, good dog."

Brant, noticing how quickly the dog calmed down, and called Pluto to him, repeating the same words in Greek that Elias used, but the dog did not respond as enthusiastically.

"Elias, do you think we should put up some barbed wire in the grotto, just to be sure?" Wade asked.

"It is not necessary with Pluto here. No one will get by him. I guarantee you that. I'll also close ancient city to public, eh? If you want to know truth, I don't think you should have opened room without authorities being there."

A feeling of guilt seized Nikos. He had worried about that also. "Maybe you are right, Elias. I'll try to call them tonight".

Brant thought about cutting the telephone line, but that wouldn't stop Nikos from using someone else's phone. He just had to hope that Nikos would not be able to get in touch with the Greek authorities over the weekend.

Merit was disappointed. "Nikos, I guess that means that I won't be able to do sketches of the treasures."

"Ah, yes that's true, and I'm sorry Merit. Maybe when authorities get here, they'll allow you to sketch."

Merit thought, I doubt I'll be here.

When they neared the compound, they could hear music and animated conversation. The colored lights strung around the perimeter were ablaze and music filled the air. Men were assembling tables and benches, and young girls were hanging garlands of flowers between the trees. Women were setting out tablecloths, flowers and candles; it was a festive sight.

Katina ran immediately to Ari when they arrived. "Oh, I'm so glad you are back. I worried about you."

Anna glanced at Nikos and raised her eyebrows. "So. She's only worried about Ari, eh?"

"Ari is lucky that Katina is not like her *mana* who is afraid to show her feelings."

Anna shook her head at Nikos. "You never give up, do you, old man?"

"Should I?" he laughed.

Matt joined them. "Nikos, don't you think it would be nice if we offered all the workers a little retsina?"

"You want to start party early, eh, Matt?" Nikos laughed.

"But not more than one glass!" Anna said emphatically, "Or they won't go home, and you won't be eating your already overcooked dinner until midnight."

In fact, it was eleven o'clock before they did get around to eating. The team was in a mood to celebrate.

When they finally rose from the dinner table to retire for the night, Anna asked Matt if he could come to her house for a little while. "I want to discuss some business with you."

He gallantly held out his arm for her to join him. "I would be delighted, my dear lady."

Nikos glared after them, wondering, why is she asking Matt to discuss her business, and not me? For the first time in his life, the anguish of jealousy raced through him as he sulked off to his house. He sat at his bedroom window, watching Anna's house until he saw Matt leave, and the lights go out. He hardly slept that night, trying to sort out his feelings about this woman whom he had known for so many years. Was he at last falling in love? No woman had ever caused him to lose sleep. Clearly, he was puzzled.

Matt had been astonished when Anna told him how much money her husband had left her. He told her that he felt it would be wise to have the finance officer at the bank assist her in investing the money. "They must be very honest people to have protected your funds and safe-deposit box all these years without hearing a word from you or Joe. I'm thrilled beyond words that you and Katina will have a secure future now. I hope you'll think about sharing it with a man now." Matt looked at her slyly and asked, "What about Nikos? I know he cares a great deal for you, probably loves you."

Anna scoffed loudly at Matt's suggestion, but Matt noticed that she also blushed deeply.

* * * *

After dinner, Brant and Merit left the table quickly, because Brant didn't feel well. Matt offered his services, but Brant insisted he'd be fine after a rest. "I've had too much wine as usual," he admitted.

Back at their house, Brant made amorous overtures to Merit, but she rejected him. He continued to try to arouse her and said in a seductive voice, "Wait until you see what I bought you for our fifth anniversary; you'll be astounded."

Without much enthusiasm she said, "I'm sure I will, Brant. Your gifts are always so special."

He suddenly grabbed her into his arms. "Listen, Merit, I'm sick of getting the cold shoulder all the time from you and everyone around here lately. What' going on?"

He hurt her, but she didn't want to fight with him. He was quite drunk. She worried that he'd get so loud the others would hear. She'd already suffered enough embarrassment today from his erratic behavior. She spoke to him softly. "Brant, let's not argue tonight. This has been such a wonderful day for all of us, especially for you. Your dream of finding a treasure has come true, and I'm so happy for you. But, I'm exhausted. Being in that damp cave all day just wears me out. I really don't know how much more of it I can take."

He released his hold and stared down at her intently. "I doubt we'll be staying here much longer anyway. Would you like to see your anniversary gift tonight?"

"No, Brant. Let's wait until tomorrow. I have something very exciting for you too." With a coquettish look that she felt might change his surly attitude. "Let's go to bed and try to guess what wonderful gifts we have for each other this time." It was a game they had played before and enjoyed. She felt that this might be the last time they'd play the game.

Brant and Merit had purchased their anniversary gifts from a well-known antiquities dealer when they stayed overnight in Athens, before they had sailed to Santorini. Prior to their arrival to Greece, the merchant had sent each of them different photographic presentations of various items he felt would be of interest to them. They each had private meetings with the dealer in Athens.

Merit had selected two Minoan artifacts. Although they were small, the two seal stones, one made of onyx and the other agate, were priceless artifacts. The stones were used to seal correspondence. They were originally found at the old palace in Knossos on Crete, which existed between 2000 and 1700 BC. She knew Brant would be thrilled with them because each carried an undeciphered script that appeared on the famous Phaistos Disc.

Long after Merit fell asleep, Brant lay awake, too excited to sleep. He thought about the magnificent gold necklace he had kept hidden in his shaving kit. It was more valuable than any treasure he had ever given Merit. He had tried to purchase it many times before but had not been successful until this year. It was part of the treasure trove that Heinrich and Sophia Schliemann had kept for themselves when they uncovered Homer's ancient city of Troy in 1871. His gift was by far one of the most artistic pieces of jewelry found in the excavations near the Hellespont.

Brant's mind was also filled with plans for tomorrow night. He would appear quite drunk all evening, staggering and feigning slurred speech. But in fact, he would drink very little until the party was over and everyone had gone to bed. He would then make his way up to the ancient city. He'd see to it that Elias got more than his share to drink. He had purchased several bottles of potent raki from the local village bootlegger. He knew which treasures he would steal. He definitely wanted the little gold figurine of the female deity, the ornate dagger and sword, and the griffin. And, of course the gold serpent ring that Merit admired so much on the skeleton's finger. He finally drifted off to sleep, a happy man.

* * * *

The brilliant rising sun on Saturday, May 25, announced that the day would be weather-perfect. The cloudless sky rapidly turned a vivid blue, and the Aegean Sea sparkled like millions of glittering diamonds. Early birds chirped noisily, insects hummed, gentle breezes wafted the fragrant scent of wild flowers throughout the village.

The residents of the compound were soon awakened by the noisy morning activities of the villagers and the tolling of the church bells of St. Demetrius.

The delicious aromas of breakfast from Anna's kitchen made Kristos, who had been waiting patiently at the gate, aware that it was now allright to come in. He was excited because before the day was over, he would be very popular with the children in his village. Merit had given him permission to decorate Zeus with flowers and give rides to village children in the field behind the compound. He now hurried to the stables to do his grooming and mucking chores.

* * * *

Brant and Merit had decided to exchange their gifts before joining the others for breakfast. Brant received his gift first and was deliriously overjoyed with the Minoan seal stones. He immediately recognized the symbols on the stones as being the same as script on the Phaistos Disc.

Brant then opened up his shaving kit and took out a velvet box. "Happy anniversary, darling, this is something I've been trying to buy you for a long time."

Merit opened the box slowly. "Oh, Brant, it's magnificent."

She held the gold necklace out and examined it carefully. The design told her it was quite ancient.

"It's had a few owners since the original. It's from Troy. It once belonged to the Schliemans. It was found when they first unearthed the golden treasures of Troy. I guess they felt they deserved a few of the trinkets they had uncovered at their own expense, much like us, darling"

"Not like us, Brant. Like you maybe, but not me."

"My, we're holier than thou this morning. Think about this Merit, Greece wouldn't be the recipient of all the beautiful treasures in the chamber if we hadn't financed this exploration."

His words upset her. "Brant, don't ever let me hear you talk like that again. You sound so mercenary." Then she kissed him lightly on the cheek and said, "Thank you for the beautiful necklace. It certainly deserves a special place of honor among my collections of antique jewelry." But privately, she pictured it in the Archaeological Museum in Athens, where it belonged.

Her enthusiasm for the golden treasure was a great deal less than Brant had expected. Annoyed, he stormed out the door, never giving a second look at the many floral bouquets that hung on it. Most had notes attached, wishing the Powers, Happy Anniversary.

One note, Merit knew she would save forever, was printed on lined paper in red crayon. It said, "happy five anniversary to mister and misses Powers. I love you and Zeus very much missus powers. I think you are very beautiful. I also like mister Mr. Powers too."

It was signed, your very good friend Kristos. The note had been written in English.

The sweet message brought tears. Sadness enveloped her as the pangs of emptiness reminded her of her childless marriage.

Nikos wasted no time in setting the party mood by playing Greek music outside, once he was sure that everyone was awake. He had tried to telephone the authorities in Athens last night, and then again this morning, but no one had answered. He even called the Archaeological Museum to see if someone there could track down the authorities for him.

This news elated Brant.

Merit was also happy. It would give her time to develop yesterday's film. She wanted to make extra prints in the event the authorities confiscated her photos and negatives.

Because the courtyard looked so festive, Anna served breakfast out there.

After breakfast, Matt and Brant took Nikos' truck and went to Fira for last minute supplies for the party. Nikos, Wade and Ari set up the large TV screen and wiring system.

The villagers were excited about seeing themselves on the screen. Many had never seen a real movie and few had seen television.

Yannis, the boss of the laborers who had worked in the cave, was the head cook for the celebration. He arrived early to fire up the giant spits. By eleven o'clock, freshly killed spring lambs had been skewered and placed over the glowing coals. The male villagers would keep the spit turning and the coals burning until dinnertime. They set up board games to pass the time, but they were interrupted constantly by women dropping by throughout the day to check on the lambs and taste a sample The young village girls had gathered plates and cutlery from the village families and set the tables. At Merit's suggestion, Katina and her friends made pretty place cards with the name of each family in the village. It had never been done before, and it pleased everyone immensely because now they would not have to scramble to get a table where their whole family could sit together.

Merit suggested to Nikos that it would be colorful if his windmill was working.

"Of course, that is wonderful idea. It has not been used for year or more maybe, but today I will put sheets up just for you."

Wade offered to help and the two men went to work hooking the white canvas sheets onto the spokes of the wheel. Once the sheets were attached, they stood back in admiration as the breeze caught the sails and the wheel began to turn and squeak. The sound of the sheets flapping in the wind caused all the workers in the compound to stop and applaud in delight.

Throughout the day, villagers arrived with food and small gifts for Brant and Merit. They insisted on giving the gifts to them personally and stood by while the Powers opened them. There were many handsome lace doilies and tablecloths of various sizes.

Kristos' mother had woven a beautiful small floor mat with a design in the center of the grotto of Hermes and Heracles She told them she appreciated their kindness to Kristos.

Some of the women and men presented bottles of homemade wine.

Even the village oracle brought them a gift of a large bulb of garlic with a blue ribbon tied to the top. She swung it back and forth in front of them murmuring words in Greek and glaring in a peculiar way at Brant then smiling at Merit.

Brant told Merit, "I think she said, 'Hang it in our kitchen for good luck.'"

Katina standing nearby, had heard the old woman say, "Ancient treasures belong to Greeks not foreigners." Katina wondered why the old oracle said that. She also wondered why Brant, who spoke Greek fluently, lied to Merit about what the old woman said.

Merit was curious. "Brant, why did she look at you so ferociously?"

"She's a weirdo. Maybe she was giving me the "evil eye." How the hell would I know?" He quickly changed the subject. "Look here comes *Papa* Ioannis."* Brant and the priest shook hands. "I hope you are joining in our celebration tonight."

"I would not miss it! If you don't think it's rude of me, I would like to ask your permission to say prayer for your marriage and make toast before we eat tonight."

"That would be lovely, *Papa,*" Merit said.

Brant said, "Yes lovely. And Merit and I have some gifts for you and your parish when our work is done here."

Merit had no idea what Brant was talking about. Actually, Brant had only thought about it last night while plotting his robbery. He wanted the priest to be on his side if anyone suspected him of stealing any treasures.

"We'd like you to have the big screen and movie equipment we bought for the party. You can rent movies and show them to the villagers. Ari will show you how to run it."

Papa Ioannis stared at them with his mouth open. He clutched his chest and cried in disbelief, "You are going to give all that to me! I don't know what to say. I'm in shock!" He held his hands out to Brant and Merit, and tears filled his eyes. He made the sign of the cross and said a brief prayer. He quickly translated, "I say thank you from everyone in village, and for God to bless your marriage for as long as you live. I must go tell my people about the equipment you have given our church!"

"No, *Papa*!" Brant said quickly. "No one is to know until our job is done here. I really prefer it that way so don't disappoint me, please. I like to keep my charitable contributions private. I'm counting on you to honor my request."

"I will try," the priest said. "I hope I can do it. I have serious fault. I'm worst person in world to keep secret, except of course when people confess sins. That I would never tell! Ah, you put big burden on my shoulders. But I'll keep promise, I hope." They shook hands, and the priest walked away, rejoicing secretly to himself.

Merit looked at Brant with a wry smile. "That was a mean trick, Brant. He's so thrilled, but he'll be in agony because he can't tell anyone. You know what he's like."

"Yes, I know," Brant said with a cocky smile. He knew the priest would not be able to keep the secret.

It was part of his plan. Who would believe that such a wealthy, generous man would steal?

By five o'clock the compound was filled with villagers. A sense of expectancy and laughter filled the air. Their everyday routines would be enlivened tonight with music, dancing, entertainment and, best of all, the movie in which each of them would play a small role. The aroma of the succulent roasting lambs permeated the compound.

The village streets were lined with large, brightly painted cans filled with candle wax. The candles would burn all through the night to guide the villagers home when the party ended. The band had arrived and was playing. Table candles flickered in the soft night breeze and cast a warm glow on the floral arrangements in the center of each table.

Most little children were in the field with Kristos, waiting in a long line for their ride on the flower-garlanded horse, Zeus. Most had never been on a horse before, only donkeys. Zeus was patient and walked slowly as the children squealed in excitement on his back. Merit dropped by occasionally to reward Zeus with an apple. He seemed to give her a pleading look with his wide eyes as if asking, 'How much longer do I have to do this?'

Kristos, dressed in his first communion suit, which was now much too tight, was enjoying his important job. His thick black hair was slicked down and parted carefully. Merit resisted an urge to hug him when she first saw him, he looked so adorable. But she knew he'd be embarrassed in front of the children.

Katina and her young friends had set up a table of their own, and Ari was her constant companion. The village girls and boys wore Western-styled clothes. Katina looked especially beautiful in a silk geometric print dress that Merit had given her. The short-sleeved bodice clung to her, and the full, short skirt swayed sensuously when she moved. Anna had bought her a matching set of gold earrings, necklace and bracelet at an expensive gold shop in Fira, a store Anna had never ventured into before.

Anna wore a pretty, soft pink dress that had been packed away years ago. Joe had bought it for her during their last trip to Athens. She had never worn it again.

Katina said as they dressed for the party, "*Mana*, your legs look sexy, in your new white sandals."

Anna frowned at Katina for using that word again. A strange feeling came over her as she stood in front of the mirror and put on her new strand of pearls. She did not recognize herself. She looked like someone else. It's true, she thought, I'm not the same person I was a week ago. There's an air of confidence and sophistication about the lady in the mirror. She then did something she had never done before. She used some of Katina's blush. She giggled when the color of her cheeks heightened. She turned to Katina, put one hand on her hip and the other on her cheek. She raised her head up in an elegant gesture. "Shall we join the party, darling daughter?" They laughed uproariously as they left their house and joined the celebration.

Sausages were grilling on a spit, and squid was frying in large pans over a pit. Every table had a selection of appetizers. The Americans'

favorite, tzatziki, yogurt with garlic, and cucumbers, was served with crusty bread for dipping.

At eight o'clock, *Papa* Ioannis, sitting at a table with elderly men and women, stood up, rang a small altar bell and strode up to the microphone. Everyone stopped talking and turned to look at him.

"Would everyone please stand?" He waited until they rose from their seats. He spoke in Greek, and Anna translated each sentence for the Americans. "This evening we have gathered here to celebrate the fifth wedding anniversary of Brant and Merit Powers of the United States of America, who are very generous people, a fact that I have been made aware of tonight, but I cannot tell all of you about it yet." He looked at the couple and put his finger over his lips. Everyone looked at the Powers and then at each other, wondering about what they gave the priest. Naturally he had aroused their curiosity. Merit groaned quietly, while Brant smiled broadly, looking at the tables of celebrants.

The priest droned on for five minutes about the sacrament of marriage and the responsibilities of the man and a woman who take the sacred vow. The partygoers were getting restless, and an undertone of muffled talking competed with his formal speech. He finally concluded by blessing Brant and Merit and asking everyone to raise their glasses to toast the couple. In unison, the entire congregation as one voice said, *"Khronia Pola"* (happy anniversary), then applauded. Everyone came to their table to shake hands, and some of the braver men kissed Merit on the cheek; Nikos kissed her lips, then went a bit farther and embraced her tightly. Fortunately, Brant did not see it.

But Anna saw it, and to her surprise, resentment ran through her. She quickly dismissed it and thought to herself, Ha, that old man will never grow up. Why should I care? She then shifted her thoughts to the more important matter of the moment, serving the main dishes.

Yannis had carved the lambs and filled large platters for each table. The women streamed in and out of Anna's kitchen carrying steaming plates of bubbling moussaka, dolmades covered with egg and lemon sauce, stuffed green and red peppers, potatoes and bowls of salata heaped with feta cheese.

Papa Ioannis moved to the table reserved for the team and Anna. He beckoned her to sit in the vacant chair between Matt and him. When the priest wasn't looking, Nikos quietly urged Matt to change places with him so he could sit on the other side of Anna. The switch was done so smoothly that a few minutes passed before Anna or the priest realized that Nikos had replaced Matt.

Anna leaned in close to Nikos, saying gruffly in his ear, "I wanted Matt to sit next to me. What are you doing in his seat, old man?"

Nikos leaned over to her. "You have never looked more beautiful than you do tonight."

Glancing suspiciously at him, she muttered, "How many women have you said that to tonight?"

"Only you, dear Anna."

She laughed loudly.

At that point *Papa* Ioannis turned toward her and was annoyed to see Nikos sitting next to her. Although the priest could not have Anna as his wife; Greek priests must marry before they are ordained, he had hopes that now they could become close friends. "What is so funny, Anna, dear?" he asked.

"Nikos, *Papa*. He's very funny!"

The priest looked past her at Nikos then back at Anna. "He's our village clown, for sure!"

That description annoyed Nikos and he leaned forward, staring intently at the priest, "Me? The village clown? Oh no, *Papa*, you are much funnier than me! Much funnier. Ask anybody, *Papa*."

Anna kicked Nikos' ankle, and he retaliated by squeezing her knee. *Papa* Ioannis saw the exchange but was too embarrassed to say more. He was no match for Nikos and knew it. Not being able to think of something clever to say, he turned to Wade who was sitting across the table from him. "I suppose you know about very generous gifts Dr. and Mrs. Powers are going to give me."

"No, *Papa*," Wade answered.

Papa Ioannis then leaned farther down the table and asked Matt. "And how about you, Doctor? I'll bet you know what wonderful gifts I am getting from Powers, eh?" His frustration at not being able to discuss it was so great that he urged Matt with his hands to speak about it.

"I have no idea either, *Papa*," Matt answered.

The young girls served coffee and trays of desserts that included baklava, fried honey diples and galatobouriko, custard between layers of filo, and a variety of Greek cookies.

Brant had purchased cases of wine and dozens of bottles of ouzo in town that day, and had distributed them personally to each table. His generosity amazed the villagers. Everyone drank freely. He kept the bottles of potent raki aside until later. He planned on the entire village consuming enough alcohol so they would all be sleeping soundly while he carried out the robbery.

Now it was show time! Nikos rose from his seat, put a glass of ouzo on his head and moved in rhythm with the music toward the center of the compound which had been left open as a stage for entertainment. He was the master of ceremonies. Once again, Anna would translate the Greek to the Americans.

Nikos raised both hands over his head, and swayed his body sensuously. The crowd hollered "*OPA!*" and began to whistle. The young people applauded loudly at his suggestive dancing while the older women appeared to be embarrassed but were nevertheless enjoying it. He stopped dancing, took the ouzo from his head and drank it down in one gulp. The crowd clapped wildly.

Matt stood up and yelled, "Boy, I wish I could dance like you!"

Nikos turned to him and in his best "Zorba" imitation, said to Matt, "You want to dahance? I teach you to dahance."

He beckoned Matt to come to the center. Matt looked at the crowd sheepishly, but it was too late to back out. Nikos borrowed two fishermen's caps and put one on Matt's head, the other on his own. He unbuttoned Matt's white shirt halfway, reached into his pocket and took out a fake moustache, which he stuck on Matt's upper lip. The crowd roared with laughter at Matt, now standing ramrod straight and looking embarrassed. Nikos signaled the band to start the "Zorba" music. Both Matt and Nikos stood with their arms over each other's shoulders and their feet close together. They slowly bent their knees up and down in time to the music, then performed crossover steps to the right and left. Matt's performance was hilarious. He kept stumbling as he tried to keep up with Nikos. Matt played the comedian well. His face was deadly serious as he kept looking sideways at Nikos, then at his feet. Nikos pretended to be utterly exasperated.

When the tempo of the music increased, suddenly, to the amazement of the crowd, Matt, finally got in step with Nikos and began dancing the intricate steps expertly. He cried out, "I've got it, by George, I've got it! I know how to dahance!"

The two men finished the frenetic dance in perfect unison kneeling on one knee with arms outstretched and bowing their heads. The crowd clapped loudly and called out "bravos!" The amazed team members had to practically carry Matt back to the table. When he recovered enough to speak, he admitted, "Nikos and I have been practicing secretly. And I've decided I'm going to be a dancer, instead of a doctor!"

Nikos, now back at the mike, announced, "Next, we will be entertained by the lovely ladies of our village performing an old Greek folk dance, the Salamis. It was taught to them by a lovely DORA STRATOU dancer, Irene Gavalas from Fira."

The music began, and a dozen women came through the crowd from all sides in colorful costumes.

Merit, was elated to be part of the women's entertainment. While moving to the music, she thought, at this moment in time, my heart and my soul are Greek. I'll be devastated when I have to leave this captivating island.

When the dance ended, the women were given a standing ovation.

"Our next act will be performed by two young men from Oia who have danced on other islands and on mainland Greece. Let's give a big welcome to Stavros and Antonis!"

The two young men were slim and handsome. They wore black tight-fitting costumes and red sashes. Whistles and yells accompanied their frenzied movements. In perfect unison, they leaped four feet in the air, twisting and turning. The Americans had never seen anything like it and were on their feet, applauding continuously. When it ended, Stavros and

Antonis walked to the team's table. Slow music began. Stavros hunched down in front of the table as Antonis asked everyone to move their chairs back. Stavros then stretched both arms out to the side while clamping his teeth on the edge of the wooden table, which was covered with glasses, plates and lighted candles. Slowly, to the amazement of the crowd, he began to lift the table with only his teeth. Standing up straight and holding the table level, he began to move gracefully around the stage until he was back to where the team sat. The crowd went wild when he set the table back down in place without spilling a drink. The applause lasted five minutes as the audience begged for an encore.

Nikos finally got the crowd's attention. "The boys need a rest," he pleaded. "Maybe later they'll dance again. Our next act was supposed to be a very exotic belly dancer, but our good *Papa* Ioannis did not think it was proper, so…"

Loud hisses and boos followed from the crowd. The poor priest was shocked. No one had told him about a belly dancer. He looked around the compound, trying to convince the crowd that he had nothing to do with it.

Nikos then held up his hand for silence. "I was only fooling. We were not planning on a belly dancer. It was just a joke, *Papa*."

The priest was fuming. He knew Nikos had done it on purpose to embarrass him.

Nikos made the announcement everyone had been waiting to hear. "It's MOVIE TIME!" The band played a somewhat familiar version of "Hollywood," as people moved their chairs to get a good view of the screen, which had been set up at the end of the stage area.

The screen came alive with bouzouki music and a long shot of the village as seen from the bottom of the one-thousand foot mountain, Mesa Vouno. It looked like a miniature make-believe town of tiny, dazzling white houses. Prominently rising above the town was the blue-domed church of St. Demetrius and its bell tower. The camera slowly zoomed up the mountain. Katina narrated in Greek. The village came into sharp focus, and the audience applauded loudly as the title, "THE VILLAGE OF SAINT DEMETRIUS" appeared over a close-up of the front of the church. Villagers were seen coming out and waving at the camera. Many stopped in front of the camera for a picture with their families. The audience giggled in embarrassment when their faces loomed large on the screen. When the old oracle hobbled down the church steps, she put her face right up to the lens, completely filling the screen. Her white, perfectly formed widow's peak grew halfway down her forehead, but the rest of her hair remained tightly covered by her black scarf. She smiled, and her heavily-lined olive skin folded into layers, and her lips caved into a toothless mouth. The audience laughed politely, but then respectfully applauded the old woman's humor. Most villagers actually feared her.

Papa Ioannis came out last, smiling broadly. Katina and Anna shook his hand. Anna said, "Isn't it a beautiful Sunday morning here in our village, *Papa?*"

Looking into the camera instead of at Anna, Father Ioannis answered stiffly, "Yes. It-is-a-very-beautiful-day. God-is-good."

The next scenes reflected religious life on the island. Inside a rustic roadside shrine, an elderly widow in black kissed a small silver icon and hung it on the wall alongside several others. Monks, at the nearby Profitas Elias Monastery, high above the village, walked slowly through a columned arcade and sang a hymn that echoed down the mountain.

In the following panoramic scenes, the audience viewed the ancient ruins of Thera. Kristo stood in front of the opening of the Grotto of Hermes and Heracles. His hair was slicked down, and his chin was raised proudly. He explained how he had discovered the hole in the back wall that led into the cave tunnels. As he spoke, he held one hand on his hip and the other pointing to the hole in the back of the grotto. The resemblance to Nikos' stance, which most villagers knew well, was not lost on the audience.

Elias, with the dog, Pluto, walked up to the ancient city of Thera and opened the gate for Merit, who was riding Zeus. The other team members followed in Nikos' dilapidated truck. Nikos gave brief descriptions of some of the less important artifacts they had found in the cave. "We hope to prove that Santorini was the lost kingdom of Atlantis."

The audience cheered that heartening news.

The screen now filled with various sights and sounds from the village square. Three young boys riding bicycles, continuously circled the waterless fountain in the center of the square. Each time they passed the camera, they performed various tricks on their bikes. Four women, gathered outside of a large white house, were deep in conversation until one of them realized they were being filmed. She alerted the others who quickly turned towards the camera. They all made funny faces, which brought on uproarious laughter from the spectators.

A wistful scene then captivated the audience. A young mother and her daughter looked out a half-shuttered window. A flower box below them, overflowed with brightly colored blossoms. The mother's long black hair, neatly tied with a pink ribbon, fell over her shoulder and flowed down her blouse. The little girl, a miniature of her mother, smiled bashfully at the camera, looked up at her mother, then took a sidelong glance at the camera, giggled and hid her face with her hands.

Two men leading a train of donkeys laden with sacks of grain on their backs, trudged up the street. The men paused and tipped their caps, and the camera followed them as they moved up the cobblestone path. The last donkey deposited a load of dung in the road, much to the delight of the audience. Instantly, two women raced out of their houses with shovels and scooped up the manure. One of the men called back, "Best fertilizer in the world!" The audience cheered in agreement.

A group of men sat under a makeshift awning at a small table outside the village taverna. They were smoking and looking intently at a backgammon board. The camera singled out each face through the haze of cigarette smoke. Not one looked up.

An elderly man on his second floor balcony leaned over the railing. He waved gently while fingering his orange worry beads.

Inside village houses, women prepared various dishes. Three women washed clothes in a creek. At the Kaldara's house, Kristos' mother instructed young village girls on how to weave on the loom.

At the top of a flight of stairs, a young girl sang along with a radio and gestured with her hands for the camera to film her stringing tomatoes and hanging them on the wall of the house to dry in the sun.

Cats continuously prowled in and out of the scenes.

A young man on a motor scooter drove by. He winked, whistled and waved when the camera followed him down the narrow street.

The final dramatic scenes, were accompanied by soft music, and narrated poetically by Katina.

"A spectacular sunrise gives birth to a new day in the village of St. Demetrius. Multi-colored swaying wildflowers cascade down a terraced hill, while a shepherd walks with his lowing flock of lambs. Figs dry in the hot sun, and in the orchards, families gather grapes, olives and pistachios. Peach, apple and cherry trees, green with buds, will soon blossom. Towards late afternoon, the sky darkens with little warning. Lightning streaks across the heavens. Rain quenches the earth. Cisterns refill. The rain stops, and puddles momentarily reflect the last rays of the sun bursting through the departing thunderheads. A final glow brightens Santorini for a moment as the celebration of sunset begins. Across the island, church bells harmonize with vibrant tolling sounds. The sunset sky, with its luminous golden disc as its focal point, presents an ever-changing tapestry, moving down slowly to meet the sea. The celestial day star that has given warmth to the island since its birth, sinks slowly into the Aegean, amid lingering traces of vivid reds, yellows and oranges that meld with the last purple storm clouds. Darkness descends and another disc, this one white, rises to guide us through the night. Santorini, survivor from ancient times and untold upheavals, home to many cultures and civilizations, continues to be sustained by the strong faith and fortitude of its people in peace and harmony."

The music heightened. The final scene, dominated by the moonlit ruins of the ancient city of Thera, and the silvery Aegean beyond, slowly fades.

The crowd rose and applauded loudly. Men whistled. Some cried unashamedly. Merit and Katina embraced, and the villagers surrounded them. Merit's film had captured the essence of Santorini, and the villagers of St. Demetrius loved her for it. When the team finally got near the girls, Matt said with great sincerity, "Ladies, I think that film should get an Academy Award." Both Nikos and Wade congratulated them. Nikos sealed it with a kiss. Brant, ignoring Katina, commented, "Merit, darling, you did a superior job! Now let's get on with the party."

The band began playing, and dancers packed the floor. Brant and Matt came out of the house, carrying boxes of dinner plates that they had purchased earlier that day.

When Nikos saw them, he smiled broadly. "*OPA*"! We break plates, eh? I have not done that for long time. You know it was outlawed by government because they thought it was uncivilized thing to do. Let's be uncivilized! I'll show you how to do it."

The three men stood on the sidelines of the dance floor and began skimming dishes at the feet of the dancers. The crowd loved it. It was an old Greek custom that had not been practiced for many years. Everyone joined in the old tradition. If villagers were not dancing, they were busy scaling the dishes. When the supply was gone, groans of disappointment filled the courtyard.

The plate smashing had intensified the audience's excitement, and the men drank much more than usual. By one o'clock, some were quite drunk and staggering. they were taken home by their families. The crowd gradually thinned out.

Brant appeared to be quite tipsy, but in fact, he'd only had one drink during the evening. Each time he filled his glass, he'd pretend to drink it but would surreptitiously empty it on the ground. He was filled with anxiety. He wanted the party to end and everyone go to bed so he could get on with his plan.

His drunken act had convinced Merit that he should not drink anymore. She suspected he was having such a wonderful time because the village men were treating him like a hero. They were drawn to him because of his generosity with wine and ouzo.

One of the men whispered drunkenly in Brant's ear, "Old *Papa* Ioannis told me your secret, eh? You gave him all things to make movie, eh? You're good man! Good to our village!" He kissed Brant's cheek.

Perfect! Brant thought. Good, old blabber-mouth Ioannis didn't fail me. He put his arm around the man and led him to a table where Elias was sitting with Nikos. He showed them the bottle of raki and put his finger up to his mouth for secrecy. They quickly turned their backs on the crowd and each man took a large slug of the potent alcohol.

Brant then wandered over to where Matt, Wade, Merit and Anna were sitting. They all seemed quite mellow.

Brant offered both Matt and Wade a drink from his bottle. Wade refused at first. "I remember what had happened the night when Elias and his dog, Pluto drank raki, and they both passed out.

"Come on," Brant urged them, slurring his words. "You know the old shaying, when in Rome, et cetera, et cetera."

"Okay, give me the bottle," Matt said. "An Irishman can drink anything if he can drink homemade Irish *poteen*, and I can drink *poteen* like nobody else. Come on Wade, lesh show old boy Powers that we can do anything he can do."

Brant emptied their drinks on the ground and put three fingers of the raki into their glasses.

"Bottoms up!" Matt said, and the two men chugalugged the potent alcohol.

Instantly, they were on their feet, holding their throats, coughing and choking. The powerful alcohol burned their gullets. Anna and Merit laughed at their antics.

Brant looked at the two women. "Of course, you two are afraid to take a little raki, huh? Women are sissies anyway."

"I'll try just a little tiny bit," Merit said, just to see how it tastes."

"Pour me a small one, too," Anna said, giving Brant a sarcastic sneer.

Brant said, "Jus a minute, ladies, and I'll get you clean glasses." He walked over to the bar, quickly opened two sleeping capsules and poured the fine powder into the new glasses. He then poured in the raki and stirred it.

"Here you go, girls, I hope you don't get drunky."

Anna clicked her glass against Merit's, and even though they drank it slowly, both coughed and made faces.

Nikos staggered over to their table, winked at Brant, put his arm around Brant's shoulder and whispered, "How about a little nightcap, old palsy?"

Brant was delighted to oblige and gave him a stiff one.

By now, only a few guests remained, and the band had packed up and left. Matt began singing Irish songs, but before long, he passed out. Wade, who was also feeling no pain, asked Brant to help him carry Matt upstairs to bed. The three men staggered off to the house.

Merit giggled. "Ya know what, Anna?"

"What?" Anna asked.

"See those three men? That's what ya call the blind leading the blind."

Anna laughed loudly and filled their glasses with more wine.

They didn't drink much, because they could hardly sit up.

Merit tried to stand but fell back down in her chair and began to sob. Brant staggered over to her and said, "Come, on honey, we're going beddy-bye."

Ari and Katina came over to the table. "Don't go, Ari said, "I want to make toast to you, please." The young couple obviously had drunk too much. Their faces were flushed, and they had trouble walking straight. Katina had her eyes closed and leaned her head on Ari's shoulder.

"Thank ya, young man. Here, have a real man's drink if you're strong nuff to take it." Brant said, offering the bottle of raki to Ari. He had forgotten about Ari. This will make him sleep soundly if he'll drink it, he thought.

Ari accepted the challenge willingly, put the bottle to his mouth and drank a large amount before he threw his head back and spit it out. Everyone laughed. When he regained his breath he choked out the words "*Stis chares sou*," (to your joys). He handed the bottle back to Brant who then offered it to Katina.

"No," Anna interceded and stuttered, "My Katina, ah, she is, ah, ah, coming home right now, with me." She was having trouble speaking and focusing.

"Well, *kakinicta*, old friends," Brant said, putting a supporting arm around Merit's waist as they staggered across the courtyard to their house.

When Anna tried to stand up, she felt dizzy.

Nikos saw her sway. "Come, Anna, dear. I'm going to tuck you in bed, cause ya drunk." He picked her up. She was so limp, she couldn't protest. He began stumbling toward the house.

Ari called to Nikos, "We put all the video equipment inside your house, Nikos. Katina and I will shut off the lights, eh?"

Nikos paused momentarily and strained to bring Ari in focus. "Shay good night to little Katina right this minute cause she's going to bed with her mana."

"Than you, Nikos." Anna moaned. "You're a good man."

Ari kissed Katina quickly on the lips and said, "I love you, Tina." Then he led her to Nikos, who was holding Anna. Katina turned to Ari, looked at him lovingly and ran into the house ahead of Nikos and Anna.

Nikos laid Anna down on her bed, and Katina fell on the bed beside her. Within minutes, both were breathing heavily. Nikos took off Anna's pearls and Katina's jewelry and set them on the bureau. He threw a light blanket over them and stood for a few moments looking down at the beautiful women. I would like them to belong to me, he thought, then staggered across the courtyard, noisily plowing through the broken dishes, and uselessly slapping cats off the tables. He crashed through his front door and passed out on his bed.

CHAPTER FOURTEEN

Brant looked at his watch, it was two o'clock. He had not undressed when Merit and he fell into bed. He quietly slipped out of the house and went behind the *banio*. Under a pile of bushes, he pulled out a burlap sack that was filled with thick chunks of lamb he'd piled on his plate several times during the party and then hid them. He cut slices into the thick lamb and emptied the contents of several sleeping capsules into the grooves.

Any sounds he might have made leaving the compound were drowned out by the erratic creaking of the windmill. Cloud formations covering the moon concealed his shadowy form as he hurried through the village. Even the candles in the tin cans along the street had either gone out or had been taken in. Luck was with him! He estimated that the steep climb up to the ruins would take him half an hour.

Reaching the summit on schedule, he stealthily moved past Elias' house, then climbed over the rickety wire gate to the ancient city. Now he breathed easier. He unlocked the office and used his flashlight to find his equipment. He suited up, grabbed a crowbar, a large lamp, and slung the sack of lamb over his shoulder. He moved swiftly through the ruins along the east side of the ancient city, then cut across toward the grotto of Hermes and Heracles.

This will be the hard part, he thought, man against animal! I've got to control Pluto. But if he doesn't cooperate, I'll use the crowbar! Well, here I go. He whistled two short whistles and one long, the way Elias signaled the dog. Instantly, Pluto raced toward him. Brant called out softly in Greek, "Good boy, Pluto, good dog."

Within seconds, they faced each other. Pluto snarled fiercely.

The dog terrified Brant, but he forced himself to hold out a large chunk of the tainted meat.

Pluto rejected Brant's soft assurances, and the lamb. He growled ferociously, opened his snarling mouth wide, bared his sharp fangs and sprang at Brant.

Brant slammed the bag of lamb at the dog's face. Pluto, stunned temporarily, sniffed and glanced down at the meat that had tumbled out of the burlap and resumed his attack stance.

Brant quickly tried the "Good boy, Pluto, good dog" tactic again.

Warily, Pluto looked at Brant, then sniffed the lamb again.

Brant realized that the well-trained dog was having a difficult time deciding whether to attack or forsake his duty.

Pluto barked sharply three times, grabbed the juicy meat in his mouth and chewed it rapidly, pausing momentarily to lick his drooling chops and glance at Brant.

Cautiously, Brant bent down to the dog, gently patted his head and spoke softly, urging him to take another piece. The dog grabbed the meat and began chewing it rapidly. Brant threw him another piece as he began to move quickly toward the grotto while continuing to throw more pieces. By the time they reached the grotto, Pluto was weak, his legs began to falter. A few moments later, he sank to the ground unconscious with part of the meat hanging from his mouth.

Pleased with his success, Brant laughed at the helpless animal. He stepped over him, turned on the large lamp and entered the grotto. Excitement filled his body when he went through the back wall and down the stairs into the tunnel.

He made his way swiftly through the familiar passageways. It was now two-thirty-five. He must hurry. When he reached the steep incline down to the cavern, he tossed the crowbar below. The reverberating sound of the iron rod hitting the floor was deafening.

"Good!" he said aloud. "If there are any critters around that'll scare them off."

Reaching the floor of the cavern, his heart began to pound wildly as he grabbed the crowbar and slowly moved between the stalagmites. A hideous smile masked his face as he thought, I'm almost there! I can just walk in and take anything I want! His excitement reached such a peak, he began giggling foolishly as he moved closer. He pointed the lamp toward the omphalos. Suddenly he stopped cold and screamed, "Jesus! What's happened! What son of a bitch did that? The chamber's sealed with limestone slabs again!" He felt like he was going crazy. He raced toward the chamber, tripped and dropped the lamp. The glass face cracked, and, although it was still shining, the beam was badly distorted. He shook his head to clear his thoughts. Get a grip on yourself, he ordered, staring at the omphalos. A moment of sanity made him remember that Nikos and Wade had put plywood over the opening.

When he reached the entrance, he pulled savagely at the plywood and it crashed to the floor. He held the battered lamp in front of him and walked inside the chamber. His breathing was labored. "Why does this room feel so cold? Oh, God, I must calm down. There's nothing here to hurt me. Now, where's my beautiful gold female deity? She'll warm me up!" He took her out of the recess and kissed her. She was so cold, his lips seemed frozen to her face. He dropped her to the floor, saying, "Bitch!"

He was becoming quite disoriented and rapidly losing his sense of reality. He reminded himself loudly, "Hurry, Dr. Powers. Take what you want. You've paid dearly for these treasures."

I must get to the sarcophagus so I can get that beautiful snake ring with the amethyst fangs that Merit admired so much."

Recklessly, he moved things aside, making his way towards the sarcophagus, knocking over pithos.

He opened the bronze box that held the gold-handled dagger and the sword with the ivory hilt. "No doubt about it! These are mine!" He stuck the dagger in his belt on one side and hung the sword through the belt on the other side. When he reached the ancient coffin, frigid air engulfed him. Although his hands were shaking, he managed to wedge the crowbar under the lid of the sarcophagus and pryed it off. Instantly, a freezing gust of air blew in his face and fog-like vapors filled the room. He dropped the lamp and the light went out completely. Only the small ray from his hard hat gave him light. He was so terrified, he couldn't move.

Suddenly, he sensed that someone was in the room with him. He could hear breathing, but he couldn't see anyone.

"Is that you, Elias? Who else is here?" he shrieked.

It must be the same specters that frightened Merit and Katina." Should I forget about the ring and get the hell out of here? Shit. No! I'm getting that snake ring for my wife." He had now lost all sense of reality, he was over the edge.

The floor under him began to shake. He pulled the dagger and sword out of his belt and slashed at the imperceptible specters that were trying to take control of him.

"Demons! Devils! Vampires! Whoever the hell you are, see what I'm doing!" He reached into the sarcophagus, pushing aside all the items that lay on top of the skeletal remains and tugged at the finger bone that wore the serpent-headed golden ring. When the finger fell away from the rest of the hand, he savagely tore the ring off.

"See! See, you evil bastards? I told you I'd get the ring for my wife!" Making his way to the door, he slipped the sharply pointed serpent ring off his finger and put it in his jacket pocket. He pulled the sword from his belt, raised the dagger and slashed the air with both weapons, then threw them back into the chamber.

The whole cavern was moving. Primal survival instincts told him he must get out of the cave quickly. He sped across the cavern floor and up the incline with ghosts and cold fog still in pursuit, partially engulfing him. Chunks of limestone struck his hard-hat, causing his ears to ring and his head to pound with pain.

He was running for his life now, and he knew it. About twenty feet from the stairs leading up to the grotto, he heard a loud crack above him. He looked up and saw an enormous piece of limestone coming down. He tried to lunge forward but lost his balance and fell backward. The huge slab crashed onto his lower left leg, crushing it and pinning him to the floor. Excruciating pain shot through his body. He couldn't move. He screamed, "Oh, Jesus Christ, someone help me! Help me! Help me, someone! I'm trapped!"

* * * *

The first tremor, which occurred at about three-fifteen A.M., was light. Not many villagers were aware of it. Although donkeys brayed continuously and small waves lapped at the sides of cisterns, only a few were alerted by those warnings. Within minutes of that tremor, a second, stronger shock shook the island. This time buildings swayed and screams of "*Seismos!*" echoed throughout the village. Families ran into the streets in their nightclothes and huddled together in fear, expecting the next jolt to collapse their homes.

Papa Ioannis raced to the church and frantically rang the bells to warn anyone who might still be asleep.

Ari, the first to be awakened in the compound, leapt out of bed, slipped on his pants and raced to Nikos' room, screaming. Pictures on the walls swayed back and forth. The hall lights flickered. He could hear objects falling downstairs. The floor under his feet pitched like a ship at sea. The windmill wheel, thrown out of balance by the shocks, slapped crookedly against the sides of the mill building. "Nikos, Nikos! Wake up! Wake up! SEISMOS! SEISMOS!" He shook Nikos vigorously, pulling him to his feet.

Nikos was so groggy that at first he didn't understand what Ari wanted. Another strong jolt hit, and the rumbling continued. Nikos jumped to his feet, grabbed his pants and pushed Ari down the stairs in front of him. He yelled loudly, racing into the courtyard towards Anna's house,

"SEISMOS! SEISMOS! SEISMOS! EARTHQUAKE! EARTHQUAKE! Ari, get the Americans out of the houses."

The old windmill wheel slowly toppled to the ground with a thundering crash.

Merit, groggy and weak and still clad in her party dress, staggered outside. "What's happening?" she asked in a frightened voice.

"It's earthquake, Mrs. Powers," yelled Ari. "Stay outside. Get Mr. Powers outside!"

Ari ran into the dining room of the middle house, calling to Matt and Wade. He saw them racing down the stairs. Light fixtures fell off the walls, and the table slid across the room.

Once outside, Matt and Wade looked around for the others. Nikos was leading Anna and Katina across the courtyard. Both women still wore their now wrinkled party dresses.

Nikos called out orders. "Ari, see if the electricity's on! Use the emergency generator if it isn't. Anna, light some candles out here. Where are the Powers?"

"Mrs. Powers was just here," Ari said, pointing to the Powers' house.

Merit ran out of her door screaming," I can't find Brant! He's not in the house or *banio*," she cried.

Another violent shock struck. They reached out to each other for support. The cobblestone surface rose and fell under their feet. Terror was etched on everyone's face!

"Did Brant go to bed with you last night, Merit?" Wade asked.

"I'm not sure. I had too much to drink. The last thing I remember, we were staggering home. Yes, I remember now, we both fell into bed."

"He was very drunk," Katina added in an apologetic tone, not wanting to hurt Merit's feelings.

"Yes, he was," Wade said. "I vaguely remember him talking to me before you went home, Merit. I wasn't in great shape, either, but I remember he wasn't too steady. He must have gotten up and wandered off someplace."

Matt looked at Merit. "Merit, you don't suppose he went up the hill, I mean, to the cave?"

Everyone looked at Merit.

She put her hands up to her mouth in horror. "Oh, my God. Do you think he could have made it up there as drunk as he was?"

"He might have taken my truck," Nikos said. "I'll go see if telephone still works, and call Elias."

Another tremor jolted the compound, although not quite so strong as the others.

Matt put his arm around Merit's shoulders and tried to comfort her. "He's probably not up there, Merit. He might just be passed out somewhere around here. Come on, everybody, let's look around the compound."

Just as they were about to disperse, Nikos came running out of his house. Yelling loudly, with a pained expression covering his face, he said, "I have some bad news. Maybe Brant is up there, but he didn't take my truck. Elias said when he whistled for Pluto, and he didn't come, he went looking for him and found him at entrance to grotto. His dog was not dead, but he couldn't wake him up. A chunk of lamb was hanging out of his mouth. He thinks someone tried to poison him. Elias and his family are very upset!"

"Has he seen Brant?" Merit asked in a quivering voice.

"No, but he was just about to call us. He found office door open. And at grotto, he saw rest of back wall of grotto had caved in and lots of limestone was piled at bottom of steps." Nikos now paused and looked anxiously from Merit to the others. "He thinks maybe ceiling caved in on, (he paused) uh, whoever hurt his dog because, oh, uh, (he paused again,) he saw boot sticking out from under big piece of stone."

Merit screamed in fright, "Oh, my God, BRANT!"

"Let's get up there fast!" Matt gave orders in rapid succession. "We'll need help getting the rubble out of the way. Everyone get shoes on! I'll get my medical bag. Ari, you and Katina stay here. It's possible he just lost his boot up there, and he's making his way back here. Keep a lookout for him just in case. If he's injured, call Kaldara's house, and we'll get right back. Anna, I'll need your help."

She nodded her willingness. "Sure. I'll get shoes and sweater and bring sheets and towels."

Katina had her arms around Merit, trying to console her.

"I'm coming with you," Merit said.

"Okay. Hurry, put on warm clothes!" Wade said.

"Everybody move!" Matt ordered. He had a premonition he might be facing a major medical crisis at the cave if Brant was trapped. He ran a quick check of his medical supplies in his mind. He only had a few surgical tools and several vials of drugs, nothing very sophisticated.

Once they were ready, they moved swiftly through the village and saw that many of the houses had been damaged.

Nikos asked each family group they passed if anyone was injured. He relayed that information to Matt. "So far, Matt no one is hurt too badly. Just scrapes and cuts!"

"Thank God for that," Matt said.

When they reached the truck, they piled in and Nikos sped up the steep hill and stopped at the Kaldaras' house.

Another tremor struck, causing the ground to quiver under their feet, but they kept moving. Elias was waiting for them. Kristos was in tears, and Dora was on her knees tending Pluto, who was wrapped in a blanket and seemed to be unconscious.

Kristos sobbed when he saw Merit, "Someone tried to kill our Pluto, Mrs. Powers."

Merit put her arms around his shoulders and tried to soothe him. "I'm sure he'll be okay, Kristos. I'll look at him when I come back."

Sobbing pathetically, Kristos blurted out, "But my *papa* says he's been poisoned. Someone gave him meat with white poison powder in it. We saw it!"

Matt instructed Elias to get towels and blankets from his house and bring them immediately to the cave. He told Elias quietly, "I think maybe the white powder was a medicine to make people sleep. I'd noticed that quite a few of the sleeping capsules I had were missing from my medicine bag. I suspected Brant had taken them because he was becoming so hyper about finding a treasure and couldn't sleep. Pluto will be fine once he sleeps off the effect. I'm sorry, Elias."

"If Mr. Powers did that, I'll report him to police."

They arrived at the office and quickly gathered their gear. Wade noticed that one of the lamps, Brant's suit and hard hat were missing. "Let's put hard hats on. Merit, give yours to Anna. She may have to go into the cave with me."

Carrying the lamp, tools and flashlights, they ran through the ancient city towards the grotto.

When they arrived, Nikos held them back. "Hold it! Let me take look first at overhead in grotto to see if there are any loose rocks that might fall on our heads." They could see that chunks of limestone had fallen from the ceiling and walls. The back wall of stones had now collapsed completely, enlarging the access into the tunnel. Nikos prodded the ceiling with a shovel, then scanned the back wall and stairs with the lamp.

At that instant they heard a low moan.

Merit screamed, "Brant!"

"Okay, everyone, let's keep cool," Matt said. "Merit, try to keep calm. Brant is obviously hurt. If he hears us panic, it won't help. Let me take a quick look at the situation."

Anna held Merit tightly. "Matt will save him," she said softly. They could do nothing but stand and wait.

The men slowly went down the steps, pushing aside the fallen chunks of limestone as best they could. When they reached the bottom, they saw Brant's right boot sticking out from under an enormous slab of thick limestone wedged between the walls.

Matt took the lamp, and with a running jump, leaped over the huge rock. "Aw, Jesus, Mary and Joseph!" he moaned, looking in horror at Brant. His left leg, from just below the knee was crushed almost flat. His pant leg was heavily soaked with blood, and a pool of blood covered the floor under his upper thigh. His right leg was flexed and somehow had miraculously escaped being trapped. His head was slumped to one side. His face was bloodied.

Matt knelt down next to him. "Brant, can you hear me?" He could tell Brant had lost a great deal of blood. His pulse was thready and rapid, his face was ashen and covered with cold sweat. He was slipping in and out of consciousness. Whenever he opened his eyes, there was little sign that he saw Matt.

Recognizing the symptoms, Matt realized Brant would soon bleed to death unless he took quick action.

"Wade, Nikos, Elias!" Matt yelled. "What are the chances of lifting the limestone off his leg with a crowbar? We have to get him out of here immediately. He's lost too much blood!"

While the three men tried to wedge the bars under the thick stone, Matt took off his belt to use as a tourniquet. He placed it around Brant's lower thigh, and prayed he could stem the bleeding quickly.

Wade called out to Matt in desperation, "Matt, it's impossible to move it. It's too tightly wedged between the walls. We could try to break it up with a sledge hammer on this side, away from his injured leg, but I'm afraid it would jar him terribly and crash down on his right leg. It's wedged against the wall, one foot above his right leg."

Matt said, "There isn't time, guys. He's critical. I'm going to have to amputate his leg. It's the only way I can save his life. Get Anna down here with my medical supplies. Hurry! Nikos, bring Merit down too, but keep her on that side! I'll give her the bad news."

Matt leaned down close to Brant's ear. "Brant, it's me, Matt. Can you hear me?"

Brant moaned slightly.

Good! Matt thought to himself.

Merit looked over the limestone that trapped her husband. "Oh, my God, Matt! Is he going to be all right?"

Wade and Elias lifted Anna over the stone and passed her the supplies. She went right to work, removing Brant's hard hat and putting a towel under his head.

Merit cried, "Matt! How badly is he hurt?"

By now Matt was working fast, picking out the necessary medical supplies and instruments from his medical bag. He looked up at Merit, "Merit, dear, there is only one way I can save Brant's life. I have to amputate his left leg."

"Oh my God, NO, Matt!" she screamed. "Is that the only way? Are you sure?"

Matt looked up at her with compassion. "It's the only way, Merit."

"Then do it." She buried her head in her hands, agonizing over how Brant would ever be able to live with only one leg. He was so vain. Nikos put his arm around her and led her outside.

Just then another tremor shook the cave. They covered their heads as limestone fragments fell from the ceiling. Anna threw herself over the medical supplies she had laid out. Matt shielded Brant with his body.

THE SANTORINI ODYSSEY

"Anna, I want to immediately start an I.V. in Brant's hand. Set up that plastic bag of saline and tubing. Hopefully it will restore his blood volume and counter the blood loss. I'm injecting a bolus of ketamine to produce anesthesia for the amputation." Matt was trying desperately to think out every move he'd have to make to save Brant's life as he inserted the I.V needle into a vein in his hand. Anna held up the bag of saline while Matt taped the needle securely in place. The life-saving solution flowed rapidly into Brant's bloodstream and the anesthesia began to take effect immediately. Brant stopped moaning, his facial expression became mask-like.

"He'll be unconscious and insensitive to the pain now for fifteen to twenty minutes," Matt said. "We'll have to work fast, Anna, Wade, get Nikos' hard hat on and come over to this side. I want you to take the IV bag from Anna and hold it up high with one hand. Shine the lamp on Brant's leg with the other. Nikos and Elias! I want you to rig some kind of a stretcher so we can carry him to the truck. Run jacket sleeves through two poles, anything! Just be ready to take him out of here after I finish, ten to fifteen minutes, at the most."

Matt and Anna donned rubber gloves and began unwrapping the instruments. He identified each one for Anna as he laid them on a sterile towel, hoping it would help her to know what to hand him. "Scalpel, blades, artery forceps, ligatures, needle-mounted sutures and a Gigli saw. That's this strand of woven wire with the burrs, and these are the handles I'll put on each end of the wire so I can cut through the bone. It's an old-fashioned saw, Anna, but for some crazy reason, I stuck it in my bag, thinking someone might get a foot caught in a crevice. I must have had a premonition."

"Thank God you did, Matt."

Anna continued laying out sponges, clamps, gauze bandages, dressings and tape. She passed Matt the scissors to cut off Brant's pant leg. Once that was done and the bare leg was exposed, Matt put his hands under Brant's buttocks and rolled him over slightly while Anna slid a clean towel under him. Then Matt placed a folded blanket under Brant's back to elevate his pelvis. He slipped a rolled towel under the upper thigh to raise it off the ground. Anna immediately began painting Brant's thigh, knee and the part of his lower leg that was accessible with an iodine solution. Then she draped more towels over Brant's torso and bare leg.

Matt was ready to begin. "Start praying everyone. Scalpel, Anna. I'm going to do what we call a guillotine amputation to save time and blood loss; I'll fashion flaps of skin to close over the stump of the bone later, after we get him to the hospital."

Anna was calm and proficient. She anticipated Matt's every move, sponging away the blood as he quickly separated and severed the muscles. He then began ligating the arteries and veins. Once that was accomplished, he began to cut through the bones with the Gigli saw.

Merit had been sitting on the top step, listening and praying. Now she heard the noise of the saw and visualized what was happening. She held back a scream and raced out of the grotto and vomited.

Wade, still holding the IV bag and lamp, felt bile rise up in his throat and turned his face away from the scene.

Matt cut through the large tibial bone, then sawed through the smaller fibula. "Done! Let's pull him away from the slab, Anna." They moved Brant back about a yard, and Matt tied off the few remaining "oozers" in the stump. Then he immediately applied a pressure dressing to the stump and wrapped it tightly with an elastic bandage.

"Nikos, Elias!" Matt yelled.

The two men came running down the stairs with a canvas stretcher and climbed over the limestone.

"I remember I have stretcher in case tourist have accident here in ancient city," Elias said. "My wife put clean sheet on it."

"Good. Okay, let's lift Brant onto the stretcher. Wrap those blankets around him, and get him outside."

Anna quickly tossed Matt's instruments and the used sponges and soiled towels into a pillowcase she had brought. She looked down at the remains of Brant's crushed leg and thought to herself in horror, the rats will clean that up fast. It was 4:20 when they raced through the dark ruins, carrying Brant on the stretcher. Merit trotted at his side, holding his hand. By now the anesthesia had begun to wear off, and he sobbed now and then. When he opened his eyes and saw Merit, he moaned, "What happened to me?"

Merit saw Matt's signal of caution. He pointed to the amputated leg, shook his index finger and head and mouthed a "no."

"You're going to be fine, darling. We're taking you to the hospital. Try to sleep."

"Can't sleep! Have to get away from ghosts! They're cold. Can't you feel them? Keep running faster, everybody! Run! Run!"

The team exchanged glances. Elias' eyes widened in fright. He looked back toward the grotto but saw nothing ghostly.

Brant squeezed Merit's hand so tightly, she thought he might break her fingers. Then he suddenly let go of her hand and patted the breast pocket of his coveralls. As hard as he tried, he couldn't quite get his hand into the pocket so he moved his other hand with the IV over to the pocket.

Merit grabbed the hand and held it tightly. "No, darling, don't move that hand. Matt has a needle in there with some medicine in it to make you better."

Brant was confused and fumbled to get his other hand in his pocket. Retrieving the ring, he squeezed it tightly in his hand. With badly slurred speech, he mumbled, "Shush, don't tell anybody, Merit. I've got it! I have something for you the ghosts didn't get. It's right here in my hand."

"Later, dear. Just rest now," Merit pleaded.

"Noooo!" he screamed. "I risked my life to get this for you. Now you take it!"

"Brant, calm down, pal," Matt said softly. "You're in a very weakened condition, and you're not going to help yourself by getting upset."

Brant became belligerent. "Oh, pardon me all to hell, Doctor. Don't worry about me. I can take care of myself." He raised his fist, with the ring still hidden inside and shook it at Matt. "I know all about snakes, especially this," He fainted.

When they reached the truck they lifted him into the back. Matt, Anna and Merit hopped in back beside him. Nikos and Wade rode up front.

Anna noticed blood trickling out between the fingers of his clenched fist. She tried to pry the fingers open without success.

Then Matt tried without any luck. "Something he's holding must have broken in his hand and cut him. I'll fix it when we get to the hospital. He doesn't seem to be losing much blood with his fist clenched so tightly."

Merit was distraught, not only because Brant had lost part of his leg, but because he had gone into the cave to steal treasures and might have one in his hand. Oh, God, how could he? He's much more mentally ill than I thought.

They were about halfway down the mountain when Brant began to shake violently, his whole body became stiff as a board.

"Jesus, what's happening?" Matt asked in anguish. "He's turning blue! He's cyanotic! He's having a seizure! But why?" Matt looked at Brant's pupils, they were dilated and his eyes stared blankly. His facial muscles were contorted, and his skin was clammy. Matt grabbed a bandage roll and stuck it between his teeth so he couldn't bite his tongue or cheeks. He felt Brant's pulse, it was rapid and feeble. His breathing was shallow, labored and irregular. Then suddenly his body seemed to relax.

"He's gone into post-seizure," Matt said as he quickly scanned Brant's body. He saw that his bloody hand was now opened wide. In it was the gold serpent ring that had been on the skeleton in the sarcophagus. The amethyst fangs on the serpent's head were almost fully embedded into Brant's palm.

Merit became hysterical. She pounded on Matt's back. "My God, do something, Matt. He looks terrible!"

Matt pulled the ring out of Brant's palm. "The fangs have broken. The tips are embedded in his palm. They must have caused the seizure. I've got to get them out." Matt looked closely with his flashlight at the broken ends of the fangs still attached to the serpent's head. "Oh God! Look, they're hollow, and there's a yellowish, salve-like substance in them." Matt smelled it. "It has an acrid odor. He's been poisoned! Anna! Get me the thin forceps quick. I must get those pieces out of his hand. Hurry! God dammit! Some of this stuff has leaked into his bloodstream!"

Anna had trouble finding the forceps in the bag, whose contents were now in disarray. Matt sponged the blood from the wound.

While he waited for Anna to find the forceps, Matt took his pen from his breast pocket and used the tip of it to extract a small dab of the yellowish salve-like substance from one of the broken fangs on the ring. He licked it with his tongue, grimaced and shivered, then spit it out and wiped his tongue on his sleeve. "Ugh, it's bitter! It's probably an ancient herb! Oh, Jesus! It could be a poison herb like strychnine! He's been poisoned by the ring! That's why he's convulsing! Jesus, it must be powerful stuff!"

Anna handed him the forceps.

"Oh my God! A poison ring!" Merit cried. "It's my fault! He stole it for me! Oh, Matt, please try to save him," she screamed.

Matt was frantic. "Oh, sweet Jesus, help me," he begged. He grabbed the end of one of the fangs and pulled it out of the hand. After much probing, he was able to recover the other tip. "I hope it's not too late." He held Brant's face in his hands. Suddenly it turned cold as marble. An ominous agonal sound gurgled from Brant's throat.

"He's gone," Matt uttered softly.

Merit threw herself over her husband, sobbing uncontrollably. Pained looks passed between Matt and Anna as they supported Merit, now prostrate on Brant's body.

"It was my fault! He was trying to get the ring for me." She sobbed.

Anna edged forward and rapped on the cab window to tell Nikos to stop. They were at a sharp curve and Nikos couldn't take his eyes off the road at that moment. When they completed the curve safely, Wade turned and read Anna's lips and understood. Wade guessed that Brant must have taken a turn for the worst. Nikos had to drive a bit further until he could safely park off the narrow road.

"Maybe we don't have to tell anyone, about this ring," Anna suddenly said, "I mean..." She had wrapped a dressing sponge around the ring and put it in a sterile paper bag. Matt looked at her in surprise. "We have to. We recorded it in the inventory, Anna. Dammit! I did such a great job saving his life back there! Shit! Damn you, Brant! You had everything in the world going for you!" Matt buried his head in his hands.

Anna took over. She had to work fast. She lifted Merit off Brant and held her close momentarily. Then she pulled Matt's hands from his face. She looked at both of them intently and said in a compelling voice, "Listen to me. We only have few seconds before they stop truck. Don't mention ring! Do you hear me? Do you both understand? Nobody, but you, Merit, and Matt and me know he stole ring. "Matt, you can say he was killed by snake. It would not be lie! Look at his hand! See! Two fang marks. he was delirious when he said he had treasure in his hand! He was drunk, too! Remember that! Everyone in village saw that. No one would believe he could steal anything from cave in his condition! How could someone so drunk make it through the cave, eh? He wasn't really drunk. He just pretended! We know that now, but nobody else knows, not even Nikos and Wade. Brant Powers was very rich man. Why would he steal? Who would believe that? He gave all those expensive movie things to our village. He went to cave to protect treasure, eh? They would believe that."

The truck was slowing down. The brakes screeched. Nikos pulled the emergency brake on.

Anna spoke rapidly now, "Merit and Matt, you do as I say if you want Brant's death to be recorded as accidental. Otherwise it's police case. That's bad thing. He's important man. Newspapers would print bad stories about him. His reputation would be ruined. If you tell truth, there will be big trouble for Elias and Nikos, too, for not protecting treasures better. Don't you see what we must do? Maybe even Elias will not want to report that his dog was not good enough to stop intruder. Do you understand what I'm saying? Bad things will happen to all of you if you don't do what I say! It will work!"

Matt and Merit both looked at each other and reluctantly nodded their agreement. The truck doors opened and shut. They heard Nikos and Wade running to the back of the truck. Both men hopped in. They didn't have to ask. They looked down at Brant whose entire body was covered with a blanket.

"Brant has died," Anna said solemnly. "Besides losing his leg, he was bitten by snake on his hand and died from venom poison. See," she said as she pulled back the blanket and showed them his hand.

Wade and Nikos looked at each other in shock.

Wade said in a questioning voice, "He said he had a treasure in his hand, Matt? Yet he did mention a snake."

Matt was terribly uncomfortable, being forced to do something so unethical as to lie about the cause of death. He chose his words very carefully. "Two fangs went into his hand and the poison killed him. I had no idea his hand had been injured. He would not have died from the amputation, but he was in a very critical condition. The poison was just too much for his weakened system."

"He had convulsions and turned blue, Anna said. There was nothing Matt could do to save him. The poison had been in him too long."

Silence ensued as the two men absorbed the news.

Merit began to cry again. Nikos moved to her side and took her in his arms.

Wade put his arm around Matt's shoulder and said, "You did the best you could, pal."

Matt shrugged Wade off. "Let's get the hell out of here and get to the hospital." Nikos insisted that Merit ride up front, but she refused and instead lay down across her husband's silent chest until they reached the hospital.

CHAPTER FIFTEEN

Lee Bradley had been waiting for a call from Matt. He had promised to call after the anniversary party was over. It was now just a little before eight-thirty, Greenwich time. Damn it, he promised, she thought. It was Saturday night, and she was lonesome and feeling sorry for herself. She missed Matt so much. Before he'd left for Greece, they'd been together almost every weekend. He probably had drunk too much and had forgotten about calling. She considered telephoning him but realized it was around three-thirty on Santorini, also, she'd have to wake up Nikos, and then he'd have to go next door to wake up Matt. Maybe she could find something worth watching on television.

Switching channels, she thought to herself, Saturday nights are the pits on TV. CNN news was about to give its 8:30 update. She was only half listening, scanning the <u>TV GUIDE</u>, when the announcer's report caught her attention.

"And now this bulletin just came in from Athens: A strong earthquake measuring five-point-seven on the Richter scale, struck a large area in the Aegean Sea about three-fifteen this morning, Athens time. First reports indicate islands in that area suffered significant damage, but there have been no reports of casualties. Because two large plates of the Earth's crust, the African and the Aegean, meet in this location, the area is prone to earthquake activity. Aftershocks are still occurring. We'll bring you an update on this quake activity on our nine o'clock news report. And now back to national news."

Lee's whole body quivered in fear. "I'm going there, I have to know if he's okay. No, that's stupid. I'll call him!" She dialed Nikos' number.

Ari and Katina, huddled in the middle of the courtyard, were terrified each time the ground moved beneath them. When the phone rang in Nikos' house, Ari ran to answer it, thinking it would be Nikos or Elias calling.

"Ari, don't leave me here alone!" Katina begged.

Ari went back and grabbed her hand. They both ran into the house. When Ari picked up the phone, another tremor hit. Katina screamed and ran outside.

Lee heard the scream. "Hello! Hello! I want to speak to Dr. Matt McGuire. What's happening there?"

"Everyone's up at cave. Someone is missing, maybe hurt. We are having bad earthquake. I can't talk anymore. Have to get out of house. Goodbye." He hung up the phone and ran outside to comfort Katina.

"Who is hurt?" Lee screamed into the dead mouthpiece.

She made an immediate decision to go to Santorini as quickly as possible. She knew there was a 10:50 P.M. Olympic Airways flight from JFK to Athens that would get her there the next day, Sunday. She called a reservation clerk she knew at Olympic and secured a seat in first class. They also arranged for a flight from Athens to Santorini. She then called the local limo service she used for clients. They could pick her up in fifteen minutes. Whether they could cover the miles from Greenwich to JFK, in time to make the flight, would be a close call. But, if Olympic was just a little late in departing, she'd make it. She quickly packed toiletries, undergarments and a few uncrushable outfits in a carry-on. She'd call her secretary from the limo phone and asked her to handle the office. "Just say, I had to go to Greece unexpectedly to assist clients who were injured in an earthquake."

On the way to JFK, Lee tried again to get through to Santorini. "All circuits to that area are out of order," the operator said.

* * * *

Bedlam filled the emergency ward of the small Santorini Hospital. Nikos and Wade remained in the truck with Merit while Matt and Anna went inside. They picked their way through distraught patients and their families to find the doctor. Matt surveyed the injured lying on gurneys and stretchers or sitting in chairs. With each injured person, at least three family members stood nearby for support.

"Matt, I think I'd better help doctor," Anna said.

"I think he could use both of us. Let me talk to him first about getting Brant's body into the morgue. Once we've done that, I can give him a hand." Matt approached the doctor who was suturing a deep wound on a child's leg. While the doctor worked, Matt explained who he was and what had happened to Brant.

"I could use Anna and another doctor very much, as you can see, eh? Put him in the body cooler drawer in morgue. It will be long time before I can examine him. Have Anna show you where. Please hurry back," he said with urgency.

Anna opened the back door of the hospital morgue, and the men carried Brant's blanket-covered body inside and laid it on a gurney.

Matt told Nikos and Wade to take Merit home and have Katina stay with her. "And Nikos, call Elias and explain that Brant has died. Ask him not to say anything to anyone about what happened tonight until we can have a talk."

Anna added, "Be sure to tell him that Brant did not steal any treasure. Tell him about Brant being poisoned by snake."

Nikos asked, "Should I call undertaker?"

"No, not until the doctor here writes a release. That won't be until later today, I'm sure," Matt said.

After the men left, Matt and Anna wrapped Brant's body in a sheet and rolled the gurney over to the refrigerator. Anna put a tag on Brant's toe, after which they slid the body into the cooler and closed the door.

"What a waste of a young life simply because of his obsession," Matt said, putting his arms around Anna and holding her close. No words were spoken for a few moments, then Matt said, "Okay nurse, it's back to work."

They both scrubbed their hands, put on rubber gloves and walked quickly to the emergency room. Anna ordered loudly, "Only one relative is allowed to stay with each patient. Everyone else who isn't injured, please go to the waiting room."

Reluctantly, a mass of relatives slowly moved away. Matt and Anna went right to work under the doctor's orders. They both were drained and hung over, but their own problems were quickly forgotten.

It was nine in the morning before all the emergencies had been dealt with. Fortunately, no serious injuries had occurred: only two broken legs, one broken arm and a multitude of contusions and abrasions. The doctor invited Matt and Anna into his office, where he served coffee and warm, crusty bread.

"So, Mr. Powers got drunk and wandered up to ancient city, eh? Why do you think he did that?"

Anna said quickly, "We knew he was very excited about some artifacts they found the day before, and we think he wanted to make sure no one went into the cave. He didn't quite trust Elias' watchdog. Course, he was very drunk, or else he would not have done such stupid thing, eh? Who would ever go up there at night? He got quite drunk at his fifth anniversary party, drinking *raki*! If he had been sober, he would not have done such a foolish thing, eh? He was a very important, rich man."

"Ah the curse of alcohol." The doctor said then asked Matt, "It must have been very difficult amputating his leg in cave. Dr. McGuire?"

"How far inside cave was he?"

Anna was about to answer again, but Matt interrupted. "He was just inside the entrance, thank God. Near the stairs that lead down to the tunnel. But by the time we reached him, he was in shock and incoherent, because of the severity of the injury to his leg, and he..."

Anna interrupted, "And because of snake bite on his hand too! He was screaming about ghosts chasing him. That's how bad off he was, eh?"

"Do you know what kind of snake it was, Dr. McGuire?"

Matt hung his head. "I don't know. I just know it was poison from a snake that killed him, not the amputation of the leg. He wouldn't have died from that." Matt was trying hard not to lie.

"Ah, you are both exhausted, I can see that. So am I. I'll look at his body this afternoon, after I've had little rest. Use my phone if you need ride home."

The two men stood and shook hands, while Anna tried to phone Nikos. "The line is dead, Doctor."

"Then please use my car. You both need to get home and get some sleep. You can bring it back later when we deal with disposition of Powers' body. There's so much paperwork you have to do to release the body of foreigner who dies here. I suppose, as usual, the wife will want to return with the body to States as soon as possible, eh?"

"I'm sure she will," Matt said.

"Then after I've slept, I'll get to it. Again, my thanks for your help. I'd still be working if it weren't for the both of you." He shook Matt's hand and kissed Anna on the cheek.

Matt and Anna said very little to each other during the difficult drive back up the mountain. Matt had to maneuver around the rubble that had tumbled down onto the road during the quake.

"I'm glad it's daylight, Anna. I doubt I could have driven home in the dark."

"I don't think there is anything you can't do, Dr. Matt McGuire!" Anna boasted proudly.

"And you, my dear Anna, I've been meaning to ask you, have you ever seen or assisted at an amputation before?" Matt asked.

"No," she answered simply.

"Then I don't think there is anything that you can't do, either, Anna Brady! You're a remarkable woman and one hell of a surgical nurse, and I love you," Matt said, smiling warmly at her.

She returned his smile, leaned back, stretched her arms and yawned. "But not like your Lee, eh?"

It was the first time he thought of Lee. "Oh, God! I'd better let her know what happened. I promised to call her after the party."

When they reached the village, they saw that some of the houses had been damaged, but men were already at work clearing the rubble and shoring up walls. At the compound, village men and women were just finishing sweeping up the broken dishes and dismantling the tables. They seemed to sense that this was not a good time to question Matt and Anna, so they looked the other way as the two crossed the compound. When Matt entered his house, Nikos, Wade and Ari were sitting around the table. They stood up.

Wade went to Matt and put his arm around his shoulder. "You must be exhausted, old pal. Go take a shower and get upstairs to bed."

"There are no words to describe how I feel. How's Merit? Was anyone hurt badly here in the village?"

"No villagers were hurt seriously, thank God." Nikos said. "Merit is asleep, and Katina is with her. She tried to call her parents in States, but phones are not working."

"That reminds me, Dr. Matt," Ari spoke up. "After you went up mountain last night, there was telephone call from woman who wanted to speak to you. I told her you are at cave. I told her we were having earthquake and had to hang up. The floor was shaking under me, and Katina was screaming."

"Did she give you her name?" Matt asked in alarm.

"No."

"Damn it! How long before the phones will be working, Nikos?"

"It's hard to say."

Matt worried that it might have been Rita Burke, his wife's nurse, who called. Something must have happened to Sarah. It wouldn't have been Lee, he was positive about that. She would never call at that hour. "Nikos, please let me know the minute the phone comes back on, and wake me up." He went out to the *banio* and showered. When he returned, he didn't speak, he just dragged himself up the stairs to bed and collapsed.

* * * *

Both Nikos and Wade were skeptical about the snake bite killing Brant. They had seen the fang marks on Brant's hand, but they felt they had not been told the whole truth. They sensed a cover-up but could not prove it. They would have to have a discussion about it with Matt.

They both agreed that Brant had probably planned on stealing some of the treasures, but they didn't know how far he went into the tunnel before the earthquake started. Could he have made it to the chamber in his drunken condition? Somehow, they must convince Elias to allow them to go back into the cave and make sure everything was secured.

Later, when Elias came to the compound to discuss the same issue. He was upset and told the men. "That Mr. Powers broke the law by entering cave. All of you had been told not to go back in cave. That was my order! He disobeyed my order. When we carried him to truck, I heard Mr. Powers say he had something for Mrs. Powers in his hand. A snake, he said. You remember that? If he made it to the chamber of treasures, he probably stole something. I intend to report it to the authorities that he went into cave against my orders!"

"We don't know that he made it to the chamber, and we don't think he stole anything, Elias," Nikos responded. "He was hallucinating because of snakebite on his hand. All he had in his hand were two fang marks and blood. We saw them. There was nothing else in his hand."

"Why did he drug my poor Pluto with sleeping pills? I think he was planning on stealing treasures."

Nikos tried to appease Elias. "He was very drunk. You saw him with your own eyes, Elias. How could Brant, so drunk, find his way into tunnel and steal anything, eh? It would be crazy. We wonder how he could have even made it up to mountain in his condition."

Wade nodded in agreement. Earlier that day, Nikos and Wade had discussed the fact that Brant probably was not as drunk as he seemed to have been. If he were, he never could have made it up the mountain. They felt he must have been putting on an act to convince everyone that he was drunk. They didn't like to admit it, but they felt there was a good possibility that he had planned to go into the cave and steal some of the treasures. They decided to share their suspicions with Matt later, when he woke up.

When Elias was leaving, he said to them, "There was one thing Mr. Powers said that I know was truth, ghosts were chasing us. I felt them, too! I've seen them before! You remember I told you that, Nikos. I think maybe it is time to tell villagers about ghosts that roam ancient city at night. That would certainly put stop to anyone trespassing at night again, eh?"

Wade begged Elias not to tell anyone that Brant had drugged his dog. "There's no reason to make Mr. Powers look more foolish than he was, Elias. His poor judgment cost him his life and has brought great sorrow to his wife. Mr. Powers was a very wealthy, important man in America. Why would he steal?" Wade was inwardly astonished at how easily he was enlarging on the story to try to prove that Brant had not done anything dishonest. Especially now, when he had so many doubts to the contrary.

Elias threw both hands up in the air in concession. "Okay, okay, I not tell anyone anything, except about ghosts maybe, okay? Mrs. Powers is fine woman. I would not want to see her hurt anymore. Matt said she was very sorry that her husband had drugged my Pluto with sleeping pills. I might have shot Pluto because I thought he was dying from poison."

When Elias left, the two men looked at each other.

"So we let Brant rest in peace now, eh?" Nikos asked.

Wade nodded. "It's the first peace I think he's had for a long time. It's too weird to think he's had two encounters with snakes."

"It was his destiny, eh? Do you remember what my friend Dr. Makrakis said to Brant?" He said, 'Let scar of viper's bite serve to remind you of high price you almost paid for your foolish obsession.' He won't be surprised to hear that Brant lost his life because of another snake."

"No, I'm sure he won't," Wade said.

* * * *

An hour later, Nikos awoke from a nap with a start, hit his forehead with the palms of both hands, jumped out of bed and ran outside. Wade was sleeping in a hammock. Nikos leaned over him and said in a hushed tone, "Wade, wake up. We have to go into cave."

Shading his eyes against the sun, he said, "What?"

"Wade, if Brant did get into cave and got as far as chamber, he might have pulled down plywood, and if he didn't wedge it back tight, critters could invade it."

"Oh, my God!" Wade looked startled. "We've got to convince Elias to let us go take a look. Let's go see him the minute Matt wakes up."

* * * *

Merit woke mid-afternoon and found herself holding the silver icon of the Blessed Virgin and Infant that Anna had given them for their anniversary. She pressed it against her face and prayed, dear Mary, give me strength to bear up under the ordeal that lies ahead of me.

Katina rose from the chair across the room, where she had been keeping watch. She moved to the bed and put her arms around Merit, weeping for her friend.

Merit hugged her, then pushed her away. "Katina," she said with a firm voice, "Please don't cry anymore. I must get a grip on myself. I have a great many things to do, and if we start crying again, I'll go to pieces. Please help me." She looked at her watch and was amazed that she had slept so long. She had used the last of the sleeping pills Matt had given her a few days ago. "Where's Matt?"

"He's sleeping. He and my *mana* didn't get back from hospital until about eleven-thirty this morning, and they were both exhausted."

"I'm going to need your help, Katina."

"I do anything you want. Just tell me."

"Is the phone working?"

"I'll go and see."

Merit looked at all of their clothes hanging on the walls. She picked out a few things and put them in a carry-on bag.

Katina came back. "Phone is working now, Merit."

"Katina, I'm leaving all of our clothes here. Don't you or your mother argue about it, because my mind is made up. You can use them yourselves or give them away, I don't care. I don't want them anymore. Also, I want you to have my Nikon and my video camera. You're a good photographer, and you can make good use of them."

"Oh, Merit, I couldn't!"

"Please don't argue with me, Katina, please."

"Okay, Merit." Katina could see that Merit was close to tears.

"*Papa* Ioannis has been here three times to pray with you for Brant's soul. We told him you were sleeping. He says he would wait here until you woke up, but Nikos told him he would call him when he was needed."

"God bless Nikos and *Papa* Ioannis."

Merit left and went to Nikos' house to use the phone. She was able to dial directly to her family's home in Greenwich.

Her mother answered on the first ring. "Oh, darling, we've been trying to get through to you ever since we heard about the earthquake on the news this morning. Are you and Brant all right?"

Trying to keep her voice steady, she said, "I'm fine, Mother, but I have some very sad news. Brant died this morning."

"Oh, my darling, in the earthquake?"

"Yes, he was trapped under a large piece of stone and his leg was crushed, but his death was caused by, ah, a poison snakebite. We didn't realize he had been bitten until after he died. Would you please call Brant's family?"

"Of course, darling, right away. We'll come as quickly as we can. Dad will charter a private jet, and we'll take you and Brant's body home."

"Oh, thank you, Mother. Yes, please come. I need you. Matt said we may have to wait a while until officials release his body. Merit could not hold back the hurt any longer and began to cry so much that she could no longer talk.

Katina had seen Merit go into Nikos' house and waited for her outside the phone closet. When she heard her break down, she went to her side, took the phone and spoke with Merit's mother. "Missus, your daughter is very brave lady, who is loved by everyone here. We'll do everything we can to help her and make things easy for her."

After she hung up, Katina put her arm around Merit and they walked out to the courtyard.

"Thank you for reassuring my folks, Katina. I'm still their little girl, you know," she said with a slight smile on her tear-stained cheeks. I'm going to take a shower and change my clothes. If Matt wakes up in the meantime, tell him I'll be out soon. I want to go with him to the hospital to see if we can get Brant's body released sooner." She spotted Kristos sitting on the ground, his knees pulled up, and his head buried in his hands. A pang of sympathy seized her heart, and she went to him.

"Kristos."

He jumped up when he heard Merit's voice and started to say something, but burst out crying and hugged her around the waist. Between sobs, he said, "I'm sorry about Mr. Powers, and I don't want you to go away, please don't!"

Merit had to fight for control as she held his sweet face in her hands. "I don't want to leave you, either, Kristos, but I must. I have a big favor to ask of you."

"I do anything you want, Mrs. Powers."

"I am going to leave Zeus here. He's so happy with you and the mountains. We don't have mountains where I live. I'd be so pleased if you would keep him. I want him to be your horse now. Will you?"

Kristos looked at her in amazement. "My horse?"

"Yes. I want you to have him. He loves you, you know."

Kristos was dumbfounded. Then he burst out crying again and hugged Merit so tightly, she almost lost her breath.

"Have your father come and see me. I want to be sure that he will let you keep Zeus."

He looked up at her lovingly. "I love you as much as I love Zeus," he said, his face now blushing scarlet. He turned away, crying loudly with joy and sadness, and raced toward town.

She watched him until he was out of sight. A penetrating sadness engulfed her. Turning toward the *banio*, she thought, I have never felt so desperate in my life. My whole being is aching with that hungry feeling of loneliness.

Coming out of her house fifteen minutes later, Merit saw Anna standing in her doorway. When they saw each other, they ran to meet and clung together without speaking.

Just then a taxi pulled into the compound and a very attractive woman stepped out. The taxi driver retrieved her bag from the back.

Merit squinted her eyes towards the woman. "My God!" she said, "That looks like Lee Bradley." Then she realized it was Lee. She ran to her with outstretched arms. "Lee! Oh my dear friend, Lee! What in the world are you doing here?"

Lee's eyes filled with tears as she spoke haltingly, "The earthquake. I, ah, heard about it on the news last night. I telephoned, and whoever answered said that someone was missing in the cave, then the line went dead." She was now fighting back tears. "I couldn't get through after that and I didn't know who was missing! Was it Matt?"

Merit dropped her eyes and spoke softly in a choked voice, "No, Lee. It was Brant, and he's dead."

Shocked, Lee uttered words of condolence as she held Merit tightly in her arms. When she released her, she noticed a woman watching them intently. She instantly knew it was Anna, recognizing her from Matt's description. She also knew that Matt was very fond of the woman. Actually, she had jealous moments about Matt's relationship with Anna but had not told Matt of her feelings. She walked to Anna, smiled through her tears and choked out, "I feel like I know you, Anna. Matt thinks the world of you."

Anna was speechless. She didn't know what to say. Matt's affair with Lee was supposed to be secret, he had told Anna.

Merit spoke up, "Anna, this is Lee Bradley, my friend from Connecticut. She's also a good friend of Matt." Merit now realized that there must be a serious relationship between Lee and Matt to warrant her rushing to Greece on such short notice. Strange she had not known about it before.

Anna and Lee shook hands warmly. Anna had the urge to say, "I know all about you, too." She thought, no wonder I couldn't seduce him. She's a lovely looking woman. She smiled faintly at Lee and pointed. "Matt is still sleeping upstairs in that house. Why don't you go wake him up. I'm sure he'll be happy to see you. He has to get up soon anyway, because there is much to be done about Brant at hospital."

Lee looked from one woman to the other, unsure if she should go up to his bedroom. What would they think?

Merit put the decision to rest for her. Putting her arm around Lee, she led her to the house. "He's had a dreadful time trying to save Brant's life. Your being here will help a great deal. He'll fill you in on the details. We'll talk later. I have to make some phone calls to the States."

Lee watched Merit walk away, her head hanging and her shoulders slumped forward. She had never seen Merit look like that. Her heart ached for her friend who now seemed nothing like the beautiful, excited woman who had looked forward so much to this adventure on Santorini. She took out her compact, dabbed at her shiny nose and fluffed her hair as she went up the stairs. She knocked lightly at the bedroom door. There was no answer except the sound of snoring. A warm feeling filled her and she smiled at the familiar sound and opened the door quietly. She looked at the man she loved more than anything else in the world. He lay nude and flat on his stomach on the rumpled bed. She slipped off her shoes and eased into the small bed beside him.

When she laid her arm across his back, he grunted softly then put his arm over her. It took a few seconds before he realized what was happening. He opened his eyes and blinked a few times, thinking he was dreaming. Suddenly he sat up and looked down at the woman next to him. "Oh my God, Lee! Lee darling! Oh sweet Jesus, what are you doing here? What time is it? I don't care! You're here, and I need you, baby. Oh God, do I need you." He burst out crying, his whole body wracked by sobs. "I've just been through the shittiest night of my life, Lee!"

"Yes, I know darling, but it's going to be okay. I'm here, and I love you, Matt."

"I know that, and it's making the pain go away already!" He took her in his arms and held her tightly, covering her face with kisses.

* * * *

Later in the day, Wade and Nikos told Matt they'd like to discuss Brant's death with him privately, before going to see Elias to get permission to go back to the cave. They had to make sure the plywood was still in place, nothing was missing. and critters didn't get in.

"Matt, you have to agree there was no way Brant could have made it up the mountain if he had been as drunk as he acted." Wade stated. "I think if the coroner takes his blood alcohol level, we could prove he was just pretending."

Nikos asked Matt, "Why did he go up to the cave alone? Why did he drug Pluto? We're sure he tried to steal treasures. And, we don't believe the snake story, Matt."

Matt, hating to lie anymore, conceded, "Okay, if what you say is true, then we should get Elias to let us go back in the cave and take a look. There are so many unanswered questions. I don't know. It seems like it was destiny that Brant Powers would die from snake fangs. He just lucked out the first time he was bitten." He hedged further, "Come on, you guys, you know he was a sick man. You saw how rapidly his personality changed in just one month. He had a very serious neurotic disorder that became worse each day. At the end, he was very different than the man who arrived on the first of May. His obsession with finding a treasure destroyed him."

Wade fixed his eyes on Matt. "Yes, we all saw that, Matt, but Nikos and I worry that he stole something. Remember, Elias has a copy of the inventory and when the authorities come and find a discrepancy, we'll all be in trouble. Why should we risk our reputations for him? We must get Elias to let us go back into the chamber room to be sure nothing is missing."

Nikos added, "Remember, Matt, it was my responsibility to my government to be sure that nothing was stolen, eh? I want to be sure, too,"

Matt looked thoughtful, "It would be a shame if he did steal something. I agree we should take a look, if Elias will let us. But what about the snake that bit him? You saw the fang marks."

"We don't think there was a real snake, Matt" Wade said.

"Okay, let's go back and take a look if Elias will let us," Matt said.

Before they left to see Elias, Matt went to see Anna on the pretense of asking her to let Lee know where he was when she woke up. "Anna, I never asked you, but now I have to know what you did with the ring?"

"I have it hidden here in my house. I needed time to think about what we should do with it."

"Nikos and Wade insist that we ask Elias to allow us to look in the chamber room to see if anything was stolen before the archaeologists from Athens arrive. If I had the ring, I might get an opportunity to put it back without anyone being the wiser. Wade and Nikos don't believe the poison snake story, and they're convinced Brant stole something."

"I know. Nikos told me same thing. I'll get ring, and say prayer that you can put it back." The ring was wrapped in a gauze packet. "I put ring in strainer and washed it with hot water to get Brant's blood and poison off. I didn't want to leave clue. I buried the broken tips in my yard, deep!"

"Anna, you're something else!"

"What else am I, eh?" Anna smiled.

"Although Brant didn't deserve it, you're the best friend he ever had."

"I did it for Merit, not him."

* * * *

After much arguing, the men convinced Elias that they'd all be in trouble with the authorities if Brant had stolen some of the treasures. Or, if he took down the plywood and didn't put it back tightly. Elias, still fearful of the ghosts was reluctant to go back into the cave.

Nikos, taking his lecture stance, won Elias over by pointing out, "You, Elias, would be in the biggest trouble with the authorities if treasures are missing from the inventory. Remember your Pluto didn't turn out to be such a great watch dog, eh?" Don't you think we should look and see, eh?"

"Okay, Okay. We should look and see!"

They went to the office, put on their suits and hard hats and picked up the other equipment and the one big lamp that was left.

They dreaded seeing the place where Matt amputated Brant's leg, but when they reached the large piece of limestone, they were startled. All that remained was a chewed boot and dark red stains on the slab and floor.

"Rats," Nikos said softly.

Matt carried the lamp and tried to stay in the lead as they made their way through the tunnel and down into the cavern. They moved slowly through the thick rubble caused by the earthquake. When they reached the chamber, Matt aimed the lamp at the doorway to the chamber. The men gasped.

"Shit!" Matt said.

Several rats came running out over the plywood that now lay on the floor.

Elias threw his fists up in the air and yelled profanities in Greek. Wade took the lamp from Matt and aimed it at the entrance.

"So, Elias, aren't you glad now that we talked you into checking the chamber?" Wade asked. "It's obvious Brant was here."

Elias was in such an agitated state, he couldn't answer. He did not want to go into the chamber because of the body in the sarcophagus, so he lingered in the doorway flashing the lamp around the room.

Wade spotted the broken lamp on the floor and picked it up. The expensive light was beyond repair.

Nikos almost stepped on the gold female deity. Examining it carefully, he said, "Look at this! Brant's beautiful gold statue must have fallen from niche up there, but it didn't break. Just scratched; that's amazing!"

Matt slowly edged his way toward the sarcophagus commenting on the broken pithoi and picking up broken shards. He noticed the cover was off the sarcophagus, but he didn't mention it just yet.

Elias shouted, "Look! There's dagger and sword laying on floor. Someone pick them up and put them back in box."

Wade brushed them off carefully, placed them back where they belonged and put the cover back on. "It's strange that Brant who thought so much of these treasures, would leave them in such disarray. When we first saw this chamber, nothing except pithoi was broken or scattered about in spite of all the many earthquakes that Santorini has suffered."

Elias answered, "It's not strange. This was sacred place. Wade."

Matt was now next to the sarcophagus. He leaned his headlight in. He couldn't believe what he was about to do, but somehow it felt right. Speaking as if to himself, he said, "Humm, everything looks okay in here."

The finger bone that had held the ring was no longer attached to the hand. Quickly, he slid the ring out of his pocket and onto the finger bone in one quick movement. A feeling of both guilt and relief filled him. He called out to the others, "The cover on the sarcophagus must have slid off during the quake. It's on the floor. Maybe we didn't put it back on correctly. I hope the rats didn't get into it and steal any small items." Matt said excitedly, "Hey guys, look, the snake ring is still on the finger, but the finger has broken off from the hand."

Elias yelled at him, "Don't touch anything, Doctor!"

Matt raised both his hands up, palms out, as if to prove he didn't have anything in his hands. He spotted the crowbar on the floor. "Here's more evidence that Brant was in the chamber." Matt held the crowbar up for them to see.

Wade holding up the smashed lamp, said, "There's no doubt about it now, Brant Powers was here."

Elias said, "Let's take inventory right now! I want to get out of here." He took out a copy of the team's inventory list.

When they came to the treasures in the sarcophagus, Elias moved into the chamber a little bit and said, "I want to see for myself that snake ring. Bring it to me, Nikos."

Nikos reached into the casket. "I wonder how this finger bone with ring became detached from the skeleton's hand, eh? He held ring and finger bone and examined them closely. Ah! Guess what? Fangs are missing on ring, but they are not here in sarcophagus.!"

The four men looked at each other.

Matt hung his head and sheepishly said, "I, ah, guess my diagnosis was right. Brant died from snake bite."

Nikos added, "And now we also know in fact, Brant did not steal anything."

"I still must report that he tried to steal!" Elias spoke in an angry voice.

Wade said to Elias, "Yes, he did try to steal and paid for it with his life."

Elias, now secure in the knowledge that nothing was missing, changed his tune somewhat. "Maybe Mr. Powers must have been crazy. No man in his right mind would come in cave at night. So, for Mrs. Powers sake, I won't report that her husband tried to steal treasures." Then making a hasty retreat out of the room, he said, "Let's get out of here."

* * * *

Mild aftershocks continued to occur periodically.

The doctor at the hospital called Nikos Sunday night to inform him that he had not been able to get either the coroner or the police to come to the hospital. They were too busy with problems created by the earthquake. There was no one else available with the authority to fill out the necessary reports and to question those who were with the victim when he died. "Maybe Monday or Tuesday we'll come," they had promised the doctor. He told Nikos to tell Matt he completed his examination of the body and had signed the death certificate as poison snake bite. But, until the other authorities completed their reports, the body would have to remain in the morgue.

Merit spent some private time with Matt and Anna to let them know how grateful she was for all they did to save Brant's life and reputation. "I'll always be eternally indebted to you, dear, Anna, for having the presence of mind to suggest a plausible alternative to the truth at that moment of despair. Your quick thinking allowed Brant to die with dignity."

By Monday night, the authorities, who were still busy with earthquake work, had not released Brant's body. The waiting seemed endless to Merit. Her parents would arrive tomorrow.

* * * *

Late that night, Nikos hung up the phone and hurried over to Anna's house, knocking loudly on the door.

Being awakened and perturbed by the loud racket, she opened the door. "What do you want, Nikos? It's almost midnight."

"I just had a phone call from the airport. A cargo plane will arrive on Wednesday morning with your Joe's remains."

Her face filled with emotion. "Oh Nikos, I'm so sorry I yelled at you. Thank you for bringing me that news." She kissed him lightly on the cheek. "You know, I feel strange. I should feel sad but actually I'm relieved that I can have a proper funeral for my Joe."

"I'll call the undertaker and Father Ioannis tomorrow to let them know."

"I don't know what I would do without you, Nikos."

"You don't have to, you know."

She looked shocked. "What did you say? What do you mean?"

"Well, I mean, ah, well, you know if you would like to maybe, ah, er...Well, you ARE a widow now for sure. I'm not making an improper suggestion."

"No. What ARE you trying to say?"

"Well, we'll talk more about this subject once we have laid Joe to rest properly."

"Ha! The thought of a permanent relationship with one woman frightens you to death, doesn't it, Nikos? Admit it!"

"Of course not! Aren't I a man? How could a woman scare me? I love women."

"And that's your problem; you're greedy." Anna gave him a sharp look and slammed the door on him. A secret, smug smile covered her face. I think maybe he's ready to settle down, but hates to admit it.

He'll choke if he has to say the word 'marriage' to me. A warm feeling filled her.

Merit's parents arrived on Tuesday. The police and the coroner interviewed Merit, Anna and Matt and finally signed the death certificates and released the body for international travel.

It also was Tuesday before Nikos was able to locate the archaeologists from Athens. They were thrilled when Nikos informed them of the chamber filled with ancient treasures. They made plans to come to Santorini quickly.

Elias was ordered not to allow anyone in the cave, and to close down the Ancient City of Thera to tourists.

It was a bittersweet farewell when Merit and her parents prepared to board the sleek private jet on Wednesday morning at the airport. Matt, Lee, Wade, Nikos, Anna and Katina kissed her fondly and promised to keep in touch.

Just as she started up the stairs, Kristos, dressed in his tight communion suit, came running across the airfield yelling to her, "Wait, Mrs. Powers, please wait!"

Merit was devastated by the sight of Kristos looking so desolate. His little face was sopping with tears. He handed her a small bouquet of wild flowers, hung his head and ran the backs of his hands across his face, roughly wiping away his tears.

Merit was so touched, she couldn't speak. She knew if she tried to say something, she'd cry. She hugged Kristos tightly to her, released him, and quickly went up the stairs into the plane, followed by her father and mother. She couldn't bear to look back at the dear friends she might never see again or the beautiful island that she had learned to love so much.

Brant's body, encased in an aluminum box, was now removed from the hearse and put in the jet's luggage compartment. As the plane lifted into the sky and headed west toward America, a cargo plane carrying the remains of Joseph Brady landed on a nearby runway. The hearse, followed by Nikos' truck carrying the others, drove across the field. The men lifted the simple wooden crate from the plane and placed it in the hearse. With a shaking hand, Anna signed the certificate that stated she claimed Joe's body.

Without saying it out loud, everyone had the same thoughts. What a strange quirk of fate that the two unrelated corpses should take off and land at this airfield at the same time. Brant's death, a senseless tragedy, brought great sorrow to his widow, Merit. Yet, the remains of Joe Brady, victim of a brutal murder, would bring comfort and closure to his widow, Anna.

The solemn pilgrimage, led by the hearse and followed by Nikos' truck, began the climb up the mountain. Anna and Lee crowded in front with Nikos, while Katina and the men stood in the back of the truck.

The tolling of the church bells announced it was time for Joe Brady's funeral. *Papa* Ioannis led the procession, out of the compound followed by the hearse. Nikos walked with Anna and Katina, their arms locked tightly together. Wade, Matt, Lee and Ari fell in behind. The villagers joined the cortege. When they reached the graveyard, *Papa* Ioannis conducted a simple, brief service. The wooden box containing Joe Brady's remains was lowered into the ground. Anna and Katina, fighting back tears, threw the symbolic handfuls of dirt onto the box and turned to the congregation.

Holding her head erect and her hand clasped tightly in Katina's, Anna said, "Thank you all for being here at my Joe's homecoming. My daughter and I are grateful to God and Dr. Matt McGuire for bringing him back to us." Then Anna and Katina left the cemetery, walking swiftly down the hill with great dignity. Nikos followed closely behind them. They hadn't cried because Anna told Katina, "We must be strong like Merit who never cried in public again after that first day. She was very ladylike." To Anna, Merit's stoic behavior had seemed proper and brave, traits she greatly admired in a woman.

* * * *

Life in the compound would never be the same again. The archaeological authorities from Athens would arrive en masse on Friday, now that the tremors had stopped completely. They were optimistic that the artifacts in the chamber would add greater credence to the theory that the island of Santorini had been part of a great lost kingdom, maybe Atlantis. Their plans included a month long extensive examination of the cave and the treasure room. Concerned that they might run into the snake that killed Brant, they invited Dr. Makrakis, to join them and hopefully, capture it. Matt felt badly that he'd have to let Mak go through the motions of the useless snake hunt.

* * * *

Wade planned to stay on Santorini for as long as the Greek authorities needed him. He intended to turn over duplicates of Merit's video film, along with her drawings, photos and all the cataloguing they had prepared. The only copy of the ghost film was missing. Did she take it with her, or destroy it? Wade wondered.

On Thursday night, Matt asked Nikos to have a drink with him after everyone had gone to bed. He wanted to talk with Nikos about Anna. He felt she needed to share her pent-up passion with a deserving man, and his instincts told him that although Anna was not deeply in love with Nikos, she cared for him a great deal. He knew that Nikos admired Anna, but also feared her a little because she knew him so well. Nikos was delighted with the opportunity to have a last drink with Matt, who intended to leave on Friday afternoon with Lee to go to Crete for a brief vacation before returning home.

Matt said, "Nikos, I have something very serious to discuss with you. Listen, old pal, I think it's about time you settled down and got yourself a wife."

"Who me?" Nikos asked, as if it were a ridiculous thing for Matt to suggest.

"Yes you, old pal. You know, you're not getting any younger. When I get home, I'd like to be sure that you're being taken care of by a loving wife."

"So, do you have anyone in mind for me, eh?"

"Of course! Anna, and I wouldn't put off asking her too much longer. She's a beautiful and sensuous woman. A man would be lucky to have her for his wife. I'll tell you the truth, Nikos. If I didn't have my wonderful, Lee, I'd have fallen for Anna."

Nikos looked startled. "You would?!"

"It's true. Anna won't remain a widow very long, pal. She tells me that she and Katina are going to America shortly to meet Joe's aunt. I can tell you that some American will very likely sweep her off her feet. Count on it, Nikos. She needs a man, old pal, and that man should be you."

"Maybe she wouldn't want an old man like me. The women today like young men, eh?" He stood up and started to pace the floor and gesture dramatically with his hands. "Besides, she is always making fun of me. She is most independent, strong and stubborn woman I know. You know, when Greek man takes woman for his wife, he is supposed to be able to order her around, tell her what to do, and what not to do. Do you think Anna would ever stand for that?"

Matt grinned at Nikos whose face was now red and angry. "Maybe she would, Nikos. You'll never know unless you try. I remember what the Greek philosopher, Socrates, said about marriage; 'By all means marry; if you get a good wife, you'll become happy; if you get a bad one, you'll become a philosopher.'" Both men laughed at the ancient words of wisdom.

Nikos hugged Matt tightly. "Thank you, my friend. You are doctor so you must know what is good for me, eh? I will do it! I WILL MARRY ANNA! There I said it! Opa! Opa!" He snapped his fingers and spun in a circle.

EPILOGUE

One year later, Merit Morton Powers donated most of Brant's antiquities, and the rare ancient pieces from her jewelry collection, to various museums all over the world. She sold many of her other priceless jewels and used the money for endowments, in Brant's name, at various schools of archaeology. She made a large contribution to support the Kalliste dig site at Akrotiri.

Nikos proposed to Anna the day after Matt and Lee left Santorini. Anna accepted happily, but laid down firm ground rules about Nikos' womanizing. "Those days are over for you, do you understand?" she warned him.

A sadness filled him. He had made so many women happy in his life. Now he would have to be content with making just one woman happy. "Ah, but that's a small price to pay to have a spirited, lovely wife and a beautiful daughter," he philosophized.

They were married by *Papa* Ioannis in a wonderful celebration of love on the fourth Sunday in June.

They took Katina with them on their honeymoon in America where they visited Joe Brady's aunt in Pasadena, and spent three days at Disneyland. They visited Merit and were shocked when they saw the mansion where she lived. They also spent a few days with Matt and Lee who were now married and living in Connecticut. Matt's wife, Sarah, had died shortly after he returned from Greece.

When Nikos, Anna and Katina returned from the States, they spent a week in Athens. They were invited to dinner at Ari's home where the four parents discussed their children's future. Although Katina and Ari did not become formally engaged, an agreeable understanding was reached. When Katina had completed her education at the University of Athens, and, if they were still in love, their marriage would take place.

Nikos and Anna purchased an apartment in one of the affluent sections of Athens where they would spend their winters. They planned to have the four houses in the compound completely redesigned and renovated with all modern conveniences. They would enjoy summers there with all their old friends and neighbors.

When Wade returned from Greece, he began to write an adventure novel about the ancient cave on Mesa Vouno.

It was months before the Department of Antiquities in Athens released the story of the priceless treasure trove to the press. The team was given many commendations in scientific journals. News stories and letters of regret about Brant's untimely death had been sent to Merit from around the world.

Today, many of the treasures are still being analyzed by experts, and are not, as yet, on display at the Archaeological Museum in Athens or the museum in Santorini.

Because most of the antiquities, found in the chamber of the Omphalos, were of Minoan origin, and obviously related to the ancient citizens of Kalliste, the age-old dispute about Plato's Lost Kingdom of Atlantis was again brought to the fore in scientific circles. Although these new finds provoked controversy among scholars, many agreed they could be much closer to solving the puzzle of the lost Kingdom that seemed to disappear overnight.

THE END

ABOUT THE AUTHOR

Peg Maddocks was a bi-coastal author. She lived on the East coast when she wrote her first book, *Cambridge Girl*. She was born in Cambridge, Massachusetts and spent a number of years living in Falmouth on Cape Cod. She moved to San Diego ten years ago and began writing *The Santorini Odyssey*. She loved to travel and visited many countries in the world. Her professional career was in politics, Advertising, Public Relations and as a writer, producer and director of many Musical Comedies. She was a volunteer for many organizations before her ultimately death on September 3, 2003. She is survived by her husband, four children, seven grandchildren and one great grandchild.

The Author, Peg Maddocks, takes a rest while exploring the ruins of the ancient city of Thera.

Lightning Source UK Ltd.
Milton Keynes UK
UKOW02f1950090615

253216UK00001B/139/P